Books by David Westheimer

SUMMER ON THE WATER

THE MAGIC FALLACY

WATCHING OUT FOR DULIE

THIS TIME NEXT YEAR

VON RYAN'S EXPRESS

MY SWEET CHARLIE

SONG OF THE YOUNG SENTRY

LIGHTER THAN A FEATHER

OVER THE EDGE

GOING PUBLIC

THE OLMEC HEAD

THE
OLMEC HEAD

THE
OLMEC HEAD

DAVID WESTHEIMER

Little, Brown and Company — Boston — Toronto

FIRST EDITION

TO 3/74

Library of Congress Cataloging in Publication Data

Westheimer, David.
  The Olmec head.

  I. Title.
PZ3.W52650l3   [PS3573.E88]   813'.5'4   73-12282
ISBN 0-316-93153-5

Published simultaneously in Canada
by Little, Brown & Company (Canada) Limited

PRINTED IN THE UNITED STATES OF AMERICA

For
Westy and Gerry
and
Joe and Elaine

THE
OLMEC HEAD

1

§ OMEHOW I'd assumed you were an older man," Otis Sandifer said after they had introduced themselves and sat down to order lunch.

This neither flattered nor offended Bell. He was twenty-eight and looked at least that. For the past several years, four of them in the military service, he had often been in positions of authority normally entrusted to older men.

"We're starting even then," he said. "I'd expected you to be younger."

Sandifer, with his longish barber-styled white hair and pink baby's complexion, had to be in his late sixties. He wore a maroon blazer, an intricately patterned wide green tie and a turquoise shirt. When he phoned Bell the night before and invited him to lunch, his brisk, vigorous voice had led Bell to expect a man in the prime of life. Sandifer had been smooth as well as vigorous on the phone, managing to persuade Bell to agree to lunch without ever revealing the purpose of the meeting.

It had not really been all that hard to do. Bell, though he had a thousand or so in the bank, was between jobs. He had left his job at Ajax Rigging ten days earlier. After two years of commanding a Marine Corps motor transport company and almost three in a supervisory position at Ajax, he wanted to stretch a little. He had felt confined, that he was growing soft and stale. And he wanted to be on his own for a change. He had gone into the Corps right out of Rice University with an ROTC commission and a four-year service obligation, and to Ajax right out of the Corps.

The waitress brought the menus and took their drink orders, a vodka martini for Sandifer and a beer for Bell. Bell craved something cooling. Despite the air conditioning and his open-necked sports shirt, he was still sweaty from the mugginess of a Houston August. Bell was the only man in Maxim's so casually dressed. It did not bother him though it had seemed to give Sandifer a moment's pause at first.

While Sandifer pored over the menu, Bell helped himself liberally to the house pâté and made an unabashed survey of the premises. He had been born, reared and educated in Houston without ever having been in the restaurant before. It was an elegant place and though elegance had a low priority in his life, he dug it. The next time he took out a girl whose thing was elegance he'd bring her here. If he still had any of his thousand left.

"May I recommend the Snapper Pontchartrain?" Sandifer asked.

Bell nodded. Steak would have been better, but if Sandifer wanted to show off the fish, he was willing to go along with the old guy. After all, Sandifer was picking up the tab.

"With that rather nice Meursault Camille's laid in," Sandifer continued.

"Meursault?" said Bell.

If Sandifer was dismayed by Bell's ignorance, he did not show it.

"You'll like it," he said. "A splendid white."

"Okay," Bell said.

He preferred beer, but he'd go along with the wine, too. If Sandifer wanted to make a big deal out of lunch, let him. He must want something awfully bad. Sooner or later the old boy would say just what.

Sandifer ordered only a salad for himself.

"Prefer getting my quota of calories in alcohol," he said with a smile.

He spread a crisp wafer of Melba toast with the merest film of pâté. His blazer sleeve pulled back to reveal his cuff links. Bell's eyes were drawn to them. They were of brownish clay and looked like oddly marked pieces of broken flowerpot.

"Pre-Columbian shards," Sandifer said. "I have them made up for me. You can't get pre-Columbian pieces any more. Not legally, that is."

He appeared to be expecting a comment but Bell said nothing.

"Not since 1970," Sandifer continued. "The Mexican government passed that infernal cultural heritage law. Means you can't bring out pre-Columbian objects."

Again he paused as if waiting for comment and again Bell remained silent.

"Hasn't stopped the traffic though," Sandifer said. "On the contrary, it's increased enormously. Enormously. It's because the risks are negligible and the rewards substantial. But I suppose you're aware of all that, with everything that gets in the papers about it."

"Not really," said Bell.

"Take my word for it. A good piece can fetch six figures."

The image this evoked in Bell's mind was not of a pre-Columbian object but of one infinitely more contemporary. He grinned.

"I see you're interested," Sandifer said, pleased.

"In what?" Bell asked.

Sandifer studied him a moment.

"Money," he said.

"Depends," Bell replied.

The red snapper was excellent. Bell ate with relish

and wiped up the last of the sauce with a hunk of one of the warm rolls with which the attentive waitress had kept him supplied. Sandifer looked on with mingled approval and envy.

"Can't eat it too often myself," he said with a sigh. "Not and keep my figger."

Sandifer dawdled over his coffee. He seemed reticent about getting back to the subject he had abandoned earlier. Finished at last, he looked at his thin gold wristwatch and said, "How are you fixed for time, Mr. Bell? Can you come back to the gallery with me? What I have to discuss is rather private."

Bell looked at his own watch, a hulking one of stainless steel. It was a reflex action. Time was what he had the most of right now, except maybe curiosity.

"I think you'll find it worth your while," Sandifer said persuasively.

"Okay," Bell said.

"Excellent," Sandifer said. "Shall we go in my machine?"

"I'll take mine," Bell replied.

No point in leaving his car downtown and having to come back after it. And having to depend on Sandifer to bring him. It was better to have his own wheels.

"It's in the Galleria," said Sandifer. "Second floor. Look for the red door or you'll miss it."

The Galleria, in the southwest suburbs, brimmed with refrigerated air and Bell plunged into it with gratitude. He lingered on the first floor a few minutes watching a mob of ice skaters toiling around the rink.

If it were not for the red door, the Otis Sandifer Gallery would have been inconspicuous among the plate glass windows and entryways of the second-floor shops. There was just the door set in the blank wall and bearing a simple brass nameplate. Inside the gallery, Bell's footsteps fell silently on a thick, pale carpet. The walls were hung only sparingly with paintings, none of which filled Bell with any great desire to make

6

a closer inspection. Over in a corner, a girl was sitting at an oval table with a top of creamy onyx. Sandifer was nowhere in sight. There was a closed door at the back of the gallery and Bell supposed he was behind it, unless he had stopped off somewhere on the way back to the gallery.

The girl rose and came toward Bell, saying, "Mr. Bell?"

She had black hair that looked as if she washed it every day. It fell straight down below her shoulders. Her brown leather skirt ended five or six inches above her knees and brown leather boots rose to three or four inches below them. She had nice knees. A belt of linked oval copper plates with a big copper buckle clasped her small waist. The sleeves of her gaudy print blouse were long and full. A gold coin hung from her strong tanned neck on a braided gold chain. Her face was a trifle too narrow, with dark eyes that seemed to be measuring him from beneath brows as thick as his own. Not exactly a beautiful face, Bell thought, but it would do. Especially if it could be coaxed into showing a little warmth.

"Yes," he said. "Sam Bell."

"Mr. Sandifer is expecting you," she said.

She led him to the closed door and opened it.

"Sandy," she said. "Bell's here."

She stood back and let Bell go past her into the room. She smelled good. Bell inhaled deeply and said, "Nice."

She shut the door behind him without changing expression.

The room was as wide as the gallery, though not nearly as deep. It was as cluttered as the gallery was uncrowded. Canvases leaned against a side wall and stood upright in a double-tiered wooden rack running the width of the rear. That surprised Bell. He thought a gallery displayed all its paintings on the walls. He had not been in many art galleries and never before in a gallery storeroom.

Just inside the door, to the right, Sandifer sat at a rolltop desk smoking a thin, dark cigar. Its aroma filled the room. He had removed his blazer and tie and folded his shirtsleeves neatly to the middle of his forearms. His arms, heavily grown with tawny hair, were corded with muscle. Bell hadn't expected that. He had associated the pink smooth complexion with flabbiness.

"Have a seat, Sam," Sandifer said, waving toward a black leather sling chair cradling a sheaf of unframed prints.

At the restaurant he had said, "Mr. Bell," never "Sam." Nonetheless, he sounded more businesslike than he had at Maxim's.

Bell gathered the prints into a neat stack and put them on the floor. The sling chair was comfortable but embraced him like an acorn in its cup. He did not like the chair much. He looked expectantly at Sandifer.

"I suppose you're wondering what led me to you," Sandifer said.

"It had crossed my mind."

"The story in the *Post* last month. The one about the job Ajax did for NASA with that big capsule. In the interview, your boss said you handled the whole enchilada. Planning, supervision, everything. That's why I thought you'd be an older man." He looked thoughtfully at Bell. "When I phoned Ajax they told me you were no longer employed there. Any particular reason?"

"Nope," said Bell.

He wanted answers, not questions.

"I take it you're available, then?"

"Depends."

"Is it understood that what I am about to propose to you is in the strictest confidence?"

Bell nodded.

"Spendid. I want something moved. Something quite heavy."

"How far and how heavy?"

Sandifer contemplated his cigar. "There are some special problems involved," he said, ignoring Bell's question.

"Special problems are my specialty."

"These are problems apart from the size of the object. Though the size does present a problem. The problems have more to do with the location of the object. Do you recall what I said about the cultural heritage law at lunch?"

"Dimly."

"To be perfectly blunt about it, I want something trucked up from Mexico that the authorities down there would rather I didn't."

"Sorry. That's not my line."

"Look, Sam, it's not drugs or anything of that nature. No one will be hurt by it."

"I would, if I'm busted."

"The chances of that are virtually nil. And I'm prepared to offer ten thousand dollars for the job."

"I don't know what you want brought in," Bell said, trying to sound unimpressed, "but that doesn't sound like enough."

He was shrewd enough to know the first offer was never enough. A man as slick as Sandifer would never open negotiations with his top offer.

"But you would be interested if the fee were adjusted upward, I take it?"

"Maybe. But I'd have to know a lot more about it."

"You shall, my boy, you shall."

Sandifer went to a locked filing cabinet, produced a key ring and unlocked it. He brought a manila envelope back to his desk and pried open the clasp. He removed a photograph from the envelope and held it out.

"Meet Chato," he said. While Bell was reaching for it he added, "Chato means 'Flat Nose' in Spanish."

Bell stared at the eight by ten print with undisguised wonder. It was a photograph of an enormous, pitted head dwarfing the human figure in droopy whites standing beside it. The head and the man were in a pit. In the foreground, a dirt ramp led down into the pit. There were trees in the background.

The head was of stone. The eyes, under beetling brows and what appeared to be a close-fitting helmet, were open but without pupils. The face was broad, the nose flat and heavy. The lips were puffy and turned down in a faintly sullen expression.

It was almost a baby face but, because of its sheer size, intimidating.

"What is it?" Bell asked, handing the photograph back.

"A colossal Olmec head," Sandifer said. "Do you know anything about the Olmecs?"

Bell shook his head, wondering how the hell would a man sneak something that big out of Mexico even if he had the equipment to haul it out of the jungle in the first place.

"Doesn't really matter," said Sandifer. "This is the fifteenth to be found, and one of the largest. The other fourteen are unavailable to collectors but the Mexican government isn't even aware of the existence of this one."

"How big is this Chato?" Bell asked.

"A little over nine feet high. Approximately eighteen tons of solid basalt. And I have a collector who's absolutely perishing to own it."

"Eighteen tons? Be a hell of a job just to get it out of the jungle. Not that I'd want to try. Considering everything."

"Getting it out of the jungle is not the problem, my boy. But I take it your principal objection is the, uh, illegality of the operation."

"You might say that, Mr. Sandifer."

"I'm sure it wouldn't sway you if I told you everyone's been bringing out pre-Columbian objects like mad. Clay figurines, gold and jade jewelry. Even seven-foot stelae. So I'll not dwell on that aspect. But in this particular case, there are aspects that might make you find it less unsavory."

"Such as?" Bell demanded.

It was true, Sandifer admitted, that the head was a Mexican national treasure even though its existence was unknown to the authorities. But, he said, the Mexican government did not seem to know what to do with the fourteen it already had. One was on display at the Museum of Anthropology in Mexico City. The much less frequented museum at Jalapa had four, two were stuck away in the tiny village of Santiago Tuxtla, south of Veracruz, where hardly anyone ever saw them except the locals, who took them for granted, and heaven knew where the others were gathering dust.

"If it hadn't been for the monero, this one would still be buried out in the jungle," Sandifer said.

"Monero?"

"The peon who found it. It comes from the Spanish word for monkey. Moneros are the monkeys who poke around for pre-Columbian artifacts. My point is, Chato would never be missed. Right?"

"I guess," said Bell.

"So, everything considered, bringing the head to this country is not so heinous a crime after all, is it?" Sandifer asked.

"You said getting it out of the jungle isn't a problem. Why? Looks to me like one hell of a problem."

"It was, indeed. But it's already been done."

"How?"

"Does it matter?"

"Look, I couldn't care less about the Olmecs but moving things is my business. I'd like to know how they did it."

The head had been cut into five slabs at the site. It had required no special equipment, just corundum powder, water, iron wire and human muscle. The wire, coated with a mud made of corundum and water, was drawn back and forth across the stone by men at either end. Once a groove was made, the mud was continuously dribbled into it by a third man.

"They used soft iron wire so the corundum particles could dig into it," Sandifer explained. "Goes through the basalt as if it were cheese."

The slabs had then been snaked through the jungle on wooden pallets to a nearby stream, loaded onto five boats and floated over a network of rivers some fifty miles to the little town of Tlacotalpán. Tlacotalpán was on the Papaloapán River, about sixty miles south of Veracruz.

"And now they're safely tucked away in Veracruz waiting to be picked up," Sandifer concluded.

"Didn't it ruin the head, cutting it up like that?" Bell asked.

"Not if the crew knew their business. And my contact knows his business. They'd be careful not to cut across any of the important features."

"I mean, wouldn't it be worth a lot less that way?" Bell said.

"Doesn't affect the value in the slightest," Sandifer replied. "Only way large pieces can be brought out, you see. I know of one case where a Mayan stela was cut into seventeen pieces and still brought six figures." He looked expectantly at Bell. "So, will you undertake to get Chato from Veracruz to Laredo for me?"

"There're still a couple of things I'd like to know," Bell said. "For one thing, why can't the same guy who got it to Veracruz for you get it to Laredo?"

"Any number of reasons, not the least of which is that he refuses to guarantee delivery by road. Laredo is nine hundred miles from Veracruz. The original arrangement was for my contact to put the head on a ship in Veracruz. Crated up as ornamental concrete garden fountains."

That arrangement had fallen through when the man who was to arrange the shipping documents was arrested before he could manage it.

"Arrested!" Bell said. "Just what are you trying to talk me into?"

"He was picked up on a completely unrelated charge," Sandifer said reassuringly. "Embezzling from his firm or something of that nature. I assure you no one has any inkling of the head's existence."

"Okay. One more thing. How am I supposed to get the thing past customs?"

"That will all be taken care of for you."

Sandifer's contact in Veracruz was to arrange for a trailer truck and a shipment of legitimate merchandise under which to hide the slabs. At the Nuevo Laredo end there was a broker who would see that Bell had the proper export documents to get the load through customs. Bell was not to drive the truck himself. Sandifer's contact would hire Mexican nationals for that. Bell's job was to supervise the loading and accompany the trailer truck in a rented car, selecting its route and taking care of any road emergencies that might arise.

"And to make sure the truck keeps going in the direction it's supposed to," Sandifer added. "It's a damned valuable load. And someone might get ideas."

"What's the rap if I'm busted?"

"Illegal possession, one to six years and a fine of one hundred to fifty thousand pesos. Four thousand dollars at most."

"It's the six years that makes me nervous," Bell said.

"You'll not be with the shipment, exactly," Sandifer said. "I told you that. You'll be in a separate machine."

"I know you did. But I'll be somewhere around. Especially when it crosses the border. What if I get busted then?"

"You won't be. You'll have your bill of lading and export permit for a legitimate load. And no one's that concerned about pre-Columbian art down there. It's drugs the Mexican and American customs people are after."

"But what if I do get busted at the border?" Bell persisted. "It's not impossible."

"Two to twelve years," Sandifer replied reluctantly.

"I'd be forty years old when I got out," said Bell.

"I'd dearly love to be forty again," Sandifer said.

"And I'd dearly love to get there without wasting the best years of my life."

"I have a feeling we're haggling over money," Sandifer said with a smile. "Are we, Sam?"

Bell smiled in return.

"Yeah," he said. "I guess that's what we're doing."

"Very well. Twelve five."

"Twenty."

"You must be mad. Fifteen."

"Twenty."

Sandifer sighed without appearing to mean it.

"All right," he said. "Twenty thousand dollars."

Bell relaxed. He hadn't really believed Sandifer would go that high. He probably would have taken on the job for the ten thousand first offered. The way Sandifer had put it, it didn't seem like so terrible a thing to do. And the challenge appealed to him even though he knew there must be considerable risk involved despite Sandifer's attempts to minimize it. Because if it was all that easy, what did Sandifer need with him in the first place?

"Who do I see in Veracruz?" he asked.

"You won't have to worry about that, Sam," said Sandifer. "You've only to play nursemaid to Chato. Someone will be going along to take care of the business arrangements."

He went to the door and opened it.

"Donna," he said. "Will you come in a minute?"

2

THE girl entered, wearing an anxious expression.

Bell struggled out of the tenacious embrace of the sling chair. He still got to his feet when a woman came into a room though, or perhaps because, he had noticed some of them resented such a display of male courtesy. The girl, however, was not looking at him but at Sandifer.

"Relax, child," Sandifer said. "We have our burro." He smiled at Bell and added, "No offense, Sam. It's slang for carrier and in no way pejorative."

"Welcome aboard, Mr. Bell," the girl said, smiling for the first time.

It was not as warm a smile as Bell would have wished but it did make her face more attractive.

"Sam," said Bell.

She was too young and good-looking to be allowed to call him mister.

"Sam," she said.

"Sam, I'd like you to meet Donna Russell," Sandifer said with a hint of formality. "My assistant. Be lost without ——"

"Have you told Mr. Bell all the details, Sandy?" Donna interrupted impatiently. "We're on a tight schedule, you know."

"—— though a bit domineering," Sandifer said. "No, Donna, not all of them."

"Exactly what has Sandy told you?" Donna demanded. "And for God's sake, sit down. I'm not carrying a flag."

Sandifer smiled, enjoying his assistant's asperity. Bell sat down, fingered the side of his sandy moustache that habitually drooped lower than the other, and looked gravely at the front of her blouse. The gold coin suspended there looked back at him like a round golden eye.

"I thought maybe you had one concealed on your person," he said.

Sandifer laughed. Donna did not even smile.

"What did Sandy tell you?" she asked.

"Mostly that it's against the law but everybody's doing it."

She made an impatient gesture.

"It's a big stone head cut into five sections and I'm supposed to load it on a trailer in Veracruz."

"Veracruz?" she demanded, staring at Sandifer.

Sandifer put the tips of his fingers together and studied them.

"Have I got something wrong?" Bell said.

"No," Donna replied. "What else?"

"And then I'm to see it gets to Laredo. And if I don't, it's twelve years in the Mexican brig."

"Did Sandy say that?"

"No. I said that."

"No way. Not if you keep your head on straight."

"Exactly what I told him," Sandifer said.

Donna sat down on Sandifer's desk with her heels on the carpet and her toes in the air. The boot heels were two or three inches high. She was shorter than Bell had thought. Five-seven, maybe. Four inches shorter than he was. He wondered how she could sit down in such a short skirt and not show anything.

"I'd like to hear the rest so I can get started," he

said. "It'll take two or three days to drive down there and check out the route."

"I'm afraid there isn't time," Sandifer said.

"We'll have to make time. The head weighs eighteen tons, you said. And you say we've got to hide it under something. That's another six, eight tons. With the tractor and trailer we'll gross out upward of forty tons. You expect me to move that over roads I never saw before?"

"Knows his business, doesn't he, Donna?" Sandifer said admiringly. "You needn't be concerned about the roads between Veracruz and Laredo, Sam. They're excellent. For Mexico. Or so I've heard."

"So you've heard," said Bell. "Beautiful."

"This is all academic," Donna said. "Isn't Vargas expecting me in Veracruz tomorrow night, Sandy?"

"Expecting *you?*" Bell demanded.

"Donna speaks fluent Spanish," Sandifer said. "And she's an expert on pre-Columbian art."

Sandifer explained that the demand for pre-Columbian art, and the prices American and European collectors were willing to pay, had encouraged rampant fakery.

"But an eighteen-ton head?" Bell protested.

"I shouldn't like to be the first victim of a colossal hoax," Sandifer replied. "Pun intended. And Donna will also handle the financial arrangements. As well as the shipping documents in Nuevo Laredo. Convinced, Sam?"

"Yep. She sounds like the right man for the job."

Donna had also already reserved two seats on Pan Am's Flight 501 leaving Houston for Mexico City at noon the next day, Wednesday. And two seats on Mexicana Flight 621, leaving Mexico City at 3:30 P.M. and arriving in Veracruz at 4:40.

"Splendid, Donna," said Sandifer. "Vargas is contacting you at the Hotel Veracruz at nine tomorrow night. I presume with your customary frightening efficiency you've already reserved a pair of rooms there?"

"One," said Donna. "And one for Mr. Bell at the Gran Hotel Diligencias."

"Y'all were pretty damn sure of me, weren't you?" Bell demanded, looking from one to the other. "Plane tickets, hotel rooms already set."

"Not necessarily you," Sandifer replied. "Though you were, of course, my first choice. We had to have someone immediately."

Bell was to pick up a tourist card and meet Donna at Houston International at 11 A.M. She would have his plane ticket for him.

Bell pushed out of the chair, stretched, and waited.

"Yes, Sam?" Sandifer asked.

"You seem to have forgotten the most important detail."

"Have I? Oh. Suppose I give you a quarter now and the balance when Chato is safely across the border?"

"I'd feel better if I had it all now. Something to come home to if I got delayed. Say twelve years."

"Nonsense, my boy. You'll be back home within a week, I assure you. Half now and the balance on delivery. That's reasonable, isn't it?"

"I guess."

Donna stood up and twirled the coin around a finger on its chain.

"Don't you have things to do, Donna?" Sandifer asked.

When she made no move to leave, he went to the filing cabinet and unlocked it. Shielding his actions with his body, he fiddled with the contents of a drawer for a minute or so. When he turned back to Bell he was holding a plain white envelope, which he gave to him. Bell put it in his pants pocket without counting the money. Donna didn't look too happy.

"See you at the airport at eleven," Bell said. "Mr. Sandifer, it's been a pleasure."

He shook hands with both of them. Donna's hand was cool, strong and impersonal. After Bell closed the office door behind him, he paused for a moment and listened.

"How much, Sandy?" came Donna's brusque voice.

"You're such a grubby child," said Sandifer's voice, not at all placating. "No more than it's worth."

Donna was waiting for him across from the Pan Am desk. She wore a tailored black and white checked pants suit and black, square-toed shoes. Her hair was tied back, showing a lot of face. She looked pretty that way, but severe. Bell wore slacks and a knit cotton sports shirt. She gave him his plane ticket and picked up a big square leather makeup box and a dress bag. Bell switched his carry-on bag and plastic suit bag containing his jacket and an extra pair of slacks to one hand and reached for the dress bag.

"I can manage," said Donna.

Donna boarded the plane as soon as the flight was called. Bell waited until the line had gone down. He had his seat assignment and he figured that he had used up his lifetime quota for waiting in line while he was in the Corps. When he walked through First Class on his way to the Tourist section, he passed Donna, who was sitting in an aisle seat with her nose buried in a book, *The Heirs of Stalin* by Abraham Rothberg.

"Did he leave much?" Bell asked.

Donna frowned without looking up. Bell could not read lips but he was certain her mouth formed the word, "jackass."

"Sandifer's idea I go Tourist?" he said.

"No. Mine."

You are a grubby child, he thought.

"Some day we'll all be one class, Comrade," he said.

Donna did not respond.

"Did you say something, sir?" a stewardess asked.

"Apparently not," said Bell.

The Mexicana flight to Veracruz was one class and Bell sat next to Donna. She seemed tense. Bell didn't think it was because she was sitting next to him.

"Something bothering you, Donna?" he asked.

"No. Well, to tell the truth, I am a little nervous. I've never brought out anything on this scale before."

"Sandifer didn't seem worried."

"Sandy stayed in Houston," she said succinctly. "Even though his Spanish is as good as mine."

The plane was ten minutes late getting into Veracruz, having encountered a little weather over Puebla. For a while Bell had thought he was going to be airsick but the turbulence hadn't seemed to bother Donna in the least. She'd have made one hell of a Marine, Bell thought.

When they landed, he reached for Donna's makeup box. This time she let him carry it.

"Be careful with it," she said. "It's got money in it."

"For Vargas?"

"And emergencies."

"How much?"

"How much is Sandy paying you?"

"Why are you so interested in what I'm getting?"

"Because I'm wondering why he wouldn't tell me."

"That's between you and Sandifer."

Veracruz was as sultry as Houston. Bell was glad to get inside the air-conditioned building. On the way to the baggage claim to pick up Donna's suitcase, Bell saw a sign with a silhouette of an automobile on it.

"Sandifer said to rent a car," Bell said. "Might as well do it here. If you know how to get into town."

"I think so. And there'll be signs."

"Can we count on that later when we get out on the road with the merchandise? Road signs, I mean?"

Donna shrugged.

"Figures," said Bell.

There were four car-rental agencies in a row behind a long counter. Only one, National Car Rental, was staffed. The clerk was a young woman in a blue dress that could have come from Sears in Houston. Somehow Bell had expected everybody this far south to be dressed like Mexicans.

Donna spoke to the young woman in Spanish. Bell heard the word, "Volkswagen."

"Hey!" he protested. "Just a minute. You're not renting a beetle, are you?"

"Why not?"

"It'll be twenty-five, thirty hours, maybe having to catch a nap in the back seat. I'll need something bigger. And air-conditioned."

"She has a Volks all ready to go. And if I can put up with the discomfort, you can too."

"You're coming with me?"

"Not that Sandy doesn't trust you with the loot. But, yes."

Bell pursued his lips. He hadn't counted on Donna being in the chase car with him. But it did make sense. She knew the ropes, she spoke Spanish. And he couldn't blame Sandifer for wanting to protect his interests.

"Do I look like a crook?" he asked, only half in jest.

"But you are, Sam. Or you will be as soon as we take delivery on Chato."

"I don't suppose it's air-conditioned. The beetle."

"This isn't Houston," she said.

She had that look in her eye that said she was thinking "jackass" again. Well, he was that, as well as a crook. He was Sandifer's burro and burro meant donkey.

Donna and the clerk were talking.

"How long will we need the car?" Donna asked Bell.

"How long will it take you to wrap things up at this end?"

"A day. Maybe two."

"How long in Nuevo Laredo?"

"Not long. If we get there during business hours. Will we?"

"If you're asking for a schedule, you better send it by Greyhound."

She should have known he had no way of telling, with the little information he had about the route and when they would be leaving. There was a little jackass in Donna, too. Somehow, that pleased him.

She took the car for a week because the rate was the same as for five days, 562.5 pesos, or $45 U.S. There was also a charge of 70 centavos a kilometer, payable when they turned the car in.

They went out front to wait for the car. Donna, he noticed, did not object to such attentions as having her suitcase carried for her. Because it was a big one, black and white checked like her pants suit, and heavy. He wouldn't have minded if she hadn't seemed to expect it.

Donna frowned when he gave a dollar tip to the man who brought the car. After their things were stowed in the back seat and they were on their way, with the windows rolled down to catch the air, she said, "I wish you'd leave the disbursements to me. And don't use American money down here. This isn't a border town."

"Yes, ma'am," Bell said.

Donna bristled.

"I wish you wouldn't say that. It's just it's such a drag keeping track of your out-of-pocket expenses."

"Why don't you put me on an allowance?" Bell said dryly.

They came to a road junction. In the middle of the junction was a grassy knoll planted with flowers. On the knoll was a colossal Olmec head.

"Look at that!" Bell cried.

"It's a replica, and not a very good one," Donna replied calmly. "Concrete."

Bell was interested anyhow. For the first time he could see with his own eyes just how imposing such a head was. Maybe he should have asked Sandifer to tell him more about the Olmecs. He stared at the head out of the back window until it was out of sight.

Donna drove north from the junction. The street sign outside of Veracruz said Alemán. After a while Alemán jogged to the left and became Allende. The houses and business establishments were mostly run-down and the street was in disrepair. Donna's face showed uncertainty. Let her work it out for herself, Bell thought. She knew everything. Allende ended at a huddle of warehouses. Donna bit her lip and turned right. After a few blocks, she cried, "Here it is, Independencia! I remember the steetcar tracks."

The street was one-way and she had to turn right. The Hotel Veracruz was four blocks away, on the west side of Independencia. Donna pulled over to the curb, cut the engine and honked for someone to come out for the luggage.

"Your hotel's across the street," she said. "Over there."

"Yours looks better," Bell said.

"Yours has the best restaurant in town."

"I don't plan on sleeping in the restaurant."

When the bellman came out, Donna said something to him and handed him the keys to the Volkswagen. He picked up Donna's suitcase and dress bag and went into the hotel, leaving Bell's things on the sidewalk.

"Your room's in the name of Clark Kent," Donna said. "When I reserved it I didn't know who'd be coming down with me."

"Don't we have things to discuss?" Bell asked.

"Not until after I see Vargas. You *can* look after yourself for a few hours, can't you?"

"I'm not sure," Bell said. "I never tried before. Where can I find some maps? All I've got is the one to three and a half million scale road map I picked up at the auto club."

"Ask at the desk. Someone will speak English."

Bell bent down for his bags.

"Adiós," he said, straightening.

But he said it to Donna's back. She was already reaching for the handle to the door into the Hotel Veracruz. Bell grinned and started walking. The Gran Hotel Diligencias was just across Miguel Lerdo, on the same side of Independencia. It was a block-long white building with shutters painted a contrasting reddish brown. A fifteen- or twenty-foot portico extended under the hotel back from the sidewalk. It was filled with tables and chairs, a good third of them occupied by dark men in short-sleeved shirts, a few of them, but only a few, sharing tables with women. Across the street was a plaza crisscrossed with paved walks, and filled with flowers and greenery. There was a splashing fountain in the center of the plaza and in back of the plaza another block-long building, this one of only two stories, with graceful arches on both floors and brilliant white in the fading minutes of the day. Over all floated the sound of marimbas and trumpets.

Bell wished he weren't in Veracruz on business, and shady business at that. And that he were with someone a bit more friendly than Donna Russell.

3

THERE was a souvenir shop and newsstand at the hotel entrance. Bell asked for a map. The girl knew just enough English to let him know she didn't have one.

The lobby of the Gran Hotel Diligencias was unprepossessing. It was dark and the armchairs and sofa in the lounge, aimed at a television set, were drab. Bell doubted if things were like that at Donna's hotel. The reception desk was a narrow quadrangle with a woman clerk standing in it. Behind her, another woman sat at an old-fashioned switchboard.

"You have a room reserved for Mr. Kent?" Bell asked.

The clerk replied in Spanish.

"Reservation," Bell said. "Kent. K-e-n-t."

She looked in a ledger, said, "Sí, señor," and slid a registration card across the counter. Bell filled out the card, signing his own name.

"Maps," he said. "Where can I find a city map and road maps from here to the border?"

"Mapa?"

She made a gesture indicating he was to wait and turned to look toward the two dinky elevators behind her station. The elevators had old-fashioned floor indicators above them, iron prongs like clock hands pointing at numbers. One indicator was moving down from four. The elevator door opened and a couple with two solemn children emerged. The clerk called to the elevator operator, a plump boy with a cheerful face. He came over and said, "Yes, mister?"

"I need some maps."

"You want paper shop. Papelería." He said it again slowly. "Papelería. Okay?"

He took Bell's key and bags and led him to the elevator. As soon as the door closed he asked, "Veracruz is good, yes?"

"Yeah," said Bell. "Veracruz is muy bueno."

The boy grinned.

The room was on the third floor overlooking Miguel Lerdo and the Hotel Veracruz. Probably nothing in it had been changed in the past twenty years but it was clean. Bell gave the boy a dollar bill, thinking he had to get some pesos and what a relief it was not to have Donna around grumbling about "disbursements."

He went down to the reception desk and exchanged $50 U.S. for 600 pesos. It was coming on dusk when he stepped out on Independencia. The lights were on all over town and the big white building across the street was bathed in illumination. Most of the tables on the portico were occupied now with people drinking coffee, beer and soda pop. The sidewalk in front of the hotel was thronged. Across the street, people were getting on and off a crowded streetcar without sides or top. Bell would have liked to take a ride on it.

Music plunged at him from every direction, from the bar to his left, from the Gran Café de la Parroquia in the block to the right and from a whole string of bars and restaurants across from the plaza on the north side of Miguel Lerdo. He hoped he would have time later on to sit at one of the tables and enjoy the music. And maybe he could persuade Donna to join him.

It did not take long to find a papelería. For eight pesos he bought a map with the city of Veracruz on one side and a 1:1,000,000 scale map of the state of Veracruz on the other. It was far more detailed than his auto-club map.

There were few empty chairs at the outside tables when he returned to the Diligencias. Marimbas, trumpets and violins were competing along Independencia and Miguel Lerdo and across the street a man was singing. Though all the groups were playing different tunes, the blend was pleasant.

Bell went up to his room, shaved with his electric razor, and showered. In the shower he washed out his shirt, underpants and socks. He combed his sandy reddish hair, put on a fresh shirt and his other slacks, and went down to dinner.

The restaurant was bright and airy but unpretentious, with a tile floor and plain wooden chairs. Donna was sitting by herself over in a corner. It puzzled him that she should be eating here until he recalled she had said the Diligencias restaurant was the best in town. Anybody connected with Otis Sandifer naturally wouldn't eat anywhere else.

Donna was already eating. When she noticed him, she surprised him by motioning for him to join her. He would have, even without that. She was good-looking even if she was so businesslike it made his teeth hurt.

"Buenas noches, Doña Donna," he said, dredging up a few words of Spanish.

He had thought it might get a smile but it didn't. At least she didn't frown. Maybe with Donna that was the equivalent of a smile.

She was eating a whole fish, heavily sauced. She and Sandifer must have a thing about fish. A waiter came over and started to pour Bell a glass of wine from the bottle on the table. Bell shook his head.

"It isn't too dreadful, for Mexican wine," Donna said.

"If you can't have a rather nice Meursault, what's the point?" Bell said.

"I forgot to tell you earlier," said Donna. "Be in your room by nine thirty."

"Is it the usual bedcheck or did you have something more personal in mind?"

"I'll want to talk to you after I've seen Vargas."

"Maybe I should go with you. There're things I need to know you may not know to ask him."

"No. He'll tell me everything you need to know."

The waiter brought a menu in a folder, two mimeo-graphed sheets under clear plastic. Bell didn't look at it.

"What's that you're eating, Donna?" he asked.

"Huachinango Veracruz. Red snapper Veracruz style. I recommend it."

She sounded like Sandifer.

"I had red snapper yesterday."

"In that case, you should try one of the other specialties."

She studied the menu, reminding him more than ever of Sandifer, except that Sandifer had charm.

"Cocktail de jaiba, rueda de róbalo en salsa verde and for dessert, papaya," she said at last.

Whatever that was, he wasn't having it. Sandifer had sent her along to handle the business arrangements, not run his life. When she started ordering his dinner, he stopped her with a gesture.

"I'll start with a shrimp cocktail," he told the waiter. "And a steak. Medium rare."

Donna had to translate the order into Spanish. When she went back to her fish, Bell watched, fasci-nated. She dissected it like a surgeon, peeling back

28

the skin and delicately removing the bones. Donna was aware of his scrutiny.

"Tell me something, Sam," she said. "Did you order steak because you don't know how to handle something civilized or because you didn't want to take a suggestion from me?"

"Was it a suggestion? I thought it was an order."

"Sandy says my suggestions always sound like orders."

It was almost an apology. Maybe she was human after all.

"Why don't you change your mind and have a glass of wine?" Donna said.

She was really thawing out, Bell thought.

"I'll never finish the bottle and it would be a shame to waste it," she said. "It cost nine dollars."

So it was frugality, not friendship.

"Are you on an expense account, too?" he asked.

"How's that? Oh. Because of the wine?" She gave a rare smile. "Yes. It's a way of making Sandy pay me what I'm worth."

"You should smile more often, Donna. You'd meet more fellows and have more fun."

"This isn't a fun trip."

"Not so far, that's for sure."

While Bell ate his steak, Donna had coffee and a platter of sliced bananas, pineapple and papaya. The coffee was served in a thick-walled water glass with a spoon in it. The waiter had a kettle with a spout in either hand and poured thick, frothing coffee from one of them until Donna signaled enough. He filled the glass with hot milk from the other kettle. It made a foamy head, like Guinness.

Donna kept looking at her watch. When she finished her coffee she had the waiter bring her check and Bell's.

"What's your hurry?" Bell said. "Why not have a glass of coffee with me?"

"It's already a quarter to nine. I want to be there when Vargas calls."

Bell did not like admitting it to himself but he was disappointed. He'd enjoyed being with her and seeing her smile, even if it was only once.

"Don't forget," she said. "Be back in your room by nine thirty. And when you order your coffee, tell the waiter café con leche."

Bell took his coffee at an outside table where he could hear the music and watch the action. It looked as if everyone in Veracruz were sitting at sidewalk tables, walking the streets or strolling in the plaza. The palatial building across the plaza was lit up like a stage. Men in white uniforms leaned on the second-floor railing looking down into the plaza. The marimbas in front of the Gran Café de la Parroquia mingled with those from the bar at the far end of the Diligencias. A boy walked through the sidewalk café carrying a huge model ship under full sail on his shoulder. He tried to sell it to Bell. Bell would have bought it for Donna as a gag if there had been room for it in the Volks. She'd probably just sneer at him anyhow for wasting good money.

He found himself wishing Donna were there with him, and were a warmer type. Then he found himself thinking about his reason for being in Veracruz. For the first time he felt nervous about it. Back in Sandifer's office it hadn't seemed like such a big deal to bring up the head, with everything all greased for him. But things could always go wrong. Even back in the States on a routine haul things sometimes went wrong. There it was just inconvenient. Here it could mean twelve years in the brig. He looked at his watch, suddenly impatient. Nine fifteen. He went up to his room, took off his shirt and shoes and lay down on one of the twin beds.

After a while he got up and spread his maps on the other bed. He had already marked a tentative route on the auto-club map with a yellow felt-tipped pen. Neither map showed contour lines or color-keyed altitude. That meant he wouldn't know much about the terrain until he actually drove through it. He had kept the first part of the 333-mile leg to Tampico as close to the coast as possible, where the terrain would be flatter. He had yet to decide which of two available routes to take from Tuxpan to Tampico. Highway 180, which he would be taking to Tuxpan, gave him a straight shot to Tampico but it meant a ferry crossing. The other route out of Tuxpan, Highway 105, eliminated the ferry but was a good forty miles longer. And might be more hilly because it was farther inland. He'd rather avoid the ferry. He didn't know what kind of load it would take or if there was a long wait. After Tampico he would be obliged to turn inland for Monterrey and Nuevo Laredo.

Maybe Vargas, or one of the truck drivers, would know more about the route. There wasn't much chance Vargas would be telling such details to Donna tonight and she sure as hell didn't know enough to ask. He should have insisted that she let him sit in with them. He looked at his watch. Almost ten. He went to the window and looked across Miguel Lerdo to the Hotel Veracruz. He wondered if that was where they were meeting. There was a nightclub on top of the hotel. He could hear the music mingling with that from below. When you were in Veracruz with a pretty girl you should be up there dancing and making time, not sweating it out in a room while she arranged to steal an eighteen-ton rock. Behind him, strange noises began struggling out of the air vent as if the air-conditioner were about to expire.

He went back to the bed and refolded his maps. He went to the window again. Ten fifteen and still no call from Donna. Maybe something had gone wrong. She'd said she was carrying a lot of bread. He ought to call her room and see if she was okay. But they might be meeting somewhere else. And, anyhow, they seemed to have worked with Vargas before, so he wasn't likely to pull anything.

It was after ten thirty when the phone rang. Bell grabbed it before it could ring a second time.

"Yeah?" he said.

"Sam?"

Donna sounded agitated.

"Something wrong?" he asked.

All he could hear was quick, shallow breathing.

"Donna? You all right?"

"We've got problems," she said at last.

"What kind of problems?"

"Not on the phone."

"I'll be right over."

"I'm not at the hotel. Meet me by the fountain in the Plaza de la Constitución in ten minutes."

"Where's that?"

"Right across from your hotel," she said impatiently, as if he were an idiot not to know.

Bell let it pass.

"You sure you're all right?" he said.

"Don't worry, I'm fine," she said more amiably. "Ten minutes. Okay?"

She hung up without waiting for an answer.

Bell slipped into his shirt and shoes and hurried downstairs, answering the friendly elevator boy's chatter in monosyllables. The sidewalk tables were crowded and the music was still unabated all along Independencia and Miguel Lerdo. Bell counted four combos playing in front of the bars and restaurants on Miguel Lerdo. In the plaza, there wasn't a vacant place on any of the benches along the walks. People were strolling among the trees and flowers or standing in small groups talking and listening to the music. Children dozed in their parents' laps or played on the sidewalk, their legs and faces smudged. It was like a carnival.

The air by the fountain was moist and at least ten degrees cooler than farther back in the plaza. Bell let it wash over him. Donna was nowhere in sight. Maybe the deal had fallen through. He wondered if Sandifer would try to get his ten thousand back. Bell resolved not to be greedy about it but to hold enough back to pay for his trouble. Traveling with Donna hadn't been exactly a weekend with your favorite chick.

He was a little relieved that he might not have to go through with it after all. Now that he'd seen what an Olmec head looked like full-size, ripping one off didn't seem like more of a prank than a crime even if Sandifer had said it would never be missed. Yet his relief was outweighed by disappointment. It wasn't just the money, though twenty thousand dollars would give him lots of options when he started looking around for a new start. He had been looking forward to moving that eighteen tons of rock nine hundred unfamiliar miles through potentially dangerous territory. It had been a good while since he'd had any real excitement.

Donna came hurrying toward him along a greenery-bordered walk. She had changed into a dark dress and was carrying a big purse. Bell went to meet her. He took her by both elbows and looked into her face.

"Take it easy, baby," he said.

She wouldn't meet his eyes.

"The head's not in Veracruz," she said apologetically.

"What?"

"Vargas never brought it up from Tlacotalpán and he hasn't hired a trailer truck."

"Beautiful," said Bell. "Why?"

"He said an agent of the Federal Judicial Police has been nosing around. So he didn't want to take any chances."

The Federal Judicial Police, she explained, was similar to the FBI in the U.S. One of its agents in

33

Veracruz, "El Azteca," Vargas had called him, apparently had heard rumors that a colossal Olmec head had been found in the jungle and removed. Vargas had acknowledged, however, that as far as he knew, the agent had no idea who had moved the head or where, or even if the rumors had foundation. Vargas was apprehensive because El Azteca knew he trafficked in pre-Columbian art.

"And he said this El Azteca's not on the take," Donna said. "You can't get to him with mordida."

"Mordida?"

"The bite. A bribe. He takes it personally when somebody tries to rip off a national treasure."

"It's all off then?"

Donna shook her head.

"Vargas said we'd have to pick it up at Tlacotalpán. He's got it tucked away on a farm."

"Will he at least arrange a tractor and trailer for us?"

"He won't touch a thing in Veracruz."

They were strolling around the plaza, speaking in low voices. The crowd was beginning to thin but the music did not flag.

"Well, hell," said Bell. "We ought to be able to find one ourselves."

"I thought you'd be a lot more uptight about it," Donna said, sounding relieved.

"I figure for what Sandifer's paying me I've got to expect a little trouble here and there. The only thing bothers me is this agent character."

"Vargas guarantees he doesn't know anything for sure."

"Yeah. And Vargas told Sandifer he had the head and a trailer waiting here for us. I wouldn't trust him any farther than I could throw Chato."

"Maybe Sandy misunderstood him."

Bell stared at her. It didn't make sense for her to defend a man who'd just let her down so badly.

34

"Sandifer wouldn't misunderstand a thing like that," he said.

"I suppose you're right. But we've got to trust Vargas now we've come this far with him. Sandy's got a lot of money tied up in this."

Don't we all, Bell thought.

"You know this Vargas character better than I do," he said. "If you're game, I am, too."

They were walking along Miguel Lerdo across from the Bar Imperial and the Restaurante Bar Palacios. A marimba band was playing in front of the Imperial, and the Palacios bar's bigger band, with violins and a trumpet, was trying to drown it out. A girl in a pink dress was between two parked cars on the plaza side of the street doing the twist all by herself. She wore a little hat and clutched a purse between her elbow and her left side. Her left hand rested lightly on the hood of one of the cars and her right hand beat the air trying to find the tempo of the competing bands.

"I could do that pretty good when I was about fifteen," Bell said. "The twist. Dance, Donna?"

She stared at him.

"Don't you dig that music?" he said.

"You must be out of your mind."

"Okay. But remember, I asked you first."

He stepped off the curb and touched the girl on the shoulder.

"May I have this dance, por favor?" he said.

She craned her head around, still dancing. She wasn't a girl. She was an old woman with mad eyes and an intent, set look on her gaunt face. Without a word, she turned away. She had not stopped dancing.

Bell looked at the people watching them and made a gesture of apology. He hoped they hadn't thought he was making fun of the mad old woman. Donna was not among them. He walked swiftly toward the corner of Independencia and Miguel Lerdo. Donna was there waiting for the light to change. It turned green before he could reach her. He sprinted and caught up with her at the Prendes restaurant on the other side of Miguel Lerdo.

"You ass!" she said through clenched teeth.

"It's your fault," Bell replied. "You shouldn't have turned me down."

"Goodnight, Sam," she said firmly, walking away from him. "I'll call you in the morning."

"Unh unh. We've got a lot to work out tonight, baby. I don't even know where Lockatalp is."

"Tlacotalpán. And don't call me baby. We can go over everything in the morning. I've got to call Sandy now."

"I'll go with you."

"It isn't necessary."

She kept walking at a brisk pace, Bell matching her stride for stride.

"Why don't you run along to your room and play with your maps?" she demanded.

He took her arm and stopped her.

"Is there any particular reason you don't want me around when you talk to Sandifer?" he said.

"Of course not. If you like, I'll call you and tell you what he advises when I get back to my room."

"I want to talk to him myself."

"It isn't necessary," she said again.

"I think it is. You're in charge of business arrangements. Transportation is my baby. Right? And we've got transportation problems. Right?"

Donna sighed, resigned.

"All right," she said.

The long distance office was a couple of blocks up Independencia. A dozen or so persons were waiting to be called to one of the booths along the right-hand wall. At the back was a counter behind which sat a girl wearing a headset. While Donna was arranging the call with her, Bell went to a soft drink machine, searched his change for coins that fit and got a couple of bottles. He brought one back to Donna. Her expression showed his thoughtfulness was unexpected.

"Thanks," she said. "Thanks, Sam."

She didn't smile, though. Bell had grown accustomed to that, but he thought now there was more to it than just her usual lack of warmth. She seemed tense, even apprehensive.

"You're more worried about this El Azteca thing than you said, aren't you?" he said quietly.

"No. It's the way Vargas's screwed everything up."

"No sweat, Donna. We'll get our own rig. Don't worry about it."

They sat down to wait for Donna's call to go through. The girl with the headset called out something and a good-looking young man in a white Navy tunic and trousers, with a short sword dangling at his hip, quit talking to a lumpy girl with a faint moustache and went to a booth. Donna stirred impatiently, started to nibble a fingernail, thought better of it, and folded her hands in her lap. She was really uptight, Bell thought. If it wasn't about the federal police, she sure was worried about something else. The girl with the headset called out again. Donna jumped up.

"That's my call," she said.

Bell followed her to the booth. She tried to shut the door but he pushed in with her. She hesitated before picking up the receiver, saw he was determined to remain, and put it to her ear.

"Hello," she said. "Sandy?"

A pause.

"Sandy, I've got Sam here with me."

It sounded to Bell like a warning.

She turned and looked at him.

"Sandy says hello," she said.

"Tell him hello for me."

"Sandy, Vargas has screwed everything up. The head's still in Tlacotalpán and he hasn't got us a trailer."

Bell strained to hear Sandifer's reply. He expected loud anger. But if Sandifer was sore it didn't make him shout. Bell couldn't hear his reply. Donna put her hand over the mouthpiece.

"He wants to know if you can handle it."

"Let me talk to him."

Bell took the receiver from Donna without waiting for a reply.

"Bell here, Mr. Sandifer."

"Hello, Sam, my boy."

Sandifer sounded calm.

"There shouldn't be any problem at this end. Except that Vargas told Donna there's a policeman nosing around."

"No problem mordida can't handle."

"Vargas told Donna this character's not on the take."

"Then we'll just have to keep out of his way, won't we?"

"Then you don't think it's anything to get uptight about?"

"No. Not at all. Let me have Donna again. And Sam?"

"Yeah?"

"If you have the opportunity, try the snapper Veracruz style at the Diligencias."

"Right."

He handed the receiver to Donna. She waited, as if expecting him to leave the booth now. He outwaited her.

"Sandy," she said reluctantly. "Vargas wants another thirty."

Now Bell could hear a loud voice, unintelligible but unmistakably angry.

"I know, I know," Donna said. "But he said things have changed."

She listened for a while and then said, "All right. I'll try ten and go the rest of the way only if I must. Yes. I understand. Good night, Sandy." She nodded and said, "I'll tell him."

She hung up and looked at Bell.

"Sandy said good night," she said.

"That all?"

"That's all."

"I think we should have a little talk, Donna."

"Can't it wait until morning? I'm very tired."

"This won't take long."

They walked back to the Diligencias and sat down at one of the outside tables. Some of them weren't occupied but the music was still going.

"I could use a beer," Bell said. "What about you? Coffee or something cold?"

"I think I'd like a beer, too."

Bell waited until the waiter left the bottles on the table before getting to the point.

"Sandifer knew the head wouldn't be in Veracruz, didn't he?" he said.

"How could he have?" Donna demanded.

"Don't try to con me, Donna. He took it like a soldier when you told him. But when you said Vargas wanted more bread, varoom! That's what you had to call him about, wasn't it? Not about the head being in Lockopan."

"Tlacotalpán." She studied the froth on her beer. "Yes. He knew."

"Then why the hell did he say everything was all set?"

"He wanted to make it sound easier than it was, I suppose. That's the way dear old Sandy is." She looked up from her glass into his face. "You're just sitting there. Don't you yell and hit people when you're mad?"

39

"Not always. And never good-looking chicks. Anyway, I'm not all that sore. For twenty thousand it figured to be more complicated than he let on."

She jerked erect in her chair, her face filled with outrage.

"Twenty thousand!" she cried. "That bastard!"

Bell was startled by her outburst.

"Look," he said. "Why are you taking it so big? It's not coming out of your pocket. Or is it?"

"Sandy's paying me five," she said grimly. "And a raise the first of the year."

"Don't be sore at me, Donna. It's not my fault Sandifer's not an equal opportunity employer."

"For two cents I'd . . ." Donna began.

She fell into a stony silence and drummed her fingers on the tabletop.

"He must be getting a bundle for that hunk of rock," Bell said. "How much?"

Donna, more controlled now, contemplated her glass.

"It must be plenty if this Vargas character wants another thirty thousand on top of whatever he was supposed to get," Bell persisted.

"Five hundred thousand dollars," Donna said softly.

Bell whistled.

"Half a million dollars?" he exclaimed.

"Don't go getting any ideas like Vargas'," she said tartly. "If anyone's entitled to a raise, it's me."

Bell smiled at her.

"If I get any ideas, it won't be about money," he said.

As usual, she did not find his attempt at dalliance amusing. Not that he could blame her, under the circumstances.

"Why would anybody pay that much for something like that?" he demanded.

"Collectors are crazy," Donna replied. Before he

could agree, she continued, "Why, indeed, when for half as much he could get an absolutely marvelous Mayan stela."

"Why, indeed," said Bell.

"And he can't even keep it in his home with his other pieces," Donna said. "He's building a special place for it on his estate. That'll cost him another fifty, seventy-five thousand dollars. Not only that, he can't let anyone know he has it except a few trusted friends. Or run the risk of having it confiscated and shipped back to Mexico."

"The poor chap," Bell murmured, his irony lost on Donna. "Just one thing," he continued. "Is it the truth about this El Azteca or just something you dreamed up to explain why Vargas didn't have the head in Veracruz?"

"There is an agent of the federal police they call El Azteca and he is in Veracruz and Vargas is concerned about him," Donna said. "But he doesn't know anything about us or the head. There are always rumors floating around about big finds out in the jungle, and I'm sure El Azteca is quite aware that's all they usually are. Rumors."

4

AT ten o'clock Wednesday morning Tomás Alvarado Ybarra sat at a sidewalk table in front of the Bar Imperial on Avenida Miguel Lerdo mopping his face and drinking a Coca-Cola. He always sat there, at the same table, when he had a few minutes to spare. It was cooler inside, where there was air conditioning, but here he had a better view of the Plaza de la Constitución and the bell tower of the Parroquia Asunción on the other side of it. He enjoyed the view of the fountain and the tulipáns and rosa de laurels with their whitewashed trunks, and he was especially fond of watching the pigeons when the Parroquia Asunción bell began its rapid clanging. They would flap out of the bell tower in clouds, wheel over the plaza and alight on the church dome. Eventually they would straggle back to the bell tower, only to do it all over again the next time the bell sounded.

Alvarado sat at the sidewalk table not only because he enjoyed doing so but also because he could see people from it, and people could see him. He sometimes learned interesting things just by sitting there and drinking Coca-Cola or café con leche. People would sometimes sit down at the table with him and speak urgently in low voices, or perhaps furtively leave scraps of paper with interesting things written on them.

Alvarado was forty-two but looked younger. He was a striking figure. He was a big man not, at six feet one inch, because of his height but because of the thickness of his chest, his heavy shoulders and big hands with clumsy-looking fingers. His nose was thick, too, but well shaped, and the bone structure above his eyes was heavy. His cheekbones were prominent and his lips thin. Were it not for his eyes, hidden now by sunglasses, it would have been a cruel face. But the eyes were not cruel. They were dark brown, alert and gentle.

Tomás Alvarado Ybarra was an Agente del Policia Judicial Federal, an agent of the Federal Judicial Police. Because of his face he was often called El Azteca, the Aztec.

Alvarado nursed the Coke glass in his big hand, feeling its coolness. He reached under the tail of his pleated white guayabera shirt and pulled the padded hook of the holster away from his side. When it was very hot and he was sitting, he was never unaware of that holster at his waistband though he never noticed the weight of the Smith and Wesson .38 Special revolver in it. The pistol was too small for his hand but was what had been issued to him long ago and he had learned to make do.

He finished his Coke and made a gesture without turning his head. A waiter came out almost immediately and brought him another. Alvarado did not pay for it. It was not expected that he should. Free drinks, an occasional free meal and other small favors were prerogatives of his position, and the only ones acceptable to him.

He sipped the cold drink, mopped his face and pulled the damp shirt away from his armpit. If ever he was transferred to a cooler, more formal place, where he would have to wear a coat, he was going to get himself a shoulder holster.

Alvarado was almost finished with the second Coke when the man for whom he had been waiting appeared — a small, portly man carrying a brown paper sack from which protruded the yellow feet of a chicken. He sat down across from Alvarado, put his chicken on a chair, removed his straw hat, and carefully wiped the sweatband with a dirty handkerchief before depositing the hat beside the chicken.

"So?" said Alvarado.

"Sorry I'm late, agente," the newcomer said. "But my wife said it was chicken with rice for lunch."

"She's a good cook, your wife?"

The man made a face.

"So, Galvez?" Alvarado said, swirling the last of the cola in its glass.

"I phoned my friend in San Andrés Tuxtla," Galvez said. "As I promised. But there is still nothing more. Only that the rumor continues something large and quite heavy was removed last month from the jungle not too distant from the Laguna de los Cerros site."

"Still only rumors?" Alvarado said.

Galvez made an apologetic gesture.

"No one wishes to admit he has certain knowledge, agente." Galvez suddenly sat up straighter and said, "Ah, ah! The talk is it was taken out by boats. That is new."

"By boats," Alvarado repeated. "To where?"

Galvez made another apologetic gesture.

"By the way," he said, "did you know Jorge Vargas is in Veracruz?"

"No, I didn't," said Alvarado. He was annoyed with himself. He should have known. "When did he get in?"

"I don't know. Only that he's in Veracruz."

"Has he made a connection?"

"I don't know that, either," Galvez said apologetically. "Look," he continued, glancing at the sack with the chicken's feet sticking out of it. "I promised my wife . . ."

"Of course," said Alvarado. "If you hear anything new . . ."

"Certainly, agente." Galvez hesitated. "About my wife's nephew . . . ?"

"I spoke with the Agente del Ministerio Público about him this morning. He definitely will see what he can do."

"Thank you," Galvez said fervently, getting up. "Thank you, agente. My wife will be pleased to hear that."

He put on his hat, picked up his chicken and ran for the streetcar discharging passengers across the plaza on Independencia. Alvarado finished his drink and started back for the comandancia. He went across to the Diligencias restaurant instead. Jorge Vargas could afford to eat well, and did. If he had arrived in Veracruz the day before, it was possible he had dined there last night. Perhaps with a companion. Someone he was seeing on business. There might be nothing to the rumors of a major find down by Laguna de los Cerros, and Vargas might be in Veracruz on legitimate business — Licenciado Vargas' law officers were in Mexico City but he did have clients here — but then again, the two things might be related. It never hurt to investigate.

The manager had been in the restaurant until closing Tuesday night. He had seen no one answering to Vargas' description. But if he saw such a person he would certainly inform the authorities without delay.

"It isn't necessary," Alvarado said. "This is unofficial."

He went outside and hailed a cab. It was too hot to walk all the way over to the Palacio Federal on Rayón and Cinco de Mayo, where the comandancia of the Federal Judicial Police was located. He did not know the driver and had to show the man his ID before he agreed to leave the meter off. That, too, was one of the small prerogatives Alvarado was willing to accept.

Alvarado got out of the taxi at the Palacio Federal and paused to look across the street at the Cine Reforma. An American detective film was playing there. Friday night he was taking the whole family to see it. He walked quickly between the peeling green arches of the Palacio Federal portico, stopped briefly to look at the posted list of winning lottery numbers — he never actually bought a lottery ticket but he sometimes picked a number — and threaded his way across the sidewalk through the pedestrians and vendors of lottery tickets, candy, cakes and chewing gum.

The Palacio Federal offices were arranged around a courtyard paved with concrete blocks. The water standpipe at the back was still dripping, Alvarado noticed. It had been doing that for weeks and still nothing had been done about it. He went down the pink tile walk past the post office to the comandancia.

The chief was engulfed in the usual litter of paperwork. He looked up, annoyed, when Alvarado rapped on the wall with his knuckles. When the chief saw who it was, the annoyance left his face but he did not smile.

"Chief, could I get a car to go to San Andrés?" Alvarado asked.

"Is that where Ramos has got to?" the chief replied, showing interest.

"It's not the Ramos case," Alvarado said reluctantly.

"Not the Ramos case? You're supposed to be on it full time. You got a girl in San Andrés?"

"I heard something," Alvarado said, stepping inside the office. "I heard the burros have been busy in a big way down south."

"And you want a car for that?"

46

"I thought I'd have a look for myself. An informant of mine said there's a lot of talk about a big find."

"What kind of big find?"

"He didn't know. But from the location, Olmec."

The chief looked pained.

"When the attorney general hears about this big find, and orders me to investigate, and if you're not busy with something else, then you can have a car. Meanwhile I'm not interested in your rumored Olmec bric-a-brac."

"Yes, chief," Alvarado said.

He was not particularly disappointed because he had expected as much. The chief did not share his views about preserving national treasures in general and Olmec in particular. Alvarado had spent a whole day in the pre-Columbian rooms at the Museum of Anthropology in Mexico City and twice had taken Sara and their three girls to visit the museum at Jalapa. Not to mention the Sundays the family had gone to Santiago Tuxtla on the bus to view the two Olmec heads on display there. The girls and Sara thought the trips boring but Alvarado never did. He had a photograph at home of the whole family posing in front of the larger of the two heads there, the one brought up from Cobato in 1970.

Alvarado was personally offended by the theft of pre-Columbian artifacts. When foreigners spirited out pieces of Mexico's past they were stealing his heritage. Despite the fact that people called him El Azteca, be believed Olmec was his true heritage because his family had lived in Veracruz State for as many generations as he could trace, and this was the region where the Olmecs had flourished thousands of years ago. When looters got their hands on an archeological site it was like tearing a page out of a history book. They took everything and left the site useless even for study. It wasn't that way when scholars and archeologists got there first. They measured and sketched and made photographs. They studied and recorded every detail. All the markings and designs and ciphers, the position of every object with relation to every other object were recorded. In that way, they were able to learn things about the ancient peoples who had made the objects and constructed the buildings. All this knowledge was lost forever when the looters got there first.

And what offended Alvarado as much as this rape of history and his heritage was the fact that foreigners and wealthy rascals like Vargas made huge profits providing pre-Columbian artifacts for American and European collectors while the impoverished peons who found them received almost nothing. It would not have made him quite so angry if the poor Mexicans who discovered the valuable objects received a just share of the profits. If the dead could help the living, it might serve some useful purpose. But when it lined the pockets of foreign dealers and their Vargases, that was something else. The real villains were the Vargases. It was one thing for a foreigner not to respect the Mexican cultural heritage, quite another for a Mexican to do so. There was one thing, and only one, to be said in defense of Vargas. At least the moneros who worked for him did not destroy the very objects themselves. Those objects too large to remove intact to be spirited across the border were cut into pieces with chain saws or corundum-coated wires, with great care taken not to mar the most intricate of the designs and carvings. Some looters acting independently were not beyond smashing such things to bits with sledgehammers and selling the more presentable shards. But then again, with Vargas it was doubtless not a sense of decency that made him forbid such barbarism, it was the fact that properly cut and rejoined specimens were what brought huge returns.

"Anything else?" the chief demanded.

"No, chief," Alvarado said.

"Then go out and catch me Luis Ramos. They've been on the Telex from the Capital every hour on the hour wanting to know what progress we've made."

Ramos was a petty criminal from Veracruz who had moved to Mexico City looking for broader horizons. A week ago he had gone up to Juárez and got hold of fifty cases of duty-free Johnny Walker Black Label to peddle in the Federal District, where whiskey was not duty free and fetched a good price. He had shot it out with the police who came to arrest him and winged one of them in the arm before escaping. What made Mexico City so interested in this relatively minor case was the fact that the wounded man was a fairly highly placed officer of the Federal Judicial Police who had gone along on the raid to keep his hand in with field operations. Now Ramos was thought to be in Veracruz. He always came home when he needed money or things got too hot in the Capital.

Alvarado had been looking for him for three days, the first two spent staking out Ramos' mother's house in the southeast part of town. At night Alvarado had prowled the bars and cantinas. Ramos was known to enjoy a good carouse. Alvarado had not caught up with Ramos but had learned he definitely was in town. And broke. Now Alvarado was checking out the people from whom Ramos might be attempting to borrow money for a stake with which to try and buy off the heat and start operating again in Mexico City. Alvarado had two names left on his list. One was Ramos' brother-in-law, who had a little shop in the Mercado de Curiosidades on the harbor across from the customs house.

The Mercado de Curiosidades was a solid block of souvenir shops dealing largely in trinkets made of seashells. The shop run by Ramos' brother-in-law, a skinny man named Fuentes, was scarcely five feet

49

across and crammed with fragile objects made of shells. Alvarado was obliged to turn sideways and tuck in his elbows to keep from turning the place into a shambles. Fuentes was very nervous. Alvarado did not know if it was because Fuentes knew him and what he wanted or merely because the shopkeeper feared for his merchandise. It was obviously the latter, because when Alvarado identified himself, Fuentes became even more apprehensive.

"Luis Ramos," Alvarado said, "you're his brother-in-law?"

Fuentes opened his mouth to speak. Only a dry croak emerged. He was obviously terrified of Ramos, Alvarado thought. It shouldn't be hard to make that work for him. Fuentes shut his mouth and nodded.

"Have you seen your brother-in-law recently?" Alvarado asked without menace.

He took off his sunglasses so Fuentes could see his eyes. Alvarado knew the impression his face made on strangers.

"No," Fuentes replied, too quickly.

"You're afraid of him, right?" Alvarado said sympathetically. "I don't blame you, friend. He's not a nice man."

Fuentes didn't say anything but he looked grateful for Alvarado's understanding.

"If one told where he might be found, one might not have to be afraid of him," Alvarado said. "He would go away for a long time. Understand?"

"Yes," said Fuentes.

"And it could be arranged he wouldn't know one provided information about him."

"Nor his sister?" Fuentes said cautiously.

Ramos' sister was Fuentes' wife.

"His sister would not know, either. You have my promise."

Fuentes squeezed past Alvarado toward the front of the shop, in the process knocking to the floor an ugly bird made of seashells. The bird shattered into fragments. Ignoring the damage, Fuentes stepped outside into the blazing sunlight and looked around in all directions. Alvarado dropped carefully to one knee and began scraping the fragments of the bird into a broad palm. They were lost in it. Fuentes came back inside, apparently satisfied that he was not being watched, while Alvarado was still kneeling.

"It is not necessary, agente," Fuentes said.

Alvarado rose, flicked the dust from his trousers and handed the fragments to Fuentes. Fuentes studied them a moment.

"It is a fine day for bathing at the Villa del Mar beach," he said, giving Alvarado a sharp look.

"Isn't it?" Alvarado replied. "It has been pleasant speaking with you, Señor Fuentes."

When he was on his way out, Fuentes called after him.

"Nor his sister, agente?"

"Nor his sister," said Alvarado.

The Playa Villa del Mar was far down Boulevard Manuel Ávila Camacho. Alvarado took a cab. He knew the driver and did not have to display his ID to keep the meter off. He got out at the thatch-roofed pavilion set on pilings at the south end of the beach. He walked between the tables and looked out over the beach in both directions. There were three solid rows of colorful umbrellas between the pavilion and the two-story restaurant with the big Superior beer sign on it a block north. Ramos might be under any one of them. The sand and the water, muddy today with six-inch wavelets marching in in widely separated white-topped columns, were clogged with sunners and bathers as far as he could see in either direction. Unless he was very lucky, Alvarado knew he was in for a long, hot search.

But first, as long as he was here, he checked the bathhouse. If Ramos had changed into his swimming trunks here, the attendant might remember him and confirm

Fuentes' information. And it would perhaps indicate that Ramos was to be found in the vicinity of the pavilion. If he could concentrate his search in the immediate area it would save a lot of walking.

Alvarado took a folded photograph out of his pocket, smoothed it open and showed it to the attendant. Yes, the man of the photograph had changed here that very morning, the attendant said.

"You're sure of that?" said Alvarado.

"I never forget a face," the attendant said.

"If he should return and I'm not around, come find me," Alvarado said.

"Is there a reward?" the attendant said.

"No," said Alvarado. "But if you let him slip by you, I would not be happy. And I never forget a face, either, friend."

"Do not disturb yourself, agente," the attendant said quickly. "I'll do exactly as you wish."

Alvarado went down the steps to the beach and began working through the throng. The sun was hot but it was good to be out in the air. Perhaps one day soon he would bring Sara and the girls to the beach. They would take a lunch and go farther down, where it was not so crowded.

A voice behind him cried, "Papá."

He turned in surprise. It was Concepción, his fourteen-year-old, and she was wearing a two-piece swimming suit. Alvarado started to order her off the beach until she could show herself in something less revealing but decided against it. He was here to apprehend a criminal and family matters should not be permitted to interfere. He would take it up with her later at home. And it wasn't as if she were here with a boy. She was with a girlfriend he approved of, the one they called Gallinita, little hen. Gallinita, he noticed sourly, was modestly dressed in a one-piece suit.

Concepción could see he was displeased with her

but it did not seem to bother her. Alvarado noticed. He had spoiled her, he knew, trying not to let Sara know how disappointed he was she was not a boy. By the time Yolanda, the third daughter, came along he no longer hid his disappointment. Still, they were all fine children, even if Concepción did steal away behind his back to display herself on a public beach in a bathing suit that revealed her bare waist.

"What are you doing here, Papá?" Concepción said.

"Working," Alvarado said curtly.

Concepción shot a mischievous smile at Gallinita.

"How exciting," she said. "Will you shoot somebody, Papá?"

Gallinita looked shocked, and so she should, thought Alvarado. Normal, quiet girls did not make jokes about Federal Judicial Policemen. Gallinita's father was a streetcar conductor.

"Only those improperly dressed," said Alvarado.

"Who could that be?" said Concepción, unabashed.

"We'll talk about it tonight," Alvarado said grimly.

He continued working the area, scanning faces, peering under umbrellas, looking out at the bathers. He spotted Ramos about the same time Ramos saw him. Ramos did not know him but apparently had a nose for policemen because he jumped up and started running. Alvarado ran after him, knocking people down. Women began screaming.

Ramos ran toward the steps leading up to the boulevard. Alvarado had anticipated that and cut him off. Ramos took off down the beach with Alvarado pounding behind him. He was younger and slighter than Alvarado but, because of the crowd, unable to open up much of a lead. He had to thread his way, Alvarado simply bowled people over. Alvarado did not take out his pistol. He would not risk a shot in a crowd. And he did not much like the thought of shooting a man, not with Concepción there to see it. And when a suspect was shot, there were always those reports to make.

Ramos ran out into the water a few feet, where there were fewer people blocking his path. It was a mistake. Alvarado followed him into the water and Alvarado's legs were much stronger. The water did not slow him down as much as it did Ramos. Ramos splashed into deeper water, not much deeper because the bottom fell off so gradually. Alvarado grew closer, bounding along like a great beast of prey.

With a lunge, Alvarado thrust out an arm like a pole and caught Ramos between his skinny shoulderblades, Ramos went down with a splash. He jumped up snorting and swinging. Alvarado ignored the blows, scarcely feeling them. Ramos was not much of a puncher. Alvarado wound his fingers in Ramos' hair and shook the fight out of him. Then he handcuffed Ramos and dragged him toward the sand.

A large crowd had gathered. It parted silently to let them through. Concepción and Gallinita were there. Gallinita looked scared to death. Concepción just looked impressed. She had spirit, that girl. And there was no doubt she admired her father. Alvarado almost did not mind that she was not a boy. If only she dressed herself properly.

He took Ramos, still in his bathing trunks, to the comandancia in a cab. The chief came out personally to look Ramos over. He was pleased, though one would not have known it unless he knew the chief as well as Alvarado did.

"How about that car to San Andrés Tuxtla?" Alvarado said.

"When you've got enough to interest the attorney general," the chief replied. "By the way, your wife called. She wants to know if you're coming home for lunch."

5

Donna was squeezing lime juice on her papaya when Bell came into the Diligencias restaurant at eight Thursday morning. He expected recriminations but she greeted him without obvious rancor. After they had parted the night before, feeling amorous and unable to sleep he had called her room after midnight. She had hung up without a word.

"If you'd worked it right, you could be having room service right now," he said, sitting down.

"If you've never tried papaya for breakfast, these are delicious," she said. "It's only a suggestion, not an order."

Bell ordered papaya with his ham and eggs. It was the least he could do, he thought.

"You got the lists?" he asked.

He had asked her to go through the phone directory and make lists of truckers and tile manufacturers. He didn't know enough Spanish to look them up himself.

Donna nodded.

"About the route to Tlacotalpán," he said. "My map shows a toll bridge on the way. They check your papers at toll bridges?"

"No."

"Then there's a ferry at Buena Vista, just before we get to Tlacotalpán. What do you know about it?"

"Nothing, I'm afraid," she said apologetically.

"Beautiful. We'll be grossing out at around forty tons. I hope the ferry'll take it. If not, we'll have to double back and come into Tlacotalpán from the west. Be an extra four, five hours."

After breakfast, they went up to Bell's room to call about trailers. Donna wrinkled her nose when she saw the room.

"Yours is better, huh?" Bell said.

"I'm management," Donna replied.

Bell couldn't believe it. Donna had made a joke. He resisted pointing out that she might be management but he was getting four times as much as she was for the job. Donna was wearing trim-fitting slacks and a blue shirt with short sleeves, the top buttons undone because the morning was already sultry. She looked the tastiest Bell had yet seen her.

"Anybody ever tell you you're a sexy-looking chick?" he asked.

"Everybody."

She sat down on the bed Bell hadn't slept in, put the list of phone numbers on the night table and looked at him for instructions.

"We want a tractor-trailer rig can take a net load of fifty thousand pounds," he said. "Oh, another thing. Vargas say he had a chain hoist down there to get Chato aboard?"

"He didn't mention it. But I imagine he would."

"We better not count on it. We'll want to rent a chain hoist, too, then. A heavy one."

None of the truckers Donna called had a trailer rig available. All of them said they could have one the next day and certainly by the day after.

"In Mexico, that could mean never," Donna said, despairing. "Sam, what will we do?"

56

"Don't panic. We'll use smaller trucks. It is in five chunks, like Sandifer said, isn't it?"

"That's what Vargas said."

"I don't suppose he told you what they weighed individually?"

"They'd be about the same size. Except the section with the eyes and nose. That would have to be larger."

Bell closed his eyes and thought about the photo he'd seen, and about the replica back at the junction. The part above the eyes would be in two pieces, also the chunk below the nose. Say roughly five tons for the center section and around three each for the other four. With enough tiles to cover, he could put the big piece in one truck and two pieces each in other trucks without going a whole lot over eight tons in any of them. Three trucks would do it.

"We want three trucks," he said. "No, make it four. I want a spare."

"A spare?"

"I don't know the trucks and I don't know the route. We've got to take a back-up vehicle."

While she was dialing he said, "And drivers. Eight experienced drivers."

She stopped dialing and said, "Eight drivers for four trucks?"

"We'll be driving straight through. Starting from Tlacotalpán it'll take maybe twenty-five, thirty hours. That means relief drivers. I don't want some jerk falling asleep at the wheel and spilling Chato's nose all over Highway One-Eighty."

The second trucker Donna called said he had two trucks on hand and could positively get two more within the hour.

"What does positively mean in Mexico?" Bell asked.

"Maybe," said Donna.

"Call him back and tell him him okay. And find out how to get to his place."

The moving company was in the rundown area

where they had been lost coming into town the day before, not far from the Diligencias. When they went to pick up the Volkswagen at the Hotel Veracruz and Donna started to get behind the wheel, Bell stopped her and took the keys. When he knew where he was going he preferred driving himself.

They stopped for a red light at Miguel Lerdo and Independencia. The marimbas were already playing at the bar on the corner. Bell tapped his foot in time with the music. He wished the car had a radio. A radio helped on a long road haul. The traffic policeman standing a few feet away had his shoulders hunched forward as if there were a pain in his chest and both hands were cupped at his mouth. Bell looked closer. The hands cupped a police whistle. Bell could hear a thin, low piping mingled with the sound of the marimbas. The policeman was playing a furtive accompaniment.

"Hey, Donna," Bell said. "Dig that."

The light changed just as she looked where he had pointed. The policeman drew himself erect, gave a blast on his whistle and waved the traffic forward.

"Dig what?" she demanded.

"You missed it. He was playing a whistle solo with the marimbas."

"So?"

Bell sighed. Donna sure as hell wasn't much fun. He whistled "Adiós Muchachos" between his teeth as he drove along Independencia.

"Do you have to do that?" Donna said.

"Do what?"

"Whistle. It goes right through me."

"Don't you like music?"

"Yes. That's why it goes right through me."

He turned right off Zamora and steered the car around broken places in the pavement. He hoped the highways were better than the streets in this part of town.

"There it is," said Donna.

Faded red block letters on a scaling stuccoed brick wall said "Auto Transportes Seguro, S.A.C.V." A broken driveway led into a muddy courtyard enclosed by unpainted wooden truck stalls. Bell had a quick glimpse of two diesel vans as he pulled past the entrance and parked in front of a small, one-story mud-colored stucco building with an air-conditioner sticking out a side window.

"It doesn't look like much," Donna said doubtfully.

"The vans looked okay," Bell replied.

"What vans?"

"Before we go in, let's get it straight what you're supposed to ask Seguro," he said.

Donna looked amused and superior.

"What's funny?" he demanded.

"The manager's name is Ochoa. Seguro means dependable in Spanish. Dependable Auto Hauling."

"Thanks for the Spanish lesson. Tomorrow I'll bring an apple to school."

He went over the things he wanted her to ask about performance, capacities, drivers and Mexican highway conditions. He told her to say they were going to Matamoros, saying, "Why advertise?" when she protested they had to cross at Nuevo Laredo. Donna thought they shouldn't use their own names when they hired the trucks. It was agreed he would be Clark Kent and she would be Donna Fairchild.

The building was divided into two offices. The door opened into the front one. A perspiring secretary was typing away at a bill of lading. Donna spoke to her in Spanish. The girl got up and opened the door into the back office. She spoke to someone inside and then to Donna, motioning them in.

It was cool in the back office. The air-conditioner was noisy but Bell didn't mind. A squat man looked across a desk at them, a solemn expression on his face. He rose when Bell stuck out his hand. He shook hands with Bell and then Donna, waved them to chairs and sat down with his elbows on his desk.

Yes, Donna translated, he had two Dina 661 diesels available. One was almost new and the other, though a bit older, was in magnificent condition. He also knew where he could get his hands on two more trucks, a U.S. International, also in top condition, and a U.S. Mack, not new but absolutely reliable. Bell did not know the Dina. He told Donna to ask about the specifications he had briefed her on outside.

The Dina diesel was Mexico's best, Ochoa assured her. The 661 was "eje sencillo" — "single axle," Donna translated, "whatever that is." It was 190 horsepower and could cruise on the flat at 100 kilometers an hour with a ten-ton load. The tank held 175 liters and the trucks used one liter per four kilometers at cruising speed, fully loaded.

Bell did some rapid calculations in his head. A hundred kilometers an hour loaded was better than 60. Not bad at all. That was on the flat, of course. If they ran into hilly terrain it would be less. The mileage worked out to about nine to the gallon. Ochoa had to be stretching things. It was probably more like five to seven miles to the gallon.

"Ask him about diesel stops between here and Matamoros," Bell said.

There were Pemex stations all along the route, Ochoa replied. Señor Kent need have no concern about fuel.

"Do you want me to find out about the Buena Vista ferry?" Donna asked.

Bell shook his head. With the load split three ways, even a small ferry could handle it. And they were hiring the trucks for Matamoros. If Donna started asking about Buena Vista, in the opposite direction, Ochoa would start wondering why she wanted to know.

"I thought . . ." Donna began.

60

"Forget it," Bell ordered.

Donna looked hurt. She had been pleased with herself for remembering about the ferry.

"I appreciate your thinking about that, but we'll be okay," Bell said. "Are the drivers experienced, ask him."

Of course, was Ochoa's reply. He hired only top drivers.

"Has he got a chain hoist we can rent?"

He did not. He had a monte carga, a fork lift, but wouldn't let it off the premises.

"Hell," Bell muttered.

There must be something down in Tlacotalpán to lift the sections with. Vargas would have had to have a way of getting them off the boats and to wherever he had them stashed.

Ochoa wanted 3,200 pesos for each truck, 3,000 for truck and driver and the other 200 for the extra driver. Donna thought it was too high and started bargaining.

"Knock it off," Bell said. "Tell him we know he's robbing us but we'll pay it if he guarantees to have all four trucks and eight drivers ready to roll by, make it one, this afternoon."

Donna had said they were to meet Vargas at the Hotel Reforma in Tlacotalpán at eight that night to close the deal and pick up the head. That would give him seven hours to load on the tiles and make it to Tlacotalpán. Even if Ochoa couldn't put it all together by one, and even if there was a wait at the ferry, it still wouldn't be cutting things too fine. If Ochoa thought he had to make it by one or lose a fat deal he'd be able to manage anyhow by three or four.

Ochoa said it could be done.

Before Bell let Donna hand over the money he went outside to check the trucks. He examined the tires and axles, looked under the hoods and fired up the motors. Both sounded fine.

Donna counted 6,400 pesos out of her handbag.

Ochoa would get the other 6,400 when he produced eight drivers and the other two trucks. Ochoa was sweating despite the refrigerated air. He'd really made himself a killing, Bell thought. Well, why not? On a half-million dollar deal, Sandifer could afford to scatter a little sunshine. He wondered why Donna had even wanted to argue, as little as she was getting out of the deal. Probably just couldn't help it. It was her nature.

They went to the nearest place on Donna's list for the tile, a large plant southwest of Auto Transportes Seguro. The walls of the sales office were lined with displays of tiles.

"Aren't some of them lovely?" Donna said. "I'd like to do over my bathroom in this one."

"Why not?" Bell said. "I figure Sandifer owes you."

Donna looked tempted. Then she shook her head.

"They must have cheaper tiles than these. We don't need fine ceramic tiles just to cover the goods," she said.

"Guess you're right," Bell said. "Tell you what, you behave yourself and we'll buy just enough of 'em for your bathroom."

"You're very generous with other people's money, aren't you, Sam?"

The girl at the sales counter would have been pretty with a trifle less nose. She gave Bell a big smile. After twenty-four hours with Donna it did wonders for him.

The cheapest tile was mosaico liso, plain tile, and mosaico bravo, embossed bathroom tile. The liso was 30 by 30 centimeters and cost 20 pesos a square meter. The bravo was only 20 by 20 and cost more, 24 pesos a square meter.

"We'll take the bravo," Bell told Donna.

"The liso's cheaper," she protested.

"I know, but the bravo would look better in your bathroom."

Donna made a face. The mosaico bravo was dull and

dun-colored and would not have been out of place in the shower room of a YMCA.

"No, really," Bell said. "The bravo's smaller and'll tuck around the load better. Ask her what it weighs."

The bravo ran 40 kilograms to the square meter. He needed 24 tons of it. That figured out to around 22,000 kilograms. At 40 kilograms a square meter, it came to 550 square meters.

"Tell her we'll take six hundred square meters," Bell said.

It wouldn't hurt to have a few extra tiles. Depending on the shape of the sections, they might have to spread the tiles pretty thin.

The girl appeared stunned at the size of the order. Maybe they should have spread it around if it was so unusual. But no, it was still better to deal with just one factory. He didn't want to be chasing all over town and dealing with more people than he had to. The girl excused herself and left.

"She's gone for the manager," Donna said.

The manager was a youngish man with black horn-rimmed glasses, lightly tinted. He wore a necktie with his white, short-sleeved shirt. It was one of the few neckties Bell had seen in Veracruz. The manager straightened the tie, ran a palm over his hair and smiled charmingly when he saw Donna. He seemed more impressed by her than by the size of their order. But, he said, there was a small problem. There were but 400 square meters of the bravo on hand. He could have the other 200 no later than the next morning.

"Tell him we'll take four hundred square meters of the bravo and two hundred of the liso," Bell said.

"Buying in quantity like this, we should get a better price than the girl quoted," Donna said.

She started bargaining with the manager. Bell did not interfere as he had at Auto Transportes Seguro. Let Donna have her fun. She'd earned it. She had been very useful so far. The manager appeared to find

Donna most persuasive. He let her have the tiles for 12,500 pesos, a saving of 1100 pesos. Twelve thousand five hundred pesos was an even thousand dollars.

Donna counted out 12,500 pesos in cash. The fact that she was rich as well as beautiful completed the conquest of the manager. He invited her to join him for a cup of coffee to commemorate the transaction. Donna refused with regrets. She could be gracious when she wanted to be, it seemed.

The manager got out a salesbook. He looked at Donna questioningly.

"Tell him it's for a firm in Corpus Christi, Texas," Bell said.

"Sandy's given me a name to use, in San Antonio," Donna said.

"We hired the trucks for Matamoros. Corpus sounds better. How about Fairchild Builders and Developers? And I want three separate invoices for two hundred square meters each."

Donna gave him a blank look.

"The load's gonna be split three ways. I want every truck to carry its own invoice."

The manager wrote out the invoices and said the tiles would be ready for loading at any time. He was a long time shaking Donna's hand when they said goodbye to him.

When they got back to Auto Transportes Seguro, one of the two promised trucks had arrived, a shabby International with 210,000 miles on the odometer. The tires were good, though, and except for a little clicking in the lifters the motor sounded smooth. Only five of the drivers had come in, but Ochoa assured him the others were on their way. He could easily have had all by now but was being careful to get only the very best.

Four of the drivers were standing around in the muddy courtyard smoking sharp-smelling cigarettes. The fifth stood a little apart from them. He had on a white dress shirt and what looked like the pants to a suit. He was maybe Bell's age and looked bright, though not like a truck driver, not that truck drivers couldn't be bright. Bell had been one himself his first six months with Ajax. It was the way the man was dressed, more than anything. Bell wondered where Ochoa had dug him up. He told Donna to ask.

The young man was Ochoa's nephew and a stupendous driver, Ochoa said. Also, he spoke English, which none of the other drivers did. He would see that the others understood their instructions and, if Señor Kent desired, attend to small details such as tolls and the men's meals. Ochoa was paying him extra out of his own pocket to provide these special services. And keep an eye on his trucks, Bell thought. The nephew's name was Alberto.

Bell called Alberto over. It was good to be able to do the talking himself and not have to go through Donna.

"Have you made the run to Matamoros, Alberto?" he asked.

"No, señor," Alberto said apologetically.

"Have any of the others? I want to ask about the route."

"I will inquire, señor."

While Alberto was questioning the drivers, the other three arrived, one at a time. Bell looked his crew over. In addition to Alberto, there was a tall one, a short one and five somewhere in between. The tall one, with his hard face and thin moustache, looked like a bandit. Bell wondered if he would be the troublemaker. With that many drivers you could almost always count on at least one of them getting in your hair. They all looked capable, even the runty one, who was an older man. Probably the most experienced of the lot, Bell thought.

None of the drivers, Alberto reported, had made the run to Matamoros before.

"Not a one?" Bell demanded. "Ochoa promised me experienced drivers."

"But they are, señor. Only they drive in the city, and sometimes to Mexico City and Orizaba. Never before to the border."

Par for the course, Bell thought.

"Please do not concern yourself, Señor Kent," Alberto said. "Our roads are very good. Maybe not like in the United States, but very good."

"I'll take your word for it, Alberto."

"Thank you, señor."

The Mack truck arrived. It was ancient, and a disaster. The tires were bald, the sides of the van looked as if someone had been at them with a hatchet, and the motor sounded as if a man were being strangled in there. Bell could tell just by listening it needed at the very least new rings and a valve job. He wondered if maybe he should just forget it.

"You're not going to take that wreck, are you?" Donna demanded.

That decided him.

"Yep," he said.

"It's two hundred and fifty dollars down the drain."

"Tell me something, Donna, why you are so worried about spending Sandifer's money when you're getting such a crummy piece of the action?"

"It's the principle of the thing," Donna said.

Sure it is, Bell thought, and maybe you intend making him jack up your end if you hold expenses down.

He asked Alberto how long it would take to equip the Mack with new tires, thought better of it and asked for good used ones. The old boat would look funny with new rubber. Alberto said he could do it in a couple of hours, perhaps less.

"And pick up a case of oil to take along," Bell said. "It sounds like a guzzler. Miss Fairchild will give you the money."

Instead of complaining, Donna said, "Well, I will say you seem to know what you're doing."

"Twenty thousand dollars' worth?"

Donna winced.

"That remains to be seen, doesn't it?" she said.

Bell went back to Alberto and said, "We're going to lunch. Get right on those tires. And keep the drivers together. We'll be back by three. Okay?"

"Yes, sir," Alberto said smartly.

Donna looked miffed. She didn't like being cut out.

"Why wait until three o'clock?" she demanded. "Why not pick up the tiles while they're changing the tires?"

"And sit around here with three truckloads of tile? We're not going to pull out until around five. That should put us in Tlacotalpán close to eight. I don't want to hang around there waiting for this Vargas cat. Somebody down there might get curious."

They had lunch at the Diligencias. Bell studied the menu as diligently as Donna. Before she could say anything he said, "May I suggest the langostinos de la plancha?"

"The grilled crayfish?" she replied.

"Oh, so that's what it is," Bell replied. "Why not?"

He had picked it because it was the most expensive thing on the menu, 50 pesos, $4 U.S.

"Why not," said Donna.

There was still time to kill after lunch.

"Why don't we go up to my room and look at my maps for a couple of hours?" Bell said.

"Why don't you just give up?" Donna replied.

When Bell got over to the Hotel Veracruz at two-thirty, Donna was watching a bellman trying to cram her big black and white suitcase into the trunk of the Volkswagen. She looked angrily at Bell, as if it were his fault the suitcase wouldn't fit.

"You're the one who rented a beetle," he said.

He had the bellman put the suitcase in the back

seat and everything else in the trunk. They'd have to move it to the front seat later on when one of them wanted to catch a nap on the road.

After they were on their way, Donna asked suddenly, "Did you remember to get a receipt for your hotel bill?"

"Yes, ma'am," said Bell.

Donna glowered.

The Mack was ready to go when they reached Auto Transportes Seguro. Six of the drivers were hunkered down with their backs against the wall, smoking and talking. The seventh, the one who looked like a bandit, sat near them, his arms folded across his chest and his eyes closed, apparently sleeping. A quiet one, Bell thought. A man to watch. Bell found Alberto in his uncle's office, where it was cool, when he went in with Donna to pay Ochoa the rest of his money.

He took Alberto outside to help him assign the men to their trucks. He put Alberto in the Mack, the most reliable man in the least reliable truck. The Mack would lead the way once they'd picked up the head. It was best to have the least reliable truck where the others could see it if it broke down and not run off and leave it behind. He instructed Alberto to put the three best men as lead drivers in the other trucks and then make a written list showing by name which men were in which trucks. Then he had Alberto introduce him to each man by name. He studied their faces until he knew who he had in each truck. He would not have time to get to know them personally on the haul but he would be talking to them through Alberto from time to time and it would make things simpler for both of them if he knew their names. And drivers were usually more conscientious if they were aware the boss knew who they were.

Two of the drivers were named Juan. One of them was the man who looked like a bandit. Bell called him

Juan One and the other Juan Two. The other drivers were Roberto, Xavier, Luis, Salomón and Francisco. Francisco was the short, older man. He was wiry, with long arms, and looked like a wise little monkey. Alberto, in fact, called him Mono, which Donna told Bell meant monkey in Spanish.

"That's where they got 'monero,' " she said. "For the finders."

Bell had Alberto send the men to their trucks and led them to the tile factory. The factory manager came out to take personal charge of the loading. The factory crew loaded the tiles by hand, stacking them on edge. Laid flat, there would be more breakage, the manager explained. Once the loading was well under way, he became more attentive to Donna than to his men. She conversed with him amiably in Spanish. Bell felt left out. His antennae went up when he heard her say "Matamoros." Donna saw his concern.

"I was telling Señor Flores about our new motel in Corpus Christi," she said. "The one we're building with the Spanish motif."

That was pretty slick of Donna. Matamoros was the nearest border town to Corpus. Everybody they'd dealt with so far would believe they were going through there instead of Nuevo Laredo. If anybody in Veracruz should start checking, which wasn't likely, they'd be expecting the tiles to show up in Matamoros.

Eight tons of tile did not stack as high in a truck as Bell had anticipated. When he got the sections of the head aboard, he couldn't use more than two tons a truck to cover them and still make the net weight jibe with his invoices if somebody put a truck on the scales. He'd seen how it looked when they loaded up in Tlacotalpán. He could always eat up space by sticking something lighter under the tiles.

The manager offered coffee. Bell told Donna to accept. They had a little time to kill. Bell wasn't worried about getting to Tlacotalpán promptly at eight anyhow. Vargas wouldn't be going anywhere. He hadn't got his money yet. That should be interesting, Bell thought, watching Donna haggle. Vargas had her over a barrel but he didn't think that would stop Donna from putting up a fight.

Before they left the tile factory, Donna wrote something on a slip of paper and gave it to Señor Flores. Señor Flores tucked it away carefully in a wallet stuffed with cards.

"What was that all about?" Bell asked on the way back to the Volks.

"He asked me if you were my husband and I said, no, my business partner, so he asked for my address in Corpus," Donna said with a half smile. "So I gave it to him."

"Didn't you even ask if he was married?" Bell said gravely.

"Didn't have to. Didn't you see his wedding band?"

"Don't you know it's bad business fooling around with married men? I'm single, you know."

"Yes. It's such a pity all the really nice men are married, isn't it?"

"I hope the poor sucker doesn't make a special trip all the way to Corpus just to look you up, Miss Fairchild."

"I hope he does, the ass. Thinking I was that easy."

"You know something, Donna? You can be right bitchy."

"You bet your life," said Donna.

The three loaded trucks were out on the street lined up behind the Mack. Alberto stood beside the Mack, looking expectantly at Bell.

"Let's roll," Bell cried.

Alberto gave the order and drivers started their engines. It reminded Bell a little bit of moving out a convoy when he was in the Corps. Only this time nobody would be shooting at him. At least he hoped so.

70

He got into the Volkswagen with Donna and pulled away from the curb. When he looked in the rearview mirror to make sure the trucks had fallen in behind him, he could see Señor Flores standing on the sidewalk, waving goodbye to Donna.

6

DONNA sat very straight in her seat.

"It's really happening, isn't it?" she said. "I'm just now starting to get excited."

"I was wondering what it took to get you excited," Bell said.

He felt a little tingle himself. This was considerably different from what he'd been doing at Ajax the past three years. Quitting Ajax had turned out just fine after all. He wished he had one of their late-model rigs and a couple of their top drivers, though. But what the hell, that might spoil the fun.

Donna kept the map open in her lap but Bell did not need it. He had studied it enough to know how to get out of town and on to Tlacotalpán. Avenida Presidente Miguel Alemán to the junction with the Olmec head replica, turn left and then south on Highway 180 to the Buena Vista ferry. Buena Vista was 50 miles south of the junction and eleven east of Tlacotalpán.

When Bell turned left instead of right at the junction, Alberto started honking in the Mack just behind him. The horn, like the truck, was feeble. Bell slowed down and gazed at the Olmec head while waiting for Alberto to pull alongside. Maybe it was only a concrete replica but it was still damned impressive, he thought. Alberto leaned across Mono, his relief man, and yelled out the window.

"Señor Kent, you have made the wrong turn. For going north it is the other way."

"That's okay, Alberto," Bell called back. "We've got to go to Tlacotalpán first."

He increased speed without further explanation. The Mack and the other trucks followed. Just beyond the knoll with the Olmec head on it, a bed of flowers spelled out the words "Feliz Viaje."

"What does that mean?" Bell asked.

"Have a nice trip."

They both laughed. It was the first time they had laughed together. Before the trip was over maybe they'd be getting along, Bell thought. But her laughter was strained. She's not just excited, he thought, she's scared. And they hadn't even picked up the head yet. He was looking forward to seeing a real one, even if it was in five pieces.

"What about those heads?" he said. "Sandifer said they've found fifteen, counting ours. What are they supposed to be?"

"No one knows for sure," Donna said. "Bernal thinks they may represent warriors or chiefs. No special ones. Just generally. And Wicke thinks they could be monuments to dead chieftains."

Bell did not see much point to asking who Bernal and Wicke might be.

"I've heard one really wild theory," Donna said. "They were carved to frighten people away from the Olmec turf. You know, if the people who live there are that big, forget it."

They passed a tiny yellow wooden box of a building marked "Caseta Fiscal." A man in a straight chair was leaning back against the side of the building. Behind him was an open window, its wooden shutter swung inward and propped up with a stick.

"What's that?" Bell demanded.

"The sign means Treasury Booth. It must be an inspection point of some sort."

"What do they inspect?"

"I don't know," Donna said apologetically. "But if it was any problem I'm sure Vargas would have mentioned it."

"I wouldn't bet on it," Bell said. "I'll ask Alberto later."

He watched in the rearview mirror to see what happened when the trucks passed the caseta. The man sitting outside it didn't stir. Bell was relieved. But maybe he was only checking trucks heading for Veracruz. Alberto should know.

Bell's mind automatically registered and filed away information as he drove along the highway. Width of road, condition of surface, grades, road signs. There was frequent minor road work in progress. To Bell it signified the highways were not particularly durable but also that they were well maintained.

"Tell me more about those heads," Bell said. "Where do they come from and how old are they? Like that."

"I didn't think you were interested in pre-Columbian art," Donna said. "You're not the type."

"I wasn't," Bell said. "Until I saw that one back at the junction yesterday."

"They come from La Venta, Tres Zapotes and San Lorenzo. Except ours."

La Venta, Tres Zapotes and San Lorenzo were three of the most important Olmec sites, Donna explained after assuring herself Bell was really interested and not just making idle conversation. La Venta was in Tabasco, the state just southeast of Veracruz, the other two in Veracruz. Tres Zapotes was only about forty miles from their destination, Tlacotalpán, near the village of Santiago Tuxtla. San Lorenzo Tenochtitlán was some thirty miles southeast of Tres Zapotes.

The heads found in the three sites ranged in size from under five feet to more than nine. Chato was among the largest. The heads all differed from one another somewhat in ways other than size. Some heads were rounder than others; some eyes, unlike Chato's, had irises; some facial expressions were more animated than others, and some heads bore more intricate carvings.

"There were Olmecs at San Lorenzo from twelve hundred to around nine hundred B.C.," Donna said. "So some of the heads could be almost three thousand years old."

Bell stared at Donna, impressed. All that information at her fingertips and, far from flaunting her knowledge, she appeared to enjoy sharing it with him.

"And these heads are all that's left to show they were around?" Bell asked.

"Oh, no. There's a wealth of evidence, from quite a large pyramid at La Venta to small jade carvings and pottery figurines. Stelae, monuments, carved votive axes, mosaics."

"What happened to them? The Olmecs?"

Donna shrugged.

"No one knows, exactly. All we know is that the Olmecs were the most ancient civilized people in the Middle Americas. Anthropologists call the region from here down to northern Tabasco the Mesopotamia of the Americas. You do know about Mesopotamia?"

Bell grinned. So she was flaunting it just a little bit. He didn't mind.

"You mean all that Tigris, Euphrates business?" he said casually. "Lately we've been calling it Iraq."

"You really don't know anything at all about the Olmecs?" Donna said suspiciously. "You haven't been just putting me on, have you?"

"Hope to die," said Bell. "Tell me more."

"Well, for one thing, dot and bar dating. The Olmecs did it first. Before archeologists discovered that, it had been attributed to the Maya."

"I've dated in a few bars myself," Bell said.

"Sometimes I think you're really as crass as you seem to be," Donna said tartly. "I don't think you actually give a damn about Olmec or any other kind of culture."

"Sorry, Donna," Bell said. "That was a pretty damn feeble joke. I am interested. Thanks for the history lesson. Really."

"Por nada," Donna said, only partially mollified. "They were really hung up on jaguars," she continued. "Stylized jaguar masks, carvings of half-human, half-jaguar babies. There's one particular carving I think would appeal to your particular hang-up. At the Potrero Nuevo site. It's in pretty poor shape but it appears to be a jaguar making it with a woman."

"Sorry," said Bell. "The thought doesn't do a thing for me. I think you're the one with the hang-up."

Donna didn't answer.

Beside the road were stands displaying mounds of pineapples and coconuts still in their husks. Beyond them, the posted speed limit was 100 kilometers an hour. Bell had been keeping the Volks at a steady 95. He took it up to 110 to see what Alberto could get out of the Mack. The Mack fell behind at first, then started catching up. But all that told Bell was that it could run pretty good empty. He had no way of knowing what it could do loaded, if things ever came to that.

They passed between the Laguna Camaronero on the Gulf of Mexico side and the Laguna Alvarado on the inland side. Bell could not always see water because low, vegetation-covered dunes obscured the view. The sun was low when they reached the town of Alvarado, six miles from Buena Vista. The road forked just beyond a service station.

"You've got the map, Donna," Bell said. "Which way do I go? Left?"

"I get nauseated when I try to read in a moving car," Donna said. "Even a map."

"Beautiful," said Bell. "Why didn't it bother you when we were bouncing around in the air on the way to Veracruz?"

"I wasn't reading."

"It's got to be the left fork."

There was a mild grade up to the bridge over the inlet joining the Gulf with the Laguna Alvarado. Bell checked the Mack in the rearview mirror. It did not appear to be laboring but the grade wasn't much and they weren't going very fast. He'd have to wait for some hills to see what it could do.

The bridge was long and arched high above the inlet. Far below, a freighter was toiling out of the lagoon.

"Nice view," said Bell.

"Yes," Donna said without enthusiasm.

Bell had expected that a girl who worked in an art gallery and knew so much about Olmecs would be interested in things like that. Maybe she was too busy thinking about what was coming up.

Just over the bridge was a row of cafés and cantinas on the right-hand side of the highway. A dozen or more trucks were parked in front of them. A good sign, Bell thought. The more truck traffic, the better. His little convoy wouldn't be noticed. The toll station, Caseta de Cobro, was astride the road beyond the cantinas. Bell automatically estimated the height of the winglike projection over his lane. A good fifteen feet. Plenty of clearance for his trucks. But there would be, naturally. There had to be enough clearance for those semis he'd seen parked farther back.

"You give Alberto money for the toll?" he asked.

"More than enough, I'm sure," said Donna.

The toll for the Volks was four pesos. The man in the collection booth gave Bell a printed receipt. Donna plucked it from Bell's hand and studied it before putting it away in the manila envelope in which she kept all her receipts.

"How many axles do our trucks have?" she demanded.

"Why?" Bell asked.

"The toll's according to number of axles. The more axles, the higher the toll. And double for out-of-state."

Bell told her.

"Good," said Donna. "I'd like to see Alberto try to hold me up now."

"I'd like to see anybody try to hold you up, baby," said Bell. "I can't understand why you didn't try to get the man to give you a rate for four."

Donna did not think it was funny.

To the right of the highway the Papaloapán River ran broad and lusterless through flatlands covered with heavy grasses and low, lush vegetation. They reached Buena Vista in minutes and joined a line of vehicles waiting for the ferry. Bell got out of the Volks and made sure his four trucks were pulled in behind it. He counted the vehicles ahead of them in line. Out in the river, the ferry was creeping toward the bank. It was dusk now but there was still enough light for Bell to see its load. Two trucks and three automobiles. That meant he could get all his trucks across in the second and third trips coming up. They were only eleven miles from Tlacotalpán and if the ferry didn't take too long for a round trip they would make it by eight o'clock easy.

Alberto got out of the Mack and came over to join him. Alberto looked troubled.

"Señor," he said. "You did not say we must come first to Tlacotalpán. My uncle said direct to Matamoros."

"A last-minute decision," Bell said. "We'll give him another hundred pesos a truck."

Alberto did not look completely satisfied but did not pursue the matter.

The other drivers had left their trucks and gathered in a group to talk and smoke. Bell told Alberto to have them get back into the trucks until after the ferry line moved up. Alberto called out an order and the drivers straggled back to their vehicles, grumbling.

"That Caseta Fiscal back on the other side of the Boca del Rio Bridge," Bell said casually. "What happens there?"

"It is an inspection station for, how do you say, agriculture, señor."

"Then we don't have to stop on the way back?"

Alberto shrugged.

"Maybe yes, maybe no. But we have mosaico, not agriculture. There will be no troubles."

"Who said anything about troubles?" Bell asked.

Alberto shrugged again.

He's sharp, Bell thought. He knows something is going on. But Alberto probably couldn't care less as long as he got his money.

"You give me a good trip and there'll be a bonus in it for you," Bell said.

"Thank you, señor. I will give you a good trip."

Donna came over to see what they were talking about.

"I was just telling Alberto there's a bonus in it if he does a good job," Bell said.

"If you want to pay it out of your own pocket," Donna said. "That wasn't in the deal I made with Ochoa."

It was about what he'd expected of her, which was why he had mentioned it.

The ferry pulled up to the riverbank — there was no slip — and a rusty iron gangway was lowered by hand-operated winches. The vehicles drove off and a bus, a truck and an automobile squeezed aboard. Bell got back in the Volks and led his trucks forward to take their places. It was a couple of minutes past seven when the ferry moved out. The round trip didn't take long. They'd be in Tlacotalpán by eight with no sweat.

Bell told Alberto to let the drivers leave their trucks. There were two cantinas side by side on the road to the ferry. Both were open sided, with concrete floors and thatched roofs standing on poles. The drivers all went into the first one. Alberto waited until Bell and Donna followed and attached himself to them. A tin tray of uncooked crab claws, blue and white and crawling with insects, sat atop a refrigerated case in front of the cantina. To the right of it, a whole boiled hog's head sat neck down on a sheet-iron grill.

"We missed supper," Bell said, nodding toward the head. "How about a big bite of that?"

Donna grimaced.

"I couldn't eat anything in this place," she said, looking distastefully at a mud-caked pig snuffling along the concrete floor. Just outside the cantina, and ignoring the pig, a lean black dog was tearing at a tortilla anchored beneath a forepaw.

"How about a Coke, then?" Bell said.

"Thanks. I'd love one."

"I will get them, señorita," Alberto said quickly.

Bell gave him the money and Alberto went back to the bar across the back of the place. The drivers were at the bar, forming a little group among the others waiting for the ferry to return. The drivers were shucking the pink shells from boiled shrimp and drinking beer. Bell went to Alberto, who was waiting for the Cokes.

"Alberto," he said. "Tell them no beer."

The drivers, all except Mono, grumbled and seemed in no hurry to comply when Alberto passed along the order. Juan One, the bandit, seemed not to have heard. Bell looked from man to man, his jaw set. He spoke directly to them, not to Alberto.

"Any one 'a you bastards doesn't do what I tell him

80

when I tell him gets his tail left right here," he said. "Tell 'em exactly what I said, Alberto."

Alberto told them. They put their beer bottles down quickly, all except Juan One. He turned his back, leaned both elbows on the bar and tilted the bottle of beer to his lips. Bell did not want to lose him. He was driving the number one Dina and Bell had a feeling he might be the best of the bunch. Bell did not know why he had that feeling, except maybe because of Juan One's aloof, self-sufficient manner, but he trusted his instincts.

Bell stepped up and touched Juan One on the shoulder. Juan turned and faced Bell stolidly, the bottle grasped like a weapon in his brown hand. Bell's hand darted out and gripped Juan's elbow, his thumb digging into the hollow. Juan winced and dropped the bottle, which somehow did not break on the concrete floor. Beer frothed out on the floor.

"Pick it up," Bell said quietly.

Alberto translated.

Juan picked up the bottle and set it on the bar. Bell stared at him a moment.

"Okay?" he said.

The ends of Juan's moustache lifted in a grin.

"Okay," he said cheerfully. "Patrón."

Bell knew what patrón meant. It meant boss.

The other drivers had been watching uneasily. Now they relaxed and whispered among themselves. Alberto slipped something into his pocket. A knife, maybe, Bell thought. Alberto had been ready to back him up. It was good to know, but if trouble developed again he'd have to tell Alberto to keep that thing in his pocket. He could handle matters without that kind of help.

They rejoined Donna with three giant bottles of Coca-Cola, apparently the size the cantina served prosperous looking customers.

"What was that all about?" Donna asked.

"What was what all about?" Bell replied, taking a swallow.

It tasted terrible. The Coke wasn't cold.

"You're just bursting with suppressed violence, aren't you?" Donna said.

"Nope. I just like my people doing what I tell 'em. When I tell 'em."

"So I gathered," Donna said dryly.

Bell stepped out into the road and looked toward the river. The ferry, lights aglow, was nosing into the bank.

"Alberto," he called. "Tell 'em to mount up."

The drivers hurried out of the cantina, some of them still eating boiled shrimp from cellophane bags. Juan was one of them. Bell pointed at the sack.

"Bueno?" he asked.

"Sí, patrón," said Juan. "Muy sabroso."

He shucked off a shell with a deft motion and handed a shrimp to Bell. Bell smelled it cautiously, then put it in his mouth. It was sweet and fresh.

"Muy bueno," he said.

He ran back into the cantina and bought a couple of bags. Donna was in the Volks when he came out and the drivers were all in place. Bell went to the Mack and told Alberto to let two of the trucks get on ahead of him and for him to wait and cross with the other two on the next trip.

"We'll wait for you on the other side," Bell said.

He got in the Volks and followed two cars onto the ferry. Two of his trucks squeezed on behind him. When he saw them safely aboard he offered a sack of shrimp to Donna. She drew back, wrinkling her nose.

"They're okay," he said. "I had one."

She shook her head.

"Thanks, anyway," she said. "I'll wait. Maybe the Hotel Reforma is cleaner."

The ferry's engine was in a little wooden shack perched out over the water. Another shack across from it on the port side housed an office. Bell got out and stood by the engine shack, eating shrimp and tossing the shells over the side into the dark water. Donna must be starved. And two little sacks of shrimp wouldn't hold him, either. Maybe she was right and there'd be something in Tlacotalpán. Juan One came up and tried to tell him something. Bell took him to Donna.

"He needs money for the ferry," Donna said. "Alberto didn't give them any. And he says it's fifty pesos. I think he's trying to cheat me. It was only six for the car."

"So ask the man," Bell said.

He didn't think Juan would cheat her. Juan wasn't the type.

"I'll do just that," Donna said, climbing out of the Volks.

She went to the number two Dina, where a ferry crewman was trying to collect the fee from Xavier. Bell watched while Donna questioned the ferryman and handed over some bills.

"How much was it?" he asked when she returned.

"Fifty pesos," she admitted. "For loaded trucks. Alberto's won't be that much and he better not say it was."

The ferry was already nosing into the riverbank on the other side. They got back in the car as the gangway clanked down. Bell drove a few hundred yards up the road and flicked his lights to get Juan One's attention. When the lights of the number one Dina flicked an answer, Bell pulled over and stopped. He was careful not to drive onto the shoulder. The whole area on that side of the river looked low and marshy. The number one Dina stopped behind him. The number two Dina started to come around it. Bell scrambled out of the Volks and waved his arms. The truck was moving slowly and despite its eight ton load mushed to a quick stop.

Bell motioned for Xavier to back it up behind the other Dina. Xavier worried it into reverse with a clashing of gears that grated on Bell's nerve endings. The truck backed past the number one Dina and cut around it onto the shoulder. It stopped abruptly with its nose still well out in the road. Bell walked back and motioned for Xavier to pull out and straighten up. Xavier emerged from the cab waving his arms and talking volubly. Together, they went to the back of the van. The right rear double tires were more than rim deep in the shoulder. Bell started swearing. Xavier hung his head.

Juan came back to investigate. He shook his head, clucked his tongue and made a reassuring gesture. He went to his truck and returned with a length of heavy chain draped over his shoulders. There was a big steel hook on one end of the chain. Juan threw a couple of hitches around the number two Dina's bumper with the other end of the chain and handed the hook to Bell. Then he got in his own truck and started the motor. Bell knew what was expected of him. He motioned Xavier into his truck. When Juan had pulled onto the road and backed close enough, Bell dropped the hook over the lead truck's rear bumper and signaled Xavier to fire up. Juan edged his truck forward. When the chain was taut and the hitches set, Bell banged on the side of the lead truck to let Juan know he should stop. He held up a hand to get Xavier's attention. Bell made a sweeping motion and shouted, "Now," loud enough for Juan to hear.

Xavier gave his truck the gas as the front Dina inched forward. The chain grew rigid and made a grinding sound. Bell stepped back to be out of range if the chain broke or the hitches pulled free. Everything held. With a sucking sound and a clatter of shifting tiles the mired truck lurched forward. When it had pulled completely free, Bell rapped the side of the front Dina again. Juan backed up to give the chain some slack. Bell unhooked the chain but could do nothing with the other end. The pulling had locked the hitches too tight. Juan came back with a pinch-bar and pried them free.

"Muy bueno," said Bell.

Juan grinned and said something ending with "patrón."

Bell looked at the luminous dial of his watch. Eleven minutes to eight. The other two trucks should be along soon. They wouldn't miss reaching Tlacotalpán at eight by too much. Fifteen or twenty minutes at the outside.

Donna was waiting in the road beside the Volks.

"We'll be late," she said icily.

"He'll wait," Bell replied. "You get there on the nose, he'll think you're anxious."

When he saw headlights coming up the road he led the two trucks out, slowly until he saw two pairs of headlights falling in behind them, then driving as fast as the pitted state of the road permitted.

Tlacotalpán lay on one side of the highway, the Papaloapán River on the other. The town looked to Bell like one long line of low buildings with their backs to the river, contiguous except where split by the single road leading from the highway into it. Between the solid row of buildings and the highway was a hard-surfaced parking area. Bell led his trucks into it and got out of the Volks to talk to Alberto.

"You stay here and don't let any of the drivers wander off," he said. "They all ate back at the ferry, didn't they?"

"Yes, señor," said Alberto.

"I'll be back in a little while. I want to find them all here, okay?"

"Yes, señor," Alberto said again.

Though Alberto asked no questions, Bell could see he was dying to know more about what was going on.

When Bell got back in the Volks, Donna said, "I forgot to ask before, but have you got a gun?"

"A gun? What would I want with a gun?"

"I'm carrying over sixty thousand dollars," Donna said.

"Don't you believe in banks?"

"I'm serious. Have you got a gun?"

"No, and if I did, I sure as hell wouldn't use it. I hired on to haul freight, not ride shotgun."

"You're a great comfort," Donna said.

There was more to Tlacotalpán than the line of joined buildings. Beyond them were more solid ranks of low buildings. The street on which they drove was paved but muddy and puddled. The town was dark except off to the left, where there were lights and the sound of music.

"Must be that way," Bell said, turning toward the lights.

The lights came from a narrow three-story building and a cantina across the street from it. The music was from the cantina and sounded like a jukebox. The three-story building was the Hotel Reforma.

7

A GENTE Alvarado was restless after dinner Thursday night. He was almost always restless when at home, surrounded as he was by women. Not that he did not cherish his family, but a man needed to be among men. And when he was too much with Sara he found himself being curt with her despite the best intentions. It might not be entirely her fault she had never managed to present him with a son but he found that difficult to accept when confronted with a household of women over a long evening. As it was, and despite the demands of his job, he spent more time with his family than any of his friends spent with theirs. If his friends thought that unusual, they knew better than to speak of it in his presence.

And Alvarado was restless for another reason. He kept thinking about what Galvez, the informer, had told him. Rumors of a big find down toward Laguna de los Cerros, below San Andrés Tuxtla. And Jorge Vargas being in Veracruz. If he could put the two together he might have something. There was no way he could comb the Laguna de los Cerros area, and in any case it would be useless, but if he could run across Vargas and keep him under surveillance he might learn something to his advantage.

Alvarado got his pistol and holster from its drawer

and clipped it inside his waistband. Sara was busy sewing. She was always working. And she was an excellent manager. She had to be, Alvarado thought, on the salary an honest agent brought home. Three thousand pesos a month was more than adequate for a single man but little enough when there were five mouths to feed and three girls always, or so they said, in need of new dresses. Sometimes he wondered, but never for long, was it truly worthwhile living that way when there were so many opportunities for supplementing one's income without particular risk or ignominy.

"I'm going out," he said.

"Will you be late?" Sara asked, which was as much as she ever did.

Alvarado never offered details of his goings and comings, nor did she expect them.

"I don't know," he said.

He went first to the Imperial bar. Two men were sitting at his table. A waiter, seeing him arrive, went to the men and whispered something. They rose immediately and moved off to share a table with another party of two. Alvarado nodded his thanks and sat down. The waiter brought him coffee and milk and a cigar with the end already punched.

"Has anyone been looking for me?" Alvarado said.

"No, agente," the waiter replied. "Would you like to eat something?"

"No. I had dinner at home."

Sara was an excellent cook. That was one of the reasons Alvarado often took dinner at home even though he could dine without charge almost anywhere he pleased. The other was that he enjoyed sitting down to a meal surrounded by his family. It was only after dinner, when the evening grew long, that he became restless.

Alvarado smoked his cigar and listened to the music. When he was a boy he had wanted to play the trumpet but there had been no money for it. He did not regret missing the opportunity. He had learned long ago he was not musical.

A man he did not know approached the table and cleared his throat.

"Agente Alvarado?" he asked diffidently.

"Yes," said Alvarado.

"Could I sit down?"

Alvarado nodded. Perhaps the man had something to tell him. It had happened many times before. But it was too much to expect that it might have to do with Vargas and his business.

"It's a warm evening, isn't it?" the man said.

"It's not so bad," Alvarado replied.

"True. Last night was warmer. Could I buy you a drink, agente?"

"Thank you," Alvarado said. "I'll have another coffee."

The waiter brought two coffees. The man sat there looking at his. Whatever it was he wanted, he was having trouble getting it out.

"Did you want to talk to me about something?" Alvarado said helpfully.

"Yes. Yes, I do."

The man looked not at Alvarado but at a marimba player, as if engrossed in the musician's technique.

"I understand you were able to help Carlos Galvez Mirelez with a problem," he said.

"It was nothing," said Alvarado.

If this man knew Galvez, perhaps the man also knew of his own interest in Jorge Vargas and the way Vargas made his money, Alvarado thought. It could very well be that he had information. What a stroke of fortune that would be. The evening was looking up.

"I, too, have a problem," the man said, still not looking at Alvarado.

Alvarado could smell what was coming. He was disappointed. It would not be information.

"Yes," he said. "Everyone has problems, don't they?"

Encouraged by this, the man said, "I thought perhaps you could help me with my problem, as you helped Galvez."

"Before you tell me exactly what your problem is, Señor . . . ?" Alvarado said.

"Tolan," the man said.

". . . Señor Tolan, did Galvez tell you the price of such help?"

"No, agente. Only that you helped. But I am sure that I could show my gratitude at least as well as Galvez."

"I see," said Alvarado. "He didn't tell you, then, I have just one fixed price?"

Tolan shook his head. "It would be worth a thousand pesos to me," he said.

"That isn't my price," Alvarado said.

Tolan rubbed his forehead with the tips of his fingers. "I can't afford more than twelve hundred at most," he said anxiously.

"That's not my price, either," said Alvarado.

Tolan looked so crestfallen Alvarado felt sorry for him.

"I deal only for information," he said.

"Information?" Tolan said, puzzled. "What kind of information, agente?"

"If you don't know what kind, you wouldn't have any I want, friend. Look, don't be so downcast. For a thousand pesos you'll have no trouble finding someone to help you. Unless it's something big."

"You're not angry with me for asking, agente?" Tolan said.

"Why should I be? No harm in asking."

Tolan looked relieved. "Perhaps you would be kind enough to tell me who . . ." he began.

Alvarado stopped him with a gesture. "I don't involve myself in that kind of business," he said. "Ask somewhere else."

He could see that Tolan wanted to leave but did not know how to manage it.

"If there's nothing else," he said.

Tolan got to his feet quickly. "Thank you for your advice," he said.

"It's nothing," said Alvarado.

He watched Tolan hurry across Miguel Lerdo, dodging traffic, and sighed. A thousand pesos was a third of a month's pay. And Tolan's problem was probably really nothing. If it was one of the usual things, it was something that could and should have been handled routinely without any money changing hands. It was a pity that things were so often done this way. Alvarado did not blame those who took a little here and there. It was hard to make ends meet on a goverment salary. But accepting money for favors was not his way. Sara couldn't understand that, not that she would dream of protesting, but Alvarado thought Concepción did, and thought the more of him for it. In that, he did not mind her being so modern.

"Tomás!" a voice exclaimed. "Why are you here all alone?"

It was César Guerra, an old friend.

"I'm on my way to the Parroquia café," said Guerra. "Old Salazar's sold his shop and we're celebrating. Come along."

Alvarado rose and embraced his friend. Guerra was a good six inches shorter than Alvarado and his face was smothered against Alvarado's big chest.

"When you greet me, Tomás," he said, laughing, "I always feel lucky to survive."

"You're getting fatter, César," Alvarado said. "I could hardly get my arms around you."

"On the day you can't, I'll place myself on exhibit and get rich," replied Guerra.

When they walked along Independencia in front of the Hotel Diligencias. Alvarado out of habit studied the faces around the sidewalk tables and looked into the restaurant to see who was there. He still entertained a diminishing hope of spotting Jorge Vargas.

Salazar and several cronies had two tables pushed together outside the Gran Café de la Parroquia. There was food, beer and a bottle of tequila on the long table thus formed. After exchanging abrazos, Alvarado sat down and helped himself to a beer. Guerra ordered a mixed drink, for which he had to endure some good-natured comment.

Salazar drank only mineral water. Besides being bald, which was unusual enough, he also had an ulcer, a relatively rare affliction in Veracruz.

"Are you going to retire, now that you've sold the shop?" Alvarado asked.

"Certainly not," Salazar replied. "I'm going to raise marijuana on my little farm, with you as partner. With your notorious influence I'll make a fortune, and without risk."

Everyone roared. They all knew about Alvarado.

"I hear you made a big arrest yesterday," someone said.

"And he gave you a fearful beating before the bystanders came to your rescue," added another.

More laughter, in which Alvarado joined.

"Tell me," said Alvarado, "does anyone have close connections in San Andrés?"

No one did.

"Always working, eh, agente?" Salazar said.

"I don't suppose any of you know a man named Vargas," Alvarado said. "Jorge Vargas."

Again, no one did.

"What's he done, Tomás?" Guerra asked.

"That's what I'd like to know," Alvarado replied.

"If you'd like to know, you will," Salazar said. "I have twenty pesos that says you will."

Salazar looked around the table, but found no takers.

"I wouldn't want Tomás after me," said Guerra. "Just being his friend is dangerous enough. I think he broke a rib or two a while ago."

After less than an hour, Alvarado found himself growing almost as restless as he had been at home. Despite the drinking and the laughter, his thoughts kept straying back to Vargas. He wondered if Vargas was still in Veracruz and, if so, what he was up to. He pushed back his chair and got up.

"I'm sorry, friends, but I've got to be going," he said.

"The evening is young," Guerra protested.

"And you've had hardly a drop to drink," Salazar added. "It isn't every day one sells his shop."

"Really," said Alvarado. "I must."

"The señorita's impatient," someone said. "He's afraid she won't wait."

Everyone laughed except Guerra, who of all those there knew Alvarado best.

"You should go into police work," Alvarado said. "You'd make a first rate detective."

He took a taxi to the Palacio Federal and had the driver wait while he went into the comandancia and got a photograph of Jorge Vargas out of the files. He went back to the Hotel Veracruz and asked to see the register. The only Vargas who had registered the past couple of days was not named Jorge. Alvarado was not surprised. If Vargas had stayed at a hotel it probably would have been the Veracruz but he most likely would have used another name. He took the photograph out of his pocket and unfolded it on the desk.

"By any chance could this man have registered under another name?" he asked.

"Not while I was on duty," the clerk said. He looked at the photograph again and said. "But I think such a man was here last night. Not as a guest. Visiting someone."

That was encouraging.

"He asked for whom?" Alvarado said.

The clerk shrugged.

"He didn't ask," the clerk said. "He went directly to the elevator."

"Did you by chance notice on which floor it stopped?"

"It isn't my job to observe such things, agente. If I had known it was important . . ."

"Never mind," said Alvarado. "Thank you for your assistance."

He went to the elevator and waited for it to come down. After it disgorged its passengers he stepped inside. The elevator boy waited for a party of three men walking across the lobby toward them.

"Shut the door, if you don't mind," Alvarado said.

The elevator boy looked startled, but he did not shut the door. The men reached the elevator and started to get in. Alvarado barred the way.

"I'm sorry," he said. "This elevator is not in service at the moment."

The largest of the three men started to say something, looked at Alvarado and thought better of it.

"Thank you," said Alvarado. "Now, shut the door."

The elevator boy did so.

"Which floor, señor?" he said.

"No floor," Alvarado replied.

He showed the boy the photograph of Vargas.

"This man was in your elevator last night?" he said.

"I don't know, señor. Maybe. We were very busy last night."

"Think hard," said Alvarado. "A maybe won't help me much."

"Yes," said the elevator boy. "I remember now."

Something about the boy's manner caused Alvarado

to understand he did not remember and was merely being overly helpful. Alvarado realized it had been a mistake to pressure the boy.

"Look," he said. "No need to be frightened. I didn't expect you to remember everyone who rode in the elevator last night. Take me all the way up."

There was a night club on the roof. Perhaps Vargas had gone there. It was well known that he liked a good time.

Alvarado showed his ID to the headwaiter and brought out the photograph of Vargas. The headwaiter recognized him. As Señor Hernández. But he had not seen Señor Hernández for several weeks. Alvarado thanked him, refusing an invitation to remain and enjoy himself as a guest of the hotel.

"If he should come here, call me at the comandancia," Alvarado said. "If I'm not there they'll know where I may be reached."

"But certainly, agente," the headwaiter said.

"He tips well?" Alvarado asked casually.

"Very well," said the headwaiter, "when he has been drinking."

Alvarado suppressed a sigh. It was not very likely that he would be hearing from the headwaiter. The headwaiter wasn't going to kill the goose that laid the golden egg.

He went across Miguel Lerdo and checked the register at the Hotel Diligencias. No Vargas. And no one acknowledged having seen the man of the photograph. Vargas obviously had not spent the night at either the Veracruz or the Diligencias. Alvarado doubted that he would have stayed at any of the other hotels in town, not a man of his tastes and income. Perhaps he hadn't spent the night in Veracruz. He could have driven in from Mexico City and returned the same night. Unless his appointment in the hotel had been for the purpose of arranging another meeting elsewhere. If there were an Olmec head, and Vargas had it, he would hardly be carrying it in his pocket. It was unfortunate Galvez had heard no rumors about where the head, if it actually existed, had been removed to.

It was very possible, of course, that there was no head at all and he had let himself jump to a false conclusion merely because Vargas chanced to show up in Veracruz on the heels of the rumors. Alvarado felt a little sour with disappointment. He had interrupted a pleasant evening for nothing.

Alvarado went to the corner of Independencia and Zamora and looked across the street toward the Gran Café de la Parroquia. Only Guerra and Salazar remained of the party that had been celebrating. They both looked somber. Alvarado decided not to rejoin them. Guerra, a childless widower, never wanted to go home. If he went back over there, he would be up all night. Not that there was any reason he shouldn't be up all night. He had the whole day off tomorrow. If Guerra had been alone he might have kept him company out of friendship. Guerra always needed a bit of cheering up in the early morning hours. But Salazar was with him. Salazar was old and wise and would know what to say to Guerra. And Salazar was sober. He would see that Guerra got home all right.

Sara and the girls would be sleeping. When they were younger, and closer, Sara always waited up for him. In those days, Sara had thought it dangerous to be a Federal agent and worried until he came home. For a moment he wished it were fifteen years ago and he were returning to an ardent bride.

Alvarado took a taxi back to the comandancia. He dismissed the taxi, then changed his mind and told the driver to wait. He was in no mood to sit on a streetcar at this hour of the night after a long day, the last part of it fruitless. He put the photograph back in the files and got in the front seat with the driver when he came back out.

When he reached his home he asked the driver how much the fare would have been if the meter were up. The driver told him. Alvarado gave him the money. A man who had been offered a thousand-peso proposition shouldn't begrudge a poor man a few pesos.

8

THE lobby of the Reforma looked less like a hotel than somebody's sparsely furnished living room. About the only thing indicating the building's function was a wooden desk with what looked like bills on it inside the entrance to the left. At the back of the longish room ordinary stairs led up to the second floor, adding to the illusion of a private home.

A woman with graying hair came forward to meet them, smiling. Donna spoke with her in Spanish. Bell heard the name "Hernández." Since there was no mention of Vargas, Bell assumed it was his alias. Vargas was certainly one cautious dude. The woman called out and a boy emerged from a door at the rear, chewing. He'd come out of the kitchen and whatever he had been eating back there smelled great. Or maybe it was just because he was so hungry, Bell thought. Donna must be even hungrier. She hadn't eaten any of the shrimp.

"He's upstairs," Donna said. "The boy will take us."

"Ask the lady if she can send up something to eat," Bell said.

"I already have."

The boy led them not up the stairs but out a back door that led past the kitchen to an outside stairway. A woman was sitting in the kitchen with a tortilla in one hand and a spoon in the other eating something dark brown and tasty looking from a bowl. The boy's bowl was across the table from her.

"Looks like chili," Bell said. "I hope she sends some up."

"Chili is peppers," Donna said in that superior tone she sometimes used. "You're thinking about chili con carne. And they wouldn't have that here."

The steps led to a newer part of the hotel, two stories around a courtyard, like a motel. The scent of flowers floated up from the courtyard and the music from the cantina could be plainly heard. The boy took them to a small, doorless public room. There were two men in it, one standing, the other seated in a rattan chair. The one standing up eyed them carefully, the seated one rose, smiling warmly, and went to Donna with his hand extended.

"Señorita Russell," he said. "It is so good to see you again."

So that was Vargas. He did not look or act at all as Bell had expected from Donna's account of her meeting with him in Veracruz. Bell had expected someone lean and shabby, with shifty eyes. Vargas was tall, well barbered and chubby. His brown eyes were steady and good-humored. His hair was chestnut, flecked with gray at the sides. He was wearing tan silk slacks and sports shirt and white loafers with silver buckles. To Bell he looked like a Mexican edition of Otis Sandifer.

Donna shook his hand without returning his smile. Vargas nodded at the other man, who was wearing a loose, light jacket despite the warmth of the evening, and the man left the room. As he turned, Bell saw the butt of a pistol protruding from his waistband. Vargas followed Bell's eyes.

"A necessary precaution, señor," he said.

"This is Sam Bell," Donna said.

"So I assumed," said Vargas. "Señorita Russell has spoken of you most highly, Señor Bell."

Bell brushed aside the pleasantry.

"Why a necessary precaution?" he demanded.

"There are those who would be happy to relieve us of our merchandise," Vargas said.

"El Azteca?" said Bell.

Now was as good a time as any to find out if Donna had invented him when she tried to cover up for Sandifer with that story about why the head wasn't waiting in Veracruz.

"No, Señor Bell," Vargas said. "Agente Alvarado is quite another matter. I speak of those who would like our merchandise for their own. El Azteca simply prefers that it remain here in Mexico."

So Donna hadn't made him up. Bell felt a little guilty.

Bell sat down in a rocker and Donna took a rattan chair near Vargas'. Vargas went to a low table on which sat a pitcher and glasses.

"Sangría, Señorita Russell?" he asked. "It is quite cold and the ice is pure."

Donna sighed impatiently. Taking that for assent, Vargas poured three glasses and handed them around. He sat down and lifted his glass in a silent toast which Bell acknowledged but Donna did not. Behind him, cool air poured into the room through a cement latticework. Donna began speaking Spanish in angry, earnest but controlled tones. Bell knew she was talking about money because he recognized numbers. When Vargas realized Bell did not understand Spanish, he smiled in amusement.

"Shouldn't we speak English for the benefit of Señor Bell?" he asked with patently feigned concern. "Certainly you have no secrets from your colleague, Señorita Russell?"

Bell wondered if she did, or if Vargas was just having a little fun trying to stir things up.

Donna caught Bell's thoughtful expression.

"Mr. Bell is here to supervise the transportation," she said. "He's not concerned with the business end."

"I see," said Vargas, with another smile. "Still, I prefer English. None of the people here speak it and it is more discreet."

"All right," Donna said testily. "Mr. S. has authorized another five thousand. But not one penny more. And only because of past performances."

Vargas laced his fingers together and put his hands behind his head.

"Correct me if I am mistaken," he said gently. "I have always received twenty percent of the moneys realized by . . . Mr. S."

He seemed to find it amusing to follow Donna's lead in referring to Sandifer by an initial.

"That's right," said Donna. "I'm not arguing about that."

"Ah, but I believe you are," Vargas said courteously. "As I said last night, a dear friend of mine in Houston . . ."

He was interrupted by the arrival of the boy with a napkin-covered tray. They all watched bemused while the boy put the tray down on the table. When the boy turned to leave, Bell caught his eye and said, "Hold on a minute."

He dredged a wad of pesos out of his pants pocket and extricated a crumpled ten peso note. The boy hesitated before accepting it, then scurried out. Vargas smiled approval.

"The people here are terribly poor," he said. "It is heartbreaking, actually."

"Yeah?" said Bell. "I didn't notice you reaching, señor."

"True," Vargas said, unabashed. "But, you see, I must deal with them every day. I should not wish to become known as an easy mark."

"Not bloody likely," Donna said.

"As I was saying," Vargas said. "I have it on the authority of my dear friend in Houston, rather than one hundred thousand dollars, your Mr. S. is disposing of the merchandise for one quarter of a million."

Donna shot Bell a cautionary glance.

"Your friend doesn't know what he's talking about," she said.

Which was true, Bell thought. It was a half million, not a quarter million.

"My friend is quite reliable," Vargas said.

"All right," Donna said with an air of defeat. "I'll level with you. It is more than a hundred thousand. After Mr. S. made the deal with you he got a better offer. A hundred and fifty thousand."

Bell dropped his head so Vargas would not see his expression. What an operator Donna was.

"But even so," Donna continued, "what about our expenses for a shipment this size? We've had to hire a specialist," with a nod toward Bell, "and I'd be embarrassed to tell you what we had to pay. And four trucks with drivers."

"Four trucks?" Vargas said.

"That's right," Bell interposed. "When you screwed up on your end it was too late to get a tractor-trailer rig."

"With all that and everything else," Donna said, continuing the attack, "our expenses will just about eat up the difference."

"Speaking of eating," Bell said.

He went to the table and removed the napkin from the tray the boy had brought. There were rolls, cheese, shrimp, fried bananas, an array of sliced fruits and the inevitable lime slices.

"And what about the risk?" Donna demanded. "We're taking all the risk. Moving eighteen tons of merchandise with that agent of the Federal Judicial Police breathing down our necks. What about that?"

"You must be starved, Donna," Bell said. "Why don't you eat something?"

It was not that he felt solicitous — a hungry lioness needed someone to look after her more than Donna did — he just wanted, perversely, to see if anything could distract her in the middle of a con.

Donna did not answer. She was glaring at Vargas as if trying to beat him down with righteous sincerity.

Bell hunkered down by the table and began eating.

"My dear young lady," Vargas said calmly. "I do take risks. Agente Alvarado is not, as you say, breathing down your neck. As I told you only last night, he has heard but the vaguest rumors of a find. He does not know you or Señor Bell. But he does know me. And unfortunately for me he considers my presence in Veracruz to be of significance. Yes, I would say if there are risks I share them. Would you not agree, Señor Bell?"

"Absolutely," Bell said.

Donna shot him a look of bleakest rage, which he ignored.

"Sure you won't have some of this cheese?" he said innocently. "It's super."

Donna shook her head impatiently.

"But," said Vargas, "I am not an unreasonable man. Suppose we say forty thousand dollars? That will make my contribution toward your expenses ten thousand. My own expenses have not been inconsiderable, you must understand."

So Vargas hadn't bought Donna's story about a $150,000 price tag on Chato. Donna had met her match, almost.

"Thirty," Donna said.

"Forty," said Vargas.

"If I don't take the head, who will?" Donna said. "Who else is in a position to take eighteen tons of contraband off your hands?"

"My dear young lady," Vargas said, "you know quite well such an object will not want for takers." He laughed. "Including some who have no intention of paying for it."

That interested Bell.

"You mean somebody might try to hijack it?" he said.

Sandifer hadn't mentioned that possibility.

"It is not inconceivable," Vargas said. "A dear friend of mine here in Tlacotalpán seems to believe there could be such an attempt."

"You have dear friends just about everywhere, don't you, Señor Vargas?" Bell said.

"Yes. It is rather important in my profession."

"He's just talking, Sam," Donna said. "He's the only holdup artist around here. Thirty-two five, Vargas, and that's my final offer."

"And you would simply leave here without it?" Vargas asked with a smile.

"You bet your sweet burro," Donna snapped.

"In that case," Vargas said with a shrug.

"It's settled then," Donna said. "Thirty-two five."

"No, dear lady. It is only settled that I am temporarily saddled with eighteen tons of merchandise. And twenty thousand pesos out of pocket in expenses. But I suspect you are out of pocket a good deal more than that."

Donna snorted like a fighter clearing his nostrils.

"Forty thousand," she said. "Sam, are you going to eat everything in sight? I'm starving."

She pulled her chair to the table and began eating ravenously. Bell had not expected her to be such a good loser. But Donna was nothing if not a realist.

"We're in business, then," Bell said. "Where's the load?"

"There is a farm a few kilometers west of town," Vargas said. "We will go whenever you are ready."

Bell asked Vargas if he could provide him with two

drivers. They could take two of the trucks and Bell would drive the third himself. He did not want any of his own men to know what they were hauling. Vargas could spare only one, his chauffeur.

"The guy who left?" Bell said.

"No. He is my bodyguard."

"How about him, then?"

"I'm afraid I cannot spare Pepe," Vargas said apologetically. "The road may be dangerous for me, under the circumstances."

So the talk about hijackers was not just a bargaining point, Bell thought.

"If it's dangerous for you it's dangerous for us," he said. "Once we take delivery."

"I'll see you safely as far as the ferry at Buena Vista," Vargas said. "After you reach the open highway it is unlikely you will be molested. Only the police would benefit from a public disturbance."

Bell left Donna with Vargas and drove back to the trucks, taking the chauffeur with him in the Volks. He had decided to let Juan One drive the third truck. Alberto seemed altogether too interested in what was going on.

Alberto wasn't too happy about being left behind with the other drivers but did not give voice to it. Bell would rather he had. He didn't much trust a man who sulked.

Bell had Juan check him out on the number two Dina's gearshift and instruments. Though it had been a good while since he had driven a truck it took him only a couple of runthroughs to learn all he would need to know for a short drive. He put Vargas' man in the middle in the International and Juan in the rear in the number one Dina.

Donna and Vargas were waiting in front of the Hotel Reforma in a new black Cadillac with Distrito Federal plates. They were in the back seat and the bodyguard was behind the wheel. When the trucks drew near, the Cadillac's lights went on and the car moved off. Bell followed. The Cadillac drove a short distance and turned right at a leafy plaza and then left to drive between more rows of joined houses, all of them with porticos facing on the street.

They crossed a small stone bridge and almost immediately were out in the country. Occasionally the headlights glinted on water-filled ditches or picked out puddled fields and stands of sugarcane. If there were hijackers out there, Bell thought, they had wet feet.

After a few minutes the Cadillac turned off the road, stopped and cut its lights. When Bell drew abreast, the lights went on again and the Cadillac moved off between weedy fields in which standing water cast reflections. Bell followed cautiously, peering ahead at the narrow dirt road. After fifty yards or so the road dipped. There were puddles in the dip and it looked muddy. Bell downshifted to the lowest gear and inched into it. He stopped when it began feeling mushy.

The lights of the following truck loomed so brightly in the side mirror Bell thought it was going to ram him but the chauffeur managed to stop in time. Bell flicked his lights. The Cadillac kept going for a few yards, then its backing lights came on. It stopped on the other side of the dip. Vargas and Donna got out and looked back at the trucks. Bell climbed out of the cab and waded into the mud. He sank in only a couple of inches but that did not signify much. He did not gross out at better than fourteen tons.

"What's the matter?" Donna asked.

"The trucks can't make it."

"Don't be an old lady. We made it easy."

"You ain't full of tiles," Bell said. "Come on over here."

"What in the world for?"

"Just do what I ask you to," Bell said curtly.

Donna's face was a study in the truck lights. She

was angry with him, but curious, too. She picked her way gingerly around the puddles. Bell reached a hand to steady her. She took it, but let go as soon as she was safely across.

"Tell my drivers to back out onto the highway," he said.

"Back out? We're not leaving without that head!"

"I just want to get turned around."

"Why?"

"Donna, you're in charge of the money, I'm in charge of transportation, right? Let's keep it that way."

Donna stalked off to give the drivers his orders.

"Vargas," Bell said, "can you get me some men out here on the double? I'm gonna need some help."

"But certainly," Vargas said.

The Cadillac drove off, swaying in the ruts. Bell got in his truck and started backing up. There was a banging on the passenger side of the cab. The door opened and Donna's angry face appeared.

"I'm not going to stay out here in the dark all alone," she said.

It wasn't easy backing the truck on the narrow road using only side mirrors. It hadn't taken Bell long to pick up on shifting but backing a big box was something else. He had grown too accustomed to looking out a rear window when he backed up.

Out on the highway, Bell went after Juan and brought him to take the wheel. He had Donna tell him to back the truck up to the dip. Juan backed the truck swiftly down the dark narrow road with casual ease. He stopped just short of the dip. Bell got out and signaled him to start coming. When the back of the van was over the mud, Bell gave him the stop and cut signal. He told Donna to send Juan back to join him and opened the van doors. He climbed inside, with Juan following, and began tossing out tiles. Juan did the same without being told.

After a while the Cadillac returned, followed by a rickety stake body truck full of men. Vargas got out of the car, saw what was going on and called out some orders. Ten men leaped out of the truck, three of them holding rifles. The seven unarmed men splashed through the mud and began heaving tiles. Bell sent Juan back to the cab and stationed himself at the rear of the truck. When there were enough tiles to make a bottom for a few feet, he signaled Juan to back up, stopping him when the rear wheels neared mud. He repeated the operation until the dip was bridged with tiles.

"That was clever," said Donna.

When Bell returned from the highway with the rest of his convoy, the farm truck was gone but the Cadillac was waiting. Its high beams were on, dazzling Bell as it backed along the road. He flicked his own high beams until Vargas' bodyguard got the message and switched to lows. Even then Bell had to shade his eyes. It was easier after the Cadillac turned around at the first solid stretch of ground.

The car led the trucks to a large farm building with white stucco sides and a tile roof. There was a wide cleared area in front of it, muddy but firm, where the trucks could park. Two men with rifles stood guard in front of the building's heavy wooden doors. Bell got out of the truck and joined Vargas and Donna. The bodyguard pulled open one of the doors and wavering yellow light streamed out.

The light came from kerosene lanterns hanging from wooden beams supporting the roof. The floor was hard-packed earth. In the middle of the barn, a heap of sugarcane pulp reached all the way to the roof. Near it was a heavy winch and derrick on broad iron rollers.

"Under there?" Bell asked, nodding toward the sugarcane pulp.

"Yes," said Vargas.

"Let's have a look," Donna said, excited, her eyes shining in the lamplight.

Vargas spoke to his bodyguard, who went out and returned with half a dozen men. They began tossing aside armloads of sugarcane pulp, quickly exposing a broad expanse of dark, pitted stone. Donna sucked in her breath. Bell was excited, too. This was what he had come for and would be hauling almost a thousand miles. Slowly, the head emerged from the heap of fiber. Then it was fully exposed, its ominous baby face bathed in the soft, wavering light of the lanterns. Bell's hackles rose. It looked alive. But blind.

"Jesus!" he said.

"Isn't it gorgeous?" Donna said.

Her voice was shaky.

"It is a nice piece, is is not?" Vargas said.

"Sandifer said it was cut up," Bell said.

"It is," said Donna. "But I insisted on seeing it whole."

Bell moved up for a closer inspection. The places where it had been sawed hardly showed, looking like nothing more than narrow grooves in the stone. It was divided as he had anticipated, with the eye and nose section the largest of the five. He'd put it in the number two Dina and load two sections each on the other trucks.

"Let's get started," he said, stepping back.

"Of course," said Vargas. "But first . . ."

He looked at Donna. She nodded.

He spoke to his bodyguard, who led the workmen out of the barn. Vargas walked aside with Donna, out of view of the open door. Donna reached into her big purse, glanced at Bell and hesitated.

"Don't you have something to do with the trucks, Sam?" she asked.

"Sure do," he said, not moving.

Seeing he intended to remain, she took a plastic envelope out of the purse, put the purse on the floor, zipped open the envelope and counted out $40,000 in U.S. currency into Vargas' outstretched hand. One hell of a lot of money, Bell thought, but not so much when you considered Sandifer would be getting half a million for the head. Vargas should really be getting a hundred thousand. He wondered what Vargas would do when he found out. He did not doubt that Vargas would, eventually.

"Now," said Vargas, "if you will excuse me."

He went to the back of the barn, faced away from them, unbuckled his belt and zipped open his trousers. Could he be going to do what it looked like he was going to do? Bell wondered. Donna turned away with an expression of distaste. Holding his trousers up by spreading his legs, Vargas fiddled with something around his waist under his shirt. He zipped up the trousers, fastened the belt and turned around. The forty thousand was nowhere in sight. Bell understood then what Vargas had been doing was stowing it in a money belt.

"Now you've been to the bank," Bell said, "how about getting me some help in here?"

Juan was asleep in the front seat when Bell went out to bring in the number one Dina. He woke Juan up and informed him by gestures he was to wait outside the barn. Juan by now knew something out of the ordinary was going on but Bell saw no reason for him to know exactly what it was they would be hauling.

Vargas' bodyguard had assembled a work crew by the time Bell backed the Dina into the barn. There were fifteen men, more than Bell really needed, but he put them all to work. Four went into the truck to unload and the others carried the tiles to the rear of the barn and stacked them. The truck was quickly emptied. Several of the men wheeled the winch and derrick to the head, looking as if they knew what they were about. Another set of men looped a heavy rope around the top slab and slid the section a couple of feet off center. The men operating the hoist slipped a padded sling under the slab, winched it up until there was room to get more slings around it, and lifted it free.

Bell backed the truck to the slab, the winch crew lowered it until it was even with the van floor and a gang of men slid it inside. After the second slab went in in the same manner, Bell had them pile sugarcane pulp around the sections. He didn't think the tiles alone would cover the sections, not and keep the net load in the neighborhood of eight tons. The two slabs weighed about six tons together. Twenty-five square meters of tile weighed about a ton. He had Vargas' men arrange fifty square meters of tile to cover the slabs and the fiber bulking out the load. The weight of the fiber wasn't enough to worry about.

The eyes and nose section went into the number two Dina with more sugarcane pulp and seventy-five square meters of tile. The two bottom slabs went into the International. The men were just covering them with the last few pieces of fifty square meters of tile when Bell heard the first shot.

9

THE shot apparently had come from somewhere near the barn. It was followed by shouts and the pounding of feet. Vargas' bodyguard slipped quickly out of the barn door and closed it behind him. The work crew bunched together around the truck they had been loading, whispering nervously. Donna looked frightened, Vargas only concerned.

"Police?" Bell asked.

Vargas shook his head.

"I think someone who would like our merchandise now that it is nicely loaded," he said. "Or perhaps it is only a man of mine firing at shadows."

If it was hijackers, they were in real trouble, Bell thought. Now that Vargas had his money, he might just slip away and leave them to take care of themselves.

Then there was more firing. It came from two sides of the barn. Something smacked into an outside wall, then again. Someone was shooting at the guards. There was still a lot of yelling but no running around. The guards were bright enough to have taken cover.

"Get back in the corner and stay there, Donna," Bell ordered.

Donna did so, looking back over her shoulder at him, her face stiff with apprehension.

"You got a gun, Vargas?" Bell asked.

They might have to defend themselves. Even if they didn't, Bell wanted to know if Vargas was armed. If Vargas tried to take off and leave them in the lurch, he intended to stop him.

"No," said Vargas. "But do not worry. I have sufficient men outside to deal with the situation."

He did not sound all that confident, though. Bell wondered what would happen if Vargas' men bugged out. Would the hijackers be content just to grab the head or would they want to get rid of Anglo witnesses? If all they wanted was Chato, he wouldn't try to stop them if it came to a standoff between him and them. He wasn't being paid to fight, just to supervise a piece of hauling.

"What kind of people are they?" he asked in a low voice so Donna could not hear.

"Very bad people, I'm afraid," Vargas replied.

So maybe he would have to fight whether he was being paid for it or not. He'd feel a lot better about it if he had a weapon.

"I want a rifle," he said.

"It is not necessary," Vargas said. "I have sufficient men."

There was a lot of firing going on, outgoing and incoming. But the barn was like a fortress. Except for one bullet that ripped through the door and into the side of the International, the return fire had no effect. The door opened and Bell darted toward it, his fist poised to deliver a blow. It was only Vargas' bodyguard. The bodyguard hurried to Vargas and began speaking in a low, urgent voice.

"What is it?" Bell demanded.

"They have many men," Vargas said, worried.

"How many?"

"Twenty at least, Pepe says. Perhaps more."

"How many you got?"

"Armed, only twelve. And Pepe, here. I think you should take your trucks and make a run for it."

"And get picked off? Not a chance."

"What is it, Sam?" Donna called from her corner. She was scared and trying not to show it.

"Nothing serious," Bell said. "You just stay where you are." He turned to Vargas and said, "Let's go outside."

"Outside? But it is much safer in here."

"I need an interpreter."

"You cannot negotiate with such men."

"Don't intend to. Tell those guys to get off their tails and put out the lights. All of 'em."

"I do not understand."

"Trust me," Bell said. "I know what I'm doing."

Vargas studied him a moment.

"I think you do, Señor Bell," he said calmly.

The man had guts, Bell thought. And apparently no intention of running out on them now that he had his money. Bell felt a little bad about Donna lying to Vargas about how much Sandifer was getting for Chato.

"Donna," he said. "We're gonna put out the lights and go outside. The bodyguard's staying with you. Okay?"

"Where are you going?"

"Just outside to reconnoiter. We won't be gone long."

"Is it bad, Sam?" Donna asked shakily.

Fear had softened her. She was no longer prickly and self-assured. Bell felt close to her for the first time, and protective.

"Don't worry about a thing, baby," he said.

The loaders put out all the lanterns. It was pitch black inside the barn.

"Pepe is to remain with Señorita Russell, correct?" Vargas said in the darkness.

"Right," said Bell. "Come on."

He groped his way toward the doors, Vargas at his heels. Bell pushed the door open and said, "Keep low."

He crouched and ran to the shelter of one of the two loaded trucks parked outside the barn. He hoped none of the shots had hit an engine or tires. Someone spoke to him calmly in Spanish. It was Juan.

"Your man would like to know if there is something you wish him to do," Vargas translated.

"Just tell him to sit tight," Bell said, glad he had picked Juan to come along.

There was still a lot of firing going on. It brought back memories. He hoped whoever it was Vargas' men were shooting at weren't as skilled at their work as some he'd run into.

"Tell your men to stop firing," Bell said.

"I don't understand," Vargas protested.

"Tell them to stop firing, man. I want to know what we're up against."

He had not believed the estimate of Vargas' bodyguard. It was his experience that in a night firefight even veteran soldiers usually thought a lot more people were shooting back at them than were really out there.

Vargas shouted an order and the firing trailed off, finally stopping altogether. Shots kept zinging in, rapping into the walls and occasionally hitting a truck. Bell listened carefully and searched the darkness for muzzle flashes.

"Eight of 'em," he said after a while. "Nine, maybe."

"I think you were once a soldier," said Vargas.

"Get me a rifle," Bell said.

Vargas called out and a man detached himself from the darkness beside a truck and ran to them. He gave Bell his rifle. Bell hefted it and held it close to his eyes in the darkness. It was an old World War II M-1. He had fired M-1s on the range. He felt for the safety. It was off. He slipped it on.

"I want some extra clips," he said.

Vargas had the man give them to him.

"I'm gonna outflank 'em," Bell said. "After I rip off a few rounds, tell your people to move out on the run. Shoot and yell and make a lot of noise. Tell 'em to move straight out. We don't want to cut those characters off from the highway."

"I do not understand," Vargas said. "Why should we permit them to reach the highway?"

"We want to chase 'em off, not wipe 'em out," Bell said. "Okay?"

"Okay," said Vargas.

"They can start shooting back now," Bell said. "But not off to the right. That's where I'll be."

When Vargas' men resumed firing, Bell felt his way along the side of the barn, moving to the right, away from the direction of the highway. Once he was off the parking surface, his shoes sank into a muddy field. If he had known what he was getting into, he would have worn boots. That wasn't quite right. If he had known what he was getting into he wouldn't have gotten into it. Bell moved out in a wide arc until he was beyond the outside man firing at the barn. He felt around for a relatively dry spot and eased down on his belly, cradling the rifle in his arms.

He waited for the next muzzle flash, then fired one round, paused and fired twice more, close together. He did not aim directly at the spot where he had seen the flash. He bracketed it. He didn't want to kill anybody, just scare him enough to make him cut and run. Bell thrashed around in the grass and began yelling.

"Let's get 'em, amigos!" he shouted.

He wished he could have said the whole thing in Spanish, but the "amigos" should be enough to make the besiegers think he had men with him on their flank.

Back at the barn, Vargas' men were yelling and running into the field, shooting wildly. Bell hoped Vargas had told them not to fire in his direction. Bell's man jumped to his feet and started running. Bell could hear the others doing the same. They weren't even shooting back. He remained where he was until the chase veered toward the highway. He had no intention of getting between Vargas' men and their fleeing quarry. Vargas' men kept running and firing. Bell didn't want that. He leaped to his feet and shouted, "Cease firing! Cease firing!"

He didn't expect them to understand but maybe Vargas would hear him and give the order. Apparently Vargas did, for the shooting and yelling tapered off. Bell returned to the barn in the same wide arc in which he had left it, and was just as careful not to make any noise. He didn't trust Vargas' men not to take pot shots at sounds in the night. When he neared the barn he heard motors roar into life and speed away out on the highway.

They were rid of the intruders, for the time being, anyhow. He wondered if they might try again out on the highway. He didn't think they would. They were routed and outnumbered, and knew Vargas' men would be ready for them if they made another try. And they had driven off to the west, going away from Tlacotalpán. If the trucks were okay, the worst was over.

The lanterns were back on in the barn. Donna and Vargas were waiting for him just outside the open doors.

"Congratulations," Vargas said. "You have won the battle of Tlacotalpán."

Now that it was over, Vargas was in high spirits. Bell felt pretty good himself. A little harmless action opened the pores and cleared away the cobwebs.

Donna surprised him by running up and giving him a big hug. She felt a good deal softer than she acted. Bell gave her a big hug in return. The trip to Mexico might have some unexpected dividends after all. Donna stiffened and pulled free.

"You're a mess!" she exclaimed. "Are you all right?"

Bell looked down at himself. He was all mud from the middle of his calves down and the rest of his body was damp and plastered with grass and twigs.

"I'm fine," he said. "Tell somebody to bring lanterns. I want to look at the trucks."

There were four bullet holes in the side of the number two Dina. Fortunately, the motor and tires had not been hit. The number one Dina had been shielded by the other truck and was unscathed. The bullet holes in the number two Dina were small and probably would not be noticed. To be on the safe side, he had Vargas put a couple of men to work plugging the holes with mud. When they had done that, he had them sling handfuls of mud against the side of the truck from a few feet away so the blobs covering the holes would not be conspicuous.

The men who had pursued the intruders straggled back, laughing and calling out to one another in celebration. Bell was washing his hands in a bucket of water drawn from a nearby well when Donna rushed to him.

"Sam," she whispered in agitation, "something terrible's happened."

She grabbed his wet hand and pulled him after her. Vargas and his men were in a semicircle just outside the barn, their backs to him. At their approach, Vargas looked back grimly at them over his shoulder. His men, boisterous, were looking at something on the ground in the yellow light from the barn. Juan was among them. He, too, looked back at Bell, neither raucous like the others nor grim like Vargas. His expression was, as usual, composed. He cleared a space among the men through which Bell could pass. A man lay there on his back, his arms still stretched back from having been dragged by them. His eyes were open but he was motionless. Bell stared at Vargas. Vargas stared back.

"Dead, I'm afraid," Vargas said.

"Oh, Jesus," said Bell.

He'd thought he had handled things so nobody would get hurt. The way Vargas' men were shooting, he hadn't thought they could hit anything. And the attackers hadn't exactly been marksmen, either. They'd been able to hit the side of a barn and that was about all. It had seemed like a game, flushing them out and chasing them hightailing for the road. It wasn't a game anymore.

"What will we do?" Donna said.

"Clear out before somebody comes to investigate all the commotion," Bell said. He looked at Vargas and nodded toward the dead man. "What about him?"

"He will be taken away," Vargas said calmly.

"Just like that?" Bell demanded.

"Yes," said Vargas. "And there is no need to rush away. No one will come to investigate. If at all."

"All the shooting and yelling," Bell protested.

"People here do not go casually to the authorities," Vargas replied. "They prefer dealing with them as little as possible." He smiled. "As in your own country, Señor Bell."

Donna didn't look good at all. Her face was white and her eyes kept straying back unwillingly to the body on the ground. Bell put his arm around her and led her away.

"Vargas, get him out of sight, will you?" he said. "And have your men finish loading the tiles. I don't want to hang around here any longer than I have to."

Two men dragged the corpse away by the arms. Bell took Donna into the barn. She looked exhausted from the strain and lack of sleep. It was after three now. Bell, except for a nagging concern that the adventure had turned sour with the death of a man, felt fine. He could miss a night's sleep easily if he could catch a couple of hours' nap the next day. Which he intended doing once they were well on their way.

There were only a few more tiles to be loaded. It

was done quickly. Bell had a brief conference with Vargas.

"They might get their nerve back and regroup for another try," he said. "You said you'd see us safely to the ferry?"

"Of course," said Vargas.

He would send armed men ahead of the convoy in a truck and bring up the rear with more armed men in his car. The guards would stand by until all three trucks were safely across the Papaloapán.

"And the tiles we took off?" Bell said. "What about them?"

There was a big stack of them in the barn, eighteen tons that had been replaced by the five slabs of Chato, minus those he had dumped in the bad place in the road.

"My friend will dispose of them," Vargas said.

"Be damn sure he does," said Bell. "If somebody comes poking around they might wonder what all those tiles are doing here."

"I had not thought you were such a cautious man," Vargas murmured.

"I wouldn't much like to get tied to a murder."

"Murder, Señor Bell? An accidental death, perhaps. Should matters proceed so far. Which I assure you is unlikely. You need not even tell our friend Sandifer. He would rather not know of such things. Correct, Señorita Russell?"

"I wish I didn't know," Donna said.

She was still shaky.

"Don't think about it," Bell said. "Once we're away from here it'll be like it never happened."

"But it did happen."

"Look at it this way. If they'd gotten in here they might have wasted us just for the fun of it. They were bad cats. Even if they couldn't shoot straight."

"I'll try, Sam," Donna said wanly.

"Good girl," said Bell.

Now that the ice was broken, he was sorry they wouldn't be stopping for the night along the way. Maybe he'd see her after they got back to Houston.

As before, Bell took the lead in the number two Dina, with one of Vargas' men behind him in the International and Juan following in the other Dina. Bell took Donna in the cab with him. He knew she would feel better away from Vargas' bandits in the Cadillac.

They reached Tlacotalpán without incident and without even seeing another vehicle on the road. The town was completely dark except for a dim light in front of the police station across from the plaza. If anyone had heard the commotion it didn't show. The police station was closed tight, and dark except for the outside light. Vargas had known what he was talking about.

Bell parked the number two Dina beside the Mack. He started to ask Donna to tell Juan not to say anything to the other drivers about what had happened but decided against it. Juan was obviously not a talker. It would be insulting to give him such an order.

Alberto was asleep in the cab of the Mack. The other drivers were sacked out in the van. Alberto came out of the cab rubbing his eyes and yawning when the three trucks lined up beside the Mack. The stake body truck carrying the guards had gone on to the highway and parked. Vargas stayed in his car, keeping his men inside with him.

"Alberto," Bell said, "did you hear anything a while ago?"

"No, señor," Alberto said. "I have been sleeping. I am sorry."

"That's okay," Bell said.

It was good to know the shooting hadn't been all that loud from this far away. Unless Alberto was an unusually heavy sleeper maybe nobody else had heard anything, either.

"Get the drivers up," he said. "I want them ready to roll in five minutes."

The drivers tumbled out of the Mack scratching and hawking. Bell had Alberto tell them they would be making a breakfast stop on the other side of Veracruz, after the sun came up, and sent them to their trucks.

Donna was in the Volks with her eyes closed. Sleeping, Bell thought. But her eyes opened immediately when he opened the door.

"It's still not like it never happened," she said.

"Give it time. Soon's it gets daylight, you'll feel better. You'll see."

He started the engine and waited for his trucks to fire up.

"The whole deal's kind of a dirty business," he said. "When you think about it."

It hadn't seemed that way in Sandifer's office, or even in Veracruz when they were running around making arrangements. It had been fun. But the fact was they were stealing eighteen tons of national treasure from the Mexicans, something somebody thought was worth half a million dollars.

"You sound like you're sorry you got into this," Donna said. "Are you?"

"Aren't you?"

"If it wasn't for that poor man back there . . ." Donna said thoughtfully. "No. I didn't expect anything like this to happen but. . . . Look, Sam, it's just business. It's not like robbing a bank. Everybody makes money and nobody gets hurt. Usually. What happened back there wasn't our fault. If they hadn't tried to rob us . . ."

She sounded as if she were trying to convince herself, and doing a pretty good job. He didn't have to worry about Donna falling apart. He wasn't so sure, himself, that it was all that harmless and simple. But he had agreed to do the job and he was going to.

122

Chances were, he'd feel better about it, too, after the sun came up.

Bell followed the stake body truck, his own trucks strung out behind him. Donna slumped over against the door, her head on her shoulder. She was sleeping. Nothing like a clear conscience, Bell thought.

When they reached the crossing, the ferry was already on its way over, the crew having seen the lights of the approaching convoy. The ferry was empty. Bell got out and told Alberto to get on with the International and the number two Dina. There wasn't room for all four trucks and the Volks.

Donna was awake when he returned to the car. Vargas had come over to join her. Bell took him aside and asked what he had done with the dead man. Vargas assured Bell his friend at the farm was taking care of everything. There was nothing to be concerned about.

When the ferry returned, Vargas let all his men out except his bodyguard and driver and followed Bell and the last truck aboard. When they drove off the ferry on the other side of the river, the Cadillac pulled up beside the Volks.

"Please give Señor Sandifer my deepest regards," Vargas said. "I wait to learn of your safe arrival."

"Feliz viaje," Bell said.

That was what had been spelled out in flowers back at the Veracruz junction. Donna had said it meant "have a nice trip."

"Thank you, Señor Bell," Vargas replied. "Feliz viaje."

The Cadillac sped away.

"How could you be so nice to him when he put the screws to me for twenty thousand dollars?" Donna demanded.

"Come off it, baby. Telling the man a hundred and fifty thousand for Chato. Ain't you ashamed?"

"No," said Donna.

"I didn't think you would be."

Alberto came back for instructions. Bell told him to maintain a steady 80 kilometers an hour and take it easy if they hit curves or grades. Bell sent the number two Dina behind the Mack, the International behind that, with Juan One bringing up the rear in the number one Dina. Bell would be driving behind the convoy for a while, assuring himself it was not being followed, but from time to time later on he would be scouting ahead. When that happened, he wanted someone reliable like Juan in back to see that no one straggled.

Except for Juan One, the drivers had no road discipline. They would fall back, opening big intervals, then gun to catch up and have to brake to keep from hitting the truck in front. As long as nobody got rear-ended, and he had Juan in back to see that no one fell out altogether, he'd be all right, Bell thought.

It was 5:25 A.M. and the darkness was paling when they reached the Caseta Fiscal on the other side of the Boca del Rio bridge. There was a light on in the caseta and across the road a sign saying "Trailers Alto Obligatorio." Bell knew what that meant without Donna saying anything. The man inside the caseta was dozing. Bell slowed after he passed the caseta, watching the convoy in his rearview mirror. All his trucks drove unchallenged past the caseta.

Bell checked the odometer at the road junction where the flowerbed spelled out "Feliz Viaje." He wrote down the number, 33,738 kilometers, and the time, 5:36 A.M., in the notebook he carried in his shirt pocket. Bell felt as if only now were they actually starting the haul. He had been prepared to bring the head from Veracruz and, despite the fact he'd had to go to Tlacotalpán to pick it up, the notion persisted. Maybe, he thought, it was because he would rather forget what happened back there.

Donna had the map open on her lap, though he did

not know what good that would do him if she couldn't read it without getting car sick. At the moment it didn't matter. He knew where he was going and it wasn't yet light enough to read a map anyhow.

There was little traffic on the road. A few pedestrians were walking along the shoulders. The convoy spun along handily. It slowed for a stretch of curvy highway with a little upgrade to it and again for another caseta, this one marked "Inspección Fiscal," where the trucks were waved on by a man standing in front.

After a while Bell said, "We should be getting close to a road junction. Place named Puente Nacional. We stay with Highway One-Eighty. Our turn should say Nautla."

"Nautla? I thought this was the highway to Jalapa."

"Jalapa's west on One-Forty. We want east on One-Eighty."

Bell was leading the convoy now. He made his turn at Puente Nacional and stopped just off the highway. He wanted to be sure all his trucks took the right turn. Alberto gave him a little toot of acknowledgment when the Mack went by. He'd have to tell Alberto not to do things like that, Bell thought. No point in advertising the Volks was part of the convoy. After the last truck went by, Juan One in the number one Dina, Bell pulled back on the highway.

The road was plain blacktop now, and narrower than before the junction. Bell told Donna to hold the wheel steady and hand him the map. The next turn, north, was at Cardel. They must be getting close to it. He sped up and took the lead again. He made the turn north and waited just past the turn until his four trucks came by.

Just inside Cardel was a grubby little movie house, Cine Modelo.

"Modelo mean model?" Bell asked.

"Yes," Donna said, her eyes closed.

"Spanish is a snap," Bell said. "What do I need you for?"

"Thanks," Donna said curtly, opening her eyes.

He'd forgotten Donna didn't have much of a sense of humor. And she was tired and hungry and wanted to wash her face. He was tired and hungry himself.

The highway passed between lush fields, with here and there a few trees. It was full light now, with still scarcely any traffic. Donna dozed. She had slept off and on from the ferry. Driving was monotonous and Bell's eyes wanted to close.

"Donna," he said. "You awake?"

"I am now."

"Talk to me. I almost dropped off just now."

"All right."

"How did you get mixed up in this kind of thing, anyway?"

"What kind of thing?" she said, a hint of amusement in her tone.

"Smuggling."

"Sandy calls it liberating."

"What do you call it?"

"The same as Sandy, I suppose."

"Don't you see anything wrong with it?"

"Not until this trip."

"Because of what happened back there?"

"Let's not talk about what happened back there. And that isn't it."

"What is it, then?"

"Because it's the largest piece by far we've ever handled, and the first one I've had to bring out by road, and Sandy's getting all that bread and only paying me five thousand."

"How'd you get the stuff out before?"

"Why? Are you thinking about going into business for yourself?"

"Not a chance. This is my first and last time."

In the past, she had several times brought out small,

126

valuable pieces in her luggage or handbag on regular commercial flights, she said. For larger items, Vargas had ways of shipping them air freight or by sea. She suspected that Vargas dealt with others besides Sandifer. Vargas was too large an operator to confine himself to a single dealer, and one without connections in Europe, at that. She would not tell Bell how much Sandifer paid her for the previous trips but he had a notion it was little more than a paid vacation in Mexico City, where she usually made her pickups.

In a way, she was responsible for Sandifer getting into pre-Columbian art. She had gone to work at the gallery four years earlier, shortly after graduating from the University of Texas with a major in art and a minor in Spanish. In her first year at the gallery she had bought herself a small Mayan jade figurine on a Mexican vacation. Wanting money to buy a painting, she had turned it over to Sandifer to sell for her. The price he obtained had been a revelation to both of them.

Bell suspected she was talking so freely because fatigue had lowered her defenses.

"What do you need Sandifer for now?" he asked. "Why don't you just bring in the stuff and sell it yourself?"

"I considered it," she said. "But Sandy's got the connections. And I like my job at the gallery. I like the work and I like the security of a regular paycheck." She looked out of the window a moment before continuing. "I never had financial security until I started working for Sandy. I thought it was a rather nice paycheck until I found out what Sandy's giving you for just one trip."

"Still gnawing on that, Donna?"

"Wouldn't you?"

"Probably."

Donna fell silent. Bell could see she regretted having unburdened herself to him.

Forty-six kilometers out of Cardel they got their first glimpse of the Gulf of Mexico. The land, vividly green, rolled right down to its edge.

"Lovely," said Donna.

So she did notice scenery after all, Bell thought. Before she'd just been too uptight to do so.

"Think your stomach'll let you look at the map?" he asked.

"I'll try. What do you want to know?"

"How far to the next town?"

Donna studied the map in spurts, looking out the window in between.

"Palma Sola," she said. "From Cardel, one side of the highway says fifty-two in black and the other side says thirty-two in red. What does that mean?"

"The black's in kilometers, the red's miles."

If Palma Sola was 52 kilometers from Cardel, they were getting close. He gunned around the convoy to beat it in. If there was a place to eat in Palma Sola, they'd stop. And there should be a service station, too, where they could top off the fuel tanks.

He pulled in front of the Mack and signaled Alberto to slow down. Palma Sola was just ahead, a small village. Just off the road to the right was a café, and beyond it a service station. The café didn't look like much but Bell wasn't feeling particular.

"How about some breakfast?" he said.

Donna's nose wrinkled.

Bell pulled off the road in front of the café anyway. It had a name, Restaurante Chelito.

"It looks terrible," Donna said. "I'll bet it hasn't even got a bathroom."

"You'll love it," Bell said. "I hear they serve the best food in town. And people come from miles around just to use the bathroom it's so great."

He looked at his watch. It was 7:50 Friday morning.

10

AGENTE Tomás Alvarado awoke at seven Friday morning and could not go back to sleep though he had the day off. He could hear Sara moving around in the kitchen. She was always up early, and always busy, cooking, sewing, cleaning. The girls were not as much help as they could be. Sara defended them as much as she dared, saying they tried to help but just got in the way because she had her own way of doing things. Concepción, Leonor and Yolanda no doubt were still sleeping. If permitted, they would sleep all day and sit up half the night giggling about boys. And Yolanda only eleven. Why could he have not had at least one boy?

It was pleasant lying in bed with the whole day ahead of him. Maybe he would take them all to the beach. But Concepción would have to dress properly. Or he could lie around all morning and in the afternoon meet César Guerra at the Imperial, have a beer or two and watch the pigeons wheel over the plaza when the Asunción bells rang. That seemed like the better idea. He was taking the family to the movies that night, an American detective film. He was not required to entertain them day and night. And his day off belonged to him. Concepción did not like going out with the family. Already she wanted to go out with boys. It would be years before he would allow that.

Or perhaps he would go to Santiago Tuxtla and have a look at the Olmec heads. Santiago was only fourteen kilometers from San Andrés Tuxtla. San Andrés was where Galvez had said there was talk of a big find out Laguna de los Cerros way. Alvarado wondered if there were anything to those rumors. If he wanted to go down there and hear them for himself he would have to do so today, when he was off. His chief wouldn't send him down officially. The chief did not share his interest in national treasures, not unless there was more to go on than rumors. The attorney general's office kept them too busy to permit the luxury of running down rumors. If he could present them with something stronger than gossip, that was another matter. There was a lot of pressure from Mexico City to crack down on looters.

Alvarado got up and looked out the window. It appeared to be a fine day. Instead of sitting around watching pigeons he would run down to San Andrés Tuxtla. Even if nothing came of it he would have an enjoyable outing. And when he had a day off, it was a good idea to be where he could not be reached. The chief had a habit of calling him on his day off.

He went into the kitchen. Sara was shelling beans.

"Why can't Concepción do that?" he demanded.

"She's not quick at it," Sara said defensively. "And she was up late last night sewing a dress. She sews so well. You should be proud of her."

"I want to see that dress before she wears it out of the house," Alvarado said.

"Oh, it's modest, Tomás," Sara said quickly. "I picked the pattern myself."

"She could change it."

"Will you have breakfast now?"

Alvarado stretched, his broad shoulders and thick arms almost filling one end of the kitchen.

"I'm hungry this morning," he said. "I think I'll take a Yankee breakfast."

That was what they called ham and eggs, toasted bread and coffee in the Alvarado household. Concepción had given it that name. She was a very clever girl. Alvarado was sure she was meant to be a boy. He could not imagine what had gone wrong. Alvarados always had plenty of boys. It was Sara's side that had the girls. He would never have a boy now. In the eleven years since Yolanda was born, Sara had not been able to give him another child.

While he was eating his ham and eggs he said, "I'm going to San Andrés this morning."

Sara looked up from the pan of beans she was shelling, then down again quickly. She said nothing. Alvarado knew the reason for the look.

"I should be back in plenty of time for the film," he said.

After breakfast, Alvarado washed his face and slipped on his trousers and a guayabera shirt. He always wore guayaberas, not the thin, see-through kind, to hide his pistol and holster. He never left the house without his pistol, even on his day off. Not since the time three years earlier when he had been obliged to stand by helplessly and see a shopkeeper robbed and killed. He had run the murderer down and beaten him unconscious with his fists, but too late to matter to the shopkeeper.

On his way out of the house he looked into the girls' room. Leonor and Yolanda slept together in the big bed. Concepción, exercising her rights as the eldest, slept alone in the little one. Despite the heat, the two younger girls were huddled together like kittens. Concepción was sleeping on her stomach with the sheet thrown off and her nightgown up to her hips. She could not even sleep like a lady. Alvarado stole into the room, not tiptoeing but nevertheless without a sound, and pulled the nightgown down where it belonged. He reached down to the pillow and touched Concepción's tousled black hair, shook his head helplessly and smiled. He bent over the two younger girls and kissed each lightly on the cheek. Everything considered, he had fine girls. It was such a pity they did not have at least one brother.

He went to town by streetcar to catch the bus for San Andrés Tuxtla. It was hot on the bus. Alvarado wondered if they would ever get air-conditioned buses for the short runs like they had for those that went to Mexico City. The man sitting beside him tugged vainly at a stuck window.

"Permit me," Alvarado said.

He leaned across his seat companion and opened the window with one powerful heave. His seatmate was impressed by Alvarado's display of strength. Alvarado took no notice, having no special pride in his physical prowess. He had not worked for it. It was merely something he happened to be born possessing. It would be the greatest of vanities to take pride in something given by God. Still, it was good to be so strong. It was often useful in his profession.

Alvarado leaned back and looked straight ahead. He had gone south by bus so many times the view no longer interested him. And in any case, he had more interest in people than in views. Movement from his seatmate caught his attention. The man, middle-aged and in need of a shave, had spread a handkerchief on his lap and now produced an avocado, a lime and a bone-handled pocketknife with a long thin blade. He divided the lime into quarters against his thumb. The knifeblade obviously was razor keen, judging from the way it sliced through the lime, but somehow did not cut into the man's thumb at the end of its stroke.

He put the sliced lime on the handkerchief and made two lengthwise cuts in the avocado, put the knife down and lifted out a neat little wedge. He squeezed lime juice on it, took the segment delicately at each end and, with a deft motion, peeled back the skin and popped the wedge into his mouth. Seeing Alvarado watching, he cut another wedge and offered it to him.

"No, thank you," Alvarado said.

The man finished the avocado methodically, threw the skin, seed and squeezed lime slices out of the window, wiped his knifeblade on the handkerchief, folded the handkerchief, put both away and leaned back with his eyes closed and a contented expression on his face.

"Where are you going, friend?" Alvarado asked.

The man's eyes popped open. He looked as if he were not really sure he had been addressed.

"San Andrés Tuxtla?" Alvarado said. "Acayucán?"

He had learned that if one asked questions, one sometimes found unexpected information from the most unlikely sources.

"Why?" the man asked suspiciously.

"Just to make conversation," Alvarado replied pleasantly. He took off his sunglasses so he would not appear so threatening. "I'm on my way to San Andrés," he said.

"I, also," the man said.

"You perhaps live in San Andrés?"

"Yes."

"Tell me, have you been to Santiago Tuxtla to see the Olmec heads?"

"No. They don't interest me."

"Is that so? I find them very interesting. You have no interest at all in such things?"

"No."

"I know of men who have made a good deal of money out of such things. Much smaller things, of course."

"Oh, that," the man said, showing more interest in the subject. "I'd like to get out and have a look around myself, one day. But I can never find the time to get away. And I wouldn't know what to do with it if I came upon something nice."

"It isn't that hard to find buyers, I understand," said Alvarado.

"Still, it's risky, I hear. The authorities on one hand, criminals who want to take it from you on the other. If it's really something nice."

He gave Alvarado a sharp look. "Tell me, señor," he said. "Are you a policeman?"

"No," Alvarado said.

"You look as if you could be a policeman."

"That's what everyone says," Alvarado replied. He looked around cautiously and said in a low, confidential voice, "Truthfully, friend, I'm sometimes on the other side of the fence, if you know what I mean."

The man looked at Alvarado as if he were not very bright to be telling such things to a stranger. Alvarado had found it was not difficult to convince strangers he was a bit slow. They were usually quick to believe the mind of an ox went with the body of an ox. And Alvarado was adept at contributing to that impression.

He looked around cautiously again. "As a matter of fact," he said, "that's why I'm on my way to San Andrés. I heard in Veracruz someone has found an entire temple down by Hidalgotitlán. And brought some fine things up to San Andrés."

"That is not what I have heard," the man said knowingly.

"Is that so?" Alvarado demanded, letting a little truculence creep into his tone. "Listen to me, friend. It's my business to know about such things and I heard it was Hidalgotitlán and a temple."

"Very well, very well," the man said, frightened.

"Look," said Alvarado. "I'm sorry I spoke up like that. I'm sure you know more about it than I do, living in San Andrés and being an intelligent man."

"I keep my eyes and ears open," the man said, mollified and complacent.

"What was it you heard?" Alvarado asked, his tone respectful now.

"It was not as far away as Hidalgotitlán. And it was not an entire temple."

"Not a temple?" Alvarado said, looking disappointed.

"No," said the man. He was enjoying himself now. "It's strange you asked me if I'd seen the Olmec heads at Santiago just now. Because that's what they say it was."

"An Olmec head? Truly?"

Alvarado did not have to pretend he was impressed now. An Olmec head was a find, indeed.

"Truly, señor," the man said. "And the biggest one ever, they say. Four meters high and more than twenty thousand kilograms in weight."

"That's even bigger than the big one at Santiago," Alvarado said. "If it's that big, it must be there still."

"Removed, they say," the man said complacently.

"But that is impossible. So large an object and no roads."

"No, they say it has been removed."

"Where did you hear of this? Perhaps there were other objects small enough for someone like myself to negotiate."

"I heard only of a head. And from no one in particular. Just talk in the cantina and elsewhere. Perhaps it's only that after all, just talk. Who could spirit away twenty metric tons? But you believed for a moment, did you not, señor?"

"No," said Alvarado. "I knew you were making sport of me. But I don't mind. I'm accustomed to it."

"Maybe one day I'll go to Santiago and have a look at the heads there," the man said, as if it were on the other side of the world and not just a few kilometers from his home.

"You should, by all means."

It was lunchtime when they reached San Andrés Tuxtla. Alvarado said goodbye to his new friend and walked over to the Hotel Zamfer, the best place in town. He was in a mood to celebrate. There just might be something to what the man had told him. After lunch he would talk with the chief of police. If the chief of police here, who was close to things, took any stock in the rumors, it would give him something with which to approach his own chief in Veracruz. If his chief took it up with the agent of the attorney general, it might get all the way to the attorney general in Mexico City and they would send a helicopter out to locate the site of the find. If anything as large as an Olmec head had been removed, the excavation almost certainly would be visible from the air unless it was so long ago the jungle had already overrun it.

If the site were located, it would confirm the rumors and perhaps then the paper-shufflers would wake up and order a full-scale investigation. They would certainly have to do that if it reached the ears of the attorney general. In Mexico City they were getting very serious about archeological looting these days. There was even a top agent of the attorney general's office working closely with the Institute of Archeology and History. And if the chief were given the job of investigating, which he would be because it was within the Veracruz jurisdiction, who but Alvarado would get the assignment?

The hotel restaurant was air-conditioned, a rare thing for San Andrés. San Andrés Tuxtla wasn't much of a town, looking smaller than its 20,000 population. The Laguna Encantada, the Enchanted Lagoon, just outside of town was supposed to be quite a tourist attraction, though. They said it was the crater of an extinct volcano and that the water level rose in dry weather, fell in wet weather. That's how it got its name. Alvarado had never bothered to visit it. Concepción had, with a group of schoolmates. She was curious about things. Like a boy.

Alvarado ordered enchiladas with green sauce, fried bananas, refried beans and a bottle of Superior beer. The television set, suspended high up in a corner, was going full blast, showing some sort of animated cartoon. There weren't many people in the restaurant. All were men. The only one watching the TV set was some young loafer with hair down to his collar.

Alvarado went over to the television set, said, "Permit me," and turned it off.

The young loafer got a sour look on his face but did not say anything. Alvarado was wearing his sunglasses so there was nothing to soften his intimidating appearance.

There was a bar alongside the wall at the back of the restaurant, just before the kitchen. The bartender leaned forward and said reprovingly, "You don't like television, señor?"

"It's too loud," Alvarado said. "All right?"

The bartender, a young man who did not look like a professional at his job, dropped the subject.

When Alvarado finished eating — the enchiladas had been good but not the way Sara made them — he went to the bar to pay.

"I've just been to see the Olmec heads at Santiago," Alvarado said. "Remarkable."

"I suppose so," the bartender said without interest.

"They say the big one weighs fifteen thousand kilos. Could that be so?"

"I wouldn't know."

"I've heard the one found last month is even bigger. Some say twenty-five thousand kilos."

The bartender chuckled. "It grows every time I hear of it," he said. "It's not much bigger than the one at Santiago."

"I heard twenty-five thousand kilos," Alvarado said doggedly. "And five meters in height."

"No," the bartender said. "Three meters, perhaps."

"How can you be so sure, friend? Have you seen it?"

"Of course not. I've better things to do with my time than go strolling around in the jungle."

"Maybe you know someone that's seen it, then? Who told you it's only three meters."

"Well, no," the bartender admitted. "But when I first heard of it last month, it was three meters. You know how a story gets exaggerated every time it's told. In another week it will be ten meters tall and made of solid jade."

"That's very true," Alvarado said. "You're very shrewd for such a young man."

"You learn a lot in this job if you keep your eyes open and your mouth shut, friend."

"I don't suppose you know anyone who has actually seen the head?"

The bartender looked thoughtful, and a little apprehensive. "Are you a policeman, perhaps?" he asked.

Alvarado chuckled. "Do I look like a policeman?" he said.

"Yes."

"You haven't learned as much as you think, friend," said Alvarado. "I'm a stonecutter. I merely happen to be interested in cultural things."

Before leaving the restaurant he went over to the television set and turned it back on.

"I hope you have missed nothing of great importance," he told the long-haired young patron, who was moodily drinking an orange soda.

Before going to the police station he stopped at the cigar factory and bought a box of Triumfo seconds. San Andrés cigars were very good but he could not afford them at the regular price. When he stopped outside to light one, he looked over the flaring match and saw a young woman eyeing him very brazenly. Alvarado was accustomed to such glances from young women, and older ones as well. It was his size and the apparent cruelty in his face that attracted them. It was flattering, but it also made him a bit angry. What had become of old-fashioned virtue and modesty? This was the kind of world Concepción and her sisters were growing up in. How lucky men were who had only sons. He scowled at the young woman and walked away.

When he walked into the police station, the chief looked up from his desk and said, "Look who's here. If it isn't the Aztec." He looked at the cigar in Alvarado's mouth and the box cradled in his massive hand and added, "The bite must be good in Veracruz these days."

Alvarado did not rise to the jibe. He knew the chief was only making the usual bad joke. It was widely known that he did not accept mordida. Alvarado gave the chief a handful of cigars, which the chief locked away in his desk.

"What are you doing in San Andrés, friend?" the chief asked.

"Buying cigars." Alvarado sat down and stuck a thumb in his waistband to ease the gouging of his holster clip. "What do you know about the Olmec head?" he said without preamble.

"What Olmec head?" the chief replied carefully.

"The one some monero ran across last month. It's all over town. I even heard about it in Veracruz."

"I don't know anything, officially."

"Unofficially, then."

"It's only gossip, you know."

"Gossip's true, sometimes. Do you believe a head was found?"

"Maybe."

"Why didn't you report it to the office of the attorney general?"

"The less I have to do with the office of the attorney general the happier I am."

Alvarado nodded. That he could understand. Local police never got more involved with the attorney general than they had to. It focused attention on them all the way from the Public Ministry down and nobody liked to be under that kind of pressure, particularly in small towns where things went at their own pace.

"I don't suppose you sent anybody out to take a look?" he said.

"Why should I? It's not in my jurisdiction."

"True. But you might have mentioned it to the PJF, you know. They might have sent someone."

"Do you think the Federal Judicial Police would really waste their time rooting around in the jungle? They could search for months and not find a thing, the way it is out there."

"Maybe."

"Anyhow, I heard it's already been moved."

"Where did you hear that?"

"Where does anyone hear such gossip? Everywhere."

"Do you believe it? That an Olmec head was found and it's been taken away already?"

"If it wasn't so large," the chief said. "It's hard to believe anyone could get something that big out without special equipment. How would they get heavy equipment into the jungle?"

"They could cut the head up. The way they do other things."

The chief shrugged.

"I heard that's how they did it," Alvarado said. "They sliced it up and put it on boats. With all the rivers, they could take it anywhere. Even to a steamer waiting at Alvarado."

The chief smiled. "Is that why you're so interested?" he said. "Because they might use your own port to smuggle something out of the country?"

"I sometimes wonder if the name came from my

family," Alvarado said. "But I doubt it. There're so many Alvarados."

There would not be any more of his immediate line, though. He had only daughters.

"They could have done that," the chief admitted.

"It's more likely they'd have to take it to Veracruz to ship it out," Alvarado said. "There's much more activity there. And it's where Vargas has his connections."

"Vargas?" the chief said.

"Jorge Vargas. Don't tell me you don't know the name."

"What has he got to do with it?"

"Nothing I'm sure of. But he was in Veracruz this week. He didn't visit San Andrés, did he?"

"Not that I know of."

"Then he didn't visit San Andrés," Alvarado said. "I don't think much happens here you don't know of."

"You're not suggesting I know more about the head than I've told you?" the chief said.

"Of course not. See here, will you do me a favor? Write up a report of what you've heard, and that in your opinion there's something to it. Send it up to me first thing in the morning to give to my chief."

"I don't want the PJF coming down here and stirring things up. I've got more than I can handle as it is."

"He'll assign me to investigate," Alvarado said. "And I've already talked with you. I wouldn't have to come back. I just need the report to start the ball rolling. I'd like to catch those bastards if I can."

"Why? There's nothing in it for you, friend, is there? Unless you've gotten available in your old age."

"I don't like seeing them get away with it. People like Vargas making millions off of things that belong to all of us."

"You're a real fanatic, aren't you, Alvarado? Very well. I'll prepare your infernal report."

"Excellent. Can you do it now?"

"You said in the morning."

"I know, but time is important. It might even be out of the country already."

"All right, all right."

The chief rolled paper into an ancient typewriter and began pecking away with two fingers. Alvarado waited patiently until he finished it, signed it and stamped it. Before handing it over the chief said, "I have your promise the PJF won't be in here turning everything upside down?"

"Of course."

Alvarado looked at his watch. He had what he had hoped for and there was still plenty of time to get back to Veracruz before the picture started.

When he got home, Leonor and Yolanda hurled themselves upon him shouting, "Papá, you're home!"

"They were afraid you'd get back too late for the picture," Concepción said. "As usual."

Alvarado kissed the little ones and went into the kitchen. Sara was busy with dinner.

"Did you have a good lunch?" she asked. "Are you hungry?"

"Good enough," he said. "But not like your cooking. I'll have a little something after the picture."

Sara and the girls had their dinner before they went to the movie. If they had not been going out, they would have waited until Alvarado felt like eating. The Alvarados rarely ate at restaurants as a family.

The film was very good. As usual, there were many things in it that were not logical to Alvarado but he accepted them because it was, after all, only a film and one did not expect a film to present police work accurately. As always in such films, he was impressed by the private automobiles of the detectives, the luxury of their homes and the expensive clothing of their wives. He was aware that in the United States policemen made a good deal of money by Mexican standards but he doubted if it was enough for them to afford such things. He wondered if the people who made the films realized that those who knew how policemen really lived, even in such a rich country as the United States, might think such luxury could only mean the detectives were getting mordida.

He had taken the trouble to explain this fallacy in American films to Sara once but she had not been interested. Concepción, however, had thought it very amusing of him to have made the observation. Sitting beside him now, she nudged him in the side when a policeman's wife, her hair expensively waved, came to pick up her husband in a new Pontiac automobile.

"Papá," she whispered, "why aren't you an American cop?"

After the film, Alvarado took them to the restaurant of the Gran Hotel Diligencias for orangeade and ice cream at a sidewalk table. He had a beer. He seldom ate sweets. Afterward, they strolled around the plaza listening to the music and looking at the people doing the same. Concepción was so busy looking at the boys to see if they were noticing her that Alvarado became irritated.

"I'm going to have to marry you off early," he said.

"Why, Papá," she said innocently. "I don't know what you're talking about."

"Yes," said Sara, with more spirit than she ordinarily displayed. "She's only fourteen."

Concepción winked at her father. It was all he could do not to smile. He was not going to encourage her in her impudence.

At eleven thirty he sent them home on the streetcar, Concepción protesting, and went to his usual table in front of the Imperial bar. He sat there for some time nursing a single Superior beer but learned nothing of great interest from those who stopped to chat with him. He did not mind. He'd had a good day already.

A boy of perhaps ten passed among the tables, singing in a dreadfully unmusical voice and accompanying himself with maracas, shouting against the sound of the Imperial's mariache. The men he tried to entertain at their tables either ignored him or ordered him to move on. When he got to Alvarado's table, however, Alvarado listened attentively to an entire atrocious song. When he finished, Alvarado patted him on the head, gave him a peso and said, "Very good."

A handsome, manly little chap, he thought. He would like to have such a son. Of course, if he had a son, the boy would not be allowed to sing on the streets and be insulted by thoughtless strangers.

Alvarado sighed and went to catch the streetcar for home.

11

DONNA went into the café at Palma Sola with her makeup box while Bell gave Alberto instructions. Bell told him to take the trucks into the village, park them off the road and bring the drivers back for breakfast. After the trucks drove off, Bell dug his other shoes, slacks and his toilet kit out of his bag and followed Donna into the café.

It was primitive but clean, and at the moment being swept cleaner by a barefoot girl. The open kitchen was just inside the door to the left. Long skinny sausages and thin panels of dark-brown meat hung like washing from a line stretched across it. Bell wondered if it was to make it easier for the flies to get at them. Wooden posts supported the roof. The oilcloth on the long tables was clean. There was a jukebox off to one side. Donna was nowhere to be seen. The girl with the broom saw Bell looking around.

"Señorita," she said, gesturing toward an opening beyond the kitchen.

Donna emerged through it with her makeup box. She looked freshly scrubbed but wore an expression of distaste.

"At least it was clean," she said.

"What was?" Bell asked.

"The john."

"I knew we should have stopped at the Palma Sola Holiday Inn," Bell said.

He went back to the toilet to change his muddy shoes and pants. Donna's expression had pretty well described it. He brushed his teeth at the one-tap wash basin, not rinsing his mouth out with the tap water. He made a quick pass at his whiskers with his cordless electric razor, washed his face and hands and felt almost as if he'd had a night's sleep.

Alberto was at a table with Donna when he came out. The other drivers were sitting together at another table. Alberto obviously considered himself a cut above the others. Juan One held up a thumb in greeting when Bell looked his way. Bell returned the gesture. He wished Juan could speak English.

"Alberto," he said, "tell the men to order whatever they want for breakfast. Miss . . ." what was it Donna had called herself? "Miss Fairchild is picking up the tab."

Donna frowned.

When Alberto went to the drivers' table to tell them about breakfast, she said, "I'm not supposed to pay for their meals."

"Write it down in your little book, then. Sandifer can deduct it from my pay."

"Don't think I won't," said Donna.

Alberto returned and the barefoot girl came to take their order. Bell interrupted while Donna was asking the girl what was available.

"The drivers first," he said. "They've got to get their trucks serviced."

Neither Donna nor Alberto appeared to like that arrangement very much.

Bell pointed to the sausages hung over the line in the kitchen.

"How about a nice plate of sausage and eggs, Donna?" he asked.

"Ugh," said Donna.

146

Bell did not feel up to sampling the cookery either. He'd seen some packaged bakery goods when he first came in. He got up and brought back Bimbo cupcakes and Tuinkies. That and coffee would do for breakfast. The drivers were having tortillas with their coffee. They were eating something that looked and smelled good. Bell wished he had been more adventurous. Coffee cup in hand, he walked over to the jukebox. There were a couple of Beatles sides, the first Beatles stuff Bell had seen in years, and the rest were Mexican records. He fed the machine a coin and punched something called "Fatalidad" by somebdy named Leo Jaramillo.

After breakfast, Donna paid the check for everyone and entered the amount in her little book.

"You subtract yours?" Bell said. "I'm only paying for the drivers."

"Yes," said Donna. "I subtracted mine."

"Good girl."

He stowed Donna's makeup box and his discarded shoes and trousers in the trunk of the Volks and followed the trucks to the service station. Alberto trailed the attendant, looking wise. Bell wonderd if Alberto really knew anything about trucks. He noticed that Juan One was also keeping an eye on things, and without having been told to do so. He toyed with the idea of putting Juan in front in the Mack but decided he would rather have him remain at the rear to chase stragglers.

Bell took down all the odometer readings. At the next stop he'd be able to figure fuel consumption. Alberto came over to tell him the Mack had taken a lot of oil. Bell wasn't surprised, considering its age and the sound of the motor. He told Alberto not to worry, just keep an eye on the oil pressure. If it dropped, he was to halt the convoy and top off from the case he had bought in Veracruz.

They were back on the road by nine. It looked like

clear sailing for at least 67 kilometers, when they would hit a toll bridge at Nautla.

The sun was well up and the day had grown sultry. They rolled the windows down to let the air blow through. It was noisy that way, but less uncomfortable. Donna cushioned her face against her palm and dozed off. Relaxed that way, she didn't look so stern. Maybe she'd be more fun to be with when her mind wasn't so fixed on business.

Bell thought before the morning was out he should catch a nap, too. There was a long drive ahead. He'd have to grab an hour or so whenever he could. He snaked the map from Donna's lap and glanced at it as he drove. No problems after Nautla until Poza Rica, a fair-sized town 62 miles the other side. He'd let Donna take over at the toll bridge and sleep until Poza Rica. He wanted to be awake when they went through town.

The road was adequate, except for the potholes. It was the rainy season and the nightly downpours washed out pockets in the blacktop. The convoy moved well. The drivers still had a tendency to accordion, but with Juan One on their tails they weren't able to spread out too much.

The road passed between acre after acre of bananas, occasionally mixed with coconut palms. The plantation houses were mansions, the fields well kept and sometimes fenced. The cattle grazing in the fields were fat and sleek, ruminating among flocks of seagulls. It was all so serene Bell found it hard to reconcile this pleasant drive with his reason for being here. Up ahead was eighteen tons of pre-Columbian art worth half a million dollars or twelve years of his life, depending on whether or not they made it across the border. And it didn't seem real that a man had been killed over it just a few hours ago. He hoped Vargas' friend had gotten rid of the body as promised.

Donna woke up when they stopped at the toll bridge. She yawned and said, "Where are we?"

"Nautla. How you feel? Rested?"

"Yes, thanks."

"Feel like taking over for a while?"

"Will it be all right, Sam?"

"Sure," he said, tracing the route on the map for her. "There's no place Alberto can go wrong between here and Poza Rica. Just wake me up before we hit town. I want to be up front when we go through."

Donna studied the toll bridge receipt before tucking it away in her manila envelope. Fat chance of Alberto padding his expenses, Bell thought, smiling to himself. He changed seats with Donna, put his head back and fell asleep immediately. He awakened when the Volks stopped.

"What is it?" he asked, without opening his eyes. He knew if he did he wouldn't go back to sleep.

"Another toll bridge," said Donna.

"Where are we?"

"Tecolutla."

"Any problems so far?"

"No."

He had scarcely fallen asleep again when Donna tugged at his elbow.

"Sam," she said urgently. "Wake up. They're stopping the trucks."

Up ahead, the Mack and the number two Dina had already pulled over at an Inspección Fiscal station and the other two trucks were slowing. The caseta was masonry, unlike the usual wooden cracker boxes, and therefore somehow more threatening.

"Don't stop," said Bell, fully awake. "Keep on going."

He turned and looked guardedly out the back window. The Mack was already being waved on. Juan Two was showing his invoice to an official.

"Slow down a little," Bell said.

The number two Dina pulled back onto the highway. One after the other, the International and the number one Dina followed.

"Pull over," Bell said. "I'll drive. That woke me up."

He let the convoy pass. Juan One gave him a discreet toot of the horn when he drove by. Bell grinned. He didn't mind Juan doing it, as he had Alberto.

"You like him, don't you?" Donna said disapprovingly. "I don't get it. He's a troublemaker."

"Best man we've got."

"Come off it. You couldn't do anything without Alberto. The rest are all peons. Including your Juan."

"You some kind of snob? I'm a peon, too."

"I know."

A sweet, heavy smell filled the air. It was strangely familiar.

"Vanilla," said Donna.

In a few minutes they were passing through Papantla. Roadside shops advertised vanilla extract and figures made of vanilla beans.

"This is called the Vanilla Route," Donna said.

"When I was a kid I tried drinking vanilla extract," Bell said.

"Ugh," said Donna.

"Yeah. It's better in cake. You ever bake a cake?"

"No."

"Figures."

He shouldn't have said that, he thought. If he wanted to thaw Donna out that wasn't the way to go about it.

A car swept by the Volks, honking. The horn played a bar of a familar tune. What was it?

" 'La Cucaracha,' " Bell said triumphantly. "My first car, the horn played 'The Colonel Bogey March.' "

"It must have made you very happy," Donna said.

"It did," said Bell, wondering if maybe thawing Donna out was a hopeless task.

They reached Poza Rica a little after eleven. The traffic was heavy and Bell was relieved when he got through town with his convoy. They crossed the Cazones River. The water was sluggish and muddy but a woman was washing clothes in it. Beyond the bridge, the highway took a right turn for Tuxpan.

"How far is Tuxpan?" Bell asked.

Donna looked at the map and said, "Thirty-six miles. Red is miles, right?"

"Right."

"Sam, if I don't look at the map too long it doesn't bother me."

"That's a big help."

"Are you being sarcastic again?"

"No. I mean it."

"Tuxpan's the only big town before Tampico. Let's stop there for lunch. Maybe they'll have a clean bathroom."

Bell started to tell her they couldn't waste time looking for a place up to her standards, but didn't. She could have been a lot worse, considering the heat and lack of sleep. If he was more accommodating, she might be more accommodating. And if all it took to make her happy was a good lunch and clean bathroom he'd try to find them for her.

They stopped for a traffic signal just outside of Tuxpan and turned right under a bridge. Bell halted the convoy and went back to give Alberto his instructions. The men were to eat and get back to their trucks. Alberto didn't hide his disappointment when he learned he was to remain with them while Bell and Donna went into town.

"Somebody's got to stay behind and take charge," Bell said.

Though he was liking Alberto less and less, he did

not want to antagonize him needlessly. Alberto was the only driver who spoke English and the others didn't mind taking orders from him because he was Ochoa's nephew.

In the Volks, Donna was fanning herself with the envelope in which she kept the expense receipts.

"Try to find an air-conditioned place," she said.

Tuxpan was a resort town. Its main street was clogged with traffic, the sidewalks with pedestrians. Among the shops lining the street were many selling tourists' goods. It reminded Bell more of a border town than of the other towns he had seen so far. There was a new-looking hotel and restaurant, the Plaza, in the heart of town. The glass doors were shut.

"That looks air-conditioned," Bell said.

It was and, even by Donna's standards, clean. The restaurant was the usual simply furnished, uncarpeted sort of place Bell had come to expect. After they placed their order for food and beer, Donna went looking for the bathroom. Bell had finished two rolls and half a beer by the time she returned with a beatific look on her face.

"It was clean, huh?" Bell said.

"Spotless."

Bell had brought the map with him. He studied it while he ate his shrimp Mexicana. They would soon be reaching Alazán, where he would have to decide which of two routes to take to Tampico, the shorter one that meant a ferry ride or the longer, more inland one that didn't. He put the map away and finished his shrimp. Very tasty. He was glad he had let Donna do the ordering.

"What's for dessert?" he said.

"Flan," said Donna. "But I really shouldn't."

She weakened when the creamy tan custard was set before Bell.

"I'll really have to start watching my weight again when I get back," she said.

"Everything's just right as it is," Bell said. "Don't lose an ounce."

"The extra pounds just don't show in these clothes."

"If you'd like a more informed judgment, Donna . . ."

On the way out of town, Donna had him stop while she ran into a shop to buy a fan. She returned with a palm-leaf fan and two small white towels. She gave one of the towels to Bell.

"Use this instead of that soppy handkerchief," she said.

It was the first time she had done anything thoughtful. He wiped his face with the towel and put it around his neck inside his sticky shirt collar.

Alberto was waiting with the trucks at the edge of town. He looked sulky. He became less so when Bell made a point of conferring with him about stopping at Alazán for information.

There was a big two-storied Pemex station at the highway junction just outside of Alazán. Though they had come only about 100 miles since being serviced at Palma Sola, Bell decided to top off the tanks while Alberto was getting route information. Diesel fuel was 43 centavos a liter here, something like 13¢ a gallon. He had Juan One supervise the servicing while Alberto asked about the two routes. The more direct route, Alberto was told, was faster and better, saving at least an hour. There was never a long wait at the ferry and, whichever route they took, the convoy would have to drive through Tampico.

After the trucks were topped off, Bell calculated their fuel consumption. Over such a short leg he didn't expect an accurate reading, only an indication. The Mack checked out at better than three kilometers a liter, close to eight miles a gallon. The other trucks had all gotten close to six miles to the gallon, not at all bad loaded as they were. All four trucks should be able to get 250 miles on a tankful of fuel even if his check was inaccurate on the high side. If he fueled up every 200 miles it would leave an ample reserve.

They left the Pemex station at 2:35 P.M. Bell took the rear of the convoy again. It was a straight shot to Tampico and there was no way Alberto could go wrong up front in the Mack.

The convoy clipped along at a hypnotic 80 kilometers an hour but dodging potholes kept Bell from falling asleep. Donna dozed again, the fan in her lap. At this rate, and if they weren't held up at inspection stations, Bell figured they would reach the Tampico ferry well before five. It was something over 500 miles from Tampico to Nuevo Laredo. Say it took an hour getting on the ferry and through town, if everything continued to go as well as it had been doing, they could make it to Nuevo Laredo from Tampico in another fourteen hours. That should put them into Nuevo Laredo before eight Saturday morning. If the paperwork at the customs broker's didn't take too long, and there were no big delays at the border, they could be in Houston with Chato by dark Saturday night. He'd have picked up twenty thousand dollars for four days' work.

Somehow he wasn't as crazy about that as he had expected. He liked picking up an easy twenty thousand, but what he was doing to earn it wasn't exactly what he would choose for a life's work. Even if the man hadn't been killed back at Tlacotalpán, ripping off a Mexican national treasure was getting less appealing. Especially now that he had been face to face with Chato and was taking him farther and farther away from where he belonged, and had been for maybe three thousand years. Bell was surprised to find himself thinking of Chato as "him," not "it."

He looked up the highway at the number one Dina. Two pieces of Chato were in there under the tiles. Cut up like that, they were just two hunks of rock. He remembered how alive Chato had looked back there in the barn, alive and, despite his size and ominous look, helpless. And back in Texas, or wherever it was Sandifer had sold him, somebody was waiting to put Chato together again and show him off to his friends, not even knowing a man had been killed getting him there. And probably not caring if he did know.

It started raining, abruptly and heavily. Water drummed on the roof and struck against the windshield in sheets, obscuring the view before Bell could start the wipers going. Rain lashed in the windows they had wound all the way down, waking Donna. The two of them scrambled to roll them up. It was quickly steamy inside the Volks, fogging up the windshield from the inside. Without being asked, Donna set to work wiping the windshield with her towel, in front of Bell first and then on her side. Bell cracked his window an inch on his side to let some of the steamy air out and Donna did the same. It helped a little, but not enough to make the interior of the Volks comfortable.

The rain continued for twenty minutes, stopping as abruptly as it had begun. Bell was drenched through now with a mixture of rain and sweat. Donna had given up trying to cool off with the fan.

"All it does is stir up the hot air," she said.

She rolled her window down and pulled her damp, clinging shirt away from her chest.

"I'd like to take everything off and wring it out," she said.

"I'd like that," Bell said.

The potholes brimmed with water and vapor shimmered over the blacktop in the sun when they passed through the small town of Ozuluama. They had come a little over half the distance from Alazán to Tampico. Because of the rain, it had taken an hour and fifteen minutes to come 48 miles. Bell recalculated the time they would reach Tampico. A few minutes one way or the other really didn't matter but he liked to carry a schedule in his head and keep to it when possible. Otherwise it was like driving aimlessly.

They got their first view of Tampico from some miles out, its skyline low and white across the Panuco River. When they reached the approach to the ferry there were seven vehicles ahead of them. People were milling around on foot among the grubby shops and refreshment stands. Vendors walked among them selling trinkets, pineapples and chewing gum. A tough-looking man in a navy-blue uniform, his trousers tucked into boots, wearing a helmet liner and carrying an automatic weapon, was directing traffic.

"That's no cop," Bell said. "What is he — Navy?"

Donna asked a vendor of paper flowers.

"He's a Marine," Donna said. "Don't you want to get out and compare notes?"

The ferry eased into its slip and began discharging vehicles. It was much larger than the one at Buena Vista and the Mack got on with the seven vehicles ahead of it. Alberto got out of the cab and looked back anxiously as the ferry pulled out. Across the Panuco River, a second ferry was already swinging out into the current for the return trip.

Children swam downstream in the muddy river. On the bank, near the ferry slip, a woman was pouring water over the head of a naked, wailing child and scrubbing its chest and shoulders with a rag.

Watching, Donna sighed and said, "How I'd love a cold shower."

"You can have one in Houston tomorrow night," Bell said. "I'll even scrub your back."

"Frankly," Donna said, "you don't interest me that way."

"I've noticed. Is it me, or men in general?"

"I wouldn't hurt your feelings by answering that."

The second ferry pulled in and discharged its load. Bell followed his trucks aboard. The car behind the

Volks was a green Chevelle sedan with five men crowded into it. They looked hot and cramped. He didn't envy them. Four minutes after the ferry departed, they reached the slip on the Tampico side of the Panuco. Alberto was waiting, pulled off to the side of a dusty, rutted street. Bell took the lead. With Juan One riding herd in the rear, he wasn't worried about losing any of his trucks in the Tampico traffic. He followed the truck route through heavy traffic, stopping once for Donna to ask directions. By 5:35 P.M. they were on Avenida Hidalgo, which Donna had been told would take them north out of the city. When they passed the Camino Real Hotel, Donna asked wistfully, "Couldn't we stop here for dinner and freshen up?"

"We'll eat when we stop for fuel," Bell said.

He took out his notebook and checked the reading he had taken down when they topped off outside of Alazán. If he was going to fill up every 200 miles they still had 60 to go.

"Is there a town about a hundred to a hundred twenty-five kilometers from here?" he asked.

"I've run out of map," Donna replied. "We're out of Veracruz state and into Tamaulipas."

Bell felt under the seat for his auto club map and handed it to her. It was marked in miles but he was now adept at converting to kilometers.

"I want something sixty to seventy miles up the road," he said. "Can you look it up or you want me to?"

"I'll manage," Donna said.

They were leaving the outskirts of Tampico. A car full of men was sitting in a service station at the right of the highway. It was the green Chevelle Bell had noticed behind them on the ferry. Not having to take the truck route, the car had gotten through town more quickly than the convoy. It was almost as if the car had waited for them. He slowed down and waved the Mack on and continued at reduced speed until all four trucks were out front. He picked up speed again and looked in the rearview mirror. A couple of hundred yards behind the Volks, the green Chevelle was pulling onto the highway.

"Is something wrong?" Donna said.

"I don't know," Bell replied. "That car back there was behind us at the ferry, too."

"So?"

"It should have made better time than us, even if they stopped for gas."

Donna looked back at the car.

"It's full of men," she said. "If they all had to go to the john . . ."

Bell laughed.

"Maybe you're right," he said. "You're the expert on that."

But maybe they had been waiting for the convoy. Vargas had said Chato was safe once they were on the open highway, but he could have said that just to get them off his hands. With Chato worth all that money, would the hijackers give up so easily? And if they were after Chato again, why had they waited so long? Waiting for darkness, probably. He should have insisted that Vargas give him guards to see him through the night. Maybe he should turn back and spend the night in Tampico. But if he did, they almost certainly wouldn't get to Nuevo Laredo until after business hours tomorrow, Saturday. That meant they would be stuck there until Monday waiting for the customs broker's office to open and fix them up with the necessary papers.

The green car swept by the Volks, going fast. Bell studied the occupants as it went by. Just five ordinary looking men, talking among themselves and paying him no attention. He edged over the center line, where he could watch the car. It passed all his trucks and kept going. Bell was relieved. It wasn't following them after all, and he wouldn't have to turn back.

"Ciudad Mante looks nice," Donna said.

"What do you mean, Ciudad Mante looks nice?"

"It's much larger than any place in between. There's more chance of getting a decent dinner there."

"And a clean john?" Bell said. "How far is it?"

"A hundred miles."

"A hundred miles? I think we can make it. I'll stop and check the fuel gauges somewhere along the way."

Fifty-one miles out of Tampico, after crossing a narrow bridge just beyond the village of Manuel, Bell stopped the convoy and checked the fuel gauges. The trucks could all make it to Mante with fuel to spare. He looked as far as he could see behind and ahead of the convoy. No sign of the green Chevelle. It was only another hour to Mante. Only a few minutes of that would be after dark.

They reached Mante at ten to eight. After a bumpy, one-block diversion, the truck route turned north on Hidalgo. Bell led the convoy into the first Pemex station he saw.

"Can't we go eat while the trucks are being serviced?" Donna said. "I'm famished."

"I want to see 'em do it," Bell said.

He made sure the oil, water, tires and batteries were checked and after the tanks were filled figured fuel consumption again. It was fairly close to what he had figured back at Alazán. After locking the trucks and giving the two attendants twenty pesos each to keep an eye on them, he led the drivers a block west to the main street, Benito Juaréz. Bell wasn't very hungry. He was too bushed to have an appetite.

There was a drugstore on the corner, the Farmacia Cruz Roja. It gave him an idea.

"Let's go in and get me some uppers for tonight," he told Donna. "And you should have some Dramamine so you can read the map."

"They put me to sleep," Donna protested.

"So sleep. It's a long drag to Nuevo Laredo."

She bought half a dozen benzedrine tablets, no prescription required, and some Dramamine. Bell gulped down a benny and discovered he was hungry after all.

Mante was a busy little town, and fairly modern, with parking meters and other signs of progress. The sidewalk was of ornamental tile. Bell liked that touch. Looking for a place to eat, they passed a grim little hotel, the Riespra.

"Fifteen pesos, double," Bell said, reading the rates posted just inside the entrance. "Tempted, Donna?"

"Don't be an ass," she said.

They found a restaurant, the Café Mante Modelo, "Servicio dia y noche." It didn't look like much but it was crowded.

"Let's give it a try," Bell said. "Maybe the local folks know something."

Donna looked doubtful. There wasn't a woman in the place and most of the customers were roughly dressed.

"Come on," Bell said. "We haven't got all night."

Alberto sat with them. When they ordered eggs rancheros and coffee, being unwilling to chance the meat, he did the same. As was his habit, Bell studied the map while he ate. Eighty-four miles to Ciudad Victoria and another 327 to Nuevo Laredo. Ciudad Victoria was on the main route from Houston to Mexico City so the roads should be first rate. They could make Nuevo Laredo in under ten hours. It was only 8:40 now. They'd be in Nuevo Laredo Saturday morning before the broker's office was open. That meant Houston by dark for sure.

"I wonder if the bathroom's clean?" Donna said, getting up.

She returned looking horrified.

"Try to hold it until we get to Nuevo Laredo,"

Bell said. "I hear they've got some of the nicest johns in Mexico."

On the way back to the Pemex station he saw a green Chevelle parked on the side street. It gave him a turn. He couldn't tell if it was the one he had last seen outside Tampico.

"I've got something in my shoe, Donna," he said. "I'll catch up."

He looked around, saw no one watching, and lifted the hood. He ripped loose every wire and cable he could get his hands on and took the distributor cap. If the car wasn't the one he'd seen earlier, or if the men weren't following the convoy, he'd played a crummy trick on someone, he thought. But if the green Chevelle did mean trouble, they'd play hell catching the convoy now. He didn't tell Donna anything when he caught up with her and the drivers. No point in worrying her, and maybe needlessly.

Back at the service station, he told Alberto to hold the Mack at 95 kilometers an hour where road conditions permitted once they reached the open highway. While the trucks were moving out, Bell scanned the area to see if they were being watched. He saw no loiterers but that didn't mean much. Someone could be watching from the shadows.

They were back on the road at nine twenty. Donna worried down a Dramamine tablet and five minutes later was fast asleep. Bell reached across her and locked the door.

The convoy rolled uneventfully through the darkness, now and then climbing or descending hills, crossing rivers with tires drumming on steel bridges, passing darkened casetas and only rarely a building in which lights showed. Donna began snoring. Well, thought Bell, nobody's perfect. He varied the monotony by alternating between the front and rear of the convoy though he spent most of his time at the rear with his eye on the mirror. If the green Chevelle had been a threat it wasn't now, but he still couldn't resist being watchful.

An hour and ten minutes out of Mante they crossed the Tropic of Cancer. Bell knew it because it was marked by a sign. They reached the Ciudad Victoria bypass at ten to eleven. There was a new-looking stucco motel, Las Fuentes, at the junction. Probably had a bathroom Donna would approve of, he thought. He wondered if he should play it safe and stop for the night in Ciudad Victoria. The thought of waiting over in Nuevo Laredo until Monday didn't appeal to him. He was probably wrong about the Chevelle, anyhow. And he had put it out of commission.

He felt like driving. It was the benzedrine. When it wore off he'd be out on his feet but by then Donna would be rested enough to take over and let him get some sleep. He'd hardly closed his eyes since Thursday morning and here it was almost Saturday.

He remained at the rear of the convoy. The road was empty, with no lights showing in his rearview mirror. The convoy was moving exceptionally well, clipping along at 95 on the straightaway, taking the curves nice and easy, staying geared down on the descents. Either Alberto was improving as lead driver or Mono, his relief man, was at the wheel. Probably Mono. The relief drivers would have taken over by now.

They crossed a one-way bridge over the Purificación River. Bell shined the flashlight on the open map in his lap. A hundred and thirty-two miles to Monterrey. And Monterrey was only 148 miles from Nuevo Laredo. They could make Nuevo Laredo with only one more fuel stop. He'd do it at Linares, coming up in under forty-five minutes. The highway became monotonous, straight and with little gradient. The air was cool, the night black and serene, with no one behind them. Bell yawned. The benzedrine was wearing off. Instead of dropping another one he would let Donna take over at Linares. It was 1:15 A.M. Just a little longer and they'd be there. Then he could sleep.

Up ahead, the stoplights of the number one Dina flashed red and the truck ground to a panic halt. Bell slowed and pulled alongside. The Dina was nose to rear with the International, which was just behind the number two Dina. Something about the number two Dina did not look right. It was canted a little, not sitting straight on the highway. The drivers were all climbing out of their cabs to investigate. Farther up the highway, the Mack was backing toward them. Bell pulled onto the shoulder in front of the number two Dina. The ground was dry and hard here, unlike down south. Donna woke up when he opened the door to get out. She looked around, startled, and saw the headlights of the trucks behind them.

"Was there an accident?" she cried.

"I don't know," said Bell.

He was wide awake now.

The number two Dina's right front wheel was off the road, jammed hub deep into a narrow, straight-walled cement culvert. Juan One, the bandit, was standing beside it. He looked at Bell and shook his head gravely. Bell squatted down and studied the wheel, then lay on his stomach and shined his flashlight under the truck. The pan was resting flush on the blacktop. There was no way they could free the wheel without a heavy crane. And even then he was not sure the Dina could continue without repairs.

And this was the truck with the heaviest section of the Olmec head, Chato's eyes and nose.

12

Aᴛ ᴛᴇʀ Agente Alvarado came home Friday night, he lay awake in bed, on his back, hands clasped behind his head. Usually he fell asleep immediately, and woke up at whatever time he had decided upon as if there were an alarm clock in his head. But tonight he lay awake, thinking. His visit to San Andrés Tuxtla had convinced him it was not rumor but fact that an Olmec head had been found and, somehow, spirited away from its site. He was both offended by the crime and stimulated by the thought of apprehending the perpetrator if it were not already too late to do so. The perpetrator being quite possibly, or so he hoped, Jorge Vargas Artega.

He did not doubt that so large an object as an Olmec head could have been removed from the place where it had rested for maybe three thousand years. Had not the ancient peoples who carved the heads themselves brought the giant blocks of stone great distances? No such stone was to be found within many miles of the low, watery lands where the Olmecs lived and laid out their sacred places. And they had brought the stones in one piece, and without modern technology of any kind. It would be child's play for looters to cut up the head with diamond-tipped chain saws, or even with soft iron wires coated with beeswax in which corundum particles were imbedded, or with a mud of water and corundum powder. And child's play to remove the head piecemeal on wooden sleds, as perhaps the Olmecs had done with greater loads, and to load the pieces on riverboats which, having engines, could swiftly transport them long distances, even to Veracruz itself, entering the Laguna Alvarado by way of the Papaloapán River and passing through it to the Gulf of Mexico. In Veracruz, a man like Vargas would have connections to get the pieces on an ocean-going vessel and ship them where he willed, camouflaged as something else. If Vargas had indeed managed to do that, he would never catch him. Alvarado could only hope that the transfer had not yet been fully accomplished.

If the Olmec head was already beyond all hope of rescue, he had at least the satisfaction that it had not been smashed to bits like so many more fragile stone sculptures. An Olmec head did not lend itself to such destruction even if the thief were not Vargas but someone less discriminating about barbarous vandalism.

Sara lay curled up on her side of the bed, as if making herself even smaller so that it could accommodate his bulk. She always slept so quietly one hardly knew she was there, Alvarado thought. He did not think she even moved, for on those rare occasions when he awoke before her in the morning she was always in the position in which she had fallen asleep. He, himself, he was aware, slept more actively. If he fell asleep on his back, he woke up on his stomach; on his stomach, he woke on his back.

His thoughts returned to the Olmec head. It could spell catastrophe if such a piece fell in the hands of an American collector, far more serious than if it were a large piece of, say, Mayan sculpture, an altar or stela. For Mayan artifacts were already well known to collectors, and highly prized by them. But, as far as he knew, there was not yet such a mad scramble for Olmec things, certainly not on the same scale as for the Mayan. And while American collectors and museums had imposing Mayan pieces by the dozens, perhaps by the hundreds, they had nothing so imposing as a colossal Olmec head. Only a handful of such heads had been found and only one had ever left Mexico, and that one under the auspices of the Mexican government itself, toured and then brought back.

But let an American collector get his hands on such a head. Word would certainly get around among other collectors. Word would get around despite the fact that the American president, Nixon, in 1972, had put his hand to a law that forbade the importation of pre-Columbian objects without the permission of the country of origin. The possessor of such a magnificent sculpture would be unable to keep it to himself. It would not be shown to the public of course, but he would be unable to resist showing it off to fellow collectors. And then everyone would want Olmec objects. The risks and penalties would not matter. The cultural heritage act of 1970 and the American law of 1972 had only seemed to encourage looting and illicit dealings by sending the prices soaring.

To the frantic, greedy traffic in Mayan art would be added a similar traffic in the art of the Olmecs. And Alvarado knew well the waste, the violence, the destruction left in the wake of such traffic. He was, in his own modest way, a student of that. For years he had gleaned, and remembered, accounts of such activities, everything that came officially into the comandancia and items from newspapers and periodicals, many of them provided by friends who received publications from throughout Mexico and knew of his interest.

There were, he knew, eleven thousand known archeological sites, and no doubt many sites as yet undiscovered, though who knew how many of them were undiscovered only by proper authorities. And he knew as well of the vast scale of the illicit trafficking resulting from the existence of so many sources and an ever-increasing market. In the first year of the formation of the attorney general's special Unit for the Defense of the Cultural Patrimony the unit had seized some fifteen thousand rare pieces. If the government had managed to find that many, how many more thousands must have slipped by?

There were those who would do anything to tap such riches. Alvarado had read of the estimate of an official at the National Museum of Anthropology in Mexico City that fifty thousand peons were out digging for pre-Columbian art every day while their crops rotted in the fields. And in the state of Campeche, fishermen searched feverishly for treasure, sometimes at the cost of their lives, despite the presence of armed guards in the region.

To such men Alvarado attached no blame. They were looking for survival, really. It was the professional looters and the Vargases, especially the Vargases, for whom he reserved his anger and contempt. They did not hesitate to destroy and kill in their greed. They killed peasants who stumbled upon their activities, they killed each other, they even killed officials of the government. In the state of Chiapas, simple Lacandone Indians out hunting with bow and arrows unwittingly interrupted the work of looters and three had been murdered. In other places police had been killed trying to prevent looting, or shot from ambush.

The sheer impudence of those who pillaged the ancient treasures angered Alvarado almost as much as their violence. He still could not think of an event that occurred as long ago as 1971 without wishing he could have been there at the time to deal with the rascals. Dr. Jorge Angulo, an archeologist of the Mexican government, was come upon by looters while excavating the site of Oaxtepec and prevented at gunpoint from continuing his work until they had stripped the site of what they wished. Even now, thinking about it, Alvarado unclasped the big hands supporting his head and clenched them into fists.

But it was not, he thought ruefully, all violence. Some of the looters, particularly those who did not depend on the moneros and the burros and came all the way from the United States, could be very clever. The cleverest of all, perhaps, were those who ravished the islet of Jaina, off the coast of Yucatán. The leader, said to be a dealer from Los Angeles in California, came to the island with a group of forty men bringing with him the proper documents to show he was there to film the excavation of an archeological site. For six weeks he had filmed the "archeologists" at work. Then, one morning, all were gone, taking with them what they had excavated.

Even the clever ones, Alvarado recalled, smiling suddenly in the darkness, were not always clever enough for the peons. Some years ago there had been a story making the rounds about a group of Americans who came to Veracruz State to wrest an illicit fortune from beneath the earth. They bought excavation rights from the local farmers for a pittance and dug up two huge loads of artifacts. Then soldiers descended upon them to confiscate the articles in the name of the Mexican government. The clever Americans bribed the soldiers to return the artifacts. When they returned to the United States they discovered their precious objects were counterfeit. Alvarado did not know if such a thing had really occurred, but he hoped it had.

He thought about Jorge Vargas and the smile left his face. It was inexcusable for the man to be in such a business. He had had all the advantages. He was a licenciado, a lawyer, with social position and wealth even before he lent his talents to the illegal traffic in pre-Columbian art, or at any rate before Alvarado had learned of any connection. It could be only greed and complete indifference to the grandeur of Mexico's past. It was true, of course, that Vargas' line, despite its position and affluence, did not go as far back in

Mexico's history as Alvarado's. There was much Indian in Alvarado's heritage. He doubted if Vargas, with his fair skin and European hair, could trace his Mexican roots back even two hundred years. Yet, if only out of guilt, Vargas should have more respect for the cultures that had preceded the Conquest, and not only the ones that had been destroyed by it. But Vargas, no doubt, thought an Olmec head grotesque and considered the Olmecs, if he thought about them at all, a barbarous race. Alvarado wondered what state of primitivism Vargas' remote ancestors had reached when the Olmec civilization had already flourished and died, leaving behind imposing monuments and works of great art as evidence of their existence.

Alvarado doubted if Vargas himself had actually killed, or even personally threatened anyone, in the conduct of his trade. But he had no doubt that those who worked for him had done so, or, even if they had not, would do so if it were expedient. Vargas, and not only Vargas but also the "respectable" foreign dealers with whom he trafficked, were as guilty of the acts committed in obtaining and protecting their contraband as the men who actually committed them.

But, if Vargas was not a killer, he was an exploiter. Alvarado had no doubt that Vargas demanded, and received, huge sums from his foreign contacts, much more than similar but less well-connected criminals of his sort. Yet the moneros who found the treasures he provided at great price received only a few pesos for their work and the burros who brought them out not a great deal more. Alvarado had seen how the peons lived, in hovels, and how Vargas lived, in a virtual palace. Not the sort of home Alvarado himself would have wanted if by some miracle he had the means, but nevertheless a palace.

On one of his infrequent trips to Mexico City, Alvarado had made a point of finding out where Vargas lived and gone out in a taxi to see it. Vargas' home was west of the University, in a suburb called Jardines del Pedregal, the Rock Gardens. It was a mansion of the most modern sort, all lava blocks and glass and oddly slanted roofs. Alvarado had thought it bizarre, even faintly offensive, while realizing that Concepción would have considered it magnificent. Even then, a year and a half ago, Concepción was already infatuated with things "modern" and American.

And the setting in which Vargas' house and those of his neighbors found themselves. Not rich, honest, Mexican earth but a grotesque frozen river of lava. There were flowers, to be sure, without which no Mexican home could be called a home, but in pockets of earth brought in from elsewhere or in pots and boxes. Not one of those costly villas had as many flowers and other growing things as his little house in Veracruz. To be perfectly fair, of course, he had to admit that, even were there earth in Jardines del Pedregal instead of stone, it would not have been as fruitful as the earth of Veracruz. Nor could a professional gardener, whom Vargas no doubt employed, coax such blossoms from it as someone like himself, who tended his own flowers.

Vargas was a corrupter as well as an exploiter. Who knew how many of the government officials he had bribed might have remained steadfast in the face of lesser offers? And not only police and customs officials, but basically honest archeologists and functionaries of smaller museums throughout Mexico? In 1972, when an inspector for a museum in the state of Guanajuato to the north of the Federal District killed himself, Alvarado's first thought on learning of the circumstances was that Jorge Vargas must be involved. The inspector had been accused of taking antiquities from archeological sites as part of a widespread conspiracy to smuggle them out of Mexico. As far as Alvarado knew, the man's guilt had never been officially established, but if he had indeed been guilty then Vargas could have well been the true culprit. It was just the sort of scheme of which he was capable.

Vargas, Alvarado thought, closing his eyes and seeing the man as if he were present in the room. Dressed in expensive clothing tailored to his personal measure, wearing a watch of solid gold with a band of gold links more fitting for a woman than a man and shoes from England. Always looking as if he had come only just that moment from his barber, his face smooth and ruddy, his brown eyes shrewd but seemingly frank, eyes that inspired confidence in one who did not know what was behind them.

Once, two years ago, right here in Veracruz, he'd almost had Licenciado Vargas. A shrimper put into port and, because its cargo was rank beyond marketability and its documents were from Campeche, and perhaps also because a government inspector was new, young and ambitious, the boat had been thoroughly searched. In the hold, under stale shrimp, had been found three cases of Mayan artifacts. They were all quite good, obviously the pick of a major find. An important man from the National Institute of Anthropology and History who came all the way from Mexico City to study them said they were among the best he had seen and as nearly as he could determine not from any known site.

Alvarado had been assigned to the investigation. The captain of the boat, in return for a promise of leniency, had quite willingly given Alvarado the name of the man for whom the shipment was intended. Alvarado was not at all surprised to discover the man was the employee of a shipping company and in a position to prepare manifests and obtain legitimate customs documents. Alvarado had brought him to the boat, still reeking of rotting shrimp, for questioning. At first he denied everything but it did not take too long for Alvarado to threaten and wheedle him into confessing his complicity. It was the first time he had ever done such a thing, the man said and, of course, he most certainly would never do it again.

Of course, Alvarado had replied, not for fifteen to thirty years. The man had been stunned by the possibility of such a long term of imprisonment, as Alvarado had intended he should be.

"But I was assured . . ." the culprit had said, sweating heavily in the sun and obviously ill from the smell of the shrimp.

"Assured?" Alvarado had said gently when the man failed to finish the sentence. "Assured of what?"

"Nothing," the man replied, even more frightened than he had been at the start of the interrogation.

"I think someone promised you everything would be taken care of," Alvarado said. "Isn't that so?"

The man did not answer but Alvarado read in his face that it was so. Alvarado sighed and said, "There is such injustice in the world, my friend."

"Injustice, agente? Is it that you agree then this is but a trivial matter for which no man should spend the rest of his years in prison?"

"Fifteen years, even thirty, is not a lifetime," Alvarado said with a shrug. "But I am not speaking of that. I am speaking of how unjust it is that a man such as you, almost innocent of any true wrongdoing, one might say, must pay such a penalty when the man who lied to you about the penalties, and would make a fortune of which I am sure you have received not a fraction, goes free."

It was quite a long speech and quite effective. Tears of self pity had filled the man's eyes and he had gone to the side to vomit into the harbor.

"You are ill, I'm afraid," Alvarado said solicitously. "Suppose we go where it is cool and more comfortable and discuss it like two men of the world."

He took the man to an air-conditioned café instead of the comandancia and bought him first mineral water to quiet his stomach and then tequila and limes. In no time at all they were old friends, or nearly enough. The man was most attentive while Alvarado explained that in the interest of justice, he would see that his friend would be dealt with gently if he revealed the name of the true culprit, the man who had lured him into such an act.

"It is he who should be sent to prison, not you," Alvarado said. "It would haunt me if you were made to suffer for his crime."

"But he is a very important person," the man said. "I'm afraid . . ."

"What is there to be afraid of? You have me for a friend and protector, and not only me, but the whole apparatus of the government."

"Still, I am afraid. If he were not to know . . ."

"I will make every attempt to keep your name out of it," Alvarado promised, knowing it was impossible.

In the end, the man had named Jorge Vargas as his employer and Alvarado was exultant. But when he took the man to the comandancia and the man learned he would, after all, have to sign a paper and confront Vargas in open court, he denied all he had told Alvarado. He stool trial, was fined and went to prison for one year without admitting anything. It would have gone much harder for him if he had not had the services of an important lawyer and, Alvarado believed, the benefit of considerable sums discreetly applied. All of which, Alvarado was convinced, could have come only from Vargas. And, during the entire proceedings, Vargas' name never came up.

Alvarado never again had come so close. But now, perhaps, he thought, he might get another chance. In the morning he would take the statement given him by the chief of police in San Andrés Tuxtla to the comandancia and ask permission to begin a thorough investigation with full cooperation from the Capital. He rolled over on his stomach and in minutes was asleep.

13

BELL thrust his hands in his pockets and looked grimly at the assembled drivers.

"How bad is it, Sam?" said Donna.

"Bad enough," Bell replied.

"If Juan will bring his chain I will pull it free for you," Alberto said helpfully.

"Not a chance, Alberto," Bell said. "That wheel's in there. You'd need a crane big enough to lift a locomotive."

Alberto's brow furrowed.

"My uncle will be most disturbed," he said.

"Screw your uncle!" Bell snapped. "Sorry, Alberto, but right now your uncle is the least of our problems."

"Sam, what are we going to do?" Donna asked tightly.

"Let me think a minute," Bell said.

He took a deep breath and forced himself to think calmly. It wasn't easy. He was weary and wanted nothing more than to put his head down somewhere and sleep. Instead, he took another benzedrine tablet. There had to be a way out, he thought. It just took a little figuring. He had Alberto tell the drivers to turn off their truck lights and send Juan One to the rear of the convoy with a flashlight.

"If anybody comes along, he's to signal 'em to go

around," Bell ordered. "If they offer to help, say we're just changing a tire."

And if it's five men in a green Chevelle, start running, he added to himself. Because if they were after Chato, and if they'd gotten a mechanic started on the car right away, they could be showing up in a couple of hours. He wondered if he should tell Donna, and decided not to. It still could be nothing and even if it were something he still had at least two hours, maybe more, to get the convoy moving. That's all he had to think about now, getting the convoy moving.

He went to the Volks and looked at the map and the odometer. He figured they were less than twelve miles out of Linares. The map symbol showed Linares to be more than merely a village. It should be big enough to have the things he needed to unload the number two Dina, because that was what he had decided to do. It was a quarter to two now and everything would be closed. But in a town that size there ought to be at least one all-night service station.

He had the number one Dina and the International moved out of the way so Mono could back the Mack to the rear of the stuck Dina. Alberto didn't like his relief man being picked over him but he kept his mouth shut. Bell waved Mono in until the Mack was right against the rear of the Dina. The right front of the Dina was down but the rear was normal height and level. The van floors of the two trucks were almost even with each other, which was what Bell had been hoping.

He called Donna aside and said, "I'm going up the road to Linares to pick up some things. I want you to stay here."

"All by myself with these men!" she exclaimed.

"Not so loud," Bell said. "You want to hurt their feelings?"

"How can you joke at a time like this?" she demanded.

"You rather I laid down and bawled? I need you back here. I want you to see they get the tiles off the truck while I'm gone."

"Why?"

"To save time. I'm gonna switch the load to the Mack. But stop 'em before they get all the way down to Chato. Okay?"

"I suppose so," Donna said reluctantly.

"Juan One'll look after you," Bell said. "Nobody'll lay a hand on you."

"I'm not worried about that, you idiot. I'm carrying a lot of money."

"That reminds me. Let me have about five thousand pesos."

"Five thousand pesos? What for?"

"Look, I'll give you whatever's left and an itemized list of what I bought with the rest. Okay?"

They got in the Volks and shut the doors so Donna could get the money out of her purse unobserved.

He took Alberto with him in the Mack to interpret for him. Xavier and Juan Two, the drivers of the incapacitated Dina, rode in the van. If things worked out as he hoped, he intended leaving them in Linares.

There was a tile-roofed building with a radio mast on it just outside Linares. It looked like a police station. That was all he needed. He asked Alberto about it. It was a public works building, Alberto said. The Pemex station up the road from the public works building had a light on, but when they drove in Bell saw it was shut tight. They drove deeper into town, having to slow to a crawl to bump over metal knobs set in a line across the street for just that purpose. Linares was larger and more modern than Tlacotalpán but reminded Bell a little of it because the low stucco buildings on either side of the street were joined together in one continuous line.

Bell took the truck route, Calle Constitución, on the theory that any all-night service station would be there.

It wasn't until they had skirted the entire business section that he saw a lighted Mobil station where the truck route rejoined the main street of Linares. The station was open but no attendant was in sight. Bell honked the feeble horn just as one came out of the office rubbing his eyes, his hair tousled.

"Ask him if he's got a portable chain hoist and a portable air compressor," Bell told Alberto.

The station had both, but when Bell saw the chain hoist he knew it was not heavy enough to handle the slab. He would have to find another way to get it out of the Dina and into the Mack. He got out his notebook and made a list.

"Find out where we can get hold of towing cables, heavy rope, pinchbars, a tarpaulin and ten or twelve long fence posts," he told Alberto.

Alberto looked puzzled.

"I do not understand, señor," he said.

"Just ask the man," Bell said.

Alberto spoke with the attendant at length. The attendant kept shaking his head.

"He has towing cables," Alberto said. "But the other things, not before seven or eight in the morning when the stores are open."

It was almost 2:30 A.M. Bell did not intend waiting another five hours with his convoy a sitting-duck on the highway. And even if no one was chasing it, he wanted the Chato section off the Dina and into the Mack under tiles while it was still dark. Plus the fact that they were still almost 250 miles from Nuevo Laredo and couldn't fool around if they wanted to be sure of getting there before the customs broker and the government offices closed for the weekend.

"Ask him where to phone to get somebody to open their stores," Bell ordered.

There was another conference and more head-shaking by the attendant.

"He is afraid to disturb anyone at this hour," Alberto said.

Bell counted out three one hundred peso notes.

"Tell him this is for him if he locates the stuff right away," he said. "And if they give him a hard time, he can tell 'em we'll pay double the regular price."

The attendant looked hungrily at the money. Probably more than he made in a week, Bell thought.

"Sí, señor," the attendant said.

He led them to the station telephone. He made several calls. Bell did not have to understand Spanish to understand the attendant was being apologetic and persuasive. When he finished his calls, Alberto said he had arranged for everything.

"But I think for more than double the accustomed price," he said.

"I don't blame 'em," Bell said. "If somebody got me out of bed at three in the morning I'd stick 'em, too."

He had to leave a deposit for the tow cables and the air compressor. They went first to the supply yard where the rope, pinchbars and tarp were available. It was easy to find. It was the only place with lights on at that hour.

The pinchbars and tarp seemed reasonable enough but the proprietor asked 80 pesos a kilogram for inch and a half manila line, and at first tried to palm off used stuff. Inch and a half line ran a bit under 45 kilograms for 50 meters. That worked out to more than $1.70 a foot, more than twice what it cost in the States. Bell paid the asking price for 15 meters of rope but insisted on new line.

They got the fence posts at a lumber yard. The proprietor was waiting out in front, anxious in a suit coat out at the elbows. Bell went through a great heap of posts, selecting the straightest, roundest and freest of protruding knots. After Xavier and Juan Two had loaded them on, he drove down the main street of Linares looking for a hotel.

178

"I want Xavier and Juan Two to stay in town," he told Alberto. "They're to wait until tomorrow afternoon and then get somebody to go after the Dina. If it's not roadworthy, I want 'em to stay here until it is and then drive it back to Veracruz. Got all that?"

"Yes, señor," Alberto said. "But who is to pay for everything? Not my uncle, I don't think."

"Of course not," Bell replied. "Is it safe to leave the money with those guys?"

"Yes, señor," Alberto said, offended. "They are honest men. Do you think because they are Mexican . . ."

"Come off it," Bell interrupted. "I'd have asked the same anywhere about guys I didn't know."

He had Alberto give them 2500 pesos, which was to cover their personal expenses in Linares as well as any charges for the Dina.

"If there's anything left," he said, "they're to give it to Ochoa for the inconvenience to him."

Alberto looked less doubtful after that. Bell had a notion if any money was left over it would end up in Alberto's pocket, not his uncle's. That was okay with him. At this point he'd rather keep Alberto happy than Ochoa. Alberto would be hauling a piece of Chato from here on out. He hoped Alberto and the Mack were up to it.

It was 3:45 A.M. when they got back to the convoy. There was no sign of trouble. So far, so good, Bell thought. The drivers were asleep in their trucks. Donna was curled up in the back seat of the Volks, snoring. Her big suitcase was gone. The tiles from the number two Dina were stacked neatly off to one side. That had been smart of Donna, Bell thought. They wouldn't have to be moved to get the Mack up to the Dina. He told Donna so when he woke her.

"It was Juan One's idea," she said. "They wanted to throw them off any which way. Did you get something to move the section with?"

"Let's hope so," Bell said.

Donna was dismayed when she saw what he had in the Mack.

"I thought you'd have something like they used at Tlacotalpán," she said.

She was so upset she forgot to ask for the change from her five thousand pesos or for his itemized expenses. But she would, Bell thought.

"What happened to your suitcase?" he asked.

"Juan put it in his truck so I'd have more room," she said. "You were right about him being the best of the bunch."

Bell sent Alberto to get some sleep in one of the trucks parked off the highway. He was not being solicitous. He did not want Alberto around when he and Juan took the last of the tiles off Chato's nose. Alberto didn't want to go. He would be pleased to assist, he said. Bell insisted.

After Alberto went off, Bell gave Juan the tarp and climbed into the van of the number two Dina. He put a flashlight on the floor for illumination. The slab was at the cab end of the van, covered with a thin layer of tiles. The floor was strewn with sugarcane pulp. They kicked it out the back and began taking off tiles. Juan shot Bell a questioning glance when the top of the slab was revealed. His interest grew as the slab emerged from the sugarcane pulp. He looked in wonder when the eyes and nose stood revealed. His face showed something close to awe. Bell, too, was stirred by the spectacle of the enormous sightless eyes and great flat nose. The massive slab, though only a portion of a face, had brooding life. Bell put his fingers to his lips and made a cautionary gesture. Juan nodded understanding.

Bell's hands were sore from the rough edges of the tile. When Juan saw him flexing them gingerly, he offered Bell his gloves. Bell refused. Juan laughed and held out his hand for Bell to feel. The palm was ridged with calluses. Bell took the gloves.

With Juan's help, he covered the slab with the tarpaulin. Donna came to the rear of the Dina to see how they were getting along and to report that all the other drivers were still asleep. She stared at the imposing bulk of the section swathed in the tarp.

"I don't see how you'll ever move it," she said.

"I'm gonna take one end and Juan's gonna take the other," Bell replied.

"I mean it," Donna said.

Bell half expected her to stamp her foot.

"Look, baby," he said, "will you just stand clear and let us get on with it?"

He went to the Mack with Juan for the hawser line and the towing cables. Together they threw a half hitch around the tarp-covered slab, leaving the two ends of the rope about equal length. When Bell bent one end of the line to a towing cable, Juan did the same with the other without having to be told. Working together, they had achieved a high degree of unspoken communication.

They slipped the hook ends of the tow cables over the steel rungs at the rear of the Mack. With gestures, Bell explained to Juan what he wanted done next. Juan got in the Mack, started the engine and eased the truck forward. The lines grew taut, drawing the slab forward over the steel-banded floor of the Dina, piling up windrows of sugarcane pulp. The Mack groaned and the engine made percolating sounds but did not falter. When the slab was almost half out of the Dina, Bell gave the cut sign to Juan, who had been watching in the side mirror.

Juan came back and helped Bell unhook the tow cables. The hitches at the other end were set too hard to untie. Juan took out his knife and, after glancing at Bell for permission, cut the hawser free from the cables. Together they got the air compressor out of the Mack and set it to one side. Juan backed the Mack to the protruding slab. The Dina rode lower now that the full weight of the slab was at the rear and the Mack floor was too high to get under it. Bell let air out of the double rear tires of the Mack until it was low enough to slide under. When that was done, he sent Donna to fetch Alberto and the other drivers.

They all looked rested, reminding Bell how long he had gone without sleep and intensifying his feeling of exhaustion. But he'd have to hang on for a while yet.

The drivers looked at the tarp-shrouded mass and began talking among themselves. All except Alberto. He stared at Bell and looked away quickly when he saw Bell watching him. He could not, however, tear his eyes away from the tarp.

"Alberto, get everybody except Juan into the Dina," Bell said.

While Alberto was doing so, Bell took Juan and Donna aside.

"Tell him to move her back until he hears me stamp on the floor," he told Donna. "Then stop. When I stamp again, start coming again."

He climbed into the Mack and rolled a fence post against the front of the slab. It looked like the slab would just clear. He stamped his foot and the truck inched back. The leading edge of the slab nosed the fence post back. Bell stamped again and the truck stopped immediately. He got a pinchbar and worked the fence post under the slab. Holding it in place with the pinchbar, he stamped on the floor. The truck started backing slowly. The edge of the slab came forward over the fence post. Bell pulled the pinchbar free. The fence post rotated as the slab rolled over it. He stopped the Mack again and rolled up another fence post. Soon the Mack was back to back with the Dina, the front end of the slab resting inside it on four parallel fence posts. It was pitch dark inside the trucks now that they were pushed together. Bell swung his flashlight around, catching Alberto trying to lift an edge of the tarpaulin. Alberto straightened guiltily.

"Send me three men, Alberto," Bell said.

He kept two of them in the Mack with him and sent the other back with three pinchbars.

"Everybody at your end take one and wedge it under the load," Bell said to Alberto. "Tell the men over here to grab hold of a rope end."

When that was done, he said, "When I say 'heave,' you and your men push. Tell mine to pull."

"Yes, sir," said Alberto.

"Heave!" Bell cried.

The men pushed and pulled, grunting. Nothing happened. The slab was too heavy for them, even with the fence posts to roll on.

"Stop," Bell said.

He sat down on the tarp and wiped the sweat off his face. He would have to tip the slab up enough for it to ride more easily on the posts.

"Donna?" he called.

"Yes?" she answered from just outside.

"Have Juan let some air out of the Dina's rear tires."

He picked up a pinchbar and joined Alberto in the Dina.

"Everybody do what I do," he said.

He jammed his pinchbar under the edge of the slab. Alberto translated and the drivers did the same with their pinchbars.

"We're gonna start sinking," Bell said. "Keep working the pinchbars underneath."

The floor of the Dina subsided slowly as the tires got lower. When the bottom of the slab was off the floor, Bell called out to Donna to have Juan stop letting out air and had Alberto tell a man to bring a fence post from the Mack.

"Where's your knife, Alberto?" Bell said.

"In my pocket, señor," Alberto said, breathing

183

heavily from the strain of pushing against his pinch-bar. "On the right side."

Bell got the knife out of Alberto's pocket and began shaving away at the end of the fence post. The knife was sharp but it was slow going. He stopped only long enough to wrap his handkerchief around the bone handle for padding when his sore hands started hurting and oozing blood. After he had shaved a taper on the end of the post, he wedged it under the slab and drove it farther under with a pinchbar.

"Donna," he called. "Let out some more air."

He kept pounding the end of the fence post with the pinchbar while the Dina settled. When he had its full thickness under the slab, he called out again.

"That's enough, Donna. Tell Juan to start inflating the Dina tires again."

He had Alberto and two men wedge pinchbars under the fencepost.

"Space 'em out so you won't break it," he cautioned.

The air compressor started up outside and he returned to the Mack, taking his man with him. He gave each of his two men a rope end.

"Same as before, Alberto," he said. "When I say 'heave,' your men lift up on the post, my men pull on the ropes."

When the air compressor stopped, he said, "Okay, Alberto. Everybody ready?"

"Yes, señor," said Alberto.

"Heave!" Bell shouted.

The slab moved slowly forward, rolling on the posts. Bell pushed another post under the advancing edge of the slab. He let his men rest a few minutes, though he was anxious to finish the job and be on his way. It was after five now, not too long before it would start getting light, but if he pushed them too hard they wouldn't be good for anything the rest of the day. He knew he wouldn't be. Every muscle ached, his torn hands itched and burned and his legs were rubbery with fatigue.

Even though he wanted to finish the job before it was full light, he would welcome the sun. There was less chance of anyone trying to pull something in broad daylight.

He sat down on the slab and closed his eyes. Despite the two bennies, he could have fallen asleep where he sat if he permitted himself. He shook himself awake and got to his feet, having to push off from the slab with both arms because his legs would not lift his weight.

"Alberto," he said. "Let's go."

Soon the entire slab rested inside the Mack on eight fence posts. He had all five men push the slab forward. As it rolled toward the front of the Mack, he took the fence posts exposed by the movement and slid them under the leading edge so that the slab was always rolling on at least seven posts. At last the section rested against the front of the van. There was no way of lifting it off the posts, so Bell wedged a pinchbar under the rearmost one to keep the sections from rolling back when they got moving again.

"Donna," Bell called, weary but triumphant. "Tell Juan to move the Mack out so we can start loading tile."

The Mack pulled away from the empty Dina. When Bell jumped to the ground his legs buckled and black spots swam before his eyes. He caught himself before he went all the way down.

"Are you all right?" Donna said anxiously.

"I'm fine," Bell said.

"Are you sure?"

"Yeah. Tell me something, Donna. You still think I'm being overpaid?"

"No," she said.

There was a hint of apology in her voice.

"Do you think you can look after things while I catch a few winks?" Bell asked. "I'm bushed."

"Of course," Donna replied.

He had her tell Juan to inflate the rear tires of the Mack and then get the tiles started aboard.

"Be sure they gather up the sugarcane pulp to pad out the load," he said. "Wake me when we're ready to pull out."

He crawled into the back seat and, despite the cramped quarters, fell asleep immediately. He dreamed about Chato. He was hitched in a harness to the Olmec head, in one solid piece now, pulling it along behind him. Chato's lips, instead of being sullen, were smiling at him in a most amiable way. Bell had the distinct impression Chato liked him. It made him feel guilty. Chato didn't know he was being dragged into captivity.

"Señor," said Chato.

Bell stirred.

"Señor," a voice said, and someone shook his foot.

Bell opened his eyes with difficulty, still drowned in sleep. It was full daylight. A face, not Chato's, was looking in the car window at him, and beside the face was a hand. The lips were smiling, not like Chato's lips, either. They were thin, not puffy, and between them glistened white teeth, one of them capped with gold. Bell was fully awake now. He had a vague recollection of having seen the face somewhere before.

In a green Chevelle automobile.

"Señor," the man said for the third time, beckoning with the hand thrust in the window.

There was a pistol in it.

14

AGENTE Tomás Alvarado's wife, Sara, was not in the house when he awoke Saturday morning. Concepción was in the kitchen eating a bowl of cornflakes and sliced bananas with milk. It made Alvarado's stomach contract just to watch her.

"How can you eat such trash?" he demanded.

"Don't be so old-fashioned, Papá," Concepción replied. "Everyone has cornflakes for breakfast in the United States."

"This isn't the United States."

Concepción sighed.

"Yes, Papá," she said. "I know. Why don't you try it? You might be surprised."

"Where's your mother?"

"She took Leonor and Yolanda to the market with her."

"I suppose you were too sleepy to go with them."

"No, Papá. Mother told me to stay and prepare your breakfast if you got up before she came back." She smiled mischievously. "What would you like, tortillas and beans?"

"Get me some coffee. I'll eat in town."

She brought him the coffee and he sat down across the table from her.

"There are worse things for breakfast than tortillas and beans," he said.

"I suppose so, Papá."

"When I was a boy, that's what we had. And I was glad to get it, I can tell you."

He sipped his coffee in silence. Concepción ate her cornflakes. She ate daintily, like a lady. Alvarado knew this was because he was there. She was often impudent, but it was true she also tried hard to please him. Occasionally Concepción looked up from her bowl of cereal and smiled at him. It was pleasant sitting there quietly with his impudent daughter, Alvarado thought. He would have preferred she were a boy, but since she was not, there was much to be said for having such a pretty, intelligent daughter.

"Are you going to the beach again today?" he asked.

"Yes, Papá."

"Who with?"

"Gallinita, of course."

"You should be more like her. There's a sensible girl."

"Maybe Señor Castillo will trade with you, Papá."

Laughing, she took his coffee cup and her bowl to the kitchen sink. "The faucet is still dripping, Papá," she said.

He had been intending to replace the washer but had been too busy. And he did not like doing things around the house. That was for Sara to look after. Incongruously, he thought about the dripping stand-pipe outside the comandancia.

"You wash those things," he said. "Don't leave them for your mother."

"It's Yolanda's day, Papá. Don't you know we take turns?"

"Don't be impudent. You're not thinking of wearing that immodest bathing suit to the beach again, are you?"

Concepción did not reply.

"Bring it to me."

"It's much too small for you, Papá."

"That's enough, Concepción."

When he called her by name he meant business. Concepción quickly fetched the two-piece bathing suit. He took it from her, held up a piece in each big hand. "And this you wore yesterday in public view?"

"Everybody wears them now, Papá."

"No daughter of mine is everybody. And I saw very few like it on the beach yesterday."

"I was very proud of you, Papá. After you left with that criminal everyone talked of nothing but how brave you were."

"Brave? That cockroach."

Concepción giggled. "It wasn't fair, was it, Papá? A giant like you and such a cockroach. But you didn't beat him up," she added seriously. "Anyone else would have. The way he struck at you. You're a good cop."

"I'm not a cop. I'm an agent."

Alvarado smiled inwardly. She thought she had succeeded in changing the subject. "You wear the suit I bought for you last year, understand?" he said.

"But it doesn't fit any more, Papá. I've grown."

And so she had. Even grown men stared at her now.

"Then borrow your mother's," he said.

"That old thing?"

"Yes, that old thing, Concepción."

Concepción sighed. She always sighed when she knew she had lost. "Yes, Papá," she said.

She wasn't sulky about it, he would say that for her. Unlike her mother, she had spirit and a mind of her own, but when she saw he was determined she accepted his decisions with good grace.

"I'll tell your mother to buy you a new bathing suit. All right?"

Sara would have to find the money somewhere.

Alvarado looked at the bathing suit and said gravely, "It is much too small for me, at that."

Concepción burst into laughter. It was too infectious for Alvarado not to join in.

Instead of stopping for breakfast Alvarado went directly to the comandancia. Now that he had the signed report from San Andrés Tuxtla perhaps the chief would give him permission to begin an official investigation.

Alvarado's chief read the report without expression. When he finished he buried it under a pile of other documents on his desk.

"You're going to Tlacotalpán this morning," he said. "The police down there need some help."

"They've heard something also, then?" Alvarado asked. This was even better than he had expected.

"About what?" the chief said dryly.

"The colossal head."

"Will you forget about that, Alvarado? You've got looters on the brain. It's a murder."

"A murder? What have we got to do with a murder in Tlacotalpán?"

Alvarado was the only agent in Veracruz who dared question the chief, and the only one who could do so unscathed. They understood each other well.

"They think it's political." With anyone else, the chief would not have bothered to explain.

"Those local police, they always say it's political," Alvarado said. "That way, we have to do their work for them."

"If that's the way it is, that's the way it is, eh, agente?"

"Chief, that report. You'll send it along to the attorney general?"

"With the rest of the routine garbage. Now pick up a car and get down to Tlacotalpán."

Alvarado parked in front of the cantina across from

the plaza in Tlacotalpán a little after eleven. He had not eaten breakfast and was hungry. He went inside and had a couple of tortas and a large Coke before going across the street to the one-story police station. The mottled green stucco of the portico arches needed repainting, but no more than the Palacio Federal in Veracruz, Alvarado thought. He wondered what he would find inside. In all the years he had been an agent he had never been inside the Tlacotalpán police station.

The interior was about what he had expected of a little village like Tlacotalpán. It certainly was not much like the police station in the film he had seen the night before. But he could not count that against the chief of the tiny force. The state of Veracruz didn't have any money to waste on needless luxuries.

He showed his ID to an officious young policeman who became stiffly respectful when he learned with whom he was dealing. The chief was not in. The policeman ran off to fetch him, leaving Alvarado alone in the office. The young simpleton should have known better than to leave the station unattended. Alvarado thought he would not mention that to the chief. He hadn't come down to Tlacotalpán to make trouble. Anyone who had to live and work here already had enough trouble.

The chief arrived out of breath. There was a fresh nick on his chin, as if he had cut himself shaving. Alvarado introduced himself and was quickly invited to sit down. The young policeman hovered around in the background. Alvarado knew the youngster wanted to see how a Federal agent from the big city operated. He acted very businesslike and knowing, putting on a little show for the policeman's benefit.

"I suppose you know if you brought me all the way down here from Veracruz, it had better be for something pretty important," he said.

"Of course," the chief said, squirming a little.

"This killing. Why do you think it's political?"

"There's been a lot of bad blood since the last election," the chief said evasively.

"And when was that?"

The chief shifted uncomfortably in his chair. "Recently," he said.

The policeman looked as if he wanted to disagree but a glance from the chief silenced him. Alvarado was at once aware there had been no election recently.

"Bad blood, eh?" he said solemnly. "You'd know among whom, naturally."

"Naturally," the chief said.

"Then you have suspects?"

"Well, no."

Alvarado let it pass. He was confident now that the killing had not been political. If it had been, the chief would have had a pretty good idea of who was involved and, if he had not made an arrest himself, the last thing he would have wanted was for the Federal Judicial Police to come poking around.

He brought out a notebook and a ballpoint pen. He seldom took notes but he thought the young policeman would expect it of him. And, of course, if the chief saw him writing things down he would be more apt to remain within reasonable bounds of accuracy.

"Now," he said. "About this murder."

The body of a man had been found on the bank of the Papaloapán River late Friday morning, apparently washed there from upstream. Not too far upstream because the body could not have been in the water very long. It was not bloated or much picked at by fish.

"Good work, observing that," Alvarado said.

The compliment caused the chief to relax somewhat.

The man had been shot in the back. The bullet had gone all the way through so it must have been a rifle.

Earlier Friday there had been gossip in the cantina about a lot of shooting west of town but at the time the chief had attached little significance to it.

"After the discovery of the corpse, you of course went out to have a look around where the shooting was heard," Alvarado said. "Did you find anything?"

The chief hesitated. He looked at the young policeman. "Why are you loafing around here, Gomez?" he demanded. "Find something useful to do."

The policeman left. The chief waited until he heard him go out the front door. "You were saying, agente?" he said.

"Did you find anything?" Alvarado repeated.

"No. Not a thing."

Alvarado did not believe the chief had stirred out of Tlacotalpán. It would not be laziness or inefficiency, necessarily. More likely, there was someone important out west of town the chief would prefer not to inconvenience openly.

"I'm sure you covered the ground thoroughly," Alvarado said. "But I suppose I'll have to take a look for myself. My chief will want a report."

That was true. Alvarado was not terribly interested in this strictly local matter but he had to go through the motions. His chief would want something in writing for the files.

"Of course," the chief said.

He appeared relieved that Alvarado was taking over so readily.

"About the victim," Alvarado said. "Local man?"

"No."

"Any identification?"

"Not a scrap."

"Hmmm," Alvarado said sagely. "My theory is he was a hired gunman."

"Why do you say that?" the chief asked, impressed and interested.

"If he was killed because of bad blood over a local

election, and he wasn't local, what else could he be but a pistolero? He was brought in by one of the disputants. And whoever he was brought in to kill got him first."

"Yes," the chief said eagerly. "Yes. That's just how it must have been."

If he really believes that cock-and-bull story, he's either stupid or terribly anxious not to get involved in the investigation, Alvarado thought, suspecting the latter. Everything pointed to it, including sending the policeman out so the youngster would be unable to gossip about what had been said in the office. Alvarado would be surprised if the chief didn't have a pretty solid notion of where the killing had taken place, and perhaps by whom. He just did not want to ruffle the wrong feathers. If the PJF handled things, the chief could always say the investigation had been taken out of his hands by higher authority. Alvarado doubted if anyone in town, even the young policeman, knew it was the chief himself who had called in Veracruz. He put his notebook and ballpoint pen away so the chief would not be intimidated by note-taking.

"Tell me," he said in his most confidential tone, one colleague to another, "who are the important people in Tlacotalpán? Someone who perhaps lives west of town."

The chief regarded him closely, as if wondering if Alvarado could be trusted to protect his source of information.

"Just between the two of us, of course," Alvarado said.

"Don Federico," the chief said guardedly. "Federico Trevino Muñoz. I suppose you've heard of him even up there in Veracruz."

"Yes, I think so," said Alvarado.

He had never heard of the man, but if the chief wished to believe the fame of a local celebrity had spread to the big city, he did not wish to disillusion him.

"His hacienda is a few kilometers out of town," the chief said. "On the road to Cosamaloapán."

Cosamaloapán was west of Tlacotalpán. So that's where the gunfight had taken place. Trevino must be a powerful man indeed if the chief of police was reluctant to involve himself in an investigation at his place.

"I must confess I don't know too much about Trevino," Alvarado said. "Tell me more about him. Just between the two of us."

"A very wealthy man. Sugarcane. Cattle. A dozen families live on his place."

"Is there more?" Alvarado asked.

There was always more.

The chief picked his words carefully. "It is said that Don Federico sometimes engages in illegal activities with a man from Mexico City," he said. "A man called Hernández."

Alvarado was immediately alert. Hernández was the name Jorge Vargas had used in Veracruz. "Hernández," he said. "I don't believe I know the name. Could you describe him?"

"I'm afraid not," the chief said. "I've never seen him, myself."

Alvarado had a feeling the chief was telling the truth. "Would you know if he's been in Tlacotalpán recently?" he asked casually.

"I'm afraid I don't know that, either," the chief said apologetically.

"I don't suppose he could have been here without you knowing it?" Alvarado said.

"I'll be frank with you," the chief replied. "It's possible. People usually tell me things, but when Don Federico is involved. . . . You know how it is."

"Of course," said Alvarado. "These illegal activities

you spoke of," he added casually. "What sort of illegal activities do they engage in?"

"I don't know," the chief said.

But of course he did. The chief was afraid of saying too much. It might lead to embarrassing questions about why he had never communicated the knowledge to Veracruz. If this Hernández was his Hernández, Alvarado thought, their illegal activities would be the theft of pre-Columbian objects. Perhaps even the Olmec head. But that would be expecting too much. Nevertheless, he would certainly take more than a cursory look around the Trevino farm.

Alvarado was still curious about one thing. Why had the chief bothered to call in the PJF if he was afraid of making himself a powerful enemy? He had only to keep quiet and the killing would have become just another unsolved local murder. It obviously was something personal.

"This Don Federico," he said. "I suppose he's a close friend of yours."

"A close friend!" the chief blurted, for the first time showing strong emotion. "That miserable son of his and my innocent little . . ."

He did not finish. He did not have to. Alvarado knew the whole story now.

"Thank you very much," Alvarado said, getting to his feet. "You've been most helpful. I'll see you get full credit for your cooperation in my report."

"Agente," the chief said, agitated. "Really, I've done nothing at all."

"Your modesty is admirable," said Alvarado. Relenting, he added, "If you prefer, you won't be mentioned in the report."

"Thank you," the chief said. "Thank you very much."

"It is nothing. I'll be getting along to Trevino's place. You needn't come with me. I can see how busy you are. If you'll just give me directions."

The chief looked enormously relieved. Alvarado wondered how the chief would have wriggled out of it if he had been asked to accompany him to Trevino's.

The young policeman was standing just outside the station, his back against the orange stucco wall at the back of the portico, looking morosely out over the plaza. He sprang to attention when Alvarado emerged.

"Relax, friend," said Alvarado. "You have a nice plaza here in Tlacotalpán."

It was a nice plaza. Not like the Plaza de la Constitución in Veracruz, but very acceptable for so small a town. It had benches, walks, flowering shrubs and slender pines whitewashed at the bottom to discourage insects. In the center was a rococo bandstand. When there was music it must be pleasant to sit out here listening in the night air. Alvarado could think of worse things.

"Agente," the policeman said hesitantly. "It must be very difficult to become an agent of the Federal Judicial Police."

"How much schooling have you, Gomez?" Alvarado said.

The policeman appeared flattered that Alvarado had remembered his name. "I completed eight years," he said with pride.

"You're more than eligible, then," said Alvarado. "Why don't you apply?"

"Thank you, agente. I will."

"Please don't take offense," Alvarado said, "but just a small word of advice. When they call you in for an interview, be sure you've shaved. And wear a clean shirt. It impresses the paper shufflers."

The policeman had felt the sparse hairs on his unshaven chin, looking stricken, but Alvarado's final words reassured him and he smiled sheepishly.

Alvarado looked back at him before he got into his car. The policeman no longer looked morose.

Alvarado did not start out immediately. He sat in

the car a moment debating with himself whether or not to phone his chief in Veracruz and get some help. More than one agent had been killed attempting to apprehend art thieves. In the end he decided against it. The chances were he would find nothing. The gun battle had taken place Thursday night. It was now after noon on Saturday. If the police chief's Hernández was actually Vargas and there had been contraband on the Trevino place, it was gone by now. Vargas was not one to sit around. If he went out there with an army, he would look like a fool. His chief already thought him a fanatic about art thefts. No, he would go to Trevino's alone and trust to common sense and his instincts not to get himself killed.

15

BELL climbed stiffly out of the Volks. His hands hurt, his legs did not want to unbend from the cramped position in which he had been sleeping and his mouth was cinder dry. They were being ripped off, his mind told him, but at the moment the realization aroused no strong emotion. He was simply too tired for strong emotions. He did not raise his hands, nor did his captor appear to want him to do so.

"What's going on?" Bell demanded, his voice hoarse because his throat was dry.

The man did not speak English.

The trucks of the convoy were in different positions now. The number one Dina was first, pointed north toward Linares, the International was next and then the Mack, riding low like a beast on its haunches. The green Chevelle was parked on the shoulder, hidden from the road by the number one Dina. The number two Dina was where it had been when he fell asleep, behind the Volks. Donna and the drivers were huddled beside it, guarded by four men. Bell's captor motioned with the pistol for Bell to join them. Bell walked the few steps, feeling life flowing back into his limbs.

Donna's face was set, masklike, but Bell knew it held fear and dismay, tightly reined. She wasn't going to let these bastards see it, he thought approvingly.

Alberto had no such control. He stared at Bell, bewildered and apprehensive, and licked his lips. Juan One also looked at Bell, then at their captors, and spat on the ground. There was drying blood on his face, a thin, crusting line from the corner of his left eyebrow down to his chin. There wasn't a whole lot of it but it made Bell feel strong emotion at last. He was enraged. Juan read Bell's expression, smiled, and held up a thumb.

"What happened?" Bell demanded hoarsely.

"We'd just finished loading on the tiles when these sons of bitches showed up," Donna said, her voice carefully controlled. "They must have been back there just waiting for that. Then they . . ."

"I can see what happened to the convoy," Bell interrupted. "What happened to Juan?"

"He tried to stop them. And one of them hit him with a gun."

They hadn't shot him, though, Bell thought. That could mean they weren't desperate enough to kill for Chato. But, on the other hand, it could also mean only that they were too shrewd to risk any shooting on the open highway in broad daylight.

The man who had fetched Bell appeared to be the leader. He gave orders in Spanish and three of his men trotted off and climbed into the three trucks.

"Is this the same bunch that hit us Thursday night, do you know?" Bell asked.

Donna nodded.

"This one said we could have saved them a lot of trouble if we had behaved sensibly back at Tlacotalpán," she said.

The man to whom she referred, the man with the gold tooth, said something and gestured with his pistol. He looked as tough as Juan, but itchy. Bell wondered if he was the one who had hit Juan, not that it made any difference.

"Everybody into the truck," Donna translated.

Bell looked thoughtfully at Gold Tooth. He wondered if they could buy him off with some of the cash Donna was carrying in her big purse. He didn't look like the type who'd be getting a whole hell of a lot for his part of the deal. But it would be stupid to try. They'd just take the money and the head, too.

The two armed men herded them all into the number two Dina and locked the doors behind them.

"God damn it to hell!" Donna cried in helpless rage.

Alberto pulled on Bell's arm.

"Señor Kent," he said desperately. "They are taking my uncle's trucks!"

Bell shrugged him loose. The other drivers, who had been quiet as rabbits until now, began talking excitedly among themselves.

"Everybody shut up!" Bell ordered.

Donna translated and they all fell quiet. Bell listened for the sound of the trucks. They fired up, made a U-turn and came back past the Dina, heading south. That figured. Whoever had hired the pistoleros would have to stash Chato until he made a connection on the other side of the border.

It was semi-dark and stifling hot in the van. Bell could feel the sweat popping out. He was still thirsty but he no longer felt so tired. Righteous anger had started the old adrenalin flowing, he thought wryly. Righteous anger. The robber robbed was what it was. But that didn't make it any easier to take. How he'd like to get his hands on those bastards. He shuffled his feet around in the darkness until he felt one of the pinchbars with which they had moved the slab. He picked it up and went to work on the doors. His hands were too sore for him to apply enough muscle.

"Donna, tell Juan to see if he can get the doors open," he said.

He handed the pinchbar to Juan. Juan began prying and pulling. Sunlight flooded into the van. He had forced the lock. Bell jumped out and ran around the

Dina to the Volks. The keys were still in the ignition. At least they weren't stranded. The brief satisfaction that gave him was quickly swept away by a deep sense of frustration. Those bastards had ripped off Chato and there wasn't a thing he could do about it. He sure as hell couldn't call the police. Maybe if Donna could phone Vargas, and Vargas could round up some men . . . But why should he? He had his split already. And it would be too late, anyhow.

Donna came up, followed by Alberto and the other drivers.

"Sandy's going to love this," she said.

"Maybe we can get it back," Bell said, surprising even himself.

Donna laughed sardonically.

"How do you propose doing that?" she demanded.

"I don't know," Bell said. "Maybe I'll think of something. They won't be expecting us to come after them."

"I thought you said you just signed on to haul a load," Donna said. "Why do you want to stick your neck out? Oh. If you don't deliver the goods you don't get the rest of your bread."

"Right," said Bell.

But that wasn't the real reason. He was not sure what his true motivation was. Anger, maybe, because those bastards thought they could just step in and take Chato away from him. He wasn't too crazy about what he'd been doing, smuggling Chato out of the country, but he had made a deal with Sandifer and a deal was a deal. The least he could do was give it a try.

"I say let them have it," Donna said. "It's not worth getting ourselves murdered."

"What about your five thousand?" Bell said.

"I'll get my five thousand," Donna said grimly. "Out of what I've got left. Let Sandy just try to stop me."

Bell called Alberto over and told him he wanted him to come with him.

"Me, señor?" Alberto said.

"Yeah. You and Juan and . . ." He looked the others over. Roberto, one of the big ones, looked the most capable. "And Roberto."

"No, Señor Kent," Alberto said.

"No? Look, I need you to translate for me."

Alberto studied the ground beneath his feet. Bell wanted to take him by the scruff of his neck and shake him. Instead he said, "What about your uncle's trucks? And that bonus Miss Fairchild promised you. She'll double it."

"I am sorry, señor," Alberto said, his voice almost inaudible.

"We're wasting time," Bell said. "Donna, tell Juan and Roberto to come with me."

"You're a damn fool," said Donna.

"You know something, baby?" Bell said. "You're right."

"You'll never catch them," Donna said.

"They won't get much out of the Mack," Bell said. "And they're running low on diesel. They'll have to stop down the road for fuel."

"They've got guns and you haven't," said Donna.

"I know all that, for Christ's sake."

"How will you communicate with Juan? You can't speak Spanish and he can't speak English."

"While you're talking they're getting farther away," Bell said.

He motioned Juan and Roberto into the Volks. Donna said something to them and they got in the back seat. While Bell was getting behind the wheel, she climbed into the passenger seat. Bell looked at her.

"I guess I'm a damn fool, too," she said.

She sounded embarrassed.

Bell headed south, flooring the accelerator. The

next town, Villagrán, was just a few miles down the road. Gold Tooth could be stopping there for fuel. They might be able to take him by surprise. Bell slowed when he saw a huddle of buildings up ahead. He didn't want to blunder into the convoy. The trucks were not there. The next town, Tomaseño, was about twenty miles farther south. Maybe they'd stop there. He floored the Volks again.

"What will you do if you catch up with them?" Donna said.

"Let me worry about that," Bell said.

"I intend to," Donna replied.

He slowed to a crawl outside of Tomaseño.

"There they are!" he cried.

The green Chevelle was parked off the road just past a service station. The Dina and the International were taking on fuel at pumps and the Mack was waiting behind them. Four men were leaning against the side of the Dina drinking soda pop. The fifth, Bell thought, must be in the Mack, waiting to drive it to a pump when one of the other trucks was finished.

Bell pulled off the highway and killed the engine.

"What now, Clark Kent?" Donna said.

Bell did not reply. He had no plan. He believed he, Juan and Roberto could handle the four men if they took them by surprise. He knew he could take two of them himself, and maybe Juan could, too. But what about the fifth man, in the Mack? And the service station people would report a brawl to the police. If he tried to take them in Tomaseño it would have to be quietly. Out on the highway he could risk a little commotion. If only he could split them up. And maybe get hold of at least one weapon. In any event, he would have to risk at least a little commotion at the service station. If things worked out, Donna could slip the attendants something to keep their mouths shut.

"I'm gonna need your help, Donna," Bell said. "Okay?"

204

"Depends," Donna said.

"What I want you to do is try to draw off Gold Tooth."

"Gold Tooth?"

"The dude in charge. I want you to drive by slow, look at 'em, and be damn sure they see you look at 'em. And then burn rubber. I'm hoping he'll follow you."

"You must be out of your mind. What if he catches us?"

"Not us, baby. You."

"That's even worse."

"Try to outrun him. If he boxes you in, pull off the road. Have your windows up and the doors locked. There's not much he can do in plain sight of the highway traffic. And if things work out right, I'll be along in a few minutes."

"And if things don't work out right?"

"Now, you tell Juan and Roberto to come with me," Bell said, ignoring her objections. "We're gonna slip around the back of the station and rush 'em while you've got their attention. I'll show 'em what to do when I want 'em to do it."

Bell would take Juan and Roberto with him and approach the station from the rear. If Gold Tooth followed the Volks, the three of them would jump Gold Tooth's men and disarm them.

"It won't be that easy," Donna said.

"They'll be watching Gold Tooth chasing you," Bell said. "They won't know what hit 'em. One more thing. You tell Juan as soon as we've taken care of those bastards he's to tell the attendants to forget the whole thing. That there's bread in it for 'em. Okay?"

"You do love to spend Sandy's money, don't you? All right. If you promise to come right away."

"Cross my heart," Bell said.

He wished he could be as positive of that as he sounded. He didn't like throwing Donna to the wolves. But if they fouled up and didn't take the other four men, the chances were Gold Tooth would be in too big a hurry to get out of there to waste time on Donna. He hoped so, anyway. If they blew it, he'd have to call the fuzz. That would blow the whole thing, but it wouldn't be anything like twelve years in the brig for them. They wouldn't have been caught trying to take Chato across the border and they could make a case for having cooperated with the authorities. They might get off with just a fine. And even if he got a couple of years, he'd owe Donna at least that much for talking her into risking her neck.

"You tell Juan and Roberto, whoever's still mobile if we blow it, to call the police," he said. "But I don't think it'll come to that."

"It better not," said Donna. "Have you heard about those Mexican jails?"

"Hell, they'll give you a medal for saving a national treasure," Bell said. "Let's get on with it."

Donna gave Juan and Roberto their instructions. Roberto didn't like the idea at all but agreed to go along. Juan looked as if he were delighted to get a crack at the pistoleros. Bell told Donna to give them just enough time to get into position, then do as he had told her. He led the two drivers to the rear of the service station, making a wide arc so there would be no chance of Gold Tooth and his men spotting them. He had Juan and Roberto stand back while he got on his stomach and peered around the edge of the service station. Close to the ground that way there would be less chance of being noticed.

He could see the Chevelle and the Dina from his vantage point, but none of the men. They must still be behind the Dina. He didn't see the Volks until it went past the station, picking up speed. The four men ran out from behind the Dina, gesturing wildly. Gold Tooth and one of the others ran for the Chevelle. The other two followed and stood looking after the

Chevelle as it sped away in pursuit. The fifth man ran up and joined them. Bell hurried to his feet and motioned to Juan and Roberto to follow him. He led them toward the three pistoleros, walking swifty but quietly. They continued to look down the highway, oblivious to Bell's approach. When he was fifteen or twenty paces away, Bell stopped his men with a signal. Then he made a swift gesture and started running toward the pistoleros. Juan ran along beside him. Roberto hung back.

At the sound of their running footsteps, the three men whirled to face them. After a moment of surprise, they began reaching under their shirts, but too late. In the brief instant before Bell and Juan reached them, Juan pointed wordlessly toward one of the pistoleros. He wanted that one himself. It must be the one who hit him, Bell thought. Bell hit the larger of the other two men, the impetus of his charge behind the blow. When it was one on two, you always eliminated the bigger man first. The man went reeling back and sprawled on the ground. At the same time, Juan leaped on his man and bore him to the ground and began pummeling him. With scarcely a glance at the man he had put down, Bell kicked the third pistolero in the shin and, while the man was still jerking forward in pain, smashed him on the side of the head with a savage right-hand blow. The man went down on his face. By the time Roberto joined them it was all over.

Juan's man lay bleeding from mouth and nose. The first man Bell hit was on his hands and knees, shaking his head and looking at the ground as if for something he had lost. Bell got his pistol and motioned for Juan and Roberto to disarm the others. As soon as this was done, Bell took Juan's arm and led him to the two service station attendants, who were watching openmouthed and frightened. Juan spoke to them. They kept nodding their heads, anxious to please.

Bell looked back at the pistoleros. The one who had been on hands and knees was on his feet and half-running, half-staggering away. Bell quickly overtook him and herded him back toward the station. With a gesture, Bell indicated Juan and Roberto were to bring the other two inside. Juan took the man he had beaten under the armpits and dragged him. Roberto picked the other up bodily. They put all three men in the washroom and jammed the knob with a chair from the station.

Bell sent Juan to the Dina and took Roberto with him in the International. In a few minutes he saw the Chevelle and the Volks parked off the highway. Gold Tooth was at one window of the Volks, his companion at the other. Gold Tooth was pointing his pistol at Donna. Bell waved Juan around to the far side of the Volks and aimed the International at Gold Tooth. Gold Tooth jumped away from the Volks and pointed his pistol at the approaching truck. Bell ducked down below the dash and kept coming. After a few seconds, he raised his head cautiously. Gold Tooth was tearing at the door of the Chevelle on the driver's side. The other pistolero was running for the car. Juan was running after him, his pistol raised. Bell honked the horn furiously.

"No, Juan!" he shouted. "No!"

Bell did not want any shooting. It wasn't just the noise. One man had already been killed. Fortunately, there was no direct connection with them. It was Vargas' men who had done that. But this was another story. He would be responsible. And Bell did not think even Chato was worth further bloodshed.

Anyhow, Gold Tooth and his man weren't a threat anymore. It was two pistols against three, and Gold Tooth had to know they would be on guard from now on. If he just let the pistoleros go, they would certainly keep heading south.

Bell got out of the truck and went to the Volks. Donna was still sitting in it, white-faced.

"You can come out now," Bell said.

Donna opened the door.

"You son of a . . ." she began shakily.

Then she looked at the two trucks boxing them in.

"You did it!" she cried. "You actually did it."

"Didn't I tell you I would?" Bell said. "Pull yourself together, baby. I don't want your hand shaking when you pay off those dudes at the service station."

By the time they finished servicing the Mack and returned to the stuck Dina it was after nine. Alberto and the drivers were sitting in the open van, their legs dangling. Alberto jumped down and ran to Bell before the International had come to a full stop.

"My uncle's trucks!" he cried. "You have them once again."

Bell climbed out of the cab and said, "That's right, Alberto."

"Señor Kent," said Alberto, "who were those men and why did they steal my uncle's trucks?"

"That's a long story, Alberto," Bell replied. "Maybe some day I'll write you a letter. Now, what say we get moving?"

Bell put Juan and his Dina up front. The Mack was next. Bell was driving that himself as far as Linares. He wanted to see how it performed loaded. Then came the International, with Donna bringing up the rear in the Volks. Bell sent Mono, Alberto's relief man, back to the Volks to drive with her.

At 80 kilometers an hour the Mack labored. Bell cut back to 70 and the motor stopped protesting. He noted that soon after he slowed and fell back, the Dina reduced speed until the interval was closed again. It was obvious that Juan was keeping track of the convoy in his side mirror.

It was about 100 miles to Monterrey and another

148 to Nuevo Laredo. At 70 kilometers, or 43 miles, an hour, and with a breakfast stop in Linares, they could reach Nuevo Laredo by four. If Sandifer's customs broker was on the ball, it should give them enough time. Bell did not know how long it normally took to get export permits but assumed Donna had in that big purse of hers whatever it took to expedite things.

He kept yawning at the wheel. Now that the excitement was over, he felt his fatigue as keenly as before. And his hands hurt, so that he had to grip the wheel gingerly.

There were two attendants on duty at the Mobil station in Linares, neither of them the man from the night shift. He had gone off duty without saying anything about the deposit on the air compressor and tow cables. Or so the attendants told Alberto. Bell told Alberto to let it pass. If they got into a hassle, Donna might come to see what it was about and, despite the day's adventures, waste half the morning arguing with the attendants.

He rejoined Donna in the Volks, letting her drive, and led the trucks back into Linares to find a restaurant where they could get breakfast.

"I think you forgot something," Donna said.

"Like what?" Bell asked.

"Shouldn't there be money left from the five thousand pesos I gave you?"

Bell started laughing. He couldn't help it. After all that had happened. Donna waited patiently, not even smiling.

"Yeah," he said, wiping the tears from his eyes.

He pulled a wad of bills from his pocket and gave them to her without counting them.

"I forgot to get receipts for what I spent," he said. "You'll just have to take my word for it. Unless you'd rather dock my wages."

"Do you really think I'd do that after the beautiful way you handled everything?" she said quietly.

"No, Donna. I guess I just can't help needling you."

"I know," she said. "It's one of the reasons I find you so charming."

They found a clean restaurant and ordered breakfast. Donna went to the lavatory. When she returned she gave it her seal of approval.

"I guess your day's made, then," Bell said.

After he said it he wished he hadn't. He shouldn't keep needling her after the way she'd come through for him with Gold Tooth and his bunch. But damn it, she asked for it.

He went to the lavatory to shave, brush his teeth, and wash up. His hand trembled with fatigue when he ran the cordless razor over his face. He longed for a shower and fresh clothes and sleep. He felt itchy. He could imagine how Donna must feel, as fastidious as she was. It was surprising, though, how good she still looked after two nights and a day on the road. And she hadn't complained, either. Donna did have her good points.

Before setting out again he had her go into a farmacia to pick up ointment for his hands.

"You poor thing!" she exclaimed when she saw the condition of his hands. "Does it hurt much?"

"Just enough to help me stay awake," he said, adding, "and thanks for asking."

They made one more stop, to get some cotton work gloves for Bell to wear over the ointment, and were back on the highway at ten thirty. Bell kept the Dina up front and the Volks in the rear. He let Donna drive while he curled up in the back seat to get some sleep. It was hot despite the rush of air through the open windows. Just before drifting off he thought if Donna hadn't been so tight, they could have at least had a roomier car if not an air-conditioned one. It seemed he had hardly closed his eyes when Donna woke him.

"Sam," she said. "I think something's wrong."

Bell sat up. They had entered a stretch of gentle

grades among scrub land interspersed with citrus groves. Up ahead, the International had slowed to a crawl. What is it this time, he wondered irritably, a caseta or another one-way bridge? The International kept moving, but slowly.

"Pull around it," he told Donna.

She stepped on the gas and swung out. The Mack was creeping along just ahead of the International, the Dina was a couple of hundred yards up the highway waiting for the other trucks to catch up. Donna pulled abreast of the Mack. It was making a loud, rapid popping noise.

"Christ!" Bell muttered.

Alberto was looking at him out of the side window, holding his hand palm up in a helpless gesture. Bell motioned for him to pull off the highway. Alberto drove onto the shoulder and stopped, the International following. The Dina pulled over as well.

"Park in front of the Mack, Donna," said Bell.

"What is it?" Donna said.

"Sounds like a burned-out intake valve," Bell replied.

He got out of the Volks and hurried back to the Mack. Donna ran after him.

"Is that something serious?" she demanded.

"Serious enough."

Alberto and Mono climbed out of the Mack. Mono began talking, making eloquent use of his hands. Bell heard the word, "valvula."

"I think he's saying what you did," Donna said. "Burned-out intake valve."

Juan came back to see what was wrong. He shook his head gravely.

"Can it be fixed?" Donna said anxiously.

"The head's got to be pulled," Bell said. "And the nearest parts are probably in Monterrey."

They could forget about reaching Nuevo Laredo before closing time.

16

ALVARADO drove through Tlacotalpán, crossed the
little bridge at the western exit and was soon among
cane fields interspersed with broad areas of swampy
ground. He anticipated no difficulty in recognizing
Trevino's place when he reached it. It would be quite
different from the thatched huts he saw in the fields.
The Papaloapán River was visible from the road.
Galvez had said the contraband had been moved by
boat. It would not have been so difficult to bring a
large, heavy object to Tlacotalpán by water. And the
river was right at Trevino's back door, so to speak.
Alvarado was intrigued by the way things seemed
to fit, but not without a keen sense of frustration. It
was galling to have hit upon such a lead but to have
done so too late. But even if he was too late to re-
cover the contraband, if indeed there had been any
at Trevino's, he still might get enough out of his investigation to nail Vargas.

As he anticipated, he recognized the Trevino place
at once. The main house was set well back from the
highway, a white mansion of two stories with a red-tile
roof. It was surrounded by a whitewashed wall, above
which was visible a graceful second-floor veranda and
the tops of palms and other trees. Lesser buildings,
some thatched and others with red-tile roofs like the

main house, were scattered among broad, grassy fields bordered by heavy stands of sugarcane. Cattle grazed in the fields.

A dirt road, deeply rutted, led into the estate. Alvarado turned onto it. The car slipped and bounced among the ruts. Trevino must have many heavy farm vehicles to have churned the road to such a state, he thought. He could see no such vehicles in the fields, nor did they seem practical here. The land was rather marshy, with water in the low places. If there were such vehicles, perhaps they were indoors, in one of the outbuildings. One building in particular, long, low, with solid white walls and a sturdy tile roof, seemed a likely place.

Some meters from the highway, a miry depression in the road was covered with crushed tile among which there was a scattering of whole tiles. That was a bit unusual, Alvarado thought. There must certainly be cheaper materials with which to mend a farm road. Perhaps there was a tile factory in Tlacotalpán where Trevino had purchased the spoilage at a reasonable price and the whole tiles had been carelessly included.

The road led to the building where Alvarado thought the heavy farm vehicles might be kept, and branched off toward the main house. Alvarado intended driving boldly to the house, identifying himself and asking for Trevino. He had his story all prepared. The body of a small-time dealer in narcotics had been found downstream shortly after gunfire had been reported in the area of the Trevino place. Perhaps Don Federico might know if the man had been pursued onto his property by business rivals and if so, had any of Don Federico's people witnessed the murder. He would appreciate an opportunity to question them about it without, of course, disturbing Don Federico. Alvarado did not think he could learn a good deal from Trevino himself. Such a man would be too clever, unless by chance he felt threatened enough to offer a bribe to end the investigation. In Alvarado's experience, that sort of thing had not been too infrequent. In that case, he could certainly learn much by pretending to accept.

Alvarado was turning toward the house when sunlight glinting off something bright in the flat-packed earth in front of the barn caught his eye. He stopped the car and looked about him. Except for a knot of workers in a distant field there was no one in sight. He got out of the car and walked across the bare area, observing as he did so that it bore the marks of many truck tires, their depth indicating the trucks had been heavily loaded. The barn, then, was where Trevino kept his vehicles.

The bright object was the half-buried case of a rifle cartridge. Alvarado picked it up, scraped off the dirt and put it in his pocket. He made a quick sweep of the area without finding another. He studied the freshly whitewashed side of the barn. There were pocks in it that could very likely have been made by bullets. And there were several small holes in the big wooden doors of the barn. Alvarado pulled open one of the doors. Inside, the wood was splintered around the holes. Definitely bullet holes. Obviously there had been a shooting scrape here. This was no doubt where the man had been killed and his body dumped in the river so conveniently near on the southern margin of the estate.

Alvarado was not terribly interested in the murder itself. It was no affair of his. The killing obviously was not a federal concern and he would throw it right back to the local authorities in Tlacotalpán. But if he could find evidence of a theft of pre-Columbian art, that was in his jurisdiction. Any scrap of hard evidence would be enough to convince his chief that a thorough investigation was in order.

He looked about again and, seeing the fields still empty except for the distant workers, went into the barn. There were no vehicles, only a heavy wheeled hoisting device and a great heap of sugarcane pulp. Alvarado poked the heap with his foot. There was something hard beneath it. He squatted down and pulled away handfuls of fiber. Underneath were stacks of brown tile much like that he had seen filling in the low spot in the road.

Why would Trevino conceal tiles in his barn, Alvarado wondered. He would not have wasted money buying perfectly good tiles to fill a hole in the road, and certainly not so many more than he needed, and certainly would have had little reason to hide what was left. He opened both doors wide to let in the sunlight and began a careful examination of the dirt floor. He found the same sort of tire marks he had observed outside, as well as a roughly circular depression four or five centimeters deep and perhaps two meters in diameter. The bottom of this depression was compacted and perfectly level. Something very heavy had stood here. An Olmec head, perhaps.

Don't jump to conclusions just because you want to believe that, Alvarado told himself. You're not even certain such a head exists. He closed his eyes and thought furiously. But supposing such a head did exist and had been brought here? With the Papaloapán River so conveniently near it would not have been difficult once the head had been brought to a connecting waterway. And if the head had been cut into pieces, as Galvez said, it could easily be loaded on trucks with that great hoisting device there. But why the tiles? To cover the pieces, of course. Hernández, or Vargas, would want to conceal them. Granted, he thought. But why so many tiles still here? There must be thousands of them. Why would Trevino provide so many more than Vargas needed?

He went to the door and looked out. Still no one in view but the workers, who had moved even farther off into the fields. He returned to his contemplation of the enormous stack of tiles. It would have been necessary to truck them in. And how except by the very trucks that took away the head? Vargas was a shrewd operator, and experienced. He would have provided himself with documents identifying the contents of his trucks as something other than contraband. Why not tiles? What simpler way to obtain legitimate bills of lading than buying a quantity of tiles equal to the weight of the head with enough left over to conceal the pieces in his trucks? His papers would show so many kilograms of tiles on each truck. Who would know there was anything concealed beneath the tiles even if the trucks were weighed?

Of course. Vargas had purchased truckloads of tiles, perhaps in Veracruz when he was there. You really want to believe that, don't you, Alvarado asked himself wryly. You're not even certain Vargas was involved in anything that happened here. At this point, there's nothing to prove he's been any nearer than Veracruz. Or that he bought tiles in Veracruz. They could have been purchased locally for some entirely different purpose. On a place the size of Trevino's, there must be many uses for tiles, innocent uses.

But supposing his conjectures were accurate. The head would have been removed Thursday night after the gun battle. Why a shooting scrape, anyhow? The only explanation could be that rival thieves had tried to take the head. It gave added weight to his theory. So. Granted there was an Olmec head and it had been brought here and taken away by trucks Thursday night. It was now already Saturday afternoon. The head could easily be across the border already and out of his grasp. Alvarado sighed. If only the chief of police in Tlacotalpán had called Veracruz a day earlier.

Even if the head was already out of the country, he could still salvage something from all this. It might still be possible to establish that an Olmec head, or something equally as large, had been removed illegally from the country and that Vargas had been involved. For that he would need evidence that Vargas had been here Thursday night and had purchased the tiles that concealed whatever had been here. Alvarado picked up one of the tiles and slipped it in his waistband under his guayabera shirt in back, where his belt could hold it in place. The edges dug into his flesh but he did not mind, not at all.

A voice said, "Who are you and what are you doing here?"

A hard-faced man, small but menacing, stood in the doorway. Alvarado reached casually under his shirt and scratched his side with a thumb, near the butt of his holstered revolver. When he saw the stranger was not armed he let the hand drop to his side.

"Looking for Don Federico," he said.

"Here? In a barn?"

"I didn't know it was a barn when I came in, friend."

"You've been snooping around," the man said, pointing to the place where Alvarado had pulled away the sugarcane pulp.

"What are you talking about?" Alvarado demanded. "It was like that when I entered."

"Do you take me for a fool?"

"If you think I waste my time poking around in barns, yes. I don't think I like your attitude, friend."

"Watch your tongue," the man said.

"Why," said Alvarado, taking a step toward him. "What will you do if I don't?"

The man backed up involuntarily, looking less sure of himself.

"Señor Hernández told me Don Federico wants to sell some cattle," Alvarado said, changing his tactics.

"You are a friend of Señor Hernández?" the man said.

218

"So I came out to have a look," Alvarado said, as if the man had not spoken. "Now I'm not sure if I want to do business with a man who would have someone like you working for him."

The man scowled and looked as if he were trying to decide how to react to this new insult.

"If you will be kind enough to take me to Don Federico, maybe I'll be kind enough not to mention your insolence," Alvarado said.

"Don Federico is away," the man said. "He's gone to Mexico City."

"Damn it all! Why didn't he mention that to Hernández Thursday when he told me about the cattle?"

"Don't ask me," the man said defensively.

"Now I've driven all the way from Acayucán for nothing!" Alvarado said angrily. He paced for a moment to demonstrate his annoyance and added, "When's he returning?"

"Don Federico does not take me into his confidence on such matters," the man replied, wavering between suspicion and fear of offending someone who might be important.

"I'm not surprised," Alvarado said, continuing to play on the man's uncertainty. "Have you the wits to remember to tell him José Elizando was here about the cattle and to call me immediately when he returns."

"He knows where to reach you, then?" the man asked, shaken that he had incurred the wrath of an acquaintance of his master.

"Would I have given you my name if he did not?" Alvarado demanded sarcastically.

"I will certainly tell Don Federico, Don José," the man said ingratiatingly.

It was difficult for Alvarado not to smile. Don, indeed.

"You can stop worrying," he said. "I won't mention how you spoke to me to Don Federico. After all, you didn't know who I was and were only doing your duty. But if I were you, I would try to be a bit more courteous with strangers."

"Thank you, Don José."

"Tell me, did Don Federico go to Mexico City with Señor Hernández? If he did, maybe I can reach him by phone at Hernández' place."

"No, señor. He went the day after. Yesterday."

Alvarado went out to his car and drove away quickly, before Trevino's man recovered his poise enough to realize that this Don José looked more like a policeman than a landed gentleman. He drove through Tlacotalpán without stopping, though he knew he should have paused long enough to pay a courtesy call on the chief of police and inform him he'd found evidence of a gun battle at Trevino's. He did not want to waste the time. It was already almost two o'clock and he had much to do in Veracruz. He would telephone the chief of police if he had a spare minute later.

There was a line of cars waiting for the ferry at the Buena Vista crossing and Alvarado did not get on until the next trip. When he was aboard he showed the fee collector his ID instead of paying and asked him when the crew shifts changed. At 6 A.M., 2 P.M. and 10 P.M., he was told. Alvarado was reasonably sure the trucks from Trevino's hacienda would have crossed after 10 P.M.

"Where can I find someone who was on the late shift Thursday night?" he asked.

"I'll get the patrón de río, agente," the fee collector said.

The ferry was already nosing against the bank on the Buena Vista side when the patrón de río, the captain of the craft, came to Alvarado. Alvarado got out of his car to speak with him.

"I want to talk with someone who was on the late shift Thursday night," Alvarado said.

The patrón de río glanced over at a couple of crewmen letting down the ramp and said, "We don't have a regular late shift, agente. It's volunteers from the other two shifts."

The cars in one of the two lines were driving off the ferry. Alvarado's car was blocking the second line. The two drivers behind it began honking impatiently.

"Tell them to go around," he ordered.

"I'm afraid there isn't room for them to back up," the patrón de río said.

"Then they'll have to wait."

The patrón de río cleared his throat uncomfortably and looked at the line of cars waiting to come aboard. He did not, however, say anything.

"I'll drive off and park my car," Alvarado said. "But don't leave. I'll be back."

"Of course, agente."

Alvarado drove off the ferry and parked the car in front of a fruit stall. The ferry was loading when he returned. He waited until the patrón de río finished supervising the loading and the raising of the ramp and the ferry chugged out into the Papaloapán.

"Who would volunteer to work an extra shift?" Alvarado asked.

"What is that, agente?" the patrón de río said. "Oh, the late shift. The men who work the ten to six shift get to keep the fees. If there's no traffic, they get their sleep anyhow. If there is, they make money."

"Do you ever work the late shift yourself, Patrón?"

The patrón de río smiled.

"Not very often, agente. I have a suitable arrangement with my crew."

"I don't suppose you worked it Thursday night."

"No."

"Did anyone on this shift?"

"I'll find out."

He went off and returned with a crewman.

"This is Armando," he said. "He worked Thursday night. Mando, the agente wishes to speak with you."

Armando looked uneasy.

"Why?" he said. "I haven't done anything."

Alvarado smiled and took off his sunglasses.

"It's no concern of mine if you had," he said pleasantly. "This has nothing to do with you. You say you worked the late shift Thursday?"

"Yes, agente."

"Did several trucks cross together?"

"Yes, they did. I remember because things had been very slow and then, four of them together."

"Four? How did you know they were together?"

"I was awake and saw them coming across the river, one behind the other."

The ferry reached the west bank of the river and Armando excused himself for a moment. It was his job to help lower the ramp, he explained. He returned when the new load was aboard and the ramp raised.

"At what hour did the trucks cross?" Alvarado said.

"I don't know. I do not have a watch. But long after midnight, I think."

"You wouldn't happen to know what they were carrying, would you?" Alvarado said. "Tiles, perhaps?"

"I don't know, agente. Except that one of them was empty. It's cheaper for trucks without a load."

"Did you notice the registration number of any of the trucks, or if they had Federal District plates? Or perhaps what kind they were?"

"No, agente. Is that something new? Will we be obliged to do that?"

"No. I was only asking."

Alvarado described Vargas.

"Tell me," he said, "was such a man with the trucks?"

"Yes, agente," Armando said, pleased to have an answer Alvarado wanted at last. "I remember him well because he was in a big American automobile. A Cadillac. With a driver."

"Thanks, friend," said Alvarado. "You've been most helpful."

It was all coming together very nicely. He had evidence to place Vargas with the trucks that had picked up something at the Trevino place. Unfortunately, he had no proof that it was contraband nor, at the moment, that Vargas was traveling with the trucks. Vargas could say it was sheer coincidence, and who could prove otherwise? Unless he could link Vargas with the purchase of a large quantity of tiles of the sort he had found in Trevino's barn, a sample of which he now had safely locked away in the trunk of his car. That was evidence.

He could be back in Veracruz by three thirty if he hurried. Still plenty of time to visit the tile factories there. If Vargas had bought thousands of tiles in Veracruz it should not prove too difficult to learn where.

17

BELL looked at his watch. He had been sleeping a little less than an hour. That meant they were still 40 miles or so from Monterrey. The Mack might be able to make it if they took it easy. He put the Mack in front and told Alberto to hold it at 35 kilometers an hour. He drove just behind it, where he could keep his eye on it, and put Juan and the Dina in the rear.

It was a quarter to twelve. Even creeping along at just over 20 miles an hour they should reach Monterrey by two. Plenty of time to locate another truck and switch loads before everybody closed. He couldn't take a chance on repairing the Mack. It would take longer to fix it anyhow than to switch loads. And, since they couldn't accomplish anything in Nuevo Laredo until Monday morning, they could spend the night in Monterrey. God knows he needed the rest. So did the drivers, though they had been able to trade off.

Beyond the next little town, Allende, the convoy hit some grades. They weren't much but it was all the Mack could do to struggle up them at 15 kilometers an hour. If they hit anything steeper, the Mack might not be able to make it at all, Bell thought. If the Mack went out, he hoped there was a tow truck in Allende big enough to take it the rest of the way in. The hills began closing in on both sides of the road but fortunately the grades did not increase. The Mack kept chugging along, popping like a lazy machine gun. After a while the highway leveled off and the truck got up to 35 again.

"Are you sure we can't go any faster?" Donna said. "This is so boring."

"Look at the bright side," Bell replied. "At this speed we're saving money on diesel."

"You were much funnier when you were sleeping," said Donna.

They reached the reservoir south of Monterrey at two o'clock and in another twenty minutes reached the outskirts of the city. The truck route, marked by an arrow and a "Camiones" sign, took them to the right instead of directly toward the heart of the city.

"Keep your eyes peeled for an auto transportes place," Bell said. "If we can, I'd rather get another truck before we get downtown. I'd just as soon not go milling around in traffic with three trucks, and the Mack sounding like a popcorn machine."

The truck route, Avenida Revolución, was a four-lane divided road with an esplanade down the middle. There wasn't anything in sight that looked like a place where they could rent a truck. Costly looking residential developments were going up on both sides of Revolución. Just beyond one of them, and looking out of place, was a sprawling tile and brick factory. The sign said "Lamosa."

"What's Lamosa mean?" Bell asked.

"Are you trying to learn Spanish at this late date, Sam?" Donna said.

"No," said Bell. "Just wondering. I have an inquiring mind."

"It doesn't show. I don't think Lamosa means anything. Just a name."

She looked at him thoughtfully.

"Sandy said you had a degree from Rice. I'm surprised you don't know any Spanish. What did they teach you there?"

"Russian. Spanish was too easy."

"You wouldn't be pulling my leg, would you?"

"Not while I'm driving. Later, if you like."

"You keep on looking back at that brick factory. Why?"

"Just thinking. If I'd known nobody would be looking in the trucks I'd have waited until we got here to buy the tiles for Chato." He shrugged. "But then all the drivers would have known right from go we were hauling contraband."

"They must all know by now, anyhow," said Donna.

"Not for sure. Except Alberto and Juan. And it doesn't matter about Juan."

"But you think it does about Alberto?"

"Maybe."

"You don't think he'd fink, do you?"

"Why should he? It's nothing to him as long as he gets his wages. First chance I get, I'll remind him about that bonus we promised."

"You promised," Donna corrected.

"Okay," Bell said. "I'll pay his bonus."

"I didn't mean it that way," Donna snapped. "Nobody expects you to pay anything out of your own pocket. After everything you did today. It's merely that I don't think he's been all that great."

"I know," Bell said contritely. "But we better keep Alberto happy."

The truck route went through an industrial district and turned north toward town again.

"I don't think we're going to find what we want out here," Bell said. "What we'll do, we'll find a good place to stash the trucks and then look for a phone."

He scouted ahead of the convoy, blinking to stay awake, until he found a vacant building with empty land behind it. He led the convoy behind the building. He got out of the Volks and leaned against it, feeling drugged and flaccid. He didn't know how much longer he could keep going without rest, real rest, not a few minutes curled up in the back seat of the Volks. He took off one of the work gloves and gulped down a benzedrine tablet. The ointment was doing its job and his hands weren't giving him any trouble. That was something, anyhow.

Alberto came up to ask why they had stopped. Bell told him it was a lunch break. And it was true that the men had to be fed. It was almost three and they'd had nothing to eat since breakfast. He wasn't hungry himself. He was too tired.

Someone would have to be sent to pick up food. It couldn't be Alberto because he didn't want Alberto going off on his own. And it couldn't be Juan because he wanted Juan to stay here and keep an eye on Alberto

"Donna," he said. "When you had Mono with you in the Volks, was he nosy about what we're hauling?"

"Couldn't have cared less. Talked me to death about his new baby. He's a sweet little man."

"New baby? That old guy?"

"He has a young wife. His third, he said."

"Give him some money and tell him to take the Dina and bring back chow for everybody. And tell Juan nobody's to leave the trucks while we're gone, especially Alberto."

Donna gave Mono the money without protest. Even if she'd done her usual number about money, Bell thought, he would have been too tired to make a joke about it.

"You drive," he said when they got back in the Volks.

God, he was tired of that car.

They drove halfway into town before they found a telephone and directory. Donna got on the phone and started calling truckers. Bell said he wanted a place with a loading dock and a tug powerful enough to move the big slab in the Mack. No more working with fence posts and pinchbars and letting air out of tires. The slab was under a tarp now and he didn't have to worry about anyone getting a look at it. He'd have the men unload the tiles and bring the Mack in with nothing but the slab in it. At the loading dock he could throw the hawser rope around the slab and have the tug haul it out and shove it into the replacement truck.

Donna used up almost all her coins without locating a trucker who had a loading dock and tug and a vehicle he could let them have for two days starting that afternoon. She did speak with one who had suitable facilities and could provide a truck first thing Sunday morning. He was willing to open his place to accommodate them.

"Call that guy back," Bell said after another unsuccessful call. "We've got to stay over anyhow. We can still get to Nuevo Laredo tomorrow night and cross first thing Monday morning."

When Donna called the trucker back with her last coins he said there would be an additional charge for performing the service on a holiday. Donna did not argue with him. Bell did not know if it was because she understood it was a reasonable demand or because she didn't want to hear any more remarks about her frugality.

When they returned to the trucks, only Juan and Alberto were not sleeping. Juan made a gesture that meant all was well.

"We will be leaving now?" Alberto asked. "You found a replacement for the Mack, señor?"

"Tomorrow," Bell said. "We spend the night in Monterrey."

"I will telephone my uncle and explain the delay."

"It won't be necessary, Alberto. I'll see he's paid for the extra time we hold his trucks."

"I have been thinking, Señor Kent," Alberto said tentatively, "would it not have been more quick to go directly to Matamoros instead of by way of Monterrey?"

"Yes, it would," Bell said. "But we had some business in Monterrey."

"I see," said Alberto.

I'll bet you do, Bell thought.

"By the way," he said. "You remember what I said about a bonus? I talked it over with Miss Fairchild and we agreed on a thousand pesos."

"Thank you very much, señor," Alberto said.

"You deserve it," Bell said. "Now get the drivers up. We're going into town to find a place to park the trucks, and rooms for the men."

Bell felt sufficiently awake to drive now. He led the convoy into the city, the Mack popping along behind the Volks. Northeast of the center of town they found a modest hotel. Bell sent Alberto in to inquire about parking facilities in the neighborhood. There was an off-street parking area within walking distance.

"Good," Bell said. "You'll stay here tonight."

There were only two rooms available. Alberto did not much relish being crowded in with ordinary drivers. Bell mollified him by assigning four men to one room and letting Alberto share the other with Juan. He left three of the drivers at the hotel and followed the trucks to the parking area. After seeing the trucks safely parked and locked, he brought the drivers back to the hotel. All of them seemed to be in a festive mood. Saturday night, Bell thought. He told Donna to give Alberto just enough money for the drivers' dinner and breakfast. He didn't want them out carousing.

"When you take them to eat," he told Alberto, "let

them have a couple of beers and then bring them back to the hotel. I don't want anybody going out on the town tonight."

"I understand, señor," Alberto said.

But who'll see that you stay put tonight, Bell wondered. He doubted if Alberto had the guts to pull anything but by now Alberto knew there must be something really valuable in the trucks. The thought of money could give even a timid man courage. He took Donna aside and told her to tell Juan to stick close to Alberto. As an added precaution, he had Alberto collect the truck ignition keys and turn them over to him.

"This way you won't have to feel responsible for 'em," he told Alberto.

He took down the hotel's address and phone number and promised Alberto he would call and give him his hotel number when he found a place to stay.

Bell knew there were several good hotels in the district just north of the Santa Catarina Canal and west of Zaragoza, a main thoroughfare. He had stayed at one of them, the Ambassador. He drove about the area until he found it, on the corner of Hidalgo and Galeana. There were no rooms. Conventions and many tourists, the reservations clerk said apologetically. The clerk called several other hotels for them before locating a room at the Jolet.

"*A* room?" Donna demanded. "We need two."

"Think of the money it saves," Bell said. "I'm so beat you won't even know I'm there."

The clerk called back and booked a second room.

"If all the good hotels are full, it must be some dump," Donna said.

"The way I feel, I wouldn't care if it's a kennel," said Bell.

"I'm sure you'd feel right at home," Donna replied, quickly adding, "I'm sorry I said that, Sam. Nobody else could have handled things the way you did today."

The Hotel Jolet was only five blocks from the Ambassador, on Padre Mier just past Garibaldi. Padre Mier was a central traffic artery, crowded and noisy. Bell would have missed its modest facade if Donna had not seen the sign. The lobby was as modest as the exterior but it was air-conditioned. That was all that really counted, Bell thought.

The clerk pushed a registration card toward Bell.

"I want to see the bathroom first," Donna said.

"If you don't like it, where do you plan on spending the night?" Bell asked.

Donna sighed and reached for the registration card. Bell held on to it for a moment. Though he felt light-headed from fatigue, he could not resist saying, "Sure you don't want to double up and save the price of a room?"

Donna snatched the card from him and filled it out.

"I guess I'll have a registration card, too," Bell told the clerk.

She gave him one, looking perplexed.

"We had a lovers' quarrel," Bell explained as he wrote. "It was her thirtieth birthday and I forgot to send flowers."

The clerk looked even more perplexed.

"Do you enjoy making an ass of yourself?" Donna demanded in a low, tight voice.

"I try not to, but that sultry charm of yours brings out the worst in me."

Donna walked away from the desk and motioned him to follow. "Did you say we'd be crossing the border Monday morning?" she said.

"Right."

"I'll call Sandy and tell him as soon as I got up to my room. He still has some arrangements to make at his end. I'm sure he's wondering where we are. He expected us tonight."

"Yeah. He must be uptight. He hasn't heard from

us since Wednesday. Unless there were telephones in those bathrooms you were using."

"I haven't been calling him behind your back, if that's what you're getting at."

"Never entered my mind. Look, I want to talk to him, too. Okay?"

Bell sent a bellman out to bring in their things. When he brought in the luggage, Donna said, "Oh, my God! We forgot my suitcase. You'll have to go back for it."

"Forget it, Donna. I couldn't drive another inch. I'll get it in the morning."

"All right," Donna said reluctantly. "But I want it first thing. These clothes are absolutely filthy."

When they stepped into the elevator, Bell said, "Your room or mine?"

"How many times must I tell you you don't turn me on?" Donna demanded.

"The phone, baby. We're phoning Sandifer, remember?"

Their rooms were on different floors. Bell went back to Donna's after seeing his bags deposited inside his door. He did not even look inside to see what the room was like. When he knocked on Donna's door she let him in without a word of greeting. She was still angry from their exchange in the elevator. Bell cast a critical eye around her room. It was nothing special but still less seedy than he'd had back at the Diligencias in Veracruz.

"Is this what they stuck you with?" he demanded. "How's the bathroom?"

"What do you mean is this what they stuck me with?" Donna replied quickly.

"Nothing."

He opened the bathroom door and looked inside. It was tiny and old-fashioned. There was a small shower stall with a plastic curtain but no tub. "They must not have remodeled this floor yet," Bell said casually.

"What do you mean?"

"You ought to see my bathroom. Twice this size and brand new. Shower over the tub with a sliding glass door. And no cracks in the toilet seat."

Donna looked upset, then thoughtful. "Sam," she said, "be a good guy and trade rooms with me."

"Nope. But if you want to share it with me I'll let bygones be bygones."

He couldn't keep a straight face. First he grinned, then he began laughing. Donna looked at him long and hard, biting her lower lip.

"It's the same as mine, isn't it?" she said.

"I don't know. I didn't look."

"You really are a bastard."

"Trouble with you, Donna, you've got no sense of humor. Besides being frigid."

"You'd like to think that, wouldn't you? Just because you don't turn me on."

"Not really," Bell said calmly. "You know, it's interesting how stingy chicks are almost always frigid."

"I'm not stingy and I'm not frigid, buster! Nobody uses me, that's all. And don't you forget it."

"I'll tell you something, Donna, and it won't cost you a dime," Bell said quietly. "If you stopped being so damned suspicious and gave people the benefit of the doubt, maybe you'd find out everybody's not out to use you. Now, what say we call Sandifer?"

"All right," Donna said just as quietly. "He should be home from the gallery by now. He's staying near the phone until we get across."

She sat on the bed and put the call through the hotel switchboard. Bell drew up a chair.

"Hello, Sandy," said Donna. She listened a moment and said, "Monterrey."

Bell heard Sandifer's voice grow louder.

"I know we should have been across by now!" Donna snapped. "I know you've been beside yourself wondering what happened to us. It hasn't exactly been a picnic for us, either. We ran into a lot of trouble." She listened again and continued. "No, not that kind of trouble. We got ripped off."

She held the receiver away from her ear. Bell could hear Sandifer yelling.

"Will you shut up a minute and listen?" Donna demanded. "For what you're paying me I don't have to take that kind of guff. Sam got it back. He could have been killed but he got it back." The yelling ceased. "I'll fill you in on the details when we get back," Donna said. "And there was trouble with the trucks, too. First one got stuck. That's why they caught up with us. And then one broke down."

Sandifer's voice grew loud again.

"We got the best trucks we could, damn it!" Donna said angrily. "What did you expect, sending Sam down thinking everything was all arranged? And you ought to be damned pleased he thought to rent a spare or we wouldn't be this far."

Sandifer's voice lowered until Bell could no longer hear it but Donna grew even angrier.

"No, Sam is not telling me I'm lovely when I'm angry!" she cried.

"But you are, Donna," Bell said.

"Shut up!" Donna said. "No, Sandy, not you. We're getting a replacement in the morning. Sam says we'll be coming across first thing Monday. All right?"

She listened for a couple of minutes, saying only "Yes," or "I understand."

She put her hand over the mouthpiece and said, "Sandy says he'll have a trailer truck in Laredo Monday morning to pick up the goods at the broker's warehouse on the U.S. side."

"Let me talk to him," Bell said, taking the phone from her. "Hello, Mr. Sandifer."

"Donna told me how beautifully you came through when you ran into trouble," Sandifer said. "Thanks."

"That's what you're paying me for. About that

tractor and trailer. I want you to be sure and get the right kind of rig."

"Oh, it will be large enough to do the job. Don't worry about that, my boy."

"That's not the point. You've got to think about gross weight. They'll be putting us on the scales on the Texas side."

Bell explained that in Texas a loaded tractor and tandem trailer was not allowed a gross weight of more than 78,000 pounds. He would be hauling a load of about 48,000 pounds.

"That means our rig can't weigh more than thirty thousand pounds empty," Bell said. "The people renting it to you can tell you the weight. Get a ragtop trailer. That's one with a fabric cover instead of a solid top. It's lighter."

"I don't know about that," Sandifer said doubtfully. "I'd prefer something with a solid top."

"No," said Bell. "I won't risk coming in overweight. It won't matter about a cloth top. If they roll it back, all they'll see is a load of tile."

"I suppose you're right. By the way, how are you getting along with Donna?"

"If you mean what I think you mean, nowhere."

Sandifer chuckled. "All business, eh?" he said. "Too bad."

"What are you talking about?" Donna said.

Bell put his hand over the mouthpiece. "He wants to know if you're holding down expenses," he said.

"I'm counting on you, Sam," Sandifer said, serious again. "I don't think I have to remind you how much is at stake."

"No," said Bell. "You don't."

Sandifer meant a half million dollars. But Bell was not thinking about what Chato was worth in dollars. He was thinking about what Chato was worth in years if he was caught trying to bring him out of Mexico.

"Relax and enjoy yourself tonight," Sandifer said.

"You've earned it. I can imagine what a terribly difficult trip it's been. Good luck, Sam. And say good night to Donna for me."

Bell hung up.

"Tell me everything he said," Donna demanded.

"He said to tell you good night. And that we should relax and enjoy ourselves tonight," Bell added wryly. "I don't know about you, but I'm ready to drop in my tracks."

"I've never been so filthy and so tired and so famished in my life," Donna said. "I don't even know whether to eat or sleep after I shower."

"You better eat something," Bell said. "I intend to, if I can stay awake that long. Just one more thing. Alberto and the drivers may be back from dinner by now. Call his hotel and tell him where we are. And tell Juan, too. Here's the number."

When Bell got to his room he ordered a steak and bottled water before removing his sweaty clothing and getting into the shower. He washed in water as hot as he could stand, then followed with cold. The cold water picked him up a little but he still craved nothing more than sleep. The waiter knocked while he was slipping on clean shorts.

Bell wolfed down the steak, which was better than it looked, or maybe it was because he was so ravenous, and fell into bed. It was after 7 P.M. Saturday and he had not had a night's sleep since Wednesday. It seemed like longer.

Despite his fatigue he did not fall asleep immediately. The highway unreeled before him as if he were still on the road and the constant throb of the Volks engine echoed in his head. He heard the popping of the crippled Mack, and the tenderness in his hands brought back vividly the labors of transferring the great slab from which Chato's eyes peered blankly. And he remembered with savage pleasure his encounter with the pistoleros.

He felt pulled in two directions. He was caught up in the challenge and excitement of overcoming the unexpected problems of the haul and yet he could not delude himself into believing what he was doing was not wrong. If he did not get Chato across the border he knew he would feel a deep sense of failure, quite apart from the possibility of being caught and jailed, but if he succeeded he would take no pleasure in the accomplishment because he knew Chato belonged here in Mexico.

And he was not out of the woods yet. He still had the load to transfer without the people at the trucking company learning what was under the tarp. The sheer bulk of it would make them wonder. Sandifer had said the original plan was to ship the pieces out of Veracruz by boat as concrete garden fountains. He'd just drop it casually that's what it was. A fountain.

Only then did he surrender to sleep.

18

AGENTE Alvarado was back at the comandancia in Veracruz by a quarter to four. The chief was out. He had gone to meet someone at the airport. Alvarado was not displeased. It would permit him to get right to work without long explanations.

He got the telephone directory and began calling tile factories. It did not take long to find the one that had sold 20,000 kilograms of tiles in a single order that week. Alvarado left a note for the chief explaining he had returned from Tlacotalpán and had gone out to follow a lead he had picked up there. He did not bother to explain that the lead concerned only indirectly the murder he had been sent to investigate. He put the tile from Trevino's barn in a folder and got the photograph of Vargas out of the files. It was not an official police photograph. Vargas had been questioned on several occasions but never booked or mugged. He had a lot of influence. The photograph had been taken surreptitiously on a street in Mexico City but was a good, clear one.

The girl in the tile factory showroom went off to fetch the manager when Alvarado showed her his ID. The manager came out looking as if he were guilty of something but did not know what. His name was Flores.

"How may I help you, agente?" he said nervously.

Alvarado was accustomed to that sort of reaction. The mere presence of a federal policeman seemed to make everyone feel guilty.

"Only a routine matter, really," he said to put the man at ease. "I understand you sold a lot of tile last Thursday. In a single order."

"Yes, indeed. Four hundred square meters of mosaico bravo and two hundred of mosaico liso."

"You remember that without having to look at the records?" Alvarado said admiringly. "You have a fantastic memory, Señor Flores."

"It was an unusual order," Flores said modestly, more at ease now.

"All the same, to remember the exact details. I don't think I would have, and I'm trained for that sort of thing."

Alvarado took his tile out of the folder and laid it on the counter. "Was it a tile such as this?" he asked.

"Yes. That's our mosaico bravo. Very nice. And not dear. But why do you wish to know, if I may ask, agente?"

Alvarado showed him the photograph of Vargas. Flores studied it.

"Is this the man who purchased the tiles?" Alvarado said.

"No, agente."

Alvarado was dismayed. He had been so certain he had a solid link to Vargas at last. "Are you sure, Señor Flores?"

Alvarado wondered if Vargas had perhaps given Flores something to influence his memory.

"Quite sure, agente. I've never seen this man before. The tiles were bought by Americans."

"Americans?"

"Yes. A man and a woman." Flores made a gesture of admiration. "And such a woman. Young. Sexy."

"I see."

That certainly made a shambles of his carefully constructed theory. Unless Vargas had bought the tiles at another factory, one of those he had not bothered to call after he learned this one had made a big sale.

"Does anyone else in the city make such tiles?" he asked.

"Similar, but not precisely identical. This is ours. I would know it anywhere."

"You're certain of that, señor?"

"Positive, agente," Flores replied. "What is this all about, please?"

"I'm not at liberty to say, Señor Flores. But it does not involve you or your firm. Be at ease about that. Did the Americans say where the tiles were going?"

"Why, yes. To their construction company in Corpus Christi, Texas. For a motor hotel. They were partners, I think."

"And how were these tiles to be delivered to Corpus Christi?"

"They had their own trucks, agente. Four of them."

"What sort of trucks?"

"Ordinary trucks. Enclosed. I didn't pay much attention, I'm afraid."

"Why should you?" Alvarado said pleasantly. "How could you know someone would be asking questions about them. Do you know where they were hired?"

"No. Just a moment! I remember now. One of them had Auto Transportes Seguro on it."

"A Veracruz firm?"

"I believe so."

"Excellent," said Alvarado. "You are being very helpful. If you only knew how unobservant most people are. These Americans, do you have their names?"

"Only the woman's. Fairchild."

"I suppose he was Señor Fairchild, then."

"No," Flores said quickly. "They weren't married."

"How do you know that, señor?"

When Alvarado saw how the question embarrassed Flores he was sorry he asked it.

"Señorita Fairchild she, she wore no wedding ring, agente."

"Of course," said Alvarado. "The check for the tiles. Was it on a Mexican bank?"

"No check. She paid cash."

"Cash? Isn't that unusual?"

"Not under the circumstances, agente. I did not know them and would not have accepted a check. Unless it was on a Veracruz bank. But she paid cash without asking."

"Did she give her full name?"

"Anna Fairchild."

Alvarado noted he did not have to pause and think. The American woman obviously had made an impression on him.

"Will you describe her, if you please?" he said.

"Very pretty," said Flores.

"Could you be just a little more specific? Her height, weight, coloring, age, anything unusual in her appearance?"

"What has she done, agente?"

"Nothing, Señor Flores," Alvarado said reassuringly. "It is not Señorita Fairchild I am interested in at all. It is the man whose photograph I showed you. But, you see, I need the information for my report. Routine."

"I wouldn't want to make trouble for her," Flores said, relieved.

"The description, please."

"Perhaps one hundred sixty-five centimeters in height. I know because she was almost as tall as I am.

Her weight, that is more difficult. You see, she was slender and yet, on the other hand, full-bodied. If you know what I mean."

"I think I do. Would you say sixty kilos, perhaps?"

"Hardly as much as that. A little too thin, really."

"Full-bodied, I thought you said."

"Well, yes. But not fleshy, you understand. And perhaps twenty-four or twenty-five years of age."

"And her hair? Eyes? Features?"

"Very dark hair. Black, I think. And long. Her eyes were also dark. She was herself dark. But from the sun, I think. She looked very American. And her features . . . let me see. Very nice features."

"I'm sure. Tell me more about them."

"A straight nose, not too small. Her mouth . . . her lips were not thin like so many American women's."

"A nice mouth," Alvarado said helpfully.

"Oh, yes, a very nice mouth. And yes, her eyebrows. Thick, like a man's."

"A truly excellent description, Señor Flores. Now tell me about her companion."

"To tell the truth, agente, I do not remember him too well."

Naturally, Alvarado thought. Señor Flores had been unable to take his eyes off the woman. "With your excellent powers of observation you must remember something about him," he said. "It was only two days ago. Was he short or tall, thin or heavy, old or young, fair or dark?"

"Young. Only a few years older than the señorita. Taller than I, but not so tall as you. Broad-shouldered like you but not so . . . so thick. And fair, perhaps. Certainly not as dark as she. Also, yes, also he had a moustache. Like Pancho Villa's. That's why I remember it."

"You remember a good deal, Señor Flores. You're a keener observer than you realized. I wish everyone was so helpful. The invoice for tiles. Could I have a copy?"

"There were three. Do you wish them all?"

"If you please."

Flores had the girl look up the office copies and set her to making duplicates.

"Would you be kind enough to find the address of Auto Transportes Seguro?" Alvarado said.

"But of course."

He gave Alvarado the address and the copies of the invoices. The invoices were made out to Fairchild Builders and Developers, Corpus Christi, Texas.

Alvarado left the tile factory reasonably pleased with his progress but nevertheless disappointed that he still had no direct link between Vargas and the tiles. The Americans could be his U.S. contacts or, more likely, representatives of his U.S. contact. From Flores' description, they seemed too young to be principals in such a scheme.

The proprietor of Auto Transportes Seguro was on the point of leaving for the day when Alvarado got there. He went back into his office with Alvarado when Alvarado introduced himself. He gave Alvarado his card. His name was Felix Ochoa.

"How may I be of assistance, agente?" Ochoa asked warily.

"Two Americans, a man and a woman, hired four of your trucks Thursday. Is that not so?"

"Yes. Two were mine and two I hired elsewhere. Ochoa looked alarmed. "But why do you ask, agente? There has been an accident?"

"No, no accident. To tell the truth, it's not your trucks I'm interested in, Señor Ochoa. It's what they were carrying."

"Oh, that. Tiles, agente. What could be wrong with that? If I had thought anything was wrong, I certainly would not have rented the trucks to them."

"Of course. Put yourself at ease. If there is anything wrong, I'm certain you're not involved, sir."

"Thank you, agente. If not tiles, what did they put in my trucks?"

"I'm not at liberty to say at this time. Where did they say they were taking the tiles?"

"Matamoros. From there across the border, I would imagine. To Brownsville, Texas. But, as you know, no farther across the border than a warehouse. For transshipment by American trucks."

"For transshipment to where, señor?"

"She did not say."

"She?"

"Señorita Fairchild. Señor Kent did not speak Spanish."

Kent. He had the man's name now as well as the woman's. He asked Ochoa to describe them. Ochoa's description tallied with Flores', though that of the woman was not nearly as detailed. And Matamoros tied in with what Flores had told him. One would go through Matamoros and Brownsville to reach Corpus Christi.

Alvarado knew of no one in Corpus Christi who dealt in pre-Columbian art on a large scale. It was a new connection, perhaps. Unless they would be taking the head on to Houston. There were several dealers, large and small, in Houston. It was not unlikely, however, that they would wish to cross the border at Matamoros even though it was not on the direct route to Houston. They would understand that a shipment to Corpus Christi would arouse less interest than a shipment to Houston. He was obviously dealing with clever people. And daring people, as well. It required audacity to carry out such a scheme.

"At any time in their conversation with one another did they mention the name Vargas?" Alvarado said.

Ochoa shook his head.

Alvarado did not believe they would have. It was

just that there was no harm in asking. He was aware he had been negligent at the Buena Vista ferry. He had been so anxious to connect Vargas with the trucks he had not bothered to ask the boatman if there was anyone else accompanying them. But, at the time, he had no indication there might be. In fact, he did not know that now, either. The Americans had hired the trucks and purchased the tiles but it did not necessarily follow that they had gone to Tlacotalpán. It was more likely that they had gone to Matamoros or Browns-ville to wait for the shipment. When he got back to the comandancia he would get in touch with Immigration and learn if their tourist cards had been turned in, and where.

"How did they come here, Señor Ochoa? he asked. "In a taxi, I suppose."

"No. They had an automobile."

"An automobile? What kind?"

"A Volkswagen, agente."

"U.S. registry?"

"No, agente. Mexican. Veracruz, in fact."

"You are very observant, señor. If you only knew how unobservant most people are."

"When you trust strangers with four valuable trucks you must learn all about them you can," Ochoa said. "And of course I sent my nephew along to see that all went well."

"Your nephew, eh? And what is his name?"

"Villareal. Alberto Villareal. Look here, agente, if there is anything illegal going on, he knew nothing of it."

"Of course," Alvarado said soothingly. "And I didn't actually say anything illegal was going on, did I?"

"But I thought. . . . Then why do you come ask-ing questions?"

"I wouldn't worry about it if I were you. Have you heard from Villareal since he left Veracruz?"

"No. He was to call me only if there were problems on the road. He wasn't to be gone that long."

"When do you expect him back, then?"

"Tomorrow night, perhaps. But Monday, certainly. They were not to stop overnight. Driving straight through to Matamoros. Each truck with a relief driver."

"You said there were four trucks, correct?"

"Yes, agente. Four. With eight drivers."

The boatmen said there were four trucks together. One of them without a load. They obviously had hired a spare. They were shrewd, all right. But Vargas would not deal with any other kind.

"I'll want to speak with him when he returns. If it's tomorrow, he can call me at home. I'll give you the number."

He wrote the number down for Ochoa, also the comandancia telephone number.

"The trucks were hired to go directly to Matamoros?" he said. "No mention of a side trip of any kind?"

"No. Only Matamoros."

"They didn't say anything about going to Tlacotalpán?"

"Tlacotalpán? Why would they go to Tlacotalpán? That's in another direction entirely."

"Driving straight through to Matamoros, how long would it take?"

"About twenty hours, counting stops for servicing the trucks and for meals."

From Tlacotalpán, say twenty-one or twenty-two hours, Alvarado thought. They had crossed on the ferry after midnight, the boatman had said. Long after midnight. Say four o'clock Friday morning. They would have arrived in Matamoros by midnight. That meant they could have picked up their export papers the first thing this morning and be across the border already. But it was possible the cargo was still in a warehouse on the American side awaiting reloading. He would call American customs at Brownsville as soon as he got back to the comandancia. The last year or two the Americans had been most cooperative about such matters. He would have preferred recovering the contraband on this side, though. Here he was thinking about a preference, Alvarado thought wryly. He had none, if the truth were known. As shrewd as Vargas and his contact were, they would see to it that trucks would be waiting across the border to pick up the load and move it out without delay.

"Is there anything else, agente?" Ochoa asked, breaking into his reverie.

"Yes. Were the Americans to accompany the trucks to Matamoros?"

"That I do not know. Señorita Fairchild did not say."

"One thing more and I'm through bothering you."

"Oh, you are not bothering me, agente. I hope I did not give the impression you are bothering me. It is a pleasure to be of service."

"I want the registration numbers of the trucks."

"Of course."

Ochoa got the information out of a filing cabinet. Alvarado took down the make of the trucks as well as the registration numbers. There were two Dina diesels and two trucks of American manufacture, an International and a Mack. If only he'd had the information a dozen hours earlier.

Alvarado returned to the comandancia feeling let down. He had been very close, he was sure, and had only missed heading off the trucks by a matter of hours. The chief had returned from the airport and left again, leaving a message that he would talk to Alvarado Monday morning unless the matter was important enough for Alvarado to call him at home. That did not displease Alvarado. He would not read the chief in just yet. The chief was good about giving him his head and protecting him when he took the initiative without going through proper channels but the chief also was not one for going out and looking for work. He preferred waiting until orders came down from the attorney general's office.

Alvarado did not think he had enough yet to persuade the chief to give him a free rein. A pair of Americans had rented trucks and bought tiles under unusual circumstances, and the trucks might have picked up contraband in Tlacotalpán, and if they had, Vargas was probably implicated, but he had no proof a crime had been committed. And in any case, it was probably too late to do anything if it had been committed. There was the murder he had been sent to investigate, of course, which no doubt tied in with it all, but he had no proof of that, either.

Without the head as evidence, if that was what had been picked up at Trevino's farm, he really didn't have anything. Because there was no proof there had ever been a contraband Olmec head. But until he knew beyond a doubt the head was out of his grasp he was going to keep plugging away. At the very least he might be able to assemble enough solid facts to get the chief to assign him to the case officially.

First of all he phoned U.S. customs in Brownsville. It was no problem finding someone on duty who spoke Spanish. He asked that a check be run for a shipment of tiles entering by truck from Veracruz and consigned to Fairchild Builders and Developers in Corpus Christi. If the shipment had entered and had not yet been picked up, it should be given a thorough going over by U.S. customs agents. If it had been picked up, he would be wanting to discuss the matter further with them. The U.S. customs agent promised his cooperation.

Alvarado wondered if it was worth taking the time to drive back down to Buena Vista tonight and learn if the Americans had accompanied the trucks. No, there was too much that was more important left to be done here. Maybe he could find out more about the Americans' activities without leaving town at all. The Volkswagen had Veracruz plates, Ochoa had said. That meant it had been hired here. At the airport, most likely. If the car had been turned in before Friday morning the Americans could not very well have accompanied the trucks.

He phoned all the car rental agencies at the airport and asked if a Volkswagen had been rented to Americans earlier in the week. They all promised to check their records and call back. While he waited, he went to the Telex and typed out the registration numbers of the trucks and a request that the garita south of Matamoros be alerted to look out for them. All traffic heading north for the border had to check through the inspection station. It wasn't likely the trucks were still on the road but he did not want to overlook any possibility.

Alvarado said the trucks were suspected of carrying contraband and the loads should be broken down for inspection. He also requested that Immigration be contacted to see if tourist cards had been turned in by one Anna Fairchild and one Kent, male, first name unknown. If so, the Veracruz comandancia was to be notified where and when.

The phone rang while he was pondering his next move. It was National Car Rental. One of its automobiles, a Volkswagen, had been hired Wednesday afternoon by an American.

"What was the name?" Alvarado asked.

The car had been rented by a Donna Russell. Alvarado was not dismayed to learn it had not been Anna Fairchild or a Señor Kent. It would be too much of a coincidence if two American women had rented Volkswagens the same afternoon. There were not that many Americans in Veracruz this time of year. And Anna was much like Donna and both last names had two syllables. A typical mistake of an amateur inventing an alias. Perhaps Miss Fairchild-Russell was not as shrewd as he thought.

"Can you give me a description?" Alvarado said. "And tell me if she was accompanied by a man?"

The girl did not know. She had not been on duty at the time. Alvarado got the name and phone number of the girl who had been on duty Wednesday afternoon.

"One other thing," he said. "Has the car been returned?"

Not at the Veracruz office, he was informed. It was probably still under hire. Donna Russell had engaged it at the weekly rate, not the daily. Could he find out if it had been returned in some other city, Alvarado asked. Not until tomorrow. Alvarado gave the girl both his home number and the number at the comandancia.

It was quite possible the Americans had accompanied the trucks to Matamoros, else why had they taken the car for an entire week? They would hardly be sightseeing for a week in this part of Mexico in August.

"Could you call Matamoros and see if it's been turned in there?" he said. "And call me right back?"

Yes, that could be done.

While he was waiting for the call, he went to another desk and phoned the girl who had been on duty Wednesday afternoon. She did not want to talk with him. She would not believe he was actually with the Federal Judicial Police and not some prankster.

"Very well," Alvarado said gruffly. "Don't leave your house. I'll be over in a few minutes and show you my badge."

The phone on the other desk rang.

"I've got another call," he said. "You stay there. I'll call you back."

The call was from National. The Volkswagen had

not been returned in Matamoros. If the Americans were accompanying the trucks it meant they had not yet reached the border. Alvarado felt excitement for the first time. It might still be possible to intercept them. He got the number of the Matamoros office and called it. He gave instructions that if the automobile was returned the person or persons doing so should be kept there on one pretext or another and the Federal Judicial Police in Matamoros notified. As soon as he hung up he called the PJF comandancia in Matamoros and explained the situation.

"At the moment, this is not exactly official," he said, "So be very discreet if you don't mind. It may turn out to be nothing. Tell whoever turns the car in that it was reported stolen. Just long enough to detain them while you notify customs to be on the lookout for trucks with these registration numbers. If they don't find any contraband in the trucks no harm will have been done."

Alvarado did not expect more than routine cooperation from Matamoros. The agent there had been enthusiastic until he learned Alvarado was after art, not drugs. Narcotics were the primary concern of people at the border comandancias. It was hard to get them stirred up over anything else.

He called the girl from National again. She had had time to reconsider and was now frightened and cooperative. Yes, the woman had been accompanied by a man. She described both. She gave a better description of the man than the woman except for the clothing they had been wearing. That did not surprise Alvarado. Both descriptions tallied with those given by Flores at the tile factory and Ochoa at the trucking firm.

Alvarado believed the name given at the tile factory and Auto Transportes Seguro was the alias. Señorita Fairchild-Russell would have been obliged to show identification when she rented the car. And if she had used an alias, the man had probably done the same. He would have to check that out and get back to PJF headquarters in Mexico City on the Telex to give them new names to look for when the tourist cards were presented for exit.

If the Americans had flown in Wednesday and hired the trucks on Thursday, they doubtless had spent the night in Veracruz. Americans who could afford it, which meant most of them who came down here, stayed at either the Veracruz or the Diligencias. He tried the Veracruz first because it was the more expensive of the two. Donna Russell had spent Wednesday night there and checked out Thursday. Her registration card gave her home address as Houston, Texas. There was no record of an Anna Fairchild. Two American males had also arrived Wednesday. One had checked out Thursday and the other was still registered. Neither was named Kent or remotely fitted the description given Alvarado. Not even without the moustache, which Alvarado thought might have been false.

At the Gran Hotel Diligencias, only one American had checked in Wednesday. His name was Samuel Bell and he was also from Houston, Texas. The description tallied with that given by Flores, Ochoa and the girl from National, including the moustache.

"The room had been reserved in another name," the clerk volunteered. "Clark Kent."

There could be no doubt about it. The Americans who had hired the trucks and bought the tiles were named Samuel Bell and Donna Russell. They were from Houston, Texas, not Corpus Christi. Alvarado was sure of that because if they had given their correct names they would also have given their correct addresses. The use of false names later had no doubt been an afterthought. More amateurism. Perhaps they would not be so difficult to apprehend after all.

Alvarado got back on the Telex and amended the

names he wanted Immigration to look out for on tourist cards. Then he called the PJF agent in Matamoros and gave him the correct names, asking him to transmit the information to the garita south of the border zone. It was there that foreign visitors turned in their tourist cards on the way back to the border if they traveled by road. Now both Immigration and Treasury would be alerted at the garita, one to look for the Americans, the other for the trucks.

When he had done that, he leaned back in his chair and put his big feet up on the desk, satisfied. For the time being, at least, he had done everything possible. If the trucks had not crossed the border, and even if they had and their cargo was waiting for pickup, he would soon know whether or not his assumptions had been correct and, incidentally, how unhappy the chief would be with him for having started things rolling without authorization.

He was not at all sure that the fact the Volkswagen had not been turned in meant the trucks had not already crossed the border and their cargo was not well on the way to its final destination, wherever that might be. He would be surprised if it were Corpus Christi, Texas. And if there actually were a Fairchild Builders and Development there. He was also not sure the American couple was still in Mexico. All he knew was that their automobile had not been turned in in Matamoros. They could have driven to Mexico City or elsewhere and taken a plane to the United States instead of accompanying the trucks. If they had, he would not know before tomorrow, when National Auto Rental got back to him, unless the PJF in Mexico City heard something about tourist cards from Immigration before then.

He went over all he had done since returning to the office. Two things nagged at him. One of them he could not quite place. It had something to do with his calls to the Hotel Veracruz and the Gran Hotel

Diligencias. The other was, had he made it clear enough to the agent in Matamoros that the important thing was to prevent the trucks from getting out of Mexico without a thorough inspection, not the detention of the Americans? If the shipment got away he would have nothing concrete to prove he had valid reasons for going outside channels and acting on his own authority. He hoped the Matamoros agent handled things right if and when the Americans showed up. If he arrested them and the trucks had already slipped through, Tomás Alvarado might find himself in trouble with the PJF, the attorney general and Immigration, trouble that even his chief couldn't get him out of.

He thought about stopping by the Imperial for a beer before going home but he was too tired. And he hadn't called home to tell Sara for her and the girls to go ahead with dinner without him. If he knew Sara, they would still be waiting.

It was not until he stepped in the front door that he realized what it was that had been annoying him as a result of his phone calls to the hotels. It was the name under which the American Bell's room had been reserved at the Diligencias. Clark Kent. He had heard that name before.

As usual, Leonor and Yolanda rushed to him, Sara held her tongue about his not calling to say he would be late and Concepción asked if he had arrested anyone interesting.

"Concepción," he said, "who is Clark Kent?"

Concepción was the resident authority on things American. "Papa," she replied. "Don't you read the comic books? Clark Kent is Superman."

19

THE ringing of the phone awakened Bell at eight o'clock Sunday morning. It must have ringing for some time because he had been deep in sleep and was still groggy when he picked up the receiver.

"Yeah?" he said sleepily.

"Oh," said Donna's voice innocently. "Did I wake you?"

"Do you know what the hell time it is?"

"It's after eight. You've had twelve hours sleep. I've been up an hour waiting for you to call me."

"About what?"

"My suitcase."

"Christ, did you get me up just for that?"

"For twenty thousand dollars I expect twenty-four-hour service."

"Then I quit," Bell said.

He hung up, grinning.

The phone rang again immediately, as he knew it would.

"I'm sorry I woke you up," Donna said, not sounding sorry at all. "But as long as you're up, will you get my suitcase for me? Please?"

He couldn't recall Donna ever saying "please" to him before.

"All right," he said, relenting. "As soon as I've had some breakfast."

He ordered breakfast and went into the bathroom to shave and wash up. His hands were stiff and there was a tightness in muscles he hadn't even known he owned, but he felt ready for whatever the day might bring. By tomorrow night he'd be in his own apartment and ten thousand dollars better off. And he would have seen the last of Donna Russell. The thought did not distress him.

When he dressed after breakfast, he found it unexpectedly pleasurable to be in clean clothes again. He really couldn't blame Donna for being impatient for her suitcase and a change of clothing. He called her and told her he was on his way.

After he climbed into the Volks he realized how much he hated it and was sick of driving it. He'd be glad to be in a full-sized car again. And with the motor up front instead of in the rear and drumming in his ears like a tail-gater.

The Mack was gone when he reached the parking lot. There was no attendant on duty to tell him what had happened to it. Bell drove straight to the drivers' hotel, double-parked and hurried inside. There was no one behind the counter in the grubby little lobby. He pounded up the dark narrow stairs and knocked on Alberto's door. It was opened by Juan. Bell shoved past him and looked around. Both beds had been slept in but Alberto wasn't there.

"Where's Alberto?" He demanded.

Juan's gesture showed plainly that he did not know.

"Where did he go? When did he leave?"

Juan gave him a helpless look. Not understanding English, he did not know what Bell was talking about.

"Oh, Christ!" Bell exclaimed in frustration. "You better come with me."

He motioned for Juan to follow him, ran down the stairs. He drove back to the Jolet recklessly, left the

Volks in the loading zone and rushed Juan inside. He waited impatiently for the elevator. Juan looked confused.

"That's okay," Bell said. "Nobody's sore at you."

Juan understood the tone if not the words.

The elevator came at last. At Donna's floor Bell hustled Juan out while the doors were still opening.

"Is that you, Sam?" she called when he knocked.

"Yeah."

She opened the door. She was cloaked in a bedspread. She did not at first see Juan or notice Bell's expression.

"You didn't bring my suitcase," she said accusingly. Then she saw Juan.

"What is it, Sam?" she said. "Is something wrong?"

"Probably," he said, signaling Juan to follow him and brushing past Donna into the room.

Donna shut the door behind them and stood with her back against it, clutching the bedspread in place. Bell wished he had taken time to pick up her suitcase. She looked so forlorn, and ridiculous, with that thing draped around her.

"The Mack's gone," he said.

"Gone?" she echoed.

"And so is Alberto."

"He took it?"

"Looks that way. That's why I brought Juan back. Talk to him. Find out what he knows."

He motioned for Juan to sit down. Juan did, looking uncomfortable. It was because of Donna, Bell knew. He and Juan had an easy relationship, but like the other drivers even the bandit Juan was a little intimidated by the no-nonsense señorita. Donna sat down on the bed. The spread opened at the top, not much but enough to bare a tanned shoulder and below it the merest edge of white skin. Juan looked away quickly, embarrassed. Bell would have thought it funny if he had not had more serious things on his mind. Donna rearranged the bedspread and began questioning Juan.

Juan did not know where Alberto had gone, or when. He apologized for having failed Señor Kent. After returning from dinner Saturday night, he and Alberto had gone right to bed, both of them very tired from the trip. Juan had remained awake as long as he could, wanting to be sure that Alberto was truly sleeping. That had proved his undoing, for it had caused him to sleep late that morning. When he awoke, Alberto was not there. Juan assumed he had gone for a look at the trucks.

"Did he say anything last night Juan thinks might give us a clue to what he had in mind?" Bell said.

When Donna questioned him, Juan shook his head. He said something in which Bell heard his own name mentioned.

"No," Donna said, "but Alberto asked him what it was Señor Kent had hidden under the tarpaulin."

"Did you tell him?" Bell demanded, speaking directly to Juan.

Donna translated the question and Juan's answer.

"He told him a big piece of dressed stone. Juan says he understands that if you wanted the others to know what it was, you wouldn't have sent them out of the truck the other night. He's very bright, Sam. And loyal."

"I know. But Alberto's no fool, either. He knew damn well Juan was lying."

"Do you think he went to the police?" Donna said.

"Why would he do that? It's no skin off his nose if we're hauling contraband. Unless we got busted and they thought he was in on it. He knows it must be something worth a hell of a lot. And he wants his share."

"What good would one piece of the head do him?"

"He wouldn't know it's a piece of something. Not until he had time to look under the tiles."

"When he finds out, maybe he'll bring it back," Donna said hopefully.

"Not a chance. He'll know we'll pay plenty to get it back."

"What will we do?"

"What can we do? Wait for him to get in touch. You did get him last night and tell him where to reach me, didn't you?"

Donna nodded. He gave her the key to his room.

"I'll take Juan back to ride herd on the drivers," he said. "Get up to my room and stay by the phone. In case Alberto calls before I get back."

"Like this?" Donna said, looking down at the spread.

"Looks great on you. I'll be right back with your suitcase. This time I won't forget. I promise."

He had Donna tell Juan to take the drivers out to breakfast and then bring them back to the hotel and keep them there. Alberto hadn't left breakfast money. Bell gave Juan a fistful of pesos when he let him out at the hotel. On the way back to the Jolet he stopped at the parking lot and got Donna's suitcase out of the Dina. Those two chunks of Chato under the tiles and the two in the International wouldn't be worth a dime without the piece in the Mack, he thought ruefully. And when Alberto saw what he had under the tarp, he'd know it, too.

Donna was in his room, wearing not the bedspread but the same slacks and blue shirt with which she'd begun the long journey. She smelled gamy under the perfume she'd put on but Bell thought it would be needlessly cruel to mention the fact.

Alberto hadn't called.

"I didn't think he would," Bell said. "Not yet. Unless he took off in the middle of the night, and he was probably too beat to do that. He'll have to find a safe place to take a look under the tiles. May take him a while."

"You should have been a cop," Donna said. "Are you really sure he'll call?"

"Sure I'm sure. Once he realizes what he took isn't worth anything to anybody but us. He'll know the rest of Chato is in the other trucks."

"Why did he take that old truck instead of one of the others?" Donna said. "It makes all that noise and it'll hardly run."

"It's the only one he could be sure had something valuable in it. He must have figured the others did, too, but he couldn't be sure."

"Another thing. Didn't you take the keys to all the trucks last night?"

"He must have jumped the ignition wires. It's not hard to do. Ask any car thief."

Donna picked up her suitcase and headed for the door, stopped, and put it back down.

"I want to be here if he calls," she said.

She got a change of clothing out of the suitcase and went into the bathroom to shower. Bell lay down on the bed and closed his eyes. What if Alberto didn't call? What if he panicked when he saw what he had was worthless and just took off, leaving the Mack God knows where? Bell thought about Chato's blank-eyed, sullen baby face. When he realized he was thinking about Chato instead of Donna bare-assed and just a few feet away, he grinned up at the ceiling.

Donna came out of the bathroom wearing a short dress and low-heeled shoes with brass buckles. He grinned at her as he had at the ceiling.

"What are you so pleased with yourself about?" she demanded. "Are you enjoying the mess we're in?"

"You know what I was thinking about just now? While you were in there with everything hanging out?"

"I can imagine."

"Wrong. I was thinking about Chato. What were

you thinking about, with a handsome dude like me so handy?"

"I was thinking about what there was to belt you with if you came busting in. And if you think any different . . ."

"Don't worry. I don't. I finally got the message. And I'll tell you something, baby. You don't turn me on, either. Not any more."

"Trying a new approach now, is that it, Sam?"

"No. It's the truth."

She walked to the bed, leaned down and kissed him on the lips. Her mouth was softer than he had expected but he did not respond. She slid a cool hand inside his shirt. He reached for her. Donna stepped back out of range, smiling triumphantly.

"The hell I don't turn you on, buster," she said.

"I really thought you didn't," Bell said, unabashed. "So I was wrong. Anyhow, I thought it might give us something to do while we waited for Alberto. Tell me something, Donna. Don't you ever fool around?"

"I pick my spots. And this isn't one of them. All right?"

"Sure. One little thing, Donna. Next time you kiss a dude, try not to clench your teeth that way. Okay?"

The maid came in to make up the room. They stood around awkwardly while she did so, hoping Alberto would not pick this time to call. When the maid left, she said something that evoked a startled smile from Donna.

"What was that all about?" Bell asked.

"She wanted to know if we were on our honeymoon."

At noon they still had not heard from Alberto.

"Maybe he won't call at all," Donna said, worried.

"He will. He wouldn't pass up a chance to make some real money."

"How much do you think he'll want?"

"Depends on his idea of real money. He's got to know it's a big deal. Four trucks, eight drivers, all that tile." He smiled at Donna and added, "And the way you throw your money around."

"You hope he sticks me for plenty, don't you, Sam?"

"No. What do you care, anyhow? It's Sandifer's money. And he can sure as hell spare it."

"It's my money," Donna said grimly.

"Your money?"

"When we get back I'm telling Sandy I expect what's left in the kitty. Him making all that bread and only giving me five thousand. With all I've been through."

Bell couldn't really blame her. With Sandifer making a fortune, Vargas getting forty thousand and himself twenty thousand, Donna had a right to want a bigger piece of the action. He couldn't even blame Alberto all that much. Why shouldn't the poor slob pick up a few crumbs? If only the little bastard wasn't screwing everything up for them just when it was beginning to look like clear sailing the rest of the way.

Bell grew hungry and ordered lunch. Donna just picked nervously at her food. The tension of the wait was getting to her. Bell's appetite was not affected.

At two o'clock Bell said, "If he doesn't call soon we'll miss that truck we ordered. Call the man and tell him not to worry. We just got delayed a little."

After she did so she started pacing up and down the room, too agitated to sit still. Nor was Bell as calm as he pretended to be. What if Alberto wasn't holding the slab for ransom but had gone to the police? They could be on their way here right now. He did not express his doubts to Donna. She was upset enough as it was.

The phone rang at three thirty. They both made a grab for it. Bell was quicker.

"Hello," he said, his voice calm.

It was Juan.

He handed the phone to Donna.

"It's not him," he said.

Juan said it was past check-out time and the hotel man wanted another night's rent. Juan did not have that much money left after paying for breakfast and lunch and what should he do? Donna had him get the manager on the phone. She explained the men were working for her and she would be in later to pay for everything.

Twenty minutes later, the phone rang again. This time they looked at each other before Bell picked up the receiver. He did not say anything.

"Hello," said Alberto. "Señor Kent?"

Bell put his hand over the mouthpiece.

"It's him," he said.

"Thank God," said Donna.

"Why, hello, Alberto," Bell said pleasantly. "What can I do for you?"

There was a moment of stunned silence. Bell had thought so casual a response would knock Alberto off balance. Donna sat next to Bell on the bed, getting as close to the phone as she could. Her face was stiff with anxiety.

At last Alberto said, "I have something of yours, Señor Kent."

He sounded almost apologetic. An amateur thief, Bell thought. Just like me. Suddenly he did not despise Alberto quite as much as before.

"I know," Bell said.

"What's he saying?" Donna whispered urgently.

"Shut up," Bell said, covering the mouthpiece.

With Donna, he didn't have to hold it in. It helped to have an outlet for his anger.

"I think it must be very valuable," Alberto said.

"Exactly how valuable?" Bell replied.

He could hear Alberto draw in a breath.

"Twenty-five thousand pesos?" Alberto said hesitantly.

Bell laughed. "Where would I get that kind of money on a Sunday afternoon?" he demanded.

"How much does he want?" Donna whispered.

Bell whispered back, "Twenty-five thousand pesos," instead of snapping at her again. He couldn't blame her for being so anxious.

"I think the Señorita Fairchild has much money with her," Alberto said.

Under other circumstances Bell would have been amused. Alberto had Donna taped, all right.

"That's two thousand dollars," Donna was saying in his other ear. "Tell him five thousand pesos."

Bell did not think two thousand dollars was that exorbitant for so valuable an item but he didn't want to make things any easier for Alberto than he had to. Alberto had made them sweat, now it was his turn. And he did not doubt that Alberto was sweating, literally. Because Alberto, though dogged, was obviously scared.

"The Señorita Fairchild suggests five thousand pesos," he said.

"Oh," said Alberto. "She is there, also. Permit me to speak with her, please."

Alberto didn't know Donna after all, Bell thought.

"If you insist," he said. "But I think you should know you'll get a better deal from me than from her."

"If you please," Alberto said.

"He wants to talk to you," Bell said, handing Donna the phone.

"Alberto," Donna began, quietly enough. Then her voice rose. "You crummy little son of a bitch! When I tell certain people . . ."

Bell grabbed the phone out of her hand.

"Don't be stupid!" he snapped. "You want to scare him into running to the police?"

"I'm not going to let him get away with this!" she cried, still furious.

"The hell you're not," Bell said. "If you want Chato back in one piece."

He took his hand away from the mouthpiece and said, "You still there, Alberto?"

"Yes, Señor Kent. I am here."

He sounded even more subdued than before. Maybe Donna's outburst hadn't been so dumb after all.

"I'll make a deal with you, Alberto," he said. "You give us back the goods and we'll let bygones be bygones. Miss Fairchild won't say anything to her friends in Mexico."

"I must have something for my trouble," Alberto said doggedly, adding unconvincingly, "I am not afraid of Señorita Fairchild's friends."

"That's not being very smart," Bell said. "Tell you what, you return the goods and I'll see if I can't persuade Miss Fairchild to do something for you."

The poor slob couldn't blackmail any better than than he could drive a truck, Bell thought, wondering how Alberto had summoned up the courage to run off with the Mack. Probably on his ass and because of it desperate enough to try and grab off some of all that money he saw floating around. And carrying a grudge, too, because the Americans had started relying on Juan more than him. Bell wasn't mad at Alberto any more. He felt sorry for him.

"How much, Señor Kent?" Alberto said. "I have a wife and five children and life is very hard for us."

"Things are tough all over, Alberto," Bell said, but without real bite. "Let's say ten thousand pesos."

He knew he could have settled for the five thousand Donna had offered, but she wouldn't miss the extra five.

"Thank you, Señor Kent," said Alberto.

He sounded as if he meant it.

Bell turned to Donna and said, "He wanted twenty but I got him down to ten. Okay?"

Donna nodded, not too happy.

"She says it's a deal," Bell said. "What now?"

Alberto gave him the name and address of a café where he would meet them in half an hour. When Bell turned over the money he would tell them where to find the truck.

After he hung up, Bell had Donna call the trucker to tell him they would be coming for their hired truck at six thirty. There was no answer to her ring. The trucker obviously had given up on them and sent everybody home.

"Alberto really screwed us up," Donna said bitterly. "I'd like to string him up by his . . ."

"That wouldn't help," Bell interrupted. "Look, maybe you better stay here while I go to meet him. You start in on him, it could blow the whole deal."

Donna refused to be left behind. Bell agreed to take her along on condition she kept her mouth shut and let him do the talking. She knew he was right but it did not prevent her from being as angry with him as she was with Alberto. She did not speak a word to him all the way to the café.

The café was a greasy little place only fifteen minutes from the Jolet but in another world. There were no smart shops and bright signs. The street was littered and some of the buildings had broken windows pasted over with newspapers. On one side of the café was a tortillería with a line of somberly dressed women, some with dirty infants in their arms, waiting to buy tortillas. The tortillas came hot from a machine and the smell reminded Bell he was hungry. On the other side of the café was a cheap shoe store.

There was a plate glass window, unexpectedly clean, to one side of the café's cramped entrance. Behind it were little mounds of shredded lettuce, cheese, tomatoes and a bubbling pan of unidentifiable chunks of meat. The place was dark and narrow, with four plain wooden tables, each with four straight chairs. At the left was a counter and several stools with split plastic seats. Behind the counter, a man in a greasy apron presided over a grill. There were three people in the café, one of them Alberto. He sat by himself at the rearmost table, anxiously watching the entrance.

When he saw them he sprang to his feet, his expression placating. Donna started for him. Bell grabbed her elbow and said, "Remember, not a damn word out of you."

He walked ahead of her and said, "Hello, Alberto. Been waiting long?"

Alberto seemed confused by his affability. He cleared his throat and croaked, "No, señor."

They all sat down and Bell said, "Would anyone besides me like a beer?"

"Let's get on with it," Donna grated.

"I would like one," said Alberto. "Very much."

He looked parched. Bell knew if he handled him gently they would not have to worry about him making trouble later. Bell waited until the beers were on the table before getting down to business. He filled his glass, motioned for Alberto to do the same, and raised it in toast.

"Here's to crime," he said.

Alberto didn't say anything. He put his glass to his lips and drained it before setting it down. Donna's face was bleak with impatience and fury but she kept her mouth shut.

"Well, Alberto," Bell said. "Where is it?"

"First, the money," Alberto replied, not looking at him.

"You heard the man," Bell said to Donna.

"I'm not handing any money over until I know where the truck is," Donna said grimly.

"Give it to him," Bell said. "He's not going anywhere."

Reluctantly, Donna opened her purse beneath the

table, out of sight, and passed the wad of bills to Alberto, still under the table. Alberto, sweating, started to stuff it in his pocket.

"Count it," Bell ordered. "Let's keep things business-like."

Alberto counted the bills so hurriedly Bell knew he was not really aware of what he was doing. He looked scared enough to faint.

"Now," said Bell. "Where's the truck?"

It was in a parking lot not half a dozen blocks from the hotel where Alberto and the other drivers had spent the night. Bell wanted to kick himself. If he had sent the drivers scouting around the neighborhood they would have found the truck and saved a lot of time and aggravation, not to mention Donna's eight hundred dollars.

Alberto had a parking check, which he handed over. He started to get up. Bell reached across the table and pushed a finger against his breastbone.

"Not so fast, Alberto," he said. "Now we find out if it's really where you say it is."

Alberto sat back down.

"Ask the man if he's got a phone," Bell told Donna.

The café did not have a phone but there was one next door in the tortillería.

"Call Juan and tell him to get over to the parking lot," Bell said. "Tell him to see if the truck's there. And to make sure everything's still in it. Then get back to the hotel and call you."

"You think I would do such a thing?" Alberto said, aggrieved, showing the most spirit he had yet displayed.

"I've heard everything," Donna said.

"Just good business, Alberto," said Bell. "Like counting the money."

Donna went next door to make the call. Alberto put his hands on the table and stared at them. They were

trembling. He put them in his lap and continued looking at them.

Donna came back and reported Juan was on his way
to the parking lot.

"I wish you'd bought some tortillas while you were
there," Bell said. "The smell's driving me crazy."

"You're already crazy," Donna said. "Being buddy-
buddy with this."

She nodded at Alberto. Alberto looked up apologetically and swiftly down again.

"Why don't we have a bite while we're waiting
for Juan to call back?" Bell said.

"Here?" Donna demanded.

"How about you, Alberto?" Bell said.

"Thank you very much, Señor Kent. But I am not
hungry."

He looked to Bell as if it might be a while before he
recovered his appetite.

Bell caught the counterman's eye, held up two fingers and said, "Dos tacos." He picked up his empty
beer bottle and said, "Una más. Another one for you,
Alberto?"

"Thank you very much," Alberto said gratefully.

"I'll have one, too," said Donna.

She watched in distaste while Bell ate the dripping
tacos filled with meat from the bubbling pan in the
window. When she left to wait for Juan's call, Bell
told her to make sure Juan had enough money for the
men's dinner. Alberto went back to his careful scrutiny
of the hands in his lap.

"You won't say anything to anybody, right?" Bell
said. "Not Ochoa or anybody."

"Oh, no, señor."

"And you'll tell him you left somebody with the
Mack to bring it back when it's fixed. Okay?"

"Yes. You will do that, will you not, señor? My
uncle, he is responsible for it."

"Don't worry. I'll take care of it."

Donna returned, looking immensely relieved.

"Everything's all right," she said.

"Well, then," Bell said, getting up. "Remember, Alberto. Not a word to a soul. You're in this up to your tail now, you know."

"Yes, señor," said Alberto.

They were almost back to the Jolet before Donna broke her stony silence. "Why did you have to handle him with kid gloves like that?" she demanded.

"You want him to go away mad?" Bell replied. "And wanting to get even when he gets back home and has time to think things over?"

"You're a scheming bastard, aren't you, Sam?" Donna said grudgingly.

"And lovable," Bell said.

"No," said Donna, unsmiling. "Definitely not lovable."

20

Aﬀer Mass Sunday morning, Alvarado returned
home with his family only long enough to get out of
his coat and tie and into his usual guayabera shirt before
going to the comandancia. There was nothing on the
Telex in answer to his queries of Saturday evening. He
had not really expected anything so soon. He typed
out a message on the Telex notifying Mexico City he
was in the office and waiting, then began making
phone calls.

The first was to the garita south of Matamoros.
The tourist cards of Donna Russell and Samuel Bell
had not yet been turned in. This neither encouraged
or discouraged Alvarado. Though it could signify that
neither the Americans nor the trucks had reached
Matamoros yet, it could also mean, as he had realized
the night before, that the Americans had flown back
to the United States instead of accompanying the
trucks. That he would not know until PJF headquarters in Mexico City had learned from Immigration if
the tourist cards had been surrendered elsewhere.

Next he phoned U.S. Customs in Brownsville to see
if any truckloads of tiles from Veracruz had entered.
The man he had spoken with the night before was,
of course, off duty now but had left word with his
relief. There had been no tiles from Veracruz or any-

where else. That did encourage Alvarado. For some reason or another the tiles had not yet left the country. Trouble on the highway, perhaps. A truck breakdown or delays because of road repair work. There was a lot of that this time of year because of the heavy rains. The delays themselves would not be enough to make the trucks lose a whole day but it could make them give up the idea of driving straight through.

Was it possible, Alvarado wondered, that the trucks had been apprehended at one of the inspection stations along the route and higher authority had not yet been informed? He got off a message to Mexico City asking that a check be run of inspection stations between Tampico and Matamoros.

He phoned home to see if National Auto Rental had tried to reach him there. The phone rang only once before Concepción answered. She sounded disappointed when she realized it was her father.

"You were expecting someone else?" Alvarado demanded.

"Gallinita," said Concepción. "I talked to her after Mass, remember? She was to call me if she didn't have to go out with her family today."

"Does Gallinita wear trousers now?" Alvarado said. "Do you think I didn't see the note that boy gave you? I wouldn't have to be a policeman not to miss that."

"Oh, Papá. That was about schoolwork."

"He was much too old to be at your grade level. A grown man."

"A grown man! Luis is only eighteen."

"So that's his name. Luis. Luis who?"

"Herrera, Papá. Don't pretend you don't know him. Señor Herrera's middle son."

"That overgrown lout was little Luis Herrera? Luis Herrera is no taller than you."

"That was last year, Papá. I don't suppose you've noticed him. He's grown."

"He certainly has. Let me talk to your mother."

When Sara came to the phone Alvarado told her if Concepción said she was going somewhere with Gallinita to be sure Gallinita came to the house to meet her.

"That Herrera boy is after her," he said.

"Luis Herrera is a very nice boy," Sara said timidly.

"Are you conspiring with Concepción behind my back?" Alvarado demanded.

"No, Tomás," Sara said quickly. "I won't let Concepción leave unless Rosa comes for her in person."

"Rosa? Who is Rosa? I said Gallinita."

"Rosa Castillo," said Sara. "Gallinita. That's what everyone calls Rosa."

"Oh. It's been so long since I heard her real name I forgot."

National Car Rental had not called. Alvarado hung up, thinking some agent he was. He carried hundreds of aliases in his head but couldn't remember the name of his daughter's best friend. Or how quickly little boys grow up into big boys. Unfortunately, he did not know as much about that as he would have liked, never having watched a little son of his own grow into a big one.

It might still be too early to call National Auto Rental. He would give them a little longer to check on the Volkswagen. To kill time he went over to the Imperial and drank coffee while he watched the pigeons for half an hour. When he got back to the comandancia there was still nothing on the Telex for him. He phoned National Auto Rental. As far as they knew, the Volkswagen had not yet been turned in.

Alvarado finished some reports he had put off working on. He sat down at the Telex but didn't send anything. They wouldn't be too pleased at headquarters if he bombarded them with follow-up messages. And if he didn't come up with anything, the chief would have that much more trouble trying to explain why one of his agents was permitted to assume such authority. It was after one and he was getting hungry. He phoned Sara and told her to bring his Sunday dinner to the comandancia. He didn't want to stray too far from the Telex and the telephones.

Sara brought his lunch in a straw hamper. It had started to cool despite the cloths in which she had wrapped it. He should have told her to come in a taxi instead of taking the streetcar, he thought. But Sara's chicken was as good cold as hot.

"Concepción and Gallinita are going to see a film this afternoon," Sara said. "I told her she could if she took Leonor and Yolanda along. Is that all right? It's the cinema where that friend of yours will admit them without charge."

"That was very wise, Sara," Alvarado said.

He meant about insisting that the girls went along. It was to be expected that Sara would be wise about saving money.

"She didn't want to," Sara said. "I told her if she objected to ask her father. That quieted her."

Sara waited until he had finished eating so she could take the dishes back. She was scarcely out the door when the Telex began clacking. There was a message for Alvarado. The tourist cards of Donna Russell and Samuel Bell had not been surrendered nor had any trucks loaded with tiles been detained at an inspection station. So, unless the Americans had left Mexico in the past few hours, they were still in the country. That still did not mean they were with the trucks. Or that the trucks were still in Mexico. The Americans could have waited somewhere in Mexico by prearrangement for a message informing them the trucks were safely across the border. Alvarado thought not, however. If they had not accompanied the trucks it would be far wiser to wait for them on the United States side. Then, if the contraband was detected they would not be trapped on the wrong side of the border. In any case, there wasn't anything he could do now but wait. He put his feet up on the desk and dozed.

The ringing of the telephone woke him up. Alvarado came awake immediately, his mind alert, and reached for the phone almost as soon as his eyes opened. It was Ochoa, of Auto Transportes Seguro, calling from home.

One of his drivers, Xavier Reyes, who had gone off with the Americans, had returned to Veracruz Saturday night but had only just now called to tell him so.

"His truck went into a culvert just this side of Linares," Ochoa said. "It is being repaired there now."

"Linares?" Alvarado said. "Hold on a minute."

He got up and looked at the wall map. Linares was not on the road to Matamoros. It was west of that, between Ciudad Victoria and Monterrey. Alvarado was furious with himself. The Americans had never intended crossing at Matamoros. They had gone instead to Nuevo Laredo. The shipment was in the United States by now and he had made a fool of himself. It had not entered his mind that the Americans would be clever enough to give a false destination to both Ochoa and Flores, the tile factory manager. He snatched up the phone.

"When did this occur?" he demanded angrily.

"Saturday morning," Ochoa replied, shaken. "Agente, do not be angry with me. I only learned of it this moment. And only think of the position I am in. This truck I hired for the Americans is now in Linares for no one knows how long and at what expense for repairs. Although Reyes did say the Americans promised to . . ."

Alvarado interrupted his babbling.

"Get hold of Reyes and send him here right away," he said. "Tell him to take a taxi."

He hung up without waiting for an answer and immediately called the Nuevo Laredo border station. He waited, interminably it seemed, while the records were checked for a shipment of tiles from Veracruz. No tiles had been passed either Saturday or that morning. Alvarado breathed a little easier. The contraband might still be in Mexico. Unless, of course, the Americans had spread around mordida and the tiles had been permitted to pass as something else.

In his haste he had neglected to ask Ochoa if Reyes had mentioned the Americans being with the trucks. But they must have been. As far as Linares, at any rate. Because Ochoa was telling him the Americans had promised to pay for repairing the truck when he cut Ochoa off.

Alvarado phoned the inspector at the garita south of Nuevo Laredo. No tourist cards had been turned in by Donna Russell or Samuel Bell. He gave the inspector the registration numbers of the trucks—all four of them because he had neglected to ask Ochoa which truck was still in Linares—and told him if the Americans should come through with them the trucks and the Americans were to be detained and the loads inspected piece by piece. If the trucks arrived without the Americans, their loads were still to be examined. But if the Americans appeared without the trucks they were to be permitted to continue and the Federal Judicial Police in Nuevo Laredo notified they were on their way.

Then he phoned the Nuevo Laredo PJF and explained the situation. He asked that if the garita reported the Americans had gone through, the Nuevo Laredo comandancia assign an agent to tail them and apprehend them if and when they rendezvoused with the trucks. The agent with whom he spoke did not sound particularly enthusiastic about it.

"Don't you know we have our hands full with the drug traffic?" he demanded. "I'll call the customs people at the border for you. They'll take care of it when your suspects try to cross."

Alvarado explained that he had already alerted Customs and Immigration at the border. He just did not want to leave anything to chance. He wanted to apprehend the suspects with the trucks. If they were apprehended separately it would not be as simple for the attorney general to make a case against them. The Nuevo Laredo agent said it might be better for everyone if the PJF could detail an agent from some less active office that could spare one.

Alvarado thought that not too bad an idea. He would prefer being in on the kill himself. It was about time, past time, if the truth were known, to let his chief know what he was up to. He had already far exceeded his authority, but if he could convince the chief he was on to something solid, the chief would overlook it and send him to Nuevo Laredo instead of asking Mexico City to provide an agent.

Out of curiosity, he phoned the airport. There was no way he could be in Nuevo Laredo before Monday afternoon. The connection to Nuevo Laredo was through Mexico City. The next flight to Nuevo Laredo left Mexico City at 11:45 A.M. Monday, with stops at Tampico and Monterrey. It landed in Nuevo Laredo at 2:15 P.M. And by 2:15 P.M. it could be all over. Alvarado was a little puzzled that it was not over already. Even with delays the trucks should have attempted to cross the border by now. He wondered if they had somehow managed to slip through despite his precautions.

Xavier Reyes arrived while Alvarado was still wondering if the chief might authorize a trip to Nuevo Laredo if nothing had broken by Monday morning. The 8:10 A.M. flight from Veracruz to Mexico City got there at nine, ample time to make connections with the plane to Nuevo Laredo. The round-trip fare was more than seven hundred pesos. The chief wouldn't like that much.

Reyes was rattled. He obviously had never had anything to do with the Federal Judicial Police before and did not know what to expect.

"Don't be nervous," Alvarado said. "You're not in trouble, friend. I deeply appreciate your coming in to help us out."

He could get a lot more, and more quickly, out of a calm man than a nervous one, unless, of course, it was a suspect he was questioning. And Reyes was not a suspect.

"I am most happy to help, agente," Reyes said, trying to look as if he really were.

"Were the two Americans both with the trucks in Linares yesterday?" Alvarado said without preamble.

"I think so, agente."

"You think so? Don't you know?"

Reyes explained that after the truck stuck, Señor Kent had taken him and his relief driver into Linares and left them there before dawn.

"Señor Ochoa's nephew, Alberto Villareal, said we were to remain there until the afternoon before sending somebody for the truck," he said. "And if it required repairs, to wait until it was done and bring it back to Veracruz."

Villareal would have been acting on instructions from the Americans, Alvarado believed. They could only have wanted Reyes to wait until afternoon because they wanted to delay Ochoa's finding out it hadn't been on the way to Matamoros.

"Did Villareal say where the trucks were going?" Alvarado said.

"Yes, agente. Before we left Veracruz. Matamoros. But we went first to Tlacotalpán for the night."

"That's valuable information you're giving me," Alvarado said to encourage him. "Didn't you wonder what you were doing at Linares if you were going to Matamoros?"

"No, agente. Why should I? I drove where they told me to."

"Didn't Villareal have anything to say about it?"

"No, agente."

Maybe Villareal was working with them. If so, he would be a valuable witness for the attorney general later on. They could put a lot of pressure on him to get the facts.

"Which truck was it they left in Linares?" he asked.

"One of the Dina diesels. The older one."

"It was carrying tiles?"

"Yes, agente."

"And nothing else?"

"I don't understand."

"They didn't pick up anything in Tlacotalpán?"

"I don't know. When they drove off with the trucks there, all of us except Juan Luna remained with the empty truck to sleep."

"Juan Luna? Who is this Luna?"

"One of the drivers. Agente, may I ask what is your interest in the matter?"

"They were, we believe they were, transporting contraband beneath the tiles."

"Contraband, agente? What kind of contraband?"

"It isn't necessary for you to know that, friend. Tell me, did they merely drive you to Linares and leave you there? Why would they want to do that?"

"Oh, no, agente. First they had us load the air compressor on the empty truck and then took us to help with the fence posts."

"Fence posts?"

"Yes, agente. In the middle of the night they bought fence posts. And ropes, pinchbars and a canvas covering."

"Did they say what they wanted with such things?"

"No. Not to me. Señor Kent and Villareal spoke always in English. I am sorry."

"That's all right," Alvarado said.

He would have to puzzle it out for himself. Pinchbars, towing cables, ropes and fence posts would be useful in freeing the truck, of course. But if the Americans intended freeing the truck, why would they leave its drivers in Linares? And why order them to drive it back to Veracruz? No, all those things were intended to assist them in transferring the contraband and the tiles from the disabled truck to the spare one. In exactly what manner he could not imagine. But in any case, without a lifting device of some sort they would have had a long and difficult time of it transferring a portion of the head unless it had been cut up into many small pieces. He doubted that it had been. The marks and the hoist he had seen in Trevino's barn indicated very heavy objects had been moved.

"So you didn't wait until afternoon to get the truck?" he said. "You went right out and pulled it free?"

As soon as he said that he realized it could not be so. If Reyes had left Linares in the truck Saturday morning he could not have reached Veracruz by Saturday afternoon. And Ochoa had said the truck needed repairs.

"You didn't wait," he said, answering his own questions.

"No, agente. I left my relief driver. It was necessary for me to return to Veracruz as soon as possible. There was no reason for two of us to remain in Linares."

"Why was it necessary?"

Maybe Reyes knew more about what was going on than he was admitting. He could have returned with information for someone. Ochoa, perhaps. Was Ochoa involved, too?

"My wife was expecting a baby, agente."

"Oh. Has she had it, by the way?"

Reyes smiled broadly.

"Yes, agente," he said. "Last night. A fat boy."

Alvarado sighed.

"Congratulations," he said.

He thanked Reyes for being so helpful and let him go back to his new son. After Reyes left, Alvarado sat inactive at his desk for a couple of minutes, depressed. Why did everyone have sons except him? He sat up straight, slapped the desk with the flat of both hands and phoned the Nuevo Laredo border station and the garita south of town to give them the number of the truck to be removed from their lists of suspect vehicles.

And now there was but one call left to make. To his chief. Alvarado did not relish making it. He had been doing a lot of things on his own without informing the chief. And the chief wasn't going to like it. Well, he had done things the chief didn't like in the past and usually it ended with the chief getting commendations from above. Which Alvarado would be the first to admit the chief passed along to him.

The chief did not wait to hear him out.

"I'm coming in," he said. "You be there, understand?"

He sounded angry. That did not disturb Alvarado particularly. It wasn't the first time he had upset the chief. And he knew it was because he hadn't kept the chief informed from the beginning. He'd had good reason for that, which the chief understood as well as he. With only what he'd had when he returned from Tlacotalpán yesterday, the chief very likely would have told him not to waste time chasing shadows and given him some more pressing assignment. Now, at least, he had accumulated enough information to keep the investigation alive whether he or other agents followed through.

When the chief arrived he listened to Alvarado's recital of events with his usual pretense of patience.

When Alvarado finished, the chief rose and took a few angry turns around the office. He stopped squarely in front of Alvarado.

"So you took it on yourself to contact the Capital?" he demanded.

Alvarado did not answer. He knew an answer was neither expected nor, at the moment, welcome. The chief had to be given time to calm himself down in his own way.

"And you took it upon yourself to bring in other field offices of the PJF, Customs, Treasury, Immigration? Tell me, how did you miss the attorney general himself?"

It was, Alvarado knew, another rhetorical question.

"Well, Alvarado," the chief demanded. "What do you have to say for yourself?"

Alvarado understood this was a question requiring an answer. "Nothing, chief," he said.

"You can sit down now, agente," the chief said.

He sat down himself and took out a cigarette. He waited a moment to see if Alvarado would produce a match and, when Alvarado did not, smiled faintly and lit it.

"What makes you think this Olmec head, if that's what it is . . . this contraband, isn't already across the border?" he demanded. "If it was at Linares before dawn yesterday, it could have already crossed before you started looking for it yesterday evening."

"Nuevo Laredo customs didn't pass any tiles from Veracruz yesterday," Alvarado replied.

"Don't you think the Americans would be shrewd enough to alter the point of origin?"

"Nuevo Laredo didn't pass tiles from anywhere," Alvarado said calmly. "I asked about that."

"Why do you suppose it hasn't reached Nuevo Laredo yet?" the chief said.

His tone was quite different now, no longer challenging.

"More trouble on the road, maybe. The truck they took along for the spare wasn't much, I understand. Maybe it took them all day to change the load from the other truck. Maybe they had to wait until they could arrange for trucks to be waiting on the American side to pick up the cargo. Or maybe . . ."

"That's enough maybes," the chief said. "I suppose you'd like to get up to Nuevo Laredo yourself, wouldn't you? Afraid customs and the PJF comandancia there don't know their jobs."

"Well, another man wouldn't hurt," Alvarado said. "One already familiar with all phases of the investigation."

"How soon could you get up there? *If* I were to be foolish enough to send you."

"Not until early tomorrow afternoon," Alvarado admitted.

"So you've already looked into that, too, agente? I should have known. By tomorrow afternoon the Americans should be in the bag. What would they need you for?"

"But suppose they aren't? And if they are, I would be there to question them on the spot. They might give us Vargas if I can get at them while they're still in shock. But I'm sure you've already thought of that yourself, chief."

"As a matter of fact, I haven't, Alvarado. I'd be very pleased to get Vargas. And so would the attorney general."

Alvarado knew then he was going to Nuevo Laredo. But the chief, as usual, did not give him his triumph too quickly. He studied his cigarette thoughtfully, as if still trying to make up his mind.

"You understand, of course," he said at last, "the Americans are more important to me than the contraband. I want Vargas, not the head. If I wish to see an Olmec head I can go to Santiago Tuxtla."

"Of course, chief," said Alvarado. "Vargas is the game we want."

But despite the chief's opinion, he would need the head as well as the Americans. Without the contraband as evidence he'd have nothing much against them. And, personally, he wanted the head. He wanted it almost as much as he wanted Vargas. The Olmec head was part of his heritage. He was not going to permit it to become the private toy of some American millionaire.

21

Donna said she was hungry but tired of Mexican cookery. She wanted a restaurant with a continental menu. Bell suggested the Luisiana on the Plaza Hidalgo, only a couple of blocks from the Hotel Ambassador. He was not too hungry himself, having eaten the two tacos, which he could still taste now and then, but he thought Donna was entitled to a good meal after all she had been through. She was still uptight from the incident in his room and the business with Alberto. It must be tough not having a sense of humor.

Bell made himself agreeable by ordering the duck with orange, as she did, and sharing a bottle of wine. And not needling her. When she seemed sufficiently receptive, he said, "Look, Donna, why don't we stop acting like a couple of kids? You don't like me, okay. And you're not exactly the chick I'd like to be marooned with on a desert island. But let's try to get along one more day. Once we get Chato across, everybody'll love everybody."

"You're absolutely right," Donna said.

They got along well enough after that. When they went to Donna's room to phone Juan, Bell was careful not to make any suggestions that might shatter their delicate truce.

He had Donna ask Juan if he was having any problems with the men, who had been caged up all day. Juan was not.

"Didn't think he would," Bell said. "They wouldn't mess around with the bandit. Ask him if they've got enough money among 'em for breakfast in the morning."

The resourceful Juan said they did not, but since the señorita had spoken with the manager of the hotel the manager had become most agreeable and Juan would borrow the money from him.

"Good," said Bell. "Tell him to have 'em ready early so we can get started as soon as we have a truck."

After Donna hung up, he said, "We better call Sandifer and let him know we won't cross in the morning. Or he'll have a hemorrhage when we don't show."

"When will we get there, do you think?" Donna asked thoughtfully.

"Tomorrow afternoon, if everything clicks. If not, it could be the morning after. Better tell him that possibility, too."

Donna picked up the phone, then put it down again.

"I just remembered," she said. "Sandy's never in on Sunday evenings. I'll have to call him later tonight."

"Okay. Just don't forget."

They agreed to have breakfast in Donna's room at seven so they could get an early start finding a truck. In his room, Bell relaxed in the shower, thinking about tomorrow. When they'd lined up a truck, he'd take the Mack to the building they had parked behind Saturday and put off the tiles. He'd pick them up again when the Chato section was transferred. Mono, Alberto's relief man, could stay in Monterrey with the Mack, get it repaired and drive it back to Veracruz. It wouldn't be fair to Ochoa to leave his trucks strung out over half of Mexico.

He wondered if the number two Dina had been

driveable when they finally got it unstuck. If it had been, Xavier and Juan Two would be back in Veracruz by now. And Ochoa would be wondering what it had been doing outside of Linares when it was supposed to be going to Matamoros. And if Ochoa was wondering, would he do anything about it? That was still on Bell's mind when he went to sleep.

Donna was dressed when he arrived at her room at ten to seven. She had already ordered his breakfast.

"Ham and eggs, toast and coffee," she said. "Did I guess right?"

"Sure did. Thanks."

There was a noticeable lessening of tension between them. Maybe it had been as much his fault as hers, Bell thought.

"I called the truck place," she said. "Nobody's there yet."

"Keep trying. What about Sandifer?"

"Sandy? I got him last night. About eleven."

"How'd he take the delay?"

"He understood. He said you'd handled Alberto exactly right."

Donna called the trucker again while they were eating breakfast. She finally reached someone about seven thirty but it was not the owner. She left her name and telephone number.

"Do you think he'll return my call?" Donna said. "After the way we stood him up yesterday?"

"If he doesn't call back by eight, try him again. And tell him we'll pay for his time yesterday. That should sweeten him up."

"That's a very good idea," Donna said.

Bell had not expected her to take his suggestion so readily. She'd been a tough enough bargainer when the money was coming out of Sandifer's pocket. Now, if she kept to her plan about keeping the bag money, it was coming out of hers.

The trucker returned Donna's call. Bell could tell

from her tone she was being very placating. He had not believed she could be. She put her hand over the mouthpiece and said, "He's all peaches and cream now. I promised him fifteen pesos an hour for the six men he claims we kept waiting all day."

"The truck," Bell said. "How about our truck?"

"He's getting to that."

Her face grew doubtful as she listened.

"No truck?" Bell demanded.

"Not the one he had yesterday. I wish you could talk to him."

"So do I. What's he got now?"

"A Dina seven sixty-one. Whatever that is. With a Remosa trailer."

"It's a tractor, then. A tractor-trailer rig. Ask him if it'll handle twenty-four tons."

"More, he says," Donna said.

"Tell him we'll take it."

"What do we want with a truck that big?"

"Tell him," Bell insisted. "I've got an idea."

Donna hired the rig. She promised to come for it later in the morning without fail.

"What's your idea?" she said after she hung up.

"We'll put all five pieces in it. Then we won't have to fool with three trucks and five drivers."

"How?" Donna demanded. "They'll see everything when we change the sections to the new truck."

"No," Bell said. "This is what we'll do."

He would buy more tarps to cover the sections in the Dina and the International. They could unload the tiles behind the building that had sheltered them Saturday. He and Juan would take off the last few after they sent the drivers out of the trucks and then lash the tarps over the sections. The drivers still wouldn't know what they'd been hauling and the trucker wouldn't know what his men were handling when they transferred the slabs at the loading dock.

"I'll tell him they're concrete garden fountains," Bell explained. "Now, before we get moving, I want you to call that brick factory we passed yesterday."

"Why, for heaven's sake?" Donna said.

"I want you to buy some bricks."

"Bricks?"

"Maybe your bathroom'll look better in Mexican brick than mosaico bravo." Before she could reply he explained the real reason. "If the number two Dina was driveable, Xavier and Juan Two are back in Veracruz by now. And Ochoa knows we didn't go to Matamoros like we said. For all he knows, we're ripping off his trucks. He'll raise a howl."

"You told Alberto you'd have the Mack fixed and send it back," Donna said. "Alberto'll tell him he can trust us."

"I don't think Alberto'll be in any hurry to check in with Ochoa. He'll want to stash his loot first. Anyhow, I doubt if he's back home yet. He probably hopped a bus. Poor folks with five kids to feed don't take planes. Take him a day and a half to make it by bus."

"You think of everything, don't you, Sam? But I still don't know what we want with bricks."

"I want to change loads. New truck, new cargo. No connection with Veracruz. If Ochoa sends up a flare for his trucks, there's no way the Mexican cops can connect 'em with us and a semi full of Monterrey bricks."

Donna looked impressed, so impressed, apparently, that she didn't even complain about the added expense that meant.

Bell told her to order 24 tons of brick, 22,000 kilograms.

"And find out what a brick weighs, and the size."

The Lamosa bricks were 6 x 10 x 20 centimeters, 2½ x 4 x 8 inches, and ran 1,800 kilograms to the thousand. They would require a bit more than 12,000 at 450 pesos a thousand.

"That's not so bad, is it?" Bell said. "Less than four hundred and fifty dollars."

"That's not too bad at all," Donna agreed.

Would wonders never cease? Bell thought. He did not say it aloud. Donna was being unexpectedly agreeable about expenses and he wasn't about to stir her up.

He sat down with pencil and paper. Eighteen hundred kilos a thousand divided out to about four pounds a brick. For Chato and the covering bricks to weigh 24 tons, they could allow themselves only six tons of brick. That was only 3,000. Bell closed his eyes and visualized the five slabs in a conventional trailer. Two of them would just about fit side by side. That meant two rows of two each, with the big slab, the one with the eyes and nose, by itself in a third row. The big slab was three feet high or better. That meant a lot of bricks on the other four if he wanted a level load, which he did. Three thousand bricks wouldn't do the job.

The trucker would have wooden pallets to stack heavy loads on so a fork lift could handle them. He'd buy enough pallets to build the shorter slabs to the level of the big one and take up the extra space in the third row, the one with only one section. The pallets would not only take up space but would also give him a level surface on which to stack the bricks. That way, 3,000 of them should be plenty. And the pallets didn't weigh enough to cause a discrepancy if somebody took the trouble to count the rows of apparently solid bricks and check it against the weight on the bill of lading

It was after nine when they checked out of the Jolet and after ten by the time they paid the drivers' bill at the other hotel, picked up the trucks, bought four tarpaulins and drove out to the abandoned building. All the drivers except Juan complained when they learned they were expected to pitch in and unload tiles again. They had had their fill of that back at

Linares. Bell got a handful of Mexican money from Donna and passed out one hundred pesos per man. They fell to without further complaint.

"I'd have paid 'em myself if I had any pesos left," Bell said.

"I wouldn't worry about it," Donna said pleasantly.

You've really changed, Bell thought, wondering why.

As outside of Linares, when the drivers got close to the load, Bell sent them out of the trucks while he and Juan finished the job. They lashed tarps firmly in place over each section. Juan worked swiftly and cheerfully. If he ever started a trucking business himself, Bell thought, he'd like to have a dozen Juans.

The trucker had a sour expression on his face when they pulled up at his loading dock at 1:20. He'd expected them earlier, he said. Donna dipped into her handbag without prompting from Bell and he cheered up instantly. The Dina 761 was a beautiful hunk of 335 horsepower tandem tractor. Bell wished he had been able to get one like it in Veracruz. He'd have long since been back home in Houston with twenty thousand dollars to help salve his conscience for helping steal Chato. The trailer was first class, too, aluminum, sturdy and clean.

The tug made short work of shifting the slabs to the trailer. The trucker did not ask what was under the tarps but Donna told him anyhow. Casually. Sections of a big fountain, custom-made in Mexico for a new office building in San Antonio, Texas. When she told Bell what she had done, he complimented her for improving on his own idea.

As Bell had hoped, the trucker sold them what wooden pallets were needed. There was only one unexpected development. The trucker insisted that one of his own drivers went along with the rig. Bell had intended for Juan to drive it and bring it back. The trucker was adamant.

"It'll be all right," Bell said. "I'll put Juan in the cab with him."

He took Donna aside and told her what to tell the drivers they were leaving in Monterrey with Ochoa's trucks. Luis, Juan's relief man, was to head back for Veracruz in the number one Dina. Salomón and Roberto were to do the same with the International. Mono would wait in Monterrey until the Mack was repaired and drive it back. Mono agreed readily and was delighted when he learned he would be paid extra for it. When they parted, Bell gave each man twenty-five dollars in U.S. bills and asked Donna to tell them to have a drink on him. Everyone shook hands and little Mono gave him a hearty Mexican abrazo, looking as if he would like to do the same to Donna. Donna settled for a handshake.

On their way to the brick factory, leading the big Dina in the Volkswagen, Donna said, "Sam, you have no idea how good it made me feel to see you part with a little of your own bread."

A gate and a check station manned by two uniformed guards barred the entrance to the brick factory. One of the guards came out and spoke with Donna and the driver of the rig. After a few words with Donna, the guard went back inside the check station to make a phone call.

"What's that all about?" Bell said.

"He said everybody has to be checked in and out," Donna said. "Company rule. That way they don't lose so many bricks."

The guard came back and told Donna how to get to the loading dock where the bricks were waiting. It was a big factory, with stacks of brick and tile overflowing onto loading docks and the ground between buildings. The new driver, whose name was Pedro, backed the Dina swiftly to the dock, braking just in time to ease it the last foot or so. Bell enjoyed the demonstration of skill. It was a relief to discover he had a man who knew what he was doing. When Donna went inside the building to pay for the bricks she learned she had to do that at another office and return with an order. Bell waited with the truck while she went to get it. When she returned, a gang of men began wheeling out bricks on hand trucks. The bricks were strapped together in sizable bundles.

"That won't do," Bell told Donna. "We'll never cover the slabs that way. Tell the foreman we want separate bricks, not big bundles."

The foreman did not want to oblige them. He said it would take too long to load that way. He offered to load smaller bundles. The large ones contained 60 bricks, the smaller only 10. Bell had a look at a 10-brick bundle. Two bricks wide and five high, it was about eight inches by eight inches by one foot. Piled short-side up, that should do it.

He went into the trailer to show the work crew how he wanted them stacked. Just a single layer high on the wooden pallets, the rest stacked to the same level from the floor up as far back as they would reach. He counted the bundles as they were wheeled in. He wanted 300 bundles, 3,000 bricks. When the load approached that number and he was satisfied it would cover adequately, he went back out, grateful to escape the heat inside the trailer.

When the last of the 300 bundles was being put on, he looked at his watch and gave an exclamation of surprise.

"Donna," he said, "tell the foreman we've got to be somewhere in fifteen minutes. We'll come back for the rest of the load later."

"What?" said Donna.

"This is all the bricks we can take. Any more'll run us over the bill of lading weight."

Donna did as he asked.

"He says they're closing for the day in an hour and a half," she told Bell. "If we're not back by then we can't get the rest until tomorrow."

"Perfect," said Bell. "That means he won't start wondering why we haven't come back until tomorrow morning."

At the gate, the guard would not let them through until he was shown the bill of lading and had a look inside the trailer. He was satisfied with what he saw. They'd passed the first test, Bell thought. The guard was thorough. He also looked in the luggage compartment of the Volks. Donna reached for the bill of lading when the guard handed it in the window.

"Unh unh," said Bell. "It stays with the truck until we get to Nuevo Laredo. If anybody wants to check it, we're not involved."

He glanced at the bill of lading when he took it back to Juan. The bricks were consigned to the H. L. Stern Construction Company of San Antonio, Texas. Bell asked Donna about that as the Dina pulled out ahead of them and the Volks fell in behind.

"I thought it would be wise to have San Antonio on the bill of lading instead of Houston," she said casually.

"Good thinking, Donna. It's smart to cover our tracks."

"I paid cash and they didn't ask for my name. Sam, are you concerned about something. Something I don't know about?"

"No. No more than anybody should be who's trying to smuggle out something that weighs thirty-six thousand pounds and is worth twelve years."

But Donna was right about him being concerned, just wrong about the reason. He wasn't too worried about being caught. They were on the last leg of the haul and it looked like clear sailing from here on out. What concerned him was what they were doing. Tomorrow Chato would be in Texas. That was a sorry trick to be playing on Chato and besides, any way you looked at it, they were committing a crime. Two crimes, really. Theft and smuggling. Not dirty crimes, like smuggling narcotics, but still crimes. He wasn't entirely sorry that he'd been a part of it, it had been a hell of an interesting experience, it was just that he didn't feel particularly proud of himself for getting away with it. One thing he was sure of, he'd never do this sort of thing again. There were more decent ways of earning a living. Donna obviously had no such compunctions. She was more bubbly than he had ever seen her.

"That was a marvelous idea of yours to put everything in one truck with a different load," she said. "I feel so much more confident now not having to worry about so many different trucks and drivers. And with absolutely nothing to connect us with Veracruz."

"This car does," Bell said.

"But we won't be crossing the border in it. We'll turn it in in Nuevo Laredo, won't we?"

"Yeah. I intended turning it in in Monterrey and getting another car for the last leg but all that business with Alberto knocked it right out of my head."

Pedro, the new driver, knew the city well and threaded his way past the downtown section to Avenida Universidad, the six-lane thoroughfare running into Highway 85 to Nuevo Laredo. They were out of Monterrey by 4:15. The big Dina barreled along ahead of them at a steady 105 kilometers an hour on the straightaway, slowing just the right amount at the occasional shallow curve. The countryside was pretty much like parts of West Texas, with mesquite, yucca and sparse grass on thirsty ground. There were more trailer rigs on the road here than anywhere else on the entire trip from Veracruz. Bell was glad to see it. The Dina was just one of many rigs heading for the border. Some of the others might be hauling bricks, too. Mexican brick was big in south Texas.

"Aren't you famished?" Donna said. "I am."

They had eaten nothing since breakfast. They had not even thought about food in the press of unloading the tiles, getting the new truck and buying the bricks.

"We'll wait until we get to Nuevo Laredo," Bell said. "It's only a couple more hours."

At the rate they were moving they would be in Nuevo Laredo by seven. And by that time Tuesday night, Chato would be in Houston.

22

AGENTE Alvarado's plane was seventeen minutes
late getting into Nuevo Laredo Monday afternoon.
Before leaving the airport he phoned the border station and the garita south of town. Neither the trucks
nor the Americans had arrived yet. That pleased
him. He was going to be on hand for the kill.

Alvarado rented a car instead of taking a taxi. It
was an extravagance he had no doubt the chief would
question but he wanted to keep mobile. The first thing
he did in Nuevo Laredo was make a courtesy call at
the Federal Judicial Police comandancia. It was the
busiest PJF office he had ever seen. Its walls were
covered with 20 by 25 centimeter glossy photos of
known and suspected narcotics smugglers. He decided
against making the office his base of operations. There
wasn't a spare desk or telephone and he knew he would
be in the way. It was obvious no one was wildly enthusiastic about turning up contraband that wasn't
narcotics.

He drove around looking for a hotel near the border
station. He found two on Ocampo, the street that led
to the weighing station in back of the customs and
immigration offices. One of them, the Montegar, was
air-conditioned. The other, the Sabinas, on Ocampo
and Victoria a couple of blocks from the border sta-

tion, was not. The Montegar was full and he had to go to the Sabinas. There was one consolation. A room at the Montegar was fifty-five pesos and at the Sabinas only twenty-five. After his extravagance with the car, the chief would be pleased about that. Alvarado was glad the comandancia budget was no affair of his. And it didn't matter that much to him if his room was not air-conditioned. His own bedroom in Veracruz wasn't and he'd managed to survive without any trouble.

After leaving the canvas bag containing an extra shirt and his toilet articles in the room, he identified himself to the man at the desk and gave him instructions to take down his telephone messages.

"And don't leave the phone unattended," he ordered. "It could be something most important. I'll be calling from time to time to see if you have anything for me."

He phoned the garita, the PJF comandancia and National Auto Rental and left the number where he could be reached. Then he walked to the border station to introduce himself to the customs people and have a look around. Automobiles and pedestrians came straight up Guerrero, the main street of Nuevo Laredo, to cross the border. Trucks turned right off Guerrero at Victoria, skirted the Plaza Juaréz to Ocampo and made a left turn for the weighing station. The truck scales were in front of a small separate brick and glass office. This was where the three trucks of the Americans would be obliged to pass.

Alvarado double-checked with the men in the border station, the weighing station and the office giving out tariff receipts to be sure everyone knew what to look for. Even if there was mordida, the trucks would never get through now. Too many people had been alerted. He left the telephone number where he could be reached. That accomplished, he walked back to the hotel to see if there were any messages. There were none.

He was hungry, having missed lunch, and he thought he might as well kill time by eating. It was best to get that out of the way while nothing was doing. He had seen several restaurants on Guerrero when he was looking for a hotel. He walked instead of taking the car. The traffic on Guerrero was bumper to bumper and it would be quicker afoot.

The Restaurante Principal looked good but was full of American tourists. That meant the prices would be high. He went in anyway. He might as well treat himself. It was his first time in Nuevo Laredo. The menu was considerably different from one in Veracruz. Less seafood and more things that appealed to American tourists — grilled fillet, roasted chicken, roasted meat and something called a Mexican Plate. The kid, shepherd style, sounded good and he ordered that, with a bottle of beer.

He looked in shop windows on his way back to the Sabinas. Nearly everything along Guerrero was for tourists and more Mexican than in Veracruz. The jewelry, the clothing, curios, everything. And more liquor stores than he had ever seen. He saw very little American-type goods of the sort popular in Veracruz. Everything was priced for Americans.

Alvarado was back at his hotel shortly after five. There were still no messages. He phoned all his contacts to be on the safe side and confirmed the fact that the Americans and their trucks had not yet arrived. He was a patient man and might have sat quietly at the hotel had he not thought it would be useful to drive out to the garita and speak with the people there in person, as he had done at the border station. If the Americans came through while he was on the way he would see them on the highway. He had excellent descriptions of them, their automobile and the trucks. He had only to keep his eyes open.

The garita straddled Highway 85, 25 kilometers south of Nuevo Laredo. Alvarado made a U-turn across the highway and parked by the checkpoint for northbound traffic. The garita was a tan building with two doors, one marked "Migración" and the other "Interventor." Alvarado spoke with both the immigration officer and the inspector. They assured him all personnel had been alerted and he would be notified the instant the Americans appeared with their trucks. Alvarado stressed again that the Americans were not to be arrested unless they could be taken with the trucks.

"If they arrive before the trucks, merely delay them long enough to be sure the trucks aren't close behind," he said. "But without arousing their suspicion. Some irregularity about their automobile, perhaps. And let me know immediately. If the trucks come along later, let them through, also. I want to take them all together."

He did not think it risky to let the Americans pass the garita. Eventually they would have to rendezvous with the trucks in Nuevo Laredo and then cross the border. And he had them blocked there.

It was after six now, and getting dark. He decided to wait around a little while on the chance the Americans would be coming through soon. He went outside and watched the traffic stream through. There were two separate lanes, one for automobiles, the other for trucks. Automobiles used the inside lane, which was covered by a portico. Trucks used the outside lane. The truck line was longer and slower because there were documents to be checked. Alvarado saw a Dina 661 but its registration number was not the one on his list. Nevertheless, he checked the celador, the guard assigned to vehicles. The Dina had a cargo of clay pots.

"For the tourists," the celador explained.

No Macks or Internationals were in the line.

Alvarado went back to the tan building and watched the automobile traffic, looking for Americans. When

Americans came through, the immigration man asked routine questions of the sort asked farther north at the border and took their tourist cards. Alvarado satisfied himself that the man was checking the cards carefully. If the man had not, Alvarado would have had a few words to say about it.

At 6:40, after a final word with the inspector, Alvarado got in his car and headed back to the Sabinas. He did not expect any messages but he thought he might take a nap. If the Americans were late in reaching the garita he would not be getting much sleep that night.

Up ahead, Bell saw the brake lights of the Dina's trailer come on. It was 6:35 P.M. and they had come 205 kilometers since leaving Monterrey. Traffic was slowing all along the highway up ahead.

"Looks like a check station," Bell said. "Everybody's stopping."

"I wonder why," Donna said anxiously.

"I think it's the main station south of the border," Bell said. "Everybody who goes outside the border area has to stop there coming and going."

"Oh," said Donna. "I didn't know that. I've always flown before."

Nearer the check station, the traffic split into two lines, cars to the right, passing under an extension of the check-station roof, trucks to the left. The truck line moved more slowly and the Volks overtook the Dina. Bell didn't look at Juan, who was on the passenger side of the cab, and Juan ignored him. At the check station, an officer in green pants and a khaki shirt rested both hands on the door and peered inside the Volks. He said something in Spanish.

"Americans," Bell said.

"You have a Mexican automobile, señor," the officer said in English.

"It's rented," said Bell. "Want to see the papers?"

"It is not necessary, señor. Your place of birth, please."

"Houston, Texas," Bell said.

"Rochester, New York," said Donna.

That surprised Bell a little. He had thought she was a native Houstonian, like himself, even if she didn't talk like one. But she didn't talk like his idea of a New Yorker, either.

"You had a good holiday?" the officer said.

"Great," said Bell.

"Your tourist cards, if you please."

Donna had hers in her purse. Bell had forgotten tourist cards were taken up before the border and had to hunt for his. It was tucked away in an outside pocket of his bag, in the luggage compartment. Donna gave him an angry, impatient look for causing a delay. The Dina had caught up with them. Bell did not know how closely it was being checked because he did not want to betray any interest in it.

The officer studied the tourist cards and asked Bell to pull the Volks over to the side. That troubled Bell. None of the cars ahead of them had had to do that.

"They're okay, aren't they?" he said casually.

"But of course," the guard said. "There is a small question about the automobile."

"We've got the papers from the rental agency," Bell said.

"It will only be a moment," the guard said.

He left them and went in a door marked "Interventor."

"What does Interventor mean?" Bell asked.

"Inspector," Donna said.

"Inspector of what, I wonder? I wonder if the word's out for us."

"How could that be?"

"We left a lot of people strung out behind us, Donna."

"Alberto's the only one who really knew anything," Donna said, alarmed. "Do you think he . . ."

"We'll know pretty quick. Sit tight and don't look so scared."

The Dina moved out while they waited.

"Damn!" said Bell. "I hope Juan knows to wait for us up the road."

"I'm not worried about that," Donna said shakily. "I'm worried about right now. Aren't you?"

"Yes."

A stranger came out of the door marked "Interventor" and hurried to the Volks. He introduced himself as the inspector and apologized profusely. A Volkswagen had been reported stolen and the guard had made a mistake about the registration number.

"Thank you for your patience, señor," he said. "Feliz viaje."

Donna sighed audibly.

"Thank you," said Bell.

He was careful to drive away not too fast and not too slowly. They did not speak for a minute or so. Donna was the first to break the silence.

"How did you manage to look so unconcerned?" she said.

"I bluff a lot at poker. Keep your eye peeled for the Dina."

It was pulled off the road a few kilometers farther on. The hood was up and Juan was pretending to tinker with the engine. Bell pulled the Volks off the road ahead of the Dina. Juan strolled over and said something in Spanish. He looked relieved at Donna's answer.

"He wanted to know what that was all about back there," Donna said.

"Good going, Juan," said Bell. "Tell him to find a motel this side of Nuevo Laredo and get a room for the night. One where he can park the rig out of sight. We'll follow him."

Bell drove away slowly while Juan returned to the truck, put the hood down and got back in the cab.

"I thought you said we'd follow him," Donna said.

"I'll let him pass after a while. I don't want it to look like we're following him."

"To whom?" Donna said.

"I don't know," said Bell. "I'm still thinking about that guy holding us up back there."

"If there was anything wrong he wouldn't have let us through," Donna replied.

"Maybe," Bell said. "But it doesn't hurt to be careful."

The Dina roared by as they were passing an outdoor movie to the right of the highway. They passed a monument of some sort and the highway became a broad avenue with an esplanade in the middle. Up ahead and off to the right was a rambling, expensive looking motel, the El Rió.

"I hope he doesn't pick that one," Bell said. "Look funny for a big rig and a couple of Mexican truck drivers to stop there."

The Dina drove past and turned into a more modest motor court. Juan always did the right thing, Bell thought gratefully. The Dina disappeared behind the motel building. Bell parked the Volks just off the road and waited, looking in the rearview mirror.

"What are we waiting for?" Donna said.

"Just want to make sure nobody's been tailing us from the check point."

"I told you, if they suspected anything they'd never have let us go," Donna said.

"I know you did."

Bell waited for five minutes by his watch. The traffic went by without pause and no one stopped up the road from the Volks. Bell was satisfied. He drove into the motel courtyard and parked by the Dina. Juan was waiting in the cab and did not get out until the

Volks headlights went out. Only then did he get out and come to them.

"Give him some money and tell him to get a room," Bell said. "Then to come back and tell us his room number and the phone number of this place." He got a twenty out of his wallet. "And tell him to treat Pedro to a good meal tonight. But somewhere within walking distance. Leave the rig here."

Juan returned with the information Bell wanted.

"Tell him if he wants me for anything we'll be at the El Río," Bell said. "Ask for, for Señor Esperson."

Esperson was the name of Houston's oldest skyscraper. Bell did not want to use either his own name or Kent, the one he had used in Veracruz.

"You're getting paranoid," Donna said. "Why bother with funny names?"

"There's nothing funny about Esperson," Bell replied. "But if you think there is, you don't have to be Mrs. Esperson."

"Thanks," said Donna.

"How about Miss Humble? Nope. They'd never believe it. Miss Shell. That's a nice building, too. Now tell Juan to stick around his room in the morning until he hears from us and let's get moving. I could eat a horse."

He shook hands with Juan and drove to the El Río motel. The office resembled that of any first-class motel on the other side of the border.

"I think you'll dig the bathrooms, Donna," Bell whispered.

They took two rooms. Bell registered as Robert Esperson of Port Arthur, Texas, giving no other information. Donna registered as Hilda Shell.

"Why Hilda?" he asked.

"I went to the University with a girl named Hilda. She was fat."

Both rooms were in a two-story building on the

other side of the swimming pool. Bell parked the car in front of it.

"I'm famished," Donna said. "Did the clerk say that's the restaurant back there?"

"Let's call Sandifer first and tell him we're here," said Bell.

"I'm sure he's having dinner somewhere himself at this hour," Donna said. "We'll call later. Why don't you go in and find us a table while I run up to my room and clean up a bit? I feel so grubby."

Bell grinned. Sandifer had called her a grubby child last week at the gallery. It seemed impossible that it was only last week.

He walked back to the restaurant in the middle of the motel complex. Inside was a lively bar with a music combo and a large dining room full of prosperous-looking Mexicans and Anglos. The dining room had its own band, a larger one than that in the bar. It was playing dance music. Bell liked the Veracruz marimbas better. The waiter brought butter and a large basket of bolillos with the menu.

"There'll be two of us," Bell said, helping himself to a roll.

He studied the menu while he waited for Donna. It was elaborate and it was printed, not mimeoed like the one at the Diligencias, and it was in Spanish and English, with the prices in pesos and dollars. Donna was taking her time, he thought, eating a second roll. Maybe the bathroom was so great she decided to take a bath. He ordered a margarita and listened to the music. He thought about the five slabs of Chato tucked away in the Dina a few hundred yards up the road. Tomorrow Chato would be in Texas and he would have got him there. While back in Veracruz, where Chato belonged, there was only a concrete imitation. It wouldn't be so bad if Chato were going into a museum or a park where anybody that wanted could see him. But Chato would be tucked away some-where in a private collection for some rich dude to drool over. And he would be the one who put Chato there. He wasn't just a smuggler. He was a pimp.

"Don't look so grim," said Donna's voice. "I haven't kept you waiting that long."

She'd combed her hair but didn't look as if she'd done a great deal more to herself.

"Is that a margarita?" she said, sitting down. "I'd like one, too."

She buttered a roll and began eating ravenously.

"What took so long," she said between bites, "I decided to take a chance on catching Sandy at home. He was there."

"And?" said Bell.

The waiter came up just then and Donna ordered a margarita. When he went away again she said, "Everything's set. The broker is expecting us in the morning. When we get to the warehouse on the other side of the border, I call the number he gave me and a trailer truck will come to pick up the goods. The warehouse will have equipment to transfer it."

The waiter returned with the margarita.

"Most people like the carne asada," he said in fluent English, without being asked. "They come over from Laredo every night for our steaks."

They ordered the carne asada.

"Donna, baby," said Bell. "Would you mind telling me why you don't want me around when you talk to Sandifer? That's twice in the last two days."

"You really are getting paranoid," Donna said. "I told you, it was a spur of the moment thing. I was saving the best for the last. If you're going to take that attitude I don't think I'll even tell you."

"Suit yourself," Bell said.

Donna appeared disappointed when he did not press her. In the middle of the carne asada, which was first-rate, Bell thought, she could contain herself no longer.

"Sandy said I could pay you off any time after I finished at the broker's," she said.

Bell's first sensation was one of relief. He wouldn't have to take Chato across the border after all. It wasn't that he been worrying about getting caught trying to cross despite his misgivings at the inspection station earlier that evening. That had proved to be a false alarm. It was what he had been thinking about when he was waiting for Donna. Pimping for Sandifer and some rich clown. He knew he was rationalizing, thinking it made any difference whether he actually took Chato across the border or not — without him Chato couldn't have reached the border in the first place — but at least it was a gesture in the right direction to pull out while the head was still in Mexico.

Donna was watching him, waiting for his reply. She looked a little anxious and trying to conceal it.

"So he finally broke down and told you what I was getting," Bell said.

"Oh, no," Donna replied. "He didn't mention it until I told him I knew. He should have known I'd find out."

"What do you think about it?" Bell said casually. "Is it okay with you?"

"If that's what you want. You'd like that, wouldn't you?"

"I'm not too crazy about the kind of work I've been doing the last few days," Bell admitted.

"It's settled, then?" Donna said.

She sat back in the chair and looked pleased with herself.

"There's something about this I don't dig," Bell said. "Why are you so willing to pay me off when it's coming out of your pocket?"

"My pocket?"

"Yeah. You were going to keep what you had left in the pot. What made you change your mind?"

Donna put the last morsel of steak in her mouth, chewed slowly and swallowed.

"When Sandy found out I knew how much you were getting," she said, "and I told him in no uncertain terms I wouldn't stand still for his miserly arrangement with me, he came around. He's doubling my bonus. And my salary. He'll certainly be able to afford it after this."

"And then some," Bell agreed. "Well, that do make it nice for everybody, doesn't it?"

Except Chato, he thought. Poor Chato.

When they said good night at the motel steps, Donna looked at him quizzically.

"No adolescent remarks about your room or mine, Sam?" she said.

"Nope," said Bell. "I think it's your turn."

Donna actually laughed. Bell was not too surprised. She'd been different since this morning, especially about money. And now that everything seemed to be locked up she was warm and euphoric. If she was ever going to be available, it was right now.

"Good night, Donna," he said.

As soon as he was in his room he tried to call Sandifer. Sandifer's home number was unlisted.

When Alvarado got back to the Sabinas there was a message waiting for him from the garita. The Americans had come through only minutes after he left. But none of the trucks on the list he had given. Alvarado phoned the inspector at once.

"They could have changed trucks," Alvarado said. "Were there any with Veracruz tiles?"

There were not.

Alvarado sat down and thought about it. It was highly unlikely the Americans would permit the contraband to get too far out of their sight. Either they had changed the covering load as well as the trucks, or something had happened to make them abandon their loot, which seemed even more unlikely. That would make his job a bit more difficult. He would have to insist that customs examine every cargo capable of concealing sections of the head. It wouldn't be as great a task as it seemed. Any cargo capable of concealing a section of the head would be a heavy one. Even if it had been cut into many small pieces the Americans would be obliged to transport a number of them in each truck. They certainly would not divide them among a whole fleet. And they might be attempting to cross even now.

He phoned the border station. Every American passing through had been required to furnish identification, he was told. There had been no Señor Bell or Señorita Russell or anyone fitting their description. And no large shipments of tiles.

"Good," said Alvarado. "And forget about examining only tiles. Look at everything weighing more than six thousand kilograms. It's possible the contraband has been placed in other trucks, and under different cover."

He wondered if the Americans would perhaps wait until tomorrow to cross the border. If they intended crossing tonight they would turn in their hired automobile. He picked up the phone to call National Auto Rental.

"Excuse me, agente," the desk clerk said. "I was supposed to finish work an hour ago. I'd like to leave now."

"I want you to wait for the night man," Alvarado said.

"There is no night man, agente. Only me."

"All right," said Alvarado. "You can go."

He would not need the man, actually. He would be dividing his time between the border station and the hotel and when he was at the hotel, instead of remaining in his room where there was no phone, he

310

could nap down here in a chair. If he should have the opportunity to nap.

Alvarado phoned National Auto Rental. The Volkswagen had not been returned. That would indicate the Americans had decided to remain in Nuevo Laredo overnight. He got out the telephone directory and began calling hotels and motels. He wished now he had not permitted the desk clerk to leave. The desk clerk could have told him which were the better places, where Americans were most likely to stay. It took him almost an hour to call all the hotels and motels in the directory. None of them had registered a Señor Bell or a Señorita Russell. And no American had arrived in a Volkswagen with Veracruz plates. Of course, many tourists did not bother to fill in that portion of the registration card, he was told.

So there was no way of knowing if the Americans would try to cross tonight. There would be no napping by the phone for him, Alvarado thought ruefully. He walked to the border station to wait for whatever the night might bring.

23

BELL woke up a little after six Tuesday morning. After he shaved and dressed he called the gallery in Houston on the chance Sandifer had come in early on his big day. It was an hour later in Houston. Texas was on Daylight Saving Time and Mexico was not.

No one answered at the gallery. Bell phoned Donna.

"I was on the verge of calling you," she said. "How can you sleep on a morning like this?"

"Throw something on," Bell said. "I'm coming over to call Juan."

Donna was already dressed and had put away the things she had brought to the room for the night. She was bright-eyed and buoyant.

"Just a few more hours," she said. "Isn't it marvelous?" She paused and added, "Sandy will be ecstatic. He's been after a coup like this for ages."

Bell had Donna call Juan and tell him to find out how to get to the customs broker's office, then have breakfast and wait for Bell to call again. He and Donna went to breakfast in the dining room. Donna ate a huge breakfast, talking between bites.

"How can you be so calm?" she demanded. "On a day like today?"

"It's Tuesday," Bell said. "I'm always calm on Tuesdays."

"It's because you have no imagination," Donna said. "You don't understand what a tremendous feat we've brought off."

"It's just a job," Bell said.

He wished he really believed that.

Bell phoned Juan from the motel office after they checked out. Juan was to wait five minutes, then start the Dina out, having Pedro hold it down until he saw the Volks in the side mirror. He was to lead them to brokers' row, park the Dina, and wait.

"I'll drop you off at the broker's and take the Volks to National Auto Rental while you're making the arrangements," Bell told Donna. "Does the broker know what's going on?"

"Not exactly," Donna said. "There's no reason he should."

The customs brokers had their offices on Avenida Mendoza in the northwest part of town across from the customs warehouses. The Dina parked just across Mendoza in a paved lot in the Plaza Cinco de Mayo. Bell dropped Donna off in front of the Salón Reforma on the corner of Mendoza and Arteaga.

"Back in a few minutes," he said.

It took longer than he expected to turn the Volks in. The girl at National Auto Rental got all flustered when he turned in the key and settled up for the mileage. She said something about Veracruz having made a mistake in the charges and Bell had to wait while the manager made a phone call to straighten it out. Everybody apologized for the inconvenience and the manager insisted on helping Bell carry the luggage to a taxi, refusing a tip. Bell got some coins from the taxi driver and had him stop at the first pay phone he saw.

Sandifer answered.

"Sam, my boy," he said, jovially. "Good to hear from you. Where are you calling from?"

"Nuevo Laredo," said Bell.

"Nuevo Laredo? Excellent. Excellent. When Donna

called me last night she was afraid you'd not be in until this afternoon."

This afternoon, Bell thought. So he hadn't been wrong in thinking Donna was up to something. Only it seemed to be aimed at Sandifer, not him.

"Operator," Sandifer said. "Are we still connected?"

"I'm still on," Bell said.

"You must have straightened out the business with the new truck more quickly than you expected," Sandifer said. "You've certainly had your share of problems with trucks, haven't you, Sam?"

"That's right," Bell replied.

"I'm afraid you'll have to wait a few hours for the trailer truck to get there from Houston," Sandifer said. "Donna said there was no point in having it in Laredo before three or so."

What Donna was doing was ripping Sandifer off, Bell realized. She had her own plans for Chato. By the time Sandifer's rig got to the warehouse she'd be long gone with a rig of her own. No wonder she'd been so cheerful about paying him off this side of the border. It was her idea, not Sandifer's. That way, he wouldn't be around when she made her move. Ten thousand dollars was a cheap enough price to pay for Chato.

Somehow he was not too surprised. He'd sensed something was fishy since last night. And he wasn't even indignant. The whole deal was a rip off and how much worse could it be for one of the rip off artists to rip off one of the others. At least Donna had intended to pay him what he had coming. Of course, it was to get him out of her hair, but she was a bright girl and might have thought of a less expensive way if she'd really wanted to take him.

"You're very quiet, Sam," Sandifer said. "Is there something I ought to know?"

"No," said Bell. "Everything's fine."

He wasn't going to let Donna get away with it. He'd rather not see Chato get across the border at all, but as long as it had to be that way Chato would go to Sandifer. He had agreed to do the job and had taken Sandifer's money. A deal was a deal. But he wasn't going to tell Sandifer what Donna had tried to do. It was no business of his. He was never going to deal with Sandifer again and if at some later date Donna did rip him off, it was strictly between them. His loyalty to Sandifer didn't extend beyond this haul.

"We'll be waiting for your rig," he said. "See you tonight."

"Good boy," said Sandifer.

Bell had the taxi drop him and the luggage in front of the Salón Reforma. There was a pushcart with a big Fiesta cigarette sign on the side in front of the Reforma. It was full of fruit and big glass jars of cold drinks. Bell was thirsty but decided not to risk it. He'd managed to avoid the turistas this far. Just across the street a tough-looking man in uniform was directing truck traffic into the loading area behind the customs warehouse. He had a pearl-handled pistol on his hip and wore a khaki shirt and green pants, like the man back at the check station. His green cap had a brown visor and he was wearing jodhpur boots. He shouldn't be staring at the man that way, Bell thought. He turned away and went looking for the broker's office.

Donna was waiting for him, drinking coffee with a sprucely dressed middle-aged man.

"This is Mr. Guzman," she said.

She did not introduce Bell. They shook hands and Guzman offered Bell coffee in excellent English.

"The girl's taking the bill of lading over to pick up our Pedimento de Exportación," Donna said. "And we have to hire a driver from the Sección de Alijadores to drive the truck across the border. Mr. Guzman is taking care of that, too."

"Yes," said Guzman. "It is necessary to have a driver licensed for the purpose to transport cargos through Mexican and United States Customs."

"U.S. Customs will let him drive to the warehouse on the other side," Donna said. "He'll wait until it's unloaded and bring the truck back across."

Bell looked at her.

"It's all right," Donna said. "I've already phoned for the truck from H. L. Stern to come after the bricks."

Bell drank coffee and discussed American baseball with Guzman while they waited. Guzman had been up to Houston several times to see games in the Astrodome. The girl returned with the export permit and a few minutes later the driver from the Sección de Alijadores arrived.

"I made arrangements for him to come to us so it would not be necessary to take your truck to the section office," Guzman explained.

Donna paid Guzman his fee and the three of them, Donna, Bell and the driver, walked across Arteaga and Mendoza and through the Plaza Cinco de Mayo to the Dina. Bell and the driver carried the luggage.

"I'm letting Juan go," Donna said. "We won't need him any longer. Pedro can wait here and drive the Dina back to Monterrey by himself."

She really thought she was taking over now, Bell thought. He wished she were. If she were taking Chato to Sandifer he'd be happy to walk away from it.

"I think he deserves a bonus, don't you?" Bell said.

If Donna hadn't tried to pull a fast one on him, he'd have paid Juan out of his own pocket. But let her do it. The only way to get to Donna was through her pocketbook.

"Of course," said Donna. "Fifty dollars, do you think?"

"Make it a hundred," said Bell.

Donna hesitated a moment, then said, "All right."

They took Juan aside and Donna gave him the

hundred. Juan was overwhelmed. When Bell added a hundred and fifty more, he was absolutely stunned. First he pumped Bell's hand, then gripped him in a crunching abrazo. Bell crunched back.

"You're a hell of a guy, you bandit," he said. "Muy macho. Donna, tell him I'll miss him."

"I never realized you were so damn sentimental," Donna said. "Just horny."

She spoke with Juan and said, "He says he'll miss you, too. If you ever need a driver again, let him know through Ochoa."

After Juan left she said, "Now it's your turn."

She took a bulging El Río Motel envelope out of her handbag and gave it to him. Bell hefted it.

"Would you like to go somewhere and count it?" Donna asked.

"No," said Bell. "I trust you."

He put it back in her hand and closed her fingers around it.

"What's that supposed to mean?" she demanded.

"I've decided to hang around a while," Bell said. "I just can't bear to part like this after all we've been to each other."

"I thought you said you wanted out," Donna said, knitting her heavy brows.

"After I dropped off the Volks I called Sandifer," Bell said quietly.

Donna went white around the lips but all she said was, "Oh?"

"Chato's going on his rig," Bell said.

"I see," said Donna.

She looked at him thoughtfully, but unabashed. You've got to hand it to her, Bell thought. She's one tough chick.

"Sam," she said cooly, "I've got another six thousand in the kitty. Let me keep five hundred for expenses and you can have the rest."

"No dice."

"Is there anything I can do to make you change your mind? Anything at all?"

Bell shook his head.

"You straight-assed son of a bitch," she said. "All right, get us a taxi."

For an instant he liked Donna. Whatever else she was, she was a good loser. He remembered how she'd shut up at Tlacotalpán after convincing herself she couldn't bargain any longer with Vargas.

Bell got a taxi and loaded the luggage into it. The new driver got into the Dina and backed it out of the Plaza Cinco de Mayo. The taxi followed the rig past the Banco Nacional de México, the Restaurante Do-Brazil and the Banco Longoria and turned right on Arteaga. The guard at the customs warehouse didn't give it a second glance. Another right and they drove past the railway depot and finally onto Guerrero. The Dina turned off at Ocampo to take the truck route to the border station and Bell had the taxi follow and park by the Plaza Juaréz until the Dina had moved up in line to the gate through the chain-link fence behind the border station, where the truck scales were. Then he had the driver return to Guerrero and join the line of passenger vehicles heading for the border. Donna had not said a word since they left the Plaza Cinco de Mayo.

There were two lanes at the border station, divided by the steel beams supporting the high cantilevered roof over the street. When the taxi reached the station, a guard leaned in the window and spoke in Spanish. When Donna answered, Bell recognized the word, "Americano."

It was unusual to be halted on the Mexican side. The guard usually just looked in from his post and waved you on, Bell thought. But before, he had always been in a car with U.S. plates. It was probably different when you crossed in a Mexican vehicle.

The guard kept asking questions.

318

"Russell," said Donna. "Donna Russell."

"Ah," said the guard, dragging out the sound like a sigh.

What's going on, Bell wondered. They never asked your name at the border.

The guard said something and Donna turned to look at Bell, her face showing consternation.

"He said to please get out," she said shakily.

"Did he say why?" Bell said in a low voice.

Donna shook her head.

During the night, Alvarado had managed to nap off and on in a chair tilted back against the wall in the border-station office. In the morning, after someone brought him breakfast, he alternated between the chair and a standing position by the back door from which he watched both the trucks lined up for the scales and the traffic feeding past the station from Guerrero. A little before nine, he received a call from the manager of National Auto Rental. Señor Bell had turned in the Volkswagen. Alvarado increased his vigilance. The Americans should be attempting to cross the border very soon now.

Around 9:30 A.M., a bustle of activity on the Guerrero side caught his eye. The station commandant hurried to him.

"We have them, agente," he said excitedly.

They looked exactly as they had been described to Alvarado, though he did not think the Señorita Russell looked as sexy as the tile-factory manager had said. In fact, she looked quite cold, though she was undeniably a handsome woman. Behind her came Señor Samuel Bell, his face set and inscrutable. It was not the sort of face Alvarado had expected to find on a man engaged in such unsavory business. It was a solid, honest, American face. But one never knew what lay behind a face. Licenciado Jorge Vargas was a case in point.

Señorita Russell stormed into the office saying in excellent Spanish, "Who's in charge here? Who's responsible for this outrage?"

Alvarado was surprised that she should be the spokesman. She appeared to be a very strong person, but the Señor Bell appeared to be much man. He was aware the woman's indignation cloaked apprehension, apprehension she was too shrewd, and perhaps to proud, to reveal. But it was impossible to judge the depth of the man's concern. His face said nothing.

The commandant nodded toward Alvarado, obviously relieved to direct the woman's anger away from himself. She strode toward Alvarado, her thick eyebrows in a straight line and her dark eyes snapping.

"Who are you and what is the meaning of this outrage?" she demanded.

"Señorita Russell," he said cordially. "Or is it Señorita Fairchild?"

She lost her composure for only a moment.

"My name is Donna Russell and I am an American citizen and I demand to be allowed to continue on to the United States," she said. "Just who the hell are you?"

Such coarse language was not at all becoming, Alvarado thought. The man was looking from one of them to the other. It was obvious to Alvarado he did not know Spanish. That no doubt was the reason he had permitted the woman to be their spokesman.

"And the gentleman with you would be Señor Samuel Bell," Alvarado said.

A flicker of expression crossed the American's face at the mention of his name. Señor Bell let a small sigh escape him.

"My name is Tomás Alvarado, señorita," Alvarado continued politely. "And I am an agent of the Federal Judicial Police."

"So?" said Señorita Russell. "What's that got to do with us?"

She was certainly a strong one, Alvarado thought.

"It would save time and perhaps future difficulties if you pointed out your trucks to me," Alvarado said.

"What trucks?"

"The trucks concealing contraband, señorita."

"I have no idea what you're talking about. My friend and I are returning from a vacation in Mexico. Are you going to stop this nonsense or must I phone my friends in Mexico City?"

"Ah," said Alvarado. "Would that be Jorge Vargas?"

The man again displayed a flicker of expression. The woman's face did not change but Alvarado saw her knuckles whiten around the strap of the heavy purse she carried.

"Are you going to let me use the phone or aren't you?" she demanded.

"It would save everyone much trouble if you would tell me in which trucks you have concealed the contraband you picked up in Tlacotalpán Thursday night, señorita."

"I want a lawyer," Señorita Russell said.

"In good time, señorita. Please sit down."

She did not look as confused as Alvarado had hoped she would. Rather, she looked wary. That was not so good.

"Is there somewhere we could speak in private, agente?" she said less belligerently.

"Of course," Alvarado said.

He led her to the back corner of the office and stood facing her, his back to the room and blocking her from the view of the commandant. He shot a quick look over his shoulder at Señor Bell, who was leaning against a wall with his arms folded across his chest. Now that he thought he was unobserved, Señor Bell looked worried. Alvarado felt less unkindly disposed toward him. A man without any human weaknesses was not much of a man. He was a machine without a soul.

"I have five hundred dollars in my purse," Señorita Russell said. "If you let me cross to the American side so I can call my lawyer, I'll let you hold it to insure my return."

"I am sorry, señorita."

"A thousand, then."

Alvarado suppressed a sigh. Never in his life had he had as much as a thousand U.S. dollars. And never would.

"Two thousand."

"Excuse me one moment, if you please," Alvarado said.

He led Señorita Russell back to join Señor Bell, then went to the rear door and looked out. There was a stake body truck on the scales. It was loaded with sacks of something. The contraband could not be on that one. Behind it was a Dina diesel with a trailer. It was large enough to contain an entire Olmec head with room to spare. The stake body truck moved on and the Dina drove onto the scales.

"What's the story?" Bell demanded in a low voice.

"He knows we picked up something in Tlacotalpán Thursday night," Donna said. "And that we're involved with Vargas. He wanted me to tell him what trucks the goods were on."

"Jesus!" said Bell.

"Maybe he won't find it," Donna said, but without conviction. "If he doesn't, there's nothing he can hold us on."

"He'll find it," Bell said.

"I think I can do business with him," Donna said. "When I offered him two thousand he didn't say no."

"I don't know," Bell said. "He doesn't look like that kind of guy."

He was churning inside. He could get twelve years

in a Mexican jail for this. Twelve years loomed like a lifetime. Why the hell hadn't he taken the money and let Donna do what she wanted with the god damned head? Why should he have cared if she ripped off Sandifer. They were both a couple of thieves. Correction. They were all three thieves. Mingled with his anxiety, Bell felt another and unexpected emotion. He was embarrassed. The big man with the cruel face and sunglasses seemed like a hell of a decent sort, an honest man doing an honest job. Bell didn't like what the big man must be thinking about him. Probably thought he did this kind of thing all the time. It was like being caught writing dirty words on the latrine wall. Only worse.

"You can buy any of them," Donna said. "It's just a matter of finding their price."

"Not this dude," Bell said. "I've got a feeling."

Alvarado looked back in the office. The Americans were whispering together. The señorita was wiping her perspiring face with a handkerchief. When she saw him looking at them, she put the handkerchief away quickly and composed her face. He went to her and said, "Would you like something to drink, señorita? A Coca-Cola, perhaps? I will send for it."

"I want a lawyer," she said.

Señor Bell was no longer so inscrutable. He still did not look frightened, however. If anything, he was shamefaced.

Alvarado returned to his position in the back door and watched the scale man open the back doors of the Dina's trailer and climb inside. After a few minutes he reappeared and motioned to Alvarado. Alvarado joined him in the trailer. It contained bricks, not tiles. Some of them had been stacked to one side to reveal a wooden platform of some sort as well as a large, roughly circular object covered with a canvas.

Alvarado took out his pocketknife and slit the covering. Underneath was solid stone. With the scale man's help he moved more bricks and pulled off the canvas. The blank eyes of an Olmec head peered at him, unseeing.

"Mother of God!" Alvarado whispered.

He told the scale man to pull the Dina out of line and see that the driver was detained, then returned to the office. Señorita Russell was biting her fingernails. Señor Bell was standing erect, his eyes looking straight ahead. Rather like a soldier, Alvarado thought.

"I'm afraid it is all over, señorita," he said gently.

"What are you talking about?"

"We have just discovered an important national treasure of Mexico in a truck which you hired. The driver has told me it is you and Señor Bell who engaged him."

He had not yet, but he would.

Señor Bell was watching them intently now. Judging from his expression, he was trying hard to understand what they were talking about.

"He's lying," Señorita Russell said. "I don't know anything about a truck or any national treasure."

"Please, señorita," Alvarado said in the kindliest tone he could muster. "You will only make it more difficult for yourself. I know everything. Who you met with in Tlacotalpán. Where you bought the tiles for the trucks you hired from Señor Ochoa. I have spoken with two of the drivers. Alberto Villareal and Xavier Reyes." He threw in Villareal's name for added effect.

The woman wilted, but only briefly.

"Look, Señor Alvarado," she said. "Surely there must be some way we can straighten out this misunderstanding."

"But of course, señorita."

She gave a sigh of relief and smiled at him. She looked at her companion and said something in English. Señor Bell looked doubtful. Señorita Russell turned back to Alvarado.

"How much?" she said briskly.

"Do not misunderstand me, señorita," Alvarado said. "I must take you into custody. But I'm sure a certain degree of cooperation will be taken into consideration by my superiors."

"I understand. I'll take care of them, too."

Alvarado shook his head sadly.

"Was it Jorge Vargas from whom you acquired the Olmec head?" he asked.

"I never heard of him."

"That is unfortunate for both of us, señorita. I will tell you something quite frankly. I am not overly concerned about you and Señor Bell. But I would most assuredly like to get my hands on Jorge Vargas. As would my superiors. Take my advice and do not shield Señor Vargas at your own expense."

"What do you mean by that?" Señorita Russell asked carefully.

"If you will pardon my saying so, Señor Vargas is more important to us than you and Señor Bell, señorita. If you take full responsibility for what you have done I'm afraid you must expect the most severe penalties. But if you share it with Señor Vargas, it would make a most favorable impression on the attorney general."

The señorita drummed on her purse with the fingers of her right hand and looked pensive. Yes, Alvarado thought, the American señorita is indeed very strong. But she is also quite aware that her first duty is to herself.

Again she looked at her companion and spoke to him in English.

"He doesn't want money," Donna said. "He wants Vargas. He says if we give him Vargas, they'll be easier on us. Do you believe him?"

Bell looked at Alvarado. Their eyes met. Alvarado had removed his sunglasses. Somehow the big man no longer looked so rough. The big man smiled and nodded, as if acknowledging an introduction.

"Yeah," said Bell. "I believe him. Donna, I want you to tell him something for me."

"Just a minute, buster," she said. "You're not making any deal that doesn't include me."

"Will you shut up and listen? I want you to tell him I'm damned sorry he caught us but I'm not sorry Chato didn't make it across."

"Idiot," said Donna.

EPILOGUE

THE taxi drove up to the knoll at the highway junction south of the city of Veracruz just as the heavy crane plucked off the concrete replica of an Olmec head and swung it around to deposit it gently on the waiting flatbed truck. Alvarado got out of the taxi, eased the pistol holster chafing his side, and watched the workmen attach slings around another, and larger, head.

It was remarkable, he thought, how well the five pieces into which it had been cut had been fitted together with one of those incredible industrial adhesives. Unless one stood very near, it was difficult to see where the pieces had been joined. Instead of locking away the head with the thousands of objects confiscated by the Unit for the Defense of the Cultural Patrimony to gather dust, the authorities in the Capital had decided to place it on permanent display here.

The Olmec head lifted off its truck, dangling from the crane. For a moment it seemed to have a certain lightness despite its bulk. The crane swung around again and placed the head in the exact spot where the replica had sat minutes earlier. The workmen undid the slings and climbed into trucks. The one with the crane clanked away, followed by the flatbed truck with the replica and the one that had brought the Olmec head. One by one, the few curious passersby who had stopped to watch the transfer got back in their automobiles and drove away.

Soon only Alvarado remained, gazing at the head. He could never look at it again without experiencing deep satisfaction. It was not merely that Veracruz now had a genuine Olmec head of its own, and one surpassing the finest to be found at Santiago Tuxtla and the museum at Jalapa, and not merely that he had been so instrumental in preventing it being spirited off to the United States, but largely because it was through this magnificent relic of Mexico's past he had at last got his hands on Jorge Vargas. In the months of his trial, Vargas had spent money like water and many influential persons had sought to intercede for him. But, to Alvarado's immense gratification, the attorney general had seen fit to make an example of him. Vargas had been heavily fined and given a sentence of fifteen years.

The merest blink of an eye in the time span of the Olmec head, Alvarado thought, but to Jorge Vargas an eternity.

In a way, Alvarado regretted that the young American, Señor Samuel Bell, had also been sent to prison. Though in repeated interrogations and throughout his trial he had refused to implicate Vargas or reveal by whom he had been employed, he had seemed genuinely contrite about his part in the attempted theft. But, for a man of his age, two years was not, after all, a lifetime. And perhaps the realization of his good fortune in receiving the minimum sentence would sustain him. Alvarado himself had been in no small degree responsible for such leniency. His report had made it clear that Señor Bell was but an employee of Señorita Russell. His investigations had revealed she handled all funds, including even Señor Bell's expenses. The señorita had kept most meticulous records.

And the Señorita Donna Russell. She might have

gotten off with as light a sentence, or possibly no sentence at all, merely a heavy fine. For she had been completely cooperative regarding Vargas and she, also, had appeared contrite. Alvarado, for one, had not been convinced of her sincerity, but apparently others had been. Señorita Russell had been permitted to go free on bail. Not unexpectedly, to Alvarado at any rate, she had attempted to flee the country. That had cost her five years and forfeiture of her bond.

After her recapture, Señorita Russell had offered to reveal for whom she had been acting, something she had evaded before. But the offer had come too late to give her a bargaining position. Alvarado had already learned without her cooperation. It had not been for anyone in San Antonio, Texas. He had quickly ascertained there was no such firm as the H. L. Stern Construction Company in San Antonio and almost as quickly that she was in the employ of one Otis Sandifer, of Houston, a notorious dealer in pre-Columbian artifacts. It was a pity he had been unable to do anything about Señor Sandifer. But another day, perhaps.

Alvarado continued to gaze at the Olmec head. Such strength, he thought. Such a representation of the oldest civilization on Mexican soil. As he gazed, it seemed to him the heavy lips were smiling. Alvarado smiled in return. He got in the taxi and with one last, lingering look, told the driver to take him to the comandancia. His chief would be waiting for his return and, if he knew the chief, impatiently.